VOICES

TIM WYNNE-JONES

VOICES

Hodder & Stoughton
LONDON SYDNEY AUCKLAND TORONTO

The author wishes to acknowledge the help and encouragement
of Alberto Manguel, who gave me a shove at the right time;
Lucinda Vardey, whose enthusiasm kept the ball rolling; Louise
Dennys, who was insightful, unflaggingly supportive and patient;
Anne Phelps, who typed draft upon draft; and, finally, Anne
Fullerton, who knows the flowering season of Cheddar Pinks.

British Library Cataloguing in Publication Data

Wynne-Jones, Tim, *1948–*
  Voices.
  I. Title
  813.54 [F]

  ISBN 0-340-51080-3

Reproduced by arrangement with
Lester & Orpen Dennys Ltd, Canada

Published by Hodder and Stoughton,
a division of Hodder and Stoughton Ltd,
Mill Road, Dunton Green, Sevenoaks, Kent TN13 2YA
Editorial Office: 47 Bedford Square, London WC1B 3DP

Printed in Great Britain by St Edmundsbury Press Ltd,
Bury St Edmunds, Suffolk

Bound by Hartnolls Ltd,
Bodmin, Cornwall

for
Virgil and Anne Burnett,
who know a castle or two,
and for
Amanda West Lewis,
who watched this one go up
brick by brick

Nothing! Thou elder brother even to shade:
Thou hadst a being ere the world was made,
And well fixed, art alone of ending not afraid.

John Wilmot, second Earl of Rochester,
Upon Nothing

We shall see the imagination build "walls" of
impalpable shadows,comfort itself with the
illusion of protection—or, just the contrary,
tremble behind thick walls, mistrust the
staunchest ramparts.

Gaston Bachelare, *The Poetics of Space*

The world is that which cannot be known.
The world is that which we each imagine.

Annie Dillard, *Living by Fiction*

Prologue

The old drunk had wandered into the alley to find a place to sleep. The others had left him around midnight. He had stopped drinking around one. Before that he had stopped drinking at six and before that, noon. He thought he knew this alley. It ran behind a taxidermist's shop and sometimes a man could find a spoilt fur or two in the trash can. Luck was with him. Not only did he find a fur piece for his pillow, but he also found a pile of collapsed cardboard boxes out back of the appliance store. With a little effort the boxes made an adequate, if stiff, sleeping bag. His pillow already had a head on it—some nasty, little, snarling vermin with a wall-eye. He tucked it out of sight.

He had nicely sandwiched himself in and had erected a cardboard roof when the rain started. It was the third night of rain—February rain, with the memory of snow frozen in every drop. Dimly the old drunk recalled a childhood camping trip. With the rain clattering down on his improvised tent, he contemplated the drunkenness of Noah and wondered where his own sons were tonight.

His head felt like a sink of dirty dish-water. He closed his eyes and pulled the plug. As on every other night, sense and memory whirled away together down the pipe.

A sigh woke him sometime later. It was still night. The rain had let up. He listened. It came again; something more than the wind in the trash cans. The old drunk's head was spinning like a record. The noise and confabulation of the evening came back to him, picked up by the worn and jumpy needle of his consciousness. He could not fall back asleep.

The old drunk was an even older sinner. Church of England— no pope, but a queen at the helm, though there had been a king when he took his first drink. It was Shrove Tuesday and the guys had been kidding him about what he was going to give up for Lent. "For the next forty days I will give up any attempt at sobriety," he had promised. "Come Holy Saturday, it will be back to drinking as usual."

The sigh came again. It was not part of his recollections. It was nearby.

"Help me," a voice whispered.

"The pillow!" squealed the old drunk. But when his shaking hands unfolded the angry little face, its mouth showed no sign of having moved.

"Down here," rasped the voice.

With great difficulty the old drunk rolled over and peered down into the shadowy darkness at the base of his cardboard bed. A light over a doorway picked out an assortment of rubble but nothing human in shape.

"By the wall," said the voice, scarcely audible. "Over here, by the wall."

The voice seemed to come from a pile of rocks.

"Make me into a circle," the rocks demanded. The drunk stayed put. There might be a rat among the rocks trying to trick him.

Again the voice implored him, "Make me into a circle."

It seemed a reasonable request.

2

"You're not a rat, are you?" the old drunk and sinner asked.

"Hurry," said the rocks.

Clambering from his rigid sheets and kneeling heavily on the wet ground, he began to sort through the pieces of stone. They proved to be more like shaped bricks, but each weighed about twenty pounds. The drunk's hands trembled.

"Don't drop me!" the disembodied voice implored hoarsely. It reminded the drunk of his old friend Jasper who had died of Parkinson's disease. It was a voice on the very edge of death. As hurriedly as his condition would allow he placed the great smooth bricks in a circle. They fit together snugly in a shape the size of a manhole. Adjusting the last piece he cut his finger.

"Be careful," said the voice, weakly but with more confidence. "My lip is sharp."

The old drunk sucked on his finger. He remembered the tests he had done at the institute. He remembered arranging blocks. He had wondered to himself then, as he did now: Am I doing the right thing?

For a moment all he heard was laboured breathing. Then the voice returned, no longer airy but focused in the dead centre of the circle.

"Thank you," said the circle of stones.

The old drunk looked around. He knew this might yet turn out to be a joke. The guys were always duping him.

"Who are you?" he asked.

"I am a hole," came the reply.

A new idea entered the drunk's mind; his thinking was growing clearer by the moment. Aliens. They could be anywhere. Perhaps, he thought, they are so dreadful in appearance they have to disguise themselves. Well, if they wanted him to think he was talking to a hole, it was just as well to go along with it.

"Pleased to meet you," he said. He waved. Then, looking past his trembling hand at the circle he had formed, he noticed the inside was darker than the pavement.

"Go on," said the hole. "I'm deep enough."

The drunk's hand hovered for a moment, then plunged into the circle between the stones. The air was colder there; he felt a draft on his palm. Soon he had lowered his whole arm up to his shoulder into a hole where there had once been concrete.

"So much of me has died tonight," said the hole.

"How'd you do that?" cried the old drunk, placing his hand protectively in his armpit.

"I am no ordinary hole."

"That much I figured."

"Did you?" asked the hole, in a wry tone the drunk didn't like. Whatever was talking to him had greatly recovered from its former desperation. He edged back, but then still another idea occurred to him. He got on all fours and cautiously leaned out over the hole, peering down into its unknown depths. It was a position he had occupied over innumerable toilets. He cupped one hand around his mouth.

"Who's down there?" he asked. His voice echoed off unseen walls, down and down until it was finally swallowed up.

"Now I expect you will want to drop a pebble down to hear it plop?" said the hole. "Man is forever dropping pebbles."

"I was thinking of it," the drunk admitted, and immediately regretted having said it for the hole began to laugh, a low gurgling laugh, as if there were something wet and heavy in its maw.

"Take your sounding if you must, old fellow, but you will not reach the end of me," said the hole. Then it stopped laughing, coughed, and sputtered.

"How'd you know I was old?" asked the drunk.

"Your voice," said the hole. "I know you right down to the colour of your socks."

"Okay, so what colour are they?"

"They aren't a colour," said the hole after a moment's gurgling cogitation. "They're too threadbare and caked with mud and sweat to be a colour."

4

"They're brown," said the old drunk. "And who the hell are you!"

"I am not anyone," said the hole. "I am nothing. Had I been anything they could have killed me. But nothing, you will understand, is immortal." The drunk couldn't understand, not quite, but the hole had no intention of him meditating on the matter. "The essential magic is still in me," the voice barrelled on. "They have not obliterated me."

"Who?" asked the drunk. The hole ignored him.

"They squabbled and fought and left me—some of them with bits of me inside—but they did not kill me."

"Who?" the drunk demanded. It sounded a lot like some guys he once knew. Just the kind of thing they'd try to pull.

"I have more life in me than they ever dreamed," the hole continued and, as if to prove its point, its voice took on a deeper, rougher texture. The drunk leaned back on his hands. The air issuing from the hole was putrid. "There is no end to me," the hole whispered dramatically.

At that moment a siren started not far off, up Queen Street. An ambulance. The hole had been about to go on with its harangue but stopped.

"Would you like to hear a story?" it asked.

There were still several hours until it would be light, thought the drunk. If all this hole planned to do was talk, it would at least be some company.

"About what?" the drunk asked, just to be prudent.

"About how I came to be piled here in this miserable alleyway, waiting for the garbage collector," said the hole.

The old drunk's spirits sagged. It sounded like a pretty boring story. It might even have been his own.

The hole seemed to read his mind. "Oh, it will be most exciting, I assure you. A romance, in fact. A pretty girl—the works! You like romances, don't you?"

5

The drunk thought for a moment. It wasn't Shrove Tuesday any more, he realized, it was Ash Wednesday. Christ was in the wilderness wrestling with the devil. And here was the old drunk in an alley off Queen Street talking to a hole.

"Okay," he said, making himself comfortable. "Out with it."

"Listen," said the hole....

PART 1

FASTYNGANGE

1

It all began a long way from here, at Fastyngange in the north-west corner of Somerset, between the Quantock and the Blackdown Hills.

Alexis was holidaying nearby in Glastonbury, recovering: Teddy had left her, they had split up, it was a trial separation. "Choose one," she would say in casual conversation, if the topic came up. Her juggling of stories was not yet pathological; it did not come that easy. Under the trying circumstances of her separation she had created for herself a recent past best suited to putting off the well-intentioned meddlers one ended up sitting next to on trains. Of her time in hospital, she said nothing. She had quit her nursing job in Toronto and gone off to find herself, or a reasonable facsimile. Teddy had talked a lot about Somerset.

"Alexis is an optimistic sort," her mother, Korrie, liked to say. "And why not? She's not yet twenty-five." Alexis would not have characterized herself so optimistically, but her brief and alarming marriage had not entirely extinguished the bedazzling prospect of true love. She had come to look for it, or a consolation prize— a baronet, perhaps. That's what she had told Korrie. "That's the spirit," Korrie had replied. Alexis fantasized it was true—that the whole trip might end up one of those Nurse Jane love-stories. But she took a wrong turn.

She was on a day trip in a rented car. Evidently her mind was on other matters. She left Glastonbury from the market cross following the B3151 along the River Brue to Meare. It was a beautiful September day. After one and a half miles she turned left onto an unclassified road, signposted Shapwick and Bridgwater, and crossed wooded Shapwick Heath. A lively wind strummed the trees. It had rained the night before and all the leaves looked freshly polished. She turned right as the guidebook advised, and climbed through Loxley Woods to the Polden Hills, turning right again onto the A39 before crossing the Sedgemoor Drain. Weston Zoyland, Bridgwater, Othery, Taunton, and finally Burrow Mump—King Alfred's stronghold—with its unfinished church. Here the guidebook proposed lunch. Alexis was hungry but she decided to go on. She was secretly enjoying the dull ache in her empty stomach. Crossing the Burrow Bridge, she paused and then veered to her right along the Parrett River, allowing the voluble scenery to distract her from the prescribed route. She was pleased with her decision, pleased with the independence of spirit it somehow affirmed. Her spontaneity was soon rewarded. She caught a glimpse of Fastyngange through the trees.

By the time she had found a spot to pull over, the castle was no longer visible. She turned to the tourist manuals strewn on the passenger seat. They were of no help, but then, she thought, in a country dotted with castles, surely not all of them were to be found in guidebooks. She sat for a moment. She had pulled onto a verge by the river. She watched the dragonflies helicoptering over the green waters, the birds darting among the withies along the bank. The air was filled with warm, buzzing life. Now that she was no longer moving, she felt drowsy. She might have been content to nap and then drive on, but her curiosity was a stronger urge than sleep. Drawn from the car, she began to stroll leisurely back along the road. She drank in the sun-splattered seclusion.

A minor breakthrough—she was alone and it was all right.

Occasionally she glanced up at the hillside to her right for some sign of the tower that had brought about this unexpected but totally delightful respite. She saw nothing. A mirage? She no longer particularly cared. As if, she thought, one could need more sensation than the bright emptiness of a country road.

She had walked half a mile when she came upon two excellent oak trees. They were very old and the trunks were hideously deformed with gall. Stopping to gaze upon the impressive disfigurement, she realized the massive trunks formed a threshold. Alexis could make out the mouth of an obsolete driveway, almost lost in the purple shadows. The drive, softened by disuse, curled up the gentle hillside. There were no fences or signs, and she saw no evidence of ownership. With a little shiver of excitement, she passed under the leafy arch. In no time the roadway had deteriorated to a pair of parallel impressions through the meadow that encroached on every side. Yews and larches grew sparsely on the smooth incline, allowing Alexis a clear prospect of the hill's conformation and grade. It was no ordinary hill; it was man-made, an Iron Age earthwork. She had seen its like elsewhere in the southwest. Though she could see no sign of more recent habitation, her discovery gave credibility to the tower she had glimpsed from the road. Castles often occupied the sites of more ancient fortifications. Climbing the earthwork's side, Alexis' mind wandered expansively, contemplating man's desperate need to rise above his fears, and that led her, inevitably, to thoughts of Teddy.

Quite suddenly the road ended at a stand of beech. Plunging ahead, Alexis emerged from the cool of the copse onto a flat expanse of meadow vibrant with maiden pinks. To her surprise she found herself on the hill's crest. And there was Fastyngange. Alexis burst out laughing. Perhaps it was the climb, the dizziness of anticipation, or just her distracted meditations on history, man's and her own, but the group of buildings huddled together within a rotted wall before her was more comic than grand. It must have been the keep she had seen from below, and while it was a stalwart structure its grandeur was not uncompromised. Its upper reaches had caved in. The summit was alive with vegetable life like an unruly mop of hair.

Alexis was far from disappointed. If she had hoped for mystery she was just as pleased with farce: a keep, a hall, and a crumbling battlement; a gate, and through it, a bailey overgrown with weeds as tall as a man's chest, something of a stable, and the corner still left standing of what must have been a church. A cloud moved over the face of the sun, plunging the castle into lively shadows. The cloud passed, and as the castle re-materialized in the light it reminded Alexis, disturbingly, of one of those dream-like Victorian photographs taken by Julia Margaret Cameron.

Suddenly Alexis was startled from her observation by a paroxysm of noisy birds rising from the castle ward. Looking up, she saw a man approaching her from that quarter. He was peering at the ground, ostensibly picking his way through the moss-covered debris in the gateway, but she knew he had seen her. He was wearing a tweed cap on a large bony head, a white shirt, dark tie and gum boots. His dark pants hung loosely from suspenders. He carried a wooden tool kit and a shovel. When he glanced up she saw that his face was older than his sinewy physique had led her to believe. His expression was grave, but his demeanour did not bother her half so much as the suddenness of his appearance.

When he was fifty feet away the man called out. "If ye'r lookin' for the 'oly Grail, ye mizzed yer turn."

One of Tom Mechelney's detractors would have described his voice as a growl. Alexis knew nothing of the man then. She heard him with the ear of a trained nurse. It sounded to her more like the gruff voice of a male patient reluctant to be administered his bed-bath.

"Am I trespassing?" she called out lightly, confidently. "I suppose I am."

Mechelney had seen her all right, long before the starlings had alerted her to his presence. He had seen a woman on stilts, taller than himself perhaps, and at five foot nine he was tall enough. She would probably stoop with age, he predicted. Suffer from back problems. Her face might be pretty enough but there was too much of it. He had assessed her features from one hundred feet as easily as he could tell the sex of a rabbit from the same distance. She wore her pale brown hair "sensibly short", a habit he found uppish, as if women were ever likely to act sensibly. She was agreeably formed but too slim for her own good, and was far too natty in her colourful frock for his taste. He had seen too many natty twenty-year-olds grow into blowsy fifty-year-olds in his day. He nodded his head in response to the question she had already answered.

"Aye, ye'r trezpazzing," he shouted. "Unlezz ye wantz to buy the place."

He had reached her now, as close as he was prepared to come. His boots were coated with a slick of mud.

"Are you the owner?" she asked.

He glanced back at the run-down estate, and then back at Alexis. His expression seemed to suggest she had been insolent. "There'z not been anything like owner 'ere zince the lazt war," he said. Alexis found herself wondering if he was referring to the Second World War or maybe to the War of the Roses. He smiled, revealing a chaos of teeth an orthodontist might have organized forty years earlier. "I'm the eztate egent, ye might zay."

"It's quite something," Alexis replied.

"It'z a far zight clozer to nothin'," the man said with a snort. "Then again," he added, coming nearer, "zomeone with a few bob might znap 'er up and give 'er a coat of paint. Zell teaz to the day-tripperz."

"'er?" Alexis asked.

"Faztyngange," said the man.

The name came as a surprise to Alexis. Fass-tin-gang-ge. Silently her tongue slipped over the name, examining it, tasting it. It was a great deal more poetic than the heap of stones it represented.

"Mind, 'e'd 'ave 'is work cut out," said the man.

Alexis looked past him at the ruin. "What happened to the keep?" she asked.

"Zome of Monmouth'z crew," he answered. "They were 'oled up 'ere, till king'z men fired a few cannon roundz and flushed 'em out. Then damned if they weren't jailed up in their own keep till Judge Jeffreyz 'ad time for 'em." Alexis wished she hadn't asked. The man had stepped closer. His teeth smelled. She was just as glad when he turned away to point at the gateway. The teeth of its rusted portcullis gave it the look of a gaping idiot. "Judge 'ad 'em 'ung. Three of 'em. Right there. But there were more what died."

With his back turned Alexis found herself more interested in the signs of wear on his collar, the dandruff in his raven hair. He turned towards her again to gauge the effect of his bloody tale. Alexis noticed the bread crumbs on his tie. "Then there are ghosts?" she asked with a sly smile. She was quite certain that the intention of the history lesson was to scare her away. That she had been irreverent was plain to see on his face.

"Mizz, it don't need zpiritz to make a place dang'rouz." His voice was gruff. "A perzon wouldn't want to go knocking about without knowing what 'e waz up to, 'z all I mean." He looked sternly at her, but Alexis could tell he was pleased with himself at having gained the upper hand. The old curmudgeon. She was smart enough not to further discompose him.

"May I just look around?" she asked, as sweetly as she dared. "I won't touch anything."

The man looked her up and down. She supposed she had licensed the perusal by asking for his blessing. It was not so much the covert sexuality of his gaze that made her uncomfortable, but her feeling that he was sizing her up for a coffin. When at last

14

he spoke again, there was an implicit warning in his voice not to dismiss what he had to say or resort to any back-chat.

"Ye may laugh, Mizz, but ye'll be laughing out t'other zide of face if ye come round 'ere to muck about. There 'ave been incidenz."

"Thank you," Alexis replied. "I'll be careful." She returned his fixed stare until he tipped his hat and set off past her down the meadow to the beech grove. She watched him go out of sight, and then returned her attention to the castle. She did not see three rebels hanging in the gateway. She saw only the sadly neglected farce she had first gazed upon when she stumbled out onto the hilltop. With its prettily variegated stone it looked as dangerous as a rockery. She started towards the castle but stopped. She heard something—a voice, it seemed. She turned, imagining it to be Mechelney hurling back one last abusive warning. The voice came again, but it was from the direction of the castle.

Had it been a cry for help she would have come. That was my mistake. For my appeal was not anguished, though there was longing in it. She could not have heard what I said from such a distance, but she did sense my longing. And it frightened her....

Under the circumstances, she might have been forgiven the sudden realization that she hadn't the time to explore. She was terribly hungry and had to find somewhere to eat lunch. With one last glance at the castle, she set off down the hill. She had not gone far when she gave in to the urgent tug of gravity and began to run. She did not see the estate agent on her descent.

2

Alexis was staying at the Marriotts' bed and breakfast on Jerusalem Street just below the market in Glastonbury. She had been there a week when she discovered Fastyngange. The Marriotts, Isabelle and Duncan, had as good as adopted her. They were old-world parents, like Teddy's parents — quick on the hug. She fell easily into their kindness, languished in it. She joined them for tea when the other guests were out touristing. She helped Duncan in his garden and Isabelle with her Eccles cakes.

The world's Isabelles will not be misled by half-truths and prevarications. She drew some of Alexis' story from her the way a poultice draws out poison.

"Teddy was under a lot of mental stress," said Alexis, one grey afternoon in the Marriotts' practical kitchen. "He couldn't see it— refused to acknowledge he was in trouble. I became increasingly frightened of him."

A timer went off and Isabelle checked a cake in the oven. "These things have a way of working themselves out," she said, as easily as if she had been commenting on the cake's doneness.

"I became so frightened that I wouldn't let him near me. Then all of a sudden I was supposed to be the one with the problem. *I* was supposed to be frigid, which was nonsense!"

"You wouldn't be the first, dear," said Isabelle, with such reassurance in her voice that Alexis wondered if perhaps abhorrence of sex was a quite ordinary female condition. Then Duncan came in from the garden with his shoulders and back splotched with fat rain-drops and it was time for tea.

So it went at the Marriotts'. But Alexis had not come there to remember, she had come there to forget. What she wished for most was to get away. What she wished for next was comfort, and she got it by the armful from the Marriotts, who gained something in return themselves. Alexis became aware of a daughter, Jill, who was "no longer with them"—whatever that meant. They treated Alexis like a daughter and it was a relationship that did not suffer from being borrowed. It was a reciprocal arrangement; Alexis adopted the Marriotts. Her parents, although still alive, still together, had shut the door quietly on one another years earlier. Korrie and Hadley Grainger were cool, distant. It was nice to borrow this old couple still in love. The domesticity at the Marriotts' was, for her, an alien joy. After a week she had realized that if her holiday did not result in romance it was certainly replete with easy affection.

Guests came and went on Jerusalem Street but one couple, the Dickeys, had been there as long as Alexis. They were from Toronto, a coincidence that delighted the couple and pervaded their every conversation with Alexis. Frank had just retired from the transportation commission. He liked to grill Alexis on bus routes and what you could and couldn't do on a transfer. Rita was equally insufferable: inquisitive and mawkish. Alexis was civil to the Dickeys but civility was not her long suit. She was glad to find them temporarily gone when she arrived home after her encounter.

It was with enthusiasm that she related to the Marriotts the events of her jaunt in the rented car. She ate cold mutton and fry-up in the kitchen and between mouthfuls she described Fastyngange as a "ludicrous little lump of a castle". How they

17

laughed. She was pleased at how well she was entertaining them with her description of the "eztate egent". She embroidered the little man's idiosyncrasies though, it occurred to her, an honest description would have been amusing enough.

Not surprisingly they knew nothing about Fastyngange, but while Isabelle put on the tea and Alexis cut slices of cake, Duncan slipped out to his study and came back with a clipping he had cut from a local paper. Duncan was forever cutting clippings from the papers for the benefit of the guests. This one was an announcement from the Somerset Society of Ancient Buildings. It encouraged historical conservation and invited new members at £10 per annum. There was an address and phone number under the name "Lucinda Harptree". Alexis phoned, admitting that, as much as anything, she couldn't pass up the opportunity of hearing the voice of a Lucinda Harptree. Isabelle and Duncan egged her on. All a tremendous lark. Mrs. Harptree enthusiastically referred her to a Dr. Troubridge up at Shepton Mallet. Troubridge, it seemed, had prepared a monograph on Fastyngange. Alexis was taken aback that someone could take such a place seriously, but she phoned the doctor anyway. And over the noise of a dog barking at his end and the kettle whistling at hers, she arranged to meet him the following day. Upon hearing that she would be motoring, he insisted on giving her an elaborately round-about and historically annotated route to his home, Chewton Cottage. They were to lunch together at noon.

The following morning, bright and early, Alexis set off, feeling happier than she had done in months. The air was apple crisp, the sun as yellow as cheese. Her map took her through the towering limestone cliffs of the Cheddar Gorge to the Castle of Comfort Inn, where the doctor had suggested she leave her car and traipse up the footpath towards Spring Farm to see the Devil's Punch Bowl. He had described the latter as a notable swallet. A swallet, so it seemed, was a hole where a stream disappeared underground.

Alexis sat for some time on a sun-splashed outcropping of rock watching the water gush noisily through the meadow grass only to be flushed suddenly downwards into the dark. The stream continued from there through a whole system of subterranean caves and grottoes which permeated the Mendip Hills. It would finally join up with a tributary of the River Axe on its own underground passage to the sea.

In the bright cool morning, the secret river coursed through Alexis' thoughts.

She wandered up the Roman road which led towards Old Sarum many miles to the east. She lost track of time. In a field, she stood in the midst of a series of earthwork rings far older than the Roman road. The Priddy Circle, Dr. Troubridge had called it. Her thoughts became imageless—not thoughts at all, really, but a kind of yearning.

A tourist bus disgorged its passengers at the Castle of Comfort, finally yanking Alexis back to reality. She was almost late for lunch.

She ran down the hill to her car and raced to Shepton Mallet, disregarding the rest of her prescribed itinerary. She arrived precisely at noon but felt something like a schoolgirl who had not quite finished her assignment.

There was a wooden gate set in a hedge wall that towered raggedly over Alexis' head. A brass plaque on the gate identified the cottage. It was like a fantasy come true. Thatched and bowed, it seemed supported by the weight of the yellow roses that climbed its stucco wall and by the chimneys to either side of the perfectly symmetrical house; a symmetry disturbed only by the puffs of woodsmoke coming from the chimney on the left. But she had no sooner stepped through the gate onto the gravel path than her dream was rudely interrupted. A massive brindle bulldog came charging from the back garden barking his ugly head off. Alexis hurried back into the lane, bringing the gate shut just in time. The bulldog pressed his slobbering face flat up against the fence-slats, revealing one old yellow fang. His eyes begged Alexis to enter. The dog was all out of place, thought Alexis. "You're ruining everything," she barked back at it.

"All right, Judge Jeffreys, all right!" The voice came from the side of the house. The doctor appeared from that quarter, shaking his head and waving a trowel at the bulldog. His hair was salt-and-pepper and as wildly luxuriant as the roses on his cottage walls. He wore an old brown cardigan and pants that were threadbare and grass-stained at the knees.

"The old dear won't bite," he said, booting the thickwaisted canine in the side. The dog waddled affectionately aside a scant few inches to allow Alexis to enter.

"Bob Troubridge," said the man, taking Alexis' hand in guidance as much as salutation. His pale grey eyes smiled out from deeply wrinkled settings. He was in his sixties, she guessed, but his tanned and freckled face made him seem younger.

"Alexis Forgeben," she said, colouring slightly, for she had not used her married name on the trip so far.

Once she was inside the garden, the doctor reached up into the foliage beside the gate and vigorously rang a hand bell that was partially hidden there. "For next time," he said. "Then I'll reach you before the Judge. He hates the damn thing."

Judge Jeffreys raced up the gravel path to the doorway, whimpering. He sat waiting for them on the porch. Having turned from fierce protector to obedient butler, he now pushed open the door with his nose and led them into the primeval dimness of Chewton Cottage.

Alexis wondered if she had tumbled down a very notable swallet. The house was like a grotto, but cosy enough. Only the chattering of an unidentifiable machine gave away the current century. Passing the entrance to a dining room she saw the source of the racket: a personal computer and printer sat on a huge oak table. They stood watching as if at a diorama.

"Prints like the Greeks," Bob said, with obvious pride. "Boustrophedon—left to right and then right to left, like oxen ploughing a field. Damn speedy for doing the Society minutes."

He led the way to a sunroom in the back. It too was a most recent addition to the cottage. The clean tang of fresh paint replaced the faint odour of mildewed plaster and musty settees. Then just as quickly the paint smell faded under the scent of flowering plants, for the room was crowded with lush vegetation. Between rattan chairs with brightly striped slipcovers sat a glass table set with a cheese platter and sparkling wine in a silver cooler. Alexis accepted a glass. Then Bob excused himself to clean up. "Lost all track of time," he apologized.

"This is so generous," thought Alexis, spreading brie on a biscuit. She stared out the window into the garden. Beyond the garden, in a wooded area, the wind pushed the leaves around. Some were turning. It was fall. Alexis loved fall. She found it strange to imagine that in her escape she had decided to return to Canada late in November, missing the one season Toronto did well. She felt lonely. It was a slightly different loneliness than that with which she was growing familiar. This one seemed to grow out of the melancholy she had felt up at the Devil's Punch Bowl. Not homesickness, she reasoned. There was no home to return to. There was always her room at Korrie and Hadley's, but that was only a room. She sipped her wine and thought of fall.

Bob returned in a tweed jacket over a blue turtleneck. He carried a tray of soup bowls and kicked Judge Jeffreys out from under his feet.

"This is so generous," said Alexis.

"It is my very great pleasure," said Bob. "There aren't many who stumble on Fastyngange." She made room for him to set down the steaming bowls filled with a fragrant mushroom soup. They pulled up chairs. The doctor broke them each thick chunks of home-made bread. His hands were as clean as a surgeon's.

"As you have gathered," he continued, "it is a very minor business—not a castle at all, strictly speaking. The keep notwith-standing, it is mostly a sixteenth-century fortified manor house." He had launched so effusively into his spiel that Alexis felt certain she should be scribbling notes in a spiral-bound notebook.

"I feel I should warn you I'm not a historian," she said.

Troubridge waved his hands in the air as he sipped his wine. "Neither am I. Stuffy bunch. But don't worry," he said, grinning. "The history of Fastyngange—what there is of it—is all in my little book. I'll give you a copy of that.

"As you have no doubt learned, history and fable—I'm not certain where one ends and the other begins—have cut a broad swathe through these parts. Your present address, for instance, Glastonbury: St. Joseph of Arimathea planting his bit of the cross, the Holy Grail buried on Chalice Hill. Then there is King Arthur's Avalon, and King Alfred's Athalon—you saw the unfinished church at Burrow Mump—lovely stuff. Lovely stuff. Don't give a tinker's damn if it's 'true' or not. In these parts, the truth is just one way of looking at what is really going on."

The doctor rambled on. When the soup was finished he took away the bowls, returning with plates of whitefish in a parsley sauce. Their glasses were never empty.

The printer stopped its clatter, and Bob sighed happily. He talked about the Society, of which he was the secretary. He talked about the local church he attended when he thought he could bear the parson. "You'll have to forgive me going on like this," he said, without a trace of penitence. But if he was loquacious, he did not seem to regret his solitude. He had cleared the dishes and they sat drinking coffee. Judge Jeffreys snored and farted at his master's feet. "There's just the Judge and me," said Bob, spanking the dog's side lovingly. "We're not lonely."

Alone but not lonely, thought Alexis. "There was a man there," she said.

"At Fastyngange?"

She nodded. "He mentioned that name, Judge Jeffreys."

Troubridge smiled. "Trying to scare you, was he?"

Alexis laughed and again recounted her meeting with the "eztate egent". Troubridge hooted, startling the dog, who had to be patted back to unconsciousness.

"Ted Mechelney," said Troubridge. "Estate agent, indeed! He's been carrying off bits of Fastyngange for most of his life. Has a kind of shambles at Huish Episcopi where he sells curios."

"Can't he be stopped?"

Troubridge shrugged his shoulders. "His collecting has its roots in a proprietorial instinct over a much larger area. Ted considers all of Somerset his for the picking."

"But what right does he have?" Alexis demanded.

Troubridge chortled. "He'll tell you his right's in his name. Mechelney's name is as old as Somerset.

"The last owner of Fastyngange left her between the wars. Abandoned her, more or less. Ted was a lad from a nearby farm. He had helped out around the manor and was left a stipend to check up on it. The Crown assumed ownership in lieu of unpaid taxes sometime in the fifties. By then Mechelney's 'caretaking' was established. I'm sure he had been pilfering from the start, mind you. I think he was given a few pence a year, but that was the last officialdom had anything much to say about the old place."

Alexis, by now, was quietly fuming.

"I've heard Mechelney called 'old man time', " said Bob. "But that's when people are being polite. I'd say he's more corrosive by half!"

"I think it's appalling," said Alexis.

Troubridge grinned at her. "It's your first castle, isn't it?" he said.

"Oh no," she replied, more defensively than she meant to. "I've seen Arundel, Carisbrook— "

He interrupted. "But you *discovered* Fastyngange," he said. Alexis blushed. "That makes it special." She nodded.

The doctor seemed pleased. "Well, I've talked your ear off enough for one day," he said. He picked an apple from the bowl on the table and stood up. Alexis, realizing with regret the session was over, stood up as well, a little wobbly on her feet. Her host went to a bookshelf and took down a slim volume paperbound in grey parchment the same colour as his eyes. There was no title on the dustcover. He handed the book to her. "Read this," he said. "If you don't find it intolerably dry."

Alexis opened the blank cover. *Fastyngange: A Monograph by M.R. Troubridge, M.D., for the Somerset Society of Ancient Buildings*. "Thank you so much," she said, cradling the book in her arm. "I'll read it immediately."

The doctor led her back through the dark little cottage to the front door. On the step they shook hands. "I shall expect you back for a progress report," he said, tapping the book with his knuckle and smiling warmly.

Alexis was brimming with fondness for this kindly stranger. "I'll do better than that," she said. "I'll return to Fastyngange and *really* discover something!"

The muscles that formed the doctor's smile constricted subtly.

"Oh, I don't mean to be rude," Alexis blathered.

A ghost of a smile returned to the man's face. "I'm sure you will discover something," he said.

Alexis shook his hand warmly and promised to return soon. Turning her car in the lane she waved as she passed the break in the hedge, but the cottage door was shut. The doctor had already retired to his minutes or his roses.

3

Alexis begged off playing cards that evening. She bathed directly after dinner and went straight to her room. It was a pretty, pink room above the kitchen and overlooking the garden. If this had been Jill's room then Alexis assumed she had left the Marriotts' life as a child, for the dresser, desk, and shelves were all low. Alexis felt like a giant bending this way and that to see herself in the mirror.

It was a cold room. Alexis dressed in a floor-length flannel nightie and, having plunked a few pence in the fireplace meter, climbed under the massive floral eiderdown. She wrote in her journal but was too impatient to be as detailed as she had become accustomed to being. Dr. Troubridge's monograph lay invitingly on the bedside table.

He launched into his treatise with an imaginative portrait of Somerset at the dawn of time. It was a poetic conjecture, not an introduction so much as an overture replete with buzzing bass and cellos and brooding kettledrums. Iron Age man entered to the tune of muted horns. There followed a panegyric on the toils of the ancients and then, *con moto*, a sweep through the epochs of successive invasions: Celt, Roman, and Saxon. Christ found his way into this invocation, and then the Dark Ages. With great drama, the pseudo-historian closed with an anonymous twelfth-century nobleman standing atop the bald earthwork at twilight, contemplating the castle he was to build.

Alexis laughed and clapped her hands with delight. Such grandiloquence and without a hint of irony! The castle she had seen could never have lived up to such a clamorous voluntary. But the onset of something like historical data, scanty though it was, put a damper on Troubridge's style. His writing became formal and stilted. Proper. There were diagrams.

Alexis learned. The original castle dated from the period of the Empress Matilda's dispute with Stephen of Blois for the English throne. Troubridge accounted for the chief players in the struggle and then speculated at length, inconclusively, on the identity of the anonymous nobleman. His nameless castle was adulterine, Troubridge deduced. There were no records of a battle in the area during the fourteen years of civil war, and Troubridge suggested the collapsed battlements were the result of demolition once Stephen was back in power. It was the practice of the day to tear down counterfeit strongholds. Only the keep, a stretch here and there of curtain wall, and a lesser donjon survived the reprise on Castle No Name. What happened to her noble tenant remained a mystery.

There followed several hundred years of mystery. Troubridge assured his reader he had scoured Somerset House and all the county registers but found nothing regarding the occupancy of the counterfeit castle. With nothing to say, the doctor's style loosened up considerably. Alexis could hear Bob's musical tenor rambling on. There was a long diversion into the history of the surrounding countryside as it might have been seen from the prospect of the Iron Age hill. The doctor also allowed himself an extensive passage describing the state of the ruin as it must have appeared to the next squire, Thomas Blagdon, the builder of Fastyngange Manor.

The arrival of Blagdon in 1550 resulted in the building of the manor and a century of solid land-ownership. Unfortunately, Alexis soon discovered, it spelled the demise of Troubridge's flights of fantasy. Blagdon was a prosperous miller. He was a man of lists and deeds and inventories — of chattel and stock. More boring still, he was a simple man with simple tastes. Nothing reflected this more effectively than the design of his new home. Fastyngange was four-square without nobility of scale, pretension in its fenestration, or idiosyncrasy in its features. Blagdon was penny-wise. The keep was closed off but used as the keystone in the hall's modest fortification. It was a period when the threat of foreign invasion was past, if not entirely forgotten.

No floor plans could be found but Troubridge was able to compile a goodly account of building supplies, receipts for payment to labourers, glaziers, and the like. A trickle of the doctor's enthusiasm and inventiveness percolated through as he literally rebuilt the hall, using supply lists to amplify what was still extant: the hall with its rather handsome cellar; the gallery linking the hall to the battlements; the keep; the kitchen facilities which formed a blind alley with the stables; and ending with the lesser donjon, ingloriously converted to cold storage. Under Troubridge's foremanship, the site rang out with phantom hammers and straining winches, until all the bailey walls were built and the manor completely enclosed. This precaution, it seemed, was to keep livestock and children in, rather than invading forces out. There was to follow an abundance of livestock and children.

Alexis fidgeted in her bed. For some reason the flourishing Blagdons annoyed her—building up holdings in the river valley, and hoarding a considerable wealth. Making children. It left her cold. She became impatient with the doctor, dutifully tallying up each success. "A plague on the Blagdons!" she murmured, and thumbed ahead.

Her expectations had been raised by the panoramic if wholly fictitious opening chapter. She had dared to hope for something which had very little to do with history and far more to do with florid, convoluted epics picked up at the convenience store when other, better forms of distraction were not available. Finally a name began to appear in the text with enough regularity to suggest a new ego at work. Augustus Blagdon III, a spendthrift son—just what the doctor ordered.

Augustus Blagdon strode lustily onto the scene prepared to set Fastyngange on its ear. By the age of twenty-three he had renovated the stodgy estate into a manor of some repute in the county. The hall was opened up with large banks of windows, and opened up still further with an Italian *trompe-l'oeil* landscape that was a constant source of amusement to the ribaldrious new master. Augustus gained a reputation as a host of elaborate parties. He countered his growing reputation as a lecher by building a very beautiful Mary Chapel in the grounds.

By the age of thirty he had depleted the family coffers disastrously by taking a London address—the first Blagdon to act in so grand a manner. London proved his undoing. He became involved with politics. He began to associate with the Protestant Duke of Monmouth, and eventually supported the Duke in his bid for the throne of James II. Dr. Troubridge speculated that this move might have been seen by Blagdon as a way out of the financial embarrassment he had brought upon his head. Nothing, the doctor mused, erases debts like a good revolution. All that remained was for young Augustus to race home and prepare for war. And, the doctor added—and Alexis could see the twinkle in his eye—get hidden as many of the Marian icons from his chapel as he could, in case the Protestant Duke should question his religious affiliations.

Below her in the kitchen Alexis heard Isabelle puttering. As the kitchen door swung open, she could hear the television in the sitting room. She heard Frank Dickey's horse laugh, the one he used when he had made a joke. Bus routes, thought Alexis sleepily. She read on, and in spite of Augustus Blagdon, her mind wandered.

Monmouth. Hadn't Mechelney mentioned the name? "Some of Monmouth's crew," he had said. She had thought he had been talking about a pack of local thugs. She marvelled at the extraordinary compression of time the native was capable of. A gift of those who live forever in one place.

Some of Monmouth's crew: a young rebel captain and some of his troops. In flight, pursued by all the king's men. Holed up in Fastyngange. Holed up in Fastyngange....

There was a knock at the door.

Alexis slipped the book under the covers.

Rita Dickey poked her head around the door, all wide-eyed and treacherous. Her face reminded Alexis of a jelly-bag full of fruit pulp. "We were thinking about you," she said, flourishing a tray with a steaming mug on it. She entered the room, her large bosom flapping under some awful gewgaw pinned there. Reluctantly Alexis moved her legs to allow the matron to sit on the edge of her bed. Horlicks.

"Thank you," said Alexis.

"So hot in here," said Rita.

She was about to expound on the English and their heating eccentricities. Alexis moved quickly to intervene. "Nice brooch," she said.

"It's St. Joseph," said Rita, staring down her front. "It's real."

"How goes the game?"

"Well," said Rita. "We gave up on bridge. Without you there Duncan decided to work in his shop. We're playing something Frank and I play back home—Spite and Malice. Frank is winning," she added, as if it were not at all sure what the final outcome might be. Her face clouded. "That skinny Paul fellow from New Zealand cheats terribly," she said. "But what can you do?"

29

With foreigners, Rita had wanted to add. "Nothing," Alexis thought. She sipped the scalding malt drink, knowing her unwanted visitor would not leave until it was drunk to the granular dregs, but dying to know the fate of the rebel captain.

"What were you reading?" Rita asked.

Guiltily Alexis noticed the shape of the book she had hidden under the covers. "It's history," she said.

Rita wrinkled her nose. "Don't like history," she said. "I thank God Frank and I have made it to our golden years. You don't see many people in history books who can say as much."

"A virtue of the quiet life," murmured Alexis.

Rita beamed. "I'll loan you my Luella Harlow, if you like, or would you rather just talk?"

Alexis thought of the thick paperback she had seen Rita with in the sitting room. There was probably a rebel captain in it too, she mused.

"Actually I'm quite sleepy," said Alexis. She settled deeper into her covers, sloshing Horlicks as she did so. Rita took the cup but not the hint.

"It must be hard to lose someone you love," she said. She sighed dreamily. "Had you been married long?"

"Not a year," mumbled Alexis.

In a light-minded moment, Alexis had told Rita that Teddy had died and then cautioned her—pleaded with her—not to let Isabelle in on the confidence. It had been a rash disclosure; intended to keep Rita at bay, it had the opposite effect of galvanizing Rita's sense of obligation to her countrywoman. Rita wore her secret duty like a medal. Her unwanted attention should have been enough to warn Alexis of the danger of playing fast and loose with the truth. It did not. It was just another ball to juggle, she told herself, remembering, with satisfaction, what Troubridge had said to her: "In these parts, the truth is just one way of looking at what is really going on."

Rita sighed. "Some sleep will do you good," she said, patting Alexis' leg. She muttered quietly about some other girl, someone's daughter, who had suffered a similar loss. Alexis drifted down into sleep. Then the lights were off and the door closed.

The dream grew out of the twilight of her evening's reading, when sleep blended her conversation with Dr. Troubridge into passages from his book and Rita's bedside ramblings and Horlicks and Alexis' own loneliness. The nugatory source of the dream was a tale told in the villages of the valley. The tale of Sally Bert.

Sally Bert was a scullery girl in Augustus Blagdon's kitchens. She was a farm wench from Burrow Mump who came to live and work at the hall when she was thirteen. (Her father had drowned patching up a dyke in the great flood of 1681—I remember her arrival well.) Sally was reasonably happy, returning one day a fortnight to her mother and siblings. Then the Monmouth business began.

With a siege laid and a handful of handsome rebels to choose from, a pretty and impressionable child found herself in the throes of first love. In more peaceful times it would have come to nothing, but under the circumstances it bloomed like some flower under a stopped sun, an accelerated and tragic affair. Sally chose nothing less than the captain as her first lover. Or he chose her.

Love, even accelerated love, was not enough to bypass the lovers' desperate predicament. Despondency flourished almost as quickly as had romance. In some secret quarter of the besieged castle Sally and her captain met one final time to sign a suicide pact, her "x" beside his illegible scrawl. They disappeared. The pact was found but not the lovers. The castle was scoured from top to bottom. It was the beginning of the end of the siege. Thrown into a panic by the double death and mysterious disappearance, the castle help soon plotted the mutiny by which the castle was taken.

Along the dyke many a parent had been known to say to a pining adolescent, "Oh, don't be such a Sally Bert."

Alexis rolled over in her sleep and the girl-child's image careered off into her unconsciousness.

"Don't be such a Sally Bert," she told herself.

4

Alexis awoke at six and lay in bed listening to the house buzzing. The light through the curtains was like thin soup, picking out the design in the carpet but not the colour. She had the strongest urge to get out of the house without having to see anyone or speak to anyone. How a dream shrivels up once you make the simplest utterance, she thought. "Good morning" alone can ruin a whole night's work: a night of Sally Bert and Fastyngange and Teddy, again.

She dressed quietly. She was hungry and needed to pee but decided to wait and go to a restaurant. She packed towel, soap, and toothpaste in her shoulder-bag and snuck down to the front hall.

Despite the earliness of the hour she could hear Isabelle in the kitchen. Alexis stood in the vestibule feeling like a fool. She stared down the hallway to the kitchen door, half hoping it would swing open—"Ah, Alexis, pet, come and help with these biscuits"—but it did not. She pulled the deadbolt like a thief and stole away. She had parked the car in the alley behind the shops across the street. She only had it until the end of the week, and then what? Wales? Scotland? She hadn't exactly followed her itinerary. So much left to tick off! That's what she thought, driving up Jerusalem Street.

She checked the Marriotts' as she passed. There were no faces in the window.

It didn't take long for her to remember that there is nowhere to eat breakfast in all of England, except where you live. And so, for the second time in three days, she was travelling to Fastyngange with a knot in her stomach and her knees crossed.

She "spent a penny", as Isabelle mysteriously called it, in the tall weeds by the river. The mist on the Parrett looked like a calendar picture. It reminded her of being a kid at the cottage.

The roadway between the oaks leading to Fastyngange was due west, so it was almost like night climbing up. She got wet to her knees in the dew. Then on the top, an amazing thing happened. She stepped out of the woods into the little meadow just as the sun reached hill-height. The shadow of the castle seemed to race towards her. The keep won, reaching her first then flying on to be lost in the shadows of the woods. She stood shivering. For a fleeting moment the castle had seemed nothing more than a shadow.

She walked through the gates and stood looking at Fastyngange from the yard. There was a wide entrance to the hall proper, and all kinds of minor entrances stretching out along the kitchen wing. Few of the doorways boasted anything like a door, but Alexis had no intention of entering the buildings. Everywhere there was evidence of Mechelney's beavering. She did not plan on him cornering her somewhere—the nasty old fart. The whole place appeared "dangerously compromised", as Troubridge had put it. One massive block of fallen wall had columns built into its side but all of the entablatures were missing, as were lengths of cornice and frieze. What was left of the wall reminded her of a picture in *National Geographic* of a dead rhino relieved of his precious tusk.

There was a well at the mouth of the servants' alley, the ground mucky around it. It was fitted with a new length of yellow acrylic cord. Mechelney had improvised a winding mechanism. She tried it out and brought up an aluminum bucket full of crystal-clear water, so cold it took her breath away. She washed in it. It was stunning. Mechelney apparently used the water for cleaning his treasures. She found a blue angel in a wheelbarrow ready to be wheeled away.

She walked along a bit of bailey wall, and could see down the valley. The sun had come up brilliantly by then. She watched a car vanish and reappear and vanish again on a wooded stretch of road miles away. The air was bracing.

She finally sat down to rest, picking up in Troubridge's monograph at Augustus Blagdon's fall, and the dreadful Judge Jeffreys—the infamous Baron Jeffreys of Wim. He was indeed a pugnacious bulldog of a man. She thought, not for the first time, what a knack the British had for torture.

The abbots of Glastonbury were the next landlords. They turned the Hall into a retreat. They refurbished the Mary Chapel and planted extensive gardens.

She read on, but sleepiness compromised the effort. She turned to her journal but her thoughts and musings became so jumbled it would have been no use to try to record any of them.

She thought a great deal about the concept of a "retreat". How different from a holiday a retreat must be. Work and prayer. Aloneness instead of loneliness. She regretted the aimlessness of travel. Travel gave her far too much time to contemplate her bruised emotions, the newly opened void.

She set off across the bailey with the thought of returning to her car by a circuitous route. Not long out of the castle compound she came upon an apple orchard on the north-eastern slope. Long grass almost obscured the gnarled, old, stunted trees. They were mostly beyond fruit-bearing, but she did discover one tree with new growth: ripe russets. They were small and wormy but she was so delighted with her find she gathered a dozen relatively clear ones in a cradle she made of the front of her sweater. With the first bite, her hunger rushed up to meet the succulent sun-warm flesh. She found it difficult to nibble around the brown spots and consumed the apple whole, core and all. Her legs suddenly felt weak and she sat down in the grass.

Clearing a spot of windfalls and stamping down the grass, she lay down with her head on her shoulder-bag and gave herself up to the unexpected and fragrant repast.

The grass rose around her like the walls of a hut. The sun poured down almost noon-high. She took off her sweater and lay back on it. She closed her eyes, feeling safely out of Mechelney's way. Her fingers felt her belt buckle grow hot. She yawned and her T-shirt pulled free of her jeans. She was below the wind but a fine stream of it trickled through the grasses and teased the skin of her belly. She thought she heard a voice, but was sleepy and secure enough to believe it was the wind.

Some time later, the sound of conversation made her sit up and peek over the top of her hut. There were several monks farther down the hill with baskets on their arms. She rubbed her eyes. They were picking rowanberries, chatting and humming. Looking up towards the castle she saw other holy brothers at work, their tonsured heads glowing with sweat. One scythed around a stretch of crumbling wall. Another seemed to be digging up roots of some kind. Another gathered bryony flowers. For healing. Then she noticed that one of the monks was sitting in the orchard, not far from her. He had noticed her and smiled contentedly when their eyes met. She nodded welcome to him. There was enough sun and hilltop for them all. She lay back on her pillow. Lazily she parted the grasses nearest her. The monk had clambered to his feet. He was stout. His face was like the full moon. He was helping himself to berries from his basket and his plump fingers were stained. Juice had trickled down a cleft in his chin from his full lips. He waved at her. She redistributed her limbs to feel more of the sun. She closed her eyes a moment, sensing that he was about to approach her, but too complacent to care.

"This place has always been holy," a voice came to her. It was a mild, soothing voice. She opened one eye and he was standing just beyond her plot of trammelled grass. But now she could see he was concealing someone behind his coarse, brown habit. A man, she thought, by the shape of the shoulder and a glimpse she caught of a knee; a man, what's more, apparently without his clothes on.

"I am Friar Rush," said the holy man. He did not introduce his naked companion.

"Alexis," she mumbled sleepily, not meeting the friar's eyes but looking past him to the stranger.

"Three druid geomancers came to this spot," said the friar and Alexis realized that he was not entirely sober. "They were led here just as the wise men were led to Bethlehem—by a star. They camped here, and after a time a voice came to them and filled them with fear and awe." He stopped for a moment and, squinting into the sun, Alexis noticed that the concealed man was tugging on the rope around Rush's fat waist.

"The voice commanded them to renounce their pagan rites," the friar continued impatiently, "and follow the Lord into hell, there to raise the wicked up to heaven." Alexis could hear the man whispering in Rush's ear. "Just a minute," Rush whispered back. "There have been many travellers and stragglers here over the years," he said, pressed by the hidden man to finish his long-winded introduction. "I have one of them with me now."

The friar stepped aside and swept his arm in a stagey manner, and for one moment the stranger was visible to Alexis in his nakedness. Then he hurried back to safety behind the friar's broad back. All Alexis could see of him was his hair blown about by the wind. Backlit by the sun, the hair was of no recognizable colour—darkness fringed with gold.

Alexis raised herself on her elbows. "Teddy?" she said. "Is that you?" She remembered him dark and gold.

37

"This traveller was a tourist like you until he came here—" Again the naked man interrupted the friar, petitioning him in a whisper. "Yes, yes," said the friar to the man, and turned to Alexis. "He says he knows you. He is wondering if he might lie with you."

It was exactly the kind of place that would have attracted Teddy, Alexis was thinking. "Of course," she said. "But why can't I see him?"

"Shhh," said the friar. "He is frail. There is not much of him."

Her mind worked quickly. He had travelled here, before she knew him. This was some part of him he had left behind. There was a kind of sense to it. Slowly Alexis lowered herself to her back. "All right," she said. "Tell him not to be frightened." It occurred to her that the situation called for more to be said, but the words "Teddy, we must talk," died in her throat. Afterwards, she thought. First things first.

She lay waiting, her eyes watering in the glare of the sun. But the man did not reveal himself. Then he whispered again in the friar's ear and the friar nodded his head.

"Perhaps if you were to pretend to be asleep...."

The sun was soporific. Alexis gave in to it. "All right," she muttered, closing her eyes.

Slowly she opened her legs to receive him. The stranger lowered himself onto her gently. The first thing that occurred to her was how big he was. He blocked out the sun, and there was no warmth to his body. "Teddy?" she murmured, shivering under him. Then she felt his hardness against her thigh and though she did not mean to, or even want to, the shock made her close her legs.

Alexis propped herself up again. A cloud had passed over the sun. The monk and the stranger were gone. An apple riddled with worm holes lay in the trough of her legs. She removed it and rubbed the spot on her thigh where it had landed. There would be quite a bruise. Her peace shattered, she gathered her belongings together and left the hill.

She had parked the car by the river where she had left it the first time. She washed the sleep out of her eyes with river water. The water was not so sweet as that from the well at Fastyngange.

She found somewhere "quaint" for lunch. It was not in her guidebook but it was the kind of place the tourist authority liked to hint was to be found in better villages the length and breadth of England. It was perfect in every way, charming right down to the gingham-aproned hostess. It was precisely the sort of inn at which Alexis had believed she would while away her afternoons. Now, somehow, it depressed her. Her mood found little solace in the knick-knackery of the place: the toby jugs along the wainscot, the fiddly china, the pretty dimity curtains.

Lunch arrived: a thick slab of ham pie with crisp brown pastry, a salad, and a generous dollop of rose chutney. The hostess, Mrs. Rowbottom, lingered a moment. Alexis thought to ask her where exactly she was, but realized it would be taken as an invitation to talk, and changed her mind. When Mrs. Rowbottom had retired again to the kitchen, Alexis turned to her food. But although she had been starving, the apples had spoiled her appetite. She found herself pecking at the pie while she thumbed through her tourist manual. To her surprise she found she was but a few minutes from Huish Episcopi. Understandably, the name had caught in her mind. "A kind of shambles," Troubridge had called Mechelney's establishment there. Finishing her lunch with renewed spirit, Alexis set off to find what a shambles might be.

It was really nothing more than a large shed, about as prepossessing as Mechelney himself, though a good deal older.

Windowless, the front of the curio shop gave little away. There was a sign painted in an oddly slanted black lettering that read, "The Museum of Olde Somerset". Alexis was almost relieved to find the door locked.

A skeleton of a woman sweeping the doormat next door came over. "'e's up north viziting 'iz zizter," she said. "Zick, she iz. Deathly zick. That's what 'e sayz."

The woman retired indoors. Alexis walked around the shed until she found a window. Blinking out the glare of the sun and the grime on the window's surface, she was able to get a glimpse of Mechelney's hotchpotch world. Her eyes alighted on a large chunk of grey-blue stone with a remnant of a carved figure, a saint perhaps, but too densely robed in lichen to identify. Lichen thrived on HamHill Stone, she had learned. She was certain the carving was from Fastyngange. She was quietly outraged.

A window opened behind her, startling her. It was the death's head who had addressed her earlier. "If ye'r the party that wantz them bull-anchorz, you should have zaid zo," the woman said.

Alexis had not understood. The woman repeated her statement good and loud. "I've got 'em 'ere," she pointed into her house. "Them and the money-lender'z table. But I won't 'aggle over the price," she said, snapping her head from side to side. "Don't mind doing a favour now and then when there'z zickness in the family, but I don't do 'iz 'aggling."

Alexis assured the lady she was only looking, and the head snapped back into the darkness of its shell. In another moment a vacuum cleaner was heard to roar. Alexis cleared a peep hole of grime. There were all manner of finds plucked from a variety of ruins, or so Troubridge had intimated: old farm equipment, cider firkins, ancient nuts and bolts, and shards of more ancient carving. A hotchpotch. Mechelney was no more methodical, she gathered, than any other hoarding creature—a mouse, a noisy squirrel. She had almost let him scare her, she grinned to herself, and the window against the dark of the shop reflected her smile. She wondered just how long he would be away.

A cat rubbed against her leg. A Siamese. Bluepoint. She stroked its warm, dusty back. It purred, then turned and nipped her hard on the finger. The cat was gone before she could kick it. She sucked on her finger, wishing she *had* kicked the little bitch. But it was towards Mechelney she turned her angry thoughts as she drove home. He had no right to meddle. None.

5

"So instead of taking blood pressure and plumping pillows, here you are attending a decrepit castle, a patient without hope of recovery."

Alexis laughed—a little inanely, she thought. Dr. Troubridge asked with his eyes if he might smoke his pipe. She assented with a nod. While he tamped down the tobacco and lit the bowl, she looked around the dark wood dining room. The word processor was gone. In its place the remains of a leg of lamb rested on a silver platter, and various half-empty bowls and boats littered the linen clothed table. A fire flickered low in the hearth.

"You've read my book," said the doctor. "You know there is no local council hammering down the National Trust's door to restore Fastyngange."

"I haven't read the end bit yet," she admitted.

"It's rather depressing," said the doctor, leaning back in his chair, his pipe going, a snifter of cognac in his hand. Judge Jeffreys rumbled. He barked half-heartedly in a dream. Someone at the gate, thought Alexis.

"After the abbots left, the Hall stood empty again until early in this century. Then a bicycle manufacturer from Bristol, with more money than sense, bought it on a lark. Husted, his name was. He had married a second time, April–December, and he apparently bought Fastyngange for his young wife. Or so she claimed. A romantic sort, Elspeth Husted. A painter. I met her, you know."

Alexis' surprise brought a smile to Troubridge's face. "I was a good deal her junior," he said. "Let's see, it was in 1960. I had just discovered Fastyngange. Husted was long dead, but I traced Elspeth to a nursing home in Cheshire." To the hopeful look in Alexis' face, the doctor only shrugged. "If she were alive now, she would be in her nineties. When I met her she was a very well preserved and attractive seventy-three. I tried to see her again when I was preparing my book—that was in '67. The home informed me she was no longer with them. They would not tell me where she had got to, or which side of the veil."

"She was a romantic?" Alexis asked.

"From what I can gather," Troubridge replied. "The home where she was staying was actually a hospital. She was not mentally fit, but she was quite lucid about Fastyngange." The doctor suddenly put his pipe in his ashtray and stood up. "Follow me," he said.

Alexis followed him down the hall and into a cold front room. When the lights were up, Alexis could see it was a sitting room, but obviously not one in which the doctor did any sitting. There were bookshelves with glass doors, uncomfortable Victorian settees with antimacassars, and a hearth that no one had sat around in some years, she suspected. She recalled a picture by Magritte of a room carved out of grey stone, waiting ponderously and immutably for something to happen. Such was the effect of this cold chamber on Alexis.

The doctor turned on a light affixed to the frame of a painting directly above the fireplace, which illuminated a tiny canvas. It was circular, no more than twelve inches in diameter. But stepping closer, Alexis could see it was not a minor kind of work. It was an intricately detailed landscape which she recognized immediately as the valley to the north-east of Fastyngange.

43

"I was there yesterday," she said, recognizing in the foreground the apple orchard where she had seen the apparition of the monks, if it had been an apparition. In the painting the orchard was in bloom. "Mrs. Husted?" asked Alexis, lingering on the lush blossoms crowning the gnarled old trees.

"Painted from memory," said the doctor. "At the nursing home."

"No!" said Alexis. She peered still more closely at the painting. She might have been staring through a tiny porthole, so perfectly did the trees and hills and the river valley align with her fresh memory. Even the difference in seasons could not hide the remarkable resemblance of the painted scene to the real thing. "From memory," Alexis mused.

"A rather disturbed memory at that," said the doctor. "Mind you, they're often the more accurate."

Alexis examined the painting from a nose-length. Every leaf glittered as if a spring shower had just passed.

"Distemper," said the doctor. "Took her five years to paint."

Alexis tried to imagine anything taking five years, let alone anything so small. She shook her head and pulled away from the painting. The doctor turned off the light and the life rushed out of the room. He took Alexis' arm and led the way back to the fire. He stoked it and they pulled up overstuffed chairs so that they could rest their feet on the fender. He poured Alexis a second cup of coffee.

"She was quite a dreamer," said the doctor, chuckling. "Quite the fabulist. At first I was all agog at the things she had to tell me, until I realized she couldn't possibly be telling me the truth."

"I suppose that's important to a historian," said Alexis, contrarily.

The doctor accepted the challenge without defensiveness. "Fiction has its place in history, I'll not deny it. It can also occupy a particularly useful place in one's own personal history. I doubt, for instance, whether you have told me the whole truth about yourself or your interest in Fastyngange. Now don't glare at me, and don't look hurt. The truth is, we need to make into fiction what we cannot fathom about the facts of our lives. As one thinker has put it: 'We imagine life, the better to test it.' What else is legend but something essential that is essentially untrue?" He stopped and regarded Alexis. She stared into the fire or through it at something the doctor could not see.

"In any case," he continued, "Elspeth Husted's life had taken on legendary proportions by the time I got to her."

"Is this part in the book?" Alexis asked.

The doctor shook his head. "Very little," he said. "Dear old thing. It would not have been right to repeat anything she said that I couldn't verify elsewhere."

Alexis imagined herself locked up in a home somewhere, chattering away to anyone who would take the time to listen, saying whatever sprang into her mind. "I feel I should tell you something," she blurted, not looking at the doctor. "My interest in Fastyngange is not entirely"—not entirely what?—"not entirely wholesome," she ventured.

The doctor nodded gravely. "No obsession ever is," he said. His gravity was tinged with affection. "But don't tell me about it." He glanced at her and must have seen something of embarrassed shock in her eyes—something of torment and, simultaneously, of relief. "Don't misunderstand me," he said. "If you have some confidence to share, I'm all ears. But my guess is you'll stop short of telling me what you really want to, and we'll both end up feeling unfulfilled by the experience." He looked uncomfortable for a moment as though recalling past unfulfilments. "What we wish to know," he said, "is inevitably compromised by what we are prepared to believe."

Alexis moved in her chair, crossed and uncrossed her legs. "All I was going to say was that the castle casts a strange kind of spell over me."

Troubridge nodded thoughtfully. Then he cast her a glance which was something of a warning. And any thoughts of continuing on the same course of conversation vanished. She returned her thoughts to Elspeth Husted.

"Imagining life the better to test it," she said, thinking of the brilliant little circle of life hanging on the doctor's other, unused fireplace. "What kind of things did *she* tell you?" Alexis asked, and he returned her grin with a wink.

"You've guessed it," said the doctor. "Fastyngange cast a spell over Elspeth as well."

He tapped his pipe thoughtfully. "Well, for one thing, she was bound and determined the Holy Grail was buried at Fastyngange."

"Mechelney said something about the Grail," said Alexis, recalling his opening gambit. She recalled his muddy boots and the shovel he had been carrying.

Troubridge was deep in a blue cloud of pipe smoke. "I daresay he did," he said, chuckling again. "He caught the bug from Elspeth. He saw something of her between the wars, a great deal more of her than her husband."

"Do you mean to say...."

Troubridge shrugged as Alexis picked up on the implications of his statement. He laughed. "Mechelney was a teenager," he said thoughtfully. "Did odd jobs for Mrs. Husted. She was twice his age. Mind you, a very beautiful woman, I'd wager." He paused for a moment, and Alexis watched the old man weigh the facts as he had obviously done before. "I doubt Mechelney would have known what to make of Elspeth Husted at *any* age," he said, seeming to dismiss the idea. Alexis didn't.

She settled her coffee cup in her saucer. The rattle seemed to give her away, for she was suddenly imagining all manner of liaison between the young farmboy and the manufacturer's lonely wife. She was also thinking, uncomfortably, that there might be more to Mechelney's aggressive territoriality than she wished to

46

allow. She placed the cup on a side table. There was only the ticking silence of the room now, and the gusting of the wind outside.

"Was it Fastyngange that drove her mad?" Alexis asked.

"How perceptive of you," said the doctor. "Rattling around in a big old place like that. Alone too much of the time. Sensitive. Who knows?"

"That's probably what it was," said Alexis. There was a tapping at the window. Alexis turned. It seemed to be the branch of a tree. There had been talk of rain. Returning her gaze to the room, she saw that the doctor had been watching her.

"There was a fire," he said. "Gutted the Mary Chapel—well, you've seen what is left. It seemed the bicycle manufacturer had been using it as a lab of some kind; the war effort affected different people in different ways. He was not there at the time the place went up. Some people thought it was a German rocket gone way off course. Whatever it was, the chapel was the only building to suffer. Nobody could find Elspeth at first. Mechelney finally did, after a couple of days. People thought she had perished in the blaze. I suppose in one way she did.

"It wasn't long after that that she moved away, back to Bristol and then to the institution in Cheshire."

Judge Jeffreys shifted his weight nearer to the fire. One of his eyelids was open a crack. Alexis could see the flames' reflection flickering there.

"She must have loved it so much," said Alexis. She sighed. "I want to possess it," she said. "Not *own* it—I don't mean that. But lock it up in my heart and take it home." Eagerly she turned to see what the doctor might have made of her outburst. He was smiling. Laughing at her? She didn't think so. "Like I was saying—not entirely wholesome," she said.

"I felt much the same about the old place," he replied. "Allow me to quote myself from the last page of my little book. 'So weary and so desolate. One is tempted to project onto that crumbling façade an image of humanity in all its comic meanness and disarray. Rebels, monks, and bicycle barons—what a pathetic sideshow, and yet, what else is history?'"

Conversation languished. Alexis and the doctor seemed to have sailed in separate boats into the lee of some dark, uninhabited island.

Troubridge coughed after a time, and put away his pipe in his pocket. He leaned forwards and made much of scratching Judge Jeffreys behind the ear.

"You will be careful, won't you?" he said, without looking at her. Alexis was at a loss for what to say. His admonition had been such a kind and fatherly gesture. Careful of what? she thought.

"There have been incidents," said the doctor.

"Incidents?" she asked, and to her own surprise there was a note of impatience in her voice.

"The ruin is not in the best of repair," the doctor said.

Alexis turned on him with an eyebrow raised. "You're prevaricating," she said.

Troubridge took heart at her cockiness. "There was a tourist," he said, cautiously. "It was some years ago now. He had gone missing in the area and there was some belief he'd made his way up to Fastyngange. There was a police enquiry. But eventually the authorities abandoned the case."

Just some straggler, thought Alexis.

Troubridge leaned back in his chair and regarded Alexis' face. She did not flinch under his observation. Alexis could see a certain tightening around his eyes.

"But then us tourists are a rum lot," she said.

Troubridge smiled, though not as brightly as she might have hoped. "You'll be all right," he said.

On the doorstep the night air was cool, and cooler still for a strong camphor-like odour. "Hyssop," said the doctor. "I transplanted it here from Fastyngange. The monks cultivated all manner of curatives, as you will have read in my book."

"The list of simples," said Alexis.

"Many of them grow wild now on the hill," replied Troubridge.

Alexis breathed deeply. "Purge me with hyssop and I shall be clean," she intoned.

Troubridge chuckled. "Yes, there are its ritualistic cleansing properties, but when I ventured into the cellars I did find evidence of a still. The hyssop probably found its way into some form of liqueur. Benedictine, I dare say."

Impulsively Alexis kissed Troubridge on the cheek. "So retreat was not without its perks," she said. He nodded.

They stared at one another for a moment in uncomfortable silence. And then, without a further word, she turned and left, the smell of hyssop filling her nostrils and bitter on her tongue.

It was ten when Alexis arrived back at the Marriotts'. Duncan and skinny Paul were watching the television. Isabelle was playing Spite and Malice with the Dickeys. They looked up at Alexis expectantly.

"You're home early," said Mrs. Dickey, inviting explication.

On the television a hijacker shoved a crippled hostage from an airplane and slammed the door behind him. Alexis watched as cowering police and Red Cross officials ran to help the cripple down the stairs.

"Yes," said Alexis. And went to her room.

6

Alexis woke up starving the morning after her dinner with Dr. Troubridge. She had slept deeply and dreamt deeply and Fastyngange had been at the centre of every dream.

She folded her hands underneath her head and looked at the sun pouring through the window. She had told the Marriotts that the next warm weather she would set off on a walking tour for a couple of days. That weather was here and she was rested and restless to go. She lay in her warm cocoon of eiderdown and let the thought of leaving percolate up through her until it filled her with delirious exuberance. She kicked her covers half-way across the room. She dressed in the grip of the idea.

First she would take the car back, she thought. But no — first she would eat. She must eat heartily this morning.

Sun drenched the dining room, glinting off the silverware and shimmering around the freshly picked flowers. The Dickeys were at their usual table. Rita wore dark glasses and waved a piece of toast at Alexis. Mr. Dickey was on his feet and holding out a chair before Alexis could politely refuse and sit elsewhere. His sunny-side-up eggs glowed, fluorescent in the light.

"In Toronto," began Mr. Dickey, resuming his seat heavily, "the hockey season is starting. Can you believe that?" He was in a boisterous mood. His purple cheeks reeked of noxious aftershave.

Alexis felt flustered. It was partially hunger, partially foreboding. "There will be quite a snarl-up at the College Street station," she said quickly, hoping to forestall a lengthier discussion of transportation administration. Mr. Dickey looked baffled.

"He means the *weather*, silly," said Rita, gesturing at the sun-filled window. "Not like this at home."

Duncan brought Alexis her tea. It already had milk in it, and sugar. Why had she never told them she took it clear? "Thank you," she said, endeavouring to give Duncan an especially cheery smile.

"Tell her our plan," said Frank Dickey to his wife.

"We are going to spend the day in Camelot," said Rita, folding her hands on her enormous breast.

"How lovely," said Alexis.

"Bus loading at 9:25 sharp," said Frank, blowing his thumb like a whistle. "Pip, pip, tally ho! Eh, Duncan?"

"I suppose so," said Duncan, as he returned to the kitchen.

" 'cept it's called Cadbury Hill in these parts," scowled Rita. She sighed.

Alexis glanced at her watch. She wanted to be at the bank as soon as it opened.

"Tell her the rest," Frank said. "Go on, Rita."

Mrs. Dickey took off her dark glasses and blinked so that her eyes disappeared into wrinkled folds of jelly-bag flesh. For the first time it occurred to Alexis that Rita might be a secret drinker.

"We'd love you to come along," she said.

"Our treat," said Frank. "The Dickey Express. High tea, the works."

Alexis was caught off guard. "Oh, but I couldn't," she said, much too quickly. To her surprise the Dickeys were not put off. They winked at each other. Frank leaned close to her. There was butter smeared on his cheek.

"You can bring your friend," he said.

Duncan entered from the kitchen with Alexis' breakfast and the teapot for refills. Frank nudged her.

"What's all this?" said Duncan. He was wearing a flowered pinafore. He wore it every morning, but it had never struck Alexis as preposterous until now.

"I've been invited to Camelot," she said. "But as I was just telling Arthur and Guinevere here, I had other plans for the day."

Frank brayed. Rita blushed. Duncan snapped his fingers. "I'd quite forgotten," he said. "You'll be wanting a lunch for your tramp in the wilds. I'll tell the boss."

Having served his guests, he returned to the kitchen, while Alexis bit into her toast noisily, glad to have her excuse corroborated and to have so narrowly avoided the unmitigated hell of an outing with the Dickeys. Her throat was dry, making it impossible to get down her mouthful. She drank some tea and made a face like someone swallowing a pill. She caught a glimpse of Rita, who was still grinning.

"Is it that doctor fellow?" asked Rita, in a girl-to-girl kind of way.

Alexis blushed. Rita looked satisfied.

"What'd I tell you?" said Frank, lightly slapping the table and then turning back to his eggs with renewed appetite.

Alexis might have left it like that. She was safe from them. The invitation to Camelot evaporated, perhaps never more than a ploy. But Alexis looked at them and was filled with ennui. She felt the same imageless yearning she had felt at the earthworks on the way to Chewton Cottage. Rita was digging through her voluminous handbag for something. Alexis had seen her do it often without actually finding anything, as though in another life perhaps Rita had been a magician and was overcome, from time to time, with the dizzy feeling of having misplaced a rabbit or a dove. And Frank was staring off through the window, munching contentedly, going over in his mind the day's itinerary, or what he'd tell the guys at the shop when he returned to Toronto. For although he was retired, he would go back to the shop—Alexis was certain of that—as often as he could, to drink bad coffee, complain about it, and chat with his mates; to get away from Rita. Something broke inside Alexis: a little bladder of bitter water. She did her best not to screw up her face at the taste of it. What did it matter what they thought, this woman of fat romances, this man of short-turns and re-routings? She had lied to them more than once when it suited her. But perhaps that was it; it had been important to her to have them believe what she wanted them to believe. Now they believed she had taken a lover and she was overcome with the urgent need to correct this impression.

"Actually the doctor is helping me," said Alexis, her mind working quickly. "You see, I've become quite interested in herbal medicine." She was glad to see the Dickeys caught off guard and hurried to further unsettle their composure. "The countryside hereabouts is famous for its abundant curatives."

Frank was not one to have his mind changed quickly. After his initial surprise, a smile crackled across his face. "You mean like pussy willow tea and that kind of hocus-pocus?"

"I don't know about pussy willows," Alexis answered without hesitation, "but bloodroot, horehound, St. John's wort, puke weed—"

"Ooo really, Alexis!" said Rita, screwing up her nose and hurriedly putting down her teacup.

Duncan re-entered the room. "Anything the matter?" he asked.

"Alexis has been pulling our leg," said Frank. "Says she's off to pick puke weed in the backwoods."

"Frank!" said Rita disapprovingly.

Duncan chuckled but gave Alexis an inquisitive look. "This is the first I've heard of it," he said.

Alexis continued, compulsively now. "Didn't I tell you?" she said. "I've found a place where there are remedies for all kinds of things just growing wild, free for the picking. All in all there is a lot to be said for the old ways, the old wives' tales."

"Quackery!" said Frank, looking Duncan's way with a devilish grin, as if not wanting to waste this intelligence on the womenfolk.

"The stuff you buy in the drugstore can't cure everything," said Alexis, too loudly and more desperately than she wanted. "Believe me, I know that better than any of you."

"She is a nurse," Duncan reminded them. Then he snapped his fingers. "Is it the old castle?"

"Yes," said Alexis, a little uncertainly now. She hadn't wanted to give away quite so much, hadn't meant her fib to come quite so close to the truth.

"Ah hah!" said Frank. "I figured this doctor fella was involved in it all somehow. You see, Rita?"

Rita did see. She blushed. She could see a field of wild, sweet-smelling flowers, an upturned basket of cuttings, and a blue-eyed doctor gathering up Alexis, limp in his strong arms, her bodice unbuttoned to the waist, a bouquet of Queen Anne's lace in her clenched fist. The doctor was kissing her throat. Rita saw it all in her Luella-Harlowed mind. Her eyes glazed over.

Alexis gave up her subterfuge. They would cling to their interpretation of her life as obstinately as she might try to change it. It had been foolish to say anything, but she trembled inside with rage.

Isabelle entered the room. "Last call for toast," she said, but it was obvious from the expression on her face as she looked from one to the other of the guests that she had sensed some kind of an uproar.

"Well, I must get ready," said Alexis, seizing the moment. She hastily wiped her lips with her napkin and got up. "Busy day ahead." She had stood up too fast, though, and had to lean on the table for a moment to get her balance.

Rita supported her by the wrist. "Are you all right?" she asked.

54

Then Paul entered in his bicycling togs.

Alexis caught her breath. She would be fine if she could get out of this room and away from these people. "I'm okay," she said with a weak smile. "A bit nervous," she added, which made Rita's day. Nervous could mean only one thing to Rita.

"You two have fun," she said under her breath, her eyes dancing.

"What, us?" said Paul, who had come to Alexis' aid and now slipped his arm around her.

Rita glared at him. "Cheeky thing," she said.

Alexis pulled herself away, annoyed at Paul's resistance, slight as it was. They all wanted her to stay. They all had plans for her.

"Camelot would have been fun," said Frank.

"Yes," said Alexis, and left. They all watched her go.

Then Frank said, "I think she's balmy, as you folks would say."

"Don't be rude, Frank," Rita added.

And then, to everyone's surprise, Isabelle piped up, "No, I'm afraid he's quite right. She's making it up as she goes along."

"Hold it," said the old drunk. "Just hold it right there. How'd you know they said that?"

"She told me everything, later," said the hole.

"She who?"

"Alexis, of course," said the hole, its impatience almost visible, a violet aura over the stone circle at the drunk's feet.

"But Alexis'd left the room," said the drunk.

"Oh?" replied the hole, mildly. "Didn't I tell you she waited in the hall? Didn't I say how she put her ear to the keyhole? Surely I did—or I would have if you hadn't interrupted me. It was that which made her mind up once and for all."

"To go?" asked the drunk.

"She didn't even return to her room," said the hole, in a pleasantly surprised tone of voice.

Everything Alexis needed for banking and shopping was in her purse. She had woken up thinking of a light-weight hiking pack. She found herself buying, instead, a large knapsack on an aluminum frame. She bought several warm sweaters and pairs of jeans, a sleeping bag, and hiking boots. Each purchase seemed to escalate a plan that had started out in the morning as a day-trip and was now growing into something more. She bought a large bottle of Benedictine.

Over lunch she wrote the Marriotts: "I might be a few days. Maybe more. You've been so thoughtful and kind, but I really need to strike off on my own. Thank you for everything."

It should have been more expressive. She added kisses and hugs above her name; that would have to do. She enclosed a cheque to bring her up to date and another to cover the cost of storing her things, signed but without the amount filled in.

And so Alexis found her way back to Fastyngange, but not in a rented car this time. She came on foot, with a backpack, like a monk on pilgrimage. It was not a symbolic act; she really had no idea how long she might stay.

7

Alexis did not come to me right away. My room in the keep could only be reached by a spiral staircase—very dark, uncompromisingly narrow, and treacherously steep. The staircase was situated at the end of a whistling gallery, which had been the scene of much of Mechelney's butchery. He had removed most of the ceiling bosses and all the traceried stonework he could. There had been cave-ins. The doorway to the keep was strewn with debris, but the entrance was by no means concealed. More than once I heard Alexis pass below, stop, reconsider, and walk away.

At first she camped in the orchard on the north-eastern slope. She chose a sheltered spot where she would not immediately be noticed by anyone arriving from the road. Just to be on the safe side, she took her tent down every morning. The sun woke her early.

She picked wild flowers and herbs using Troubridge's list of simples, augmented by some musty old field guides she had found in Glastonbury at a second-hand bookstore. There were a fair number of species still flowering as the weather was unseasonably warm, but with so much time on her hands she was content to gather dead plants as well. Often she could not recognize the withered stalks, but that did not stop her. She worked with what she found. She was always hanging up a bouquet to dry or pulverizing seeds in a mortar or boiling up this or that in a billycan over her camp stove: betony flower for anxiety, piquant lovage for menstrual disturbances, rue for nervous congestion, juniper as an aphrodisiac, and winter savoury to counteract the juniper. Though for the most part these astringents and tonics had little effect, there were exceptions; her medical background did not stop her from recklessness. She aged yellow broom in a sealed jar and after ten days smoked the molding leaves. The euphoric result was compromised by a severe bout of uterine contractions. On another occasion she overdosed on lobelia-leaf tea and fell into a mild coma. She kept herself busy.

She went on many walking trips, circumnavigating the earth-work, visiting the nearer towns; but as the days wore on she stayed closer to home. She made her provisions last longer. She learned to be frugal. She was certain the naked man on the hill had been Teddy but searching for him was futile, she soon decided. She determined to make the waiting as tranquil as possible.

She discovered passion flowers in bloom on a dilapidated stretch of the south wall. They fascinated her—the large white flower with the corona like Christ's crown of thorns, ten petals like the ten true disciples, three styles like the nails of the crucifixion, and an ovary like a hammer. She made an extract from the flowering heads. It made her very calm.

She was happy, some days, just to explore the castle, or write in her journal out in the yard. I could sometimes hear her singing, talking to herself. She argued out loud—won and lost. I came to know her quite well. My hearing is "tuned to a worm's turn", as one of your poets puts it.

Gradually I noticed her growing confidence in her own presence there. Her step changed. She learned where the floor dipped, where the railing was no longer secure. Sometimes she stood in the roofless, wall-less church remembering hymns and snatches of the service from her Anglican childhood. It took me back. She was playing house in the bones of Fastyngange. Then one day, she moved in. Perhaps she noticed the weather was about to change. It was October, and though there was still fine weather ahead, there would be rain on and off through the cooler days and lengthening nights. Perhaps she was emboldened by Mechelney's failure to appear.

She picked a snug retreat. She moved into the buttery, in the old servant's alley behind the lesser donjon. She cleaned it out with an evergreen bough and sprinkled the floor with fragrant grasses from the meadow—a veritable Snow White. The room was well chosen for her surreptitious occupancy. The roof was sound and there was a door she could secure from the inside.

It was strange for Alexis to sleep indoors again. She hardly closed her eyes the whole night. She thought she heard voices—someone yelling, whispering, calling. Kids, she suspected. The hill would make a great spot for necking. She did not imagine they would venture up to the castle. Who could contemplate love-making in such a place? Her first night in the orchard she had worried about prowling animals; in the buttery there was only one kind of animal she anticipated. Every cell in her body was on the alert. She willed Teddy to find her there. This time she would not flinch. She had cut balsam boughs for a mattress. She slept, at last, or at least she woke up. The second night was just the same—filled with fear and longing.

On the third night she dreamed of her parents' cottage, of sitting on the dock in the still of the night and hearing snatches of converstion from unseen cottagers across the lake. It had always impressed her as a girl how clearly she could hear voices on the water. Drifting in and out of her dream, the voices all seemed to be talking about her and Teddy. Straining to hear them more closely she heard his name again and again. Dreaming, she recalled Teddy's first time at the cottage, finding her parents there unexpectedly. She recalled Korrie managing everything without blinking an eye—getting Hadley to cart Teddy's bag off to the sleeping lodge on the beach while she lugged Alexis' bag to her room in the main cottage.

Alexis awoke under the strain of the dream and lay on her balsam bed sweating. The strangest feeling came over her. She became quite certain the voices had stopped talking just as she woke up. A coincidence, not the end of a dream. She listened. Nothing. She imagined others listening to her listening. She dozed off. Sometime later she heard singing. Gilbert and Sullivan. She recalled her parents' G&S parties and, just as she had done as a child, she wanted to leave her little room and go to join the party, or at least watch it from the shadows at the top of the stairs. It frightened her at first, but the merriness of the singing eventually allayed her fears, though not enough to make her stir from the safety of her retreat. If these were ghosts, she told herself, then they were not averse to human company. Soon, she told herself, he would come.

She spent her days preparing for the night and her nights longing for the day. Teddy had been here. There was something of him here still. All her life she had been a woman of action, but there was nothing she could do now but drink her extract of passion flower and wait.

She shopped in Othery, buying all the kinds of food she remembered the heroes and heroines of Enid Blyton adventures taking with them on picnics: canned hams, potted this and that, sweet gherkins, sweetened condensed milk, and Peek Frean biscuits. She wrote a long and chatty letter to Isabelle, describing an imaginary hostel she had reached and how friendly all the people were there. It only occurred to her after she had mailed it that the postmark would be wrong.

She found a piece of glass she used as a mirror. "Mirror, Mirror, on the wall, who's the skinniest of them all?" she chanted, astonished at the image the pane presented her. If she sucked in her breath she could see her xiphoid process sticking down from her sternum like a little dagger into her diaphragm. She could grasp it in her hand. It was exhilarating.

Finally, one night, after a week in the buttery and the last few ounces of Benedictine, he came. She was sure it was him. He stood outside her door for some time. Then he walked away down the alley to the well. He lingered there; she heard him muttering, she thought, staring back down the alley towards her little room, where she waited, listening, scarcely able to breathe.

"Teddy?" she dared to whisper. It was obvious to Alexis that he expected her to make the first move. She knew her little latch could not keep him out. He could breathe on her door and it would cave in. He paced back and forth and then, as quickly as he had come, he was gone again.

Alexis had no idea when she fell asleep. She lay thinking of the afternoon under the apple tree. She became aroused for the first time since leaving Toronto. She fought it and then gave in. It was depressing but at least she slept afterwards. This was her life in the buttery.

But Alexis was not in the buttery the rainy day Mechelney returned. She was down in the great gutted hall, standing in the deep bay with its wide-mullioned glassless window, looking out across the overgrown ward to the Mary Chapel. There was only a corner of the transept and something of the choir left. It made, I'm told, an evocative set-piece, especially on a wet, grey day. There was nothing beyond the church to mar the view but the meadow gently rolling down to the Parrett and, in the distance, the Mendip Hills. In any case, her thoughts must have been miles away because she saw the agent before she heard him. Luckily he did not look up. She was caught completely off guard. With the other's footsteps loud in the antechamber of the hall itself, she removed her shoes and I heard the scrape of her bare feet flying across the floor, up the stairs to the covered bridge, and down into the obscurity of the whistling gallery. Alexis hovered at the dark end of that passage, near the doorway to the keep. She was safe enough for the moment. Mechelney was busy elsewhere. I could hear his hammer ringing as he chiselled away at some ornament.

Alexis was on the brink of the keep, the stronghold, the last resort. Her thoughts turned to Augustus Blagdon and Monmouth's rebel crew. They preceded her up the stairway with their torches and their wounds. She was wounded herself. She had cut her foot in her shoeless flight from the hall. The hammering stopped. Alexis trained her eyes on the light at the end of the gallery. By the time Mechelney entered the long room, Alexis had slipped through the doorway into the keep. I listened to her tentatively climbing the stairs. She gasped as she entered my chamber, for the pitch blackness suddenly gave out onto a landing lit by a small window. Alexis stood on the top step. When the footsteps below still seemed to approach, she looked around the room for further means of egress. My chamber was the end of the line. The collapsed tower above had suffocated the uppermost stretch of the keep. The chamber was strewn with broken stones. With nowhere left to go, Alexis looked for either something to bar the way or a weapon of some kind. It did not occur to her that she could have obliterated her rival by rolling one of the great square stones down the narrow stairwell. That was the essence of the keep's design—all advantage to the besieged. The idea must have occurred to Mechelney though, for he did not enter the stairwell. There was a little table and chair in the room. Alexis grabbed up the chair and waited at the top of the stairs.

" 'ello up there!" Mechelney shouted. Alexis whimpered. "I know ye'r up there," he called. Alexis shook when the words had wound their way up to her. "I'll not cum up," he said. "But ye'r acting like a bloody little fool." Alexis' face turned scarlet. Her cheeks burned as they had not done in years. Suddenly she was at home again, locked in the bathroom, with her father shouting at her, reprimanding her for some adolescent foolishness. She was momentarily paralysed with rage. Then he shouted, "Ye can't keep thiz up for ever, Mizzy!"

What right had he! It was her business. This was between her and Teddy. They could solve it themselves if he would just leave. "Go away. For God's sake just go away!" she whispered, inaudible to anyone but me. The voice came again.

"I'd az zoon find no trace of ye when I next cum 'bout," he shouted. Then his footsteps retreated along the whistling gallery. Alexis' storm of indignation abated. The incident had left her weak. She wrapped her arms around herself and paced the dimly lit little room.

The rain picked up. It soothed her ragged nerves. She righted the chair which was to have been her weapon. She sat down on it to examine the cut on her foot. She wet a handkerchief with spit and began to clean the dirty clotted wound. Nursing brought her round to her senses. Not willing yet to venture from her refuge, she took the time to look it over more closely. Her glance at last travelled to the little niche in the wall with the *oeil-de-boeuf* window, not entirely choked by lichen. I took that moment to introduce myself.

"The window is an architectural conceit," I said.

From what I know of social intercourse, it seems important to make one's opening remarks innocuous and yet, at the same time, encourage some kind of lively riposte. I failed, for I received no response whatsoever from Alexis. She stared at the bull's-eye in the wall, transfixed. She could see the rain slanting down outside. She could see a pool of rain collecting on the curved and worn sill.

"Don't you see," I continued, "the window is invitingly at eye level, but in order to peek through it one must stand directly over the oubliette." Alexis' glance travelled down the wall as slowly as a raindrop, falling at last on the manhole-sized opening set in the floor. The cover of my mouth, the trapdoor, had long since become unhinged and lost. "The window is a little joke, in the worst of taste," I said. I could feel her eye fix on me. "The prisoner is granted one last fleeting view of the world he will never see again."

Alexis' body tensed and her hands firmly grasped the back of the chair in which she was seated. She turned slowly to take in the entirety of the round chamber. Not one square inch of it escaped her inspection. Inexorably, her eyes returned to me.

"I am a hole," I said. "An oubliette. Such a pretty word, from the French, to forget, to be forgotten...." As I spoke, the breeze drifting in through the window stalled and my voice faded with it to a whisper. For a moment Alexis did not breathe, then, when my voice had faded altogether, she sighed with relief and leaned heavily on the back of the chair. She had been dreaming after all, she told herself. Her relief was short-lived though, for the breeze returned.

"You'll have to forgive me," I said, reanimated and in full voice. "We are none of us perfect. I myself am particularly susceptible to drafts." Alexis did not grasp my literary allusion, or at least she did not laugh. I heard her trying to make the sounds the human voice makes when it is unsuccessfully attempting to lubricate itself for speech. I filled the silence.

"I am very deep," I said. "My voice originates from within, which is where it gains its character. However, it gets most of its strength from the currents of air which play around this room and across my mouth—a pity, that. If you care to look closer, you will see that erosion has crafted a fine embouchure of my lip."

Alexis did not look any closer. She struggled to speak. "You are *not* a hole," she said in a rasp.

"You think I am a ghost, perhaps?"

"No," she said.

"People inevitably find it easier to believe I am a ghost rather than merely a hole."

"You are a trick," she interrupted with forced conviction. "You're a sound system," she insisted.

"Do I sound like old Mechelney perhaps?" I asked. She obviously had not registered the hollow resonance of my voice, its liquid-centred gravity of tone, not to mention my impeccable diction. "Or am I something else, Alexis?"

She rose from her chair. "Something else!" she cried with less assurance. "A horrible trick!"

Hearing the scrape of the chair's legs, I said, "Are you leaving now?" There was no reply. "If my voice is reaching you by electronic means," I continued, "then, presumably, my embodiment is elsewhere in the castle." On tiptoe, Alexis started down the stairs. "And if I am elsewhere in the castle," I added quickly, "presumably you are safer here."

This gave her pause. She sat on the step, not daring to turn back.

"I am nothing but a voice," I said, soothingly. "And there is so much we can talk about."

She got to her feet and began her descent.

"Wait," I called.

"I am not going to stay here and argue with a...with a hole," she muttered.

I was not defeated. "If you suppose you have nothing to learn from a hole," I shouted after her, "I suggest you have not examined your life closely enough."

It is, I feel, imperative in social intercourse to get in the last word.

With her hand on either wall for support, Alexis made her escape. She took each step as if it might crumble beneath her and leave her falling into nothingness.

8

Back on terra firma, Alexis found neither Mechelney nor any sign of electronic gadgetry—not so much as a wire. A bad night followed. She would have considered leaving but for the rain and the exhaustion of her ordeal in the tower. She expected company; she knew Mechelney might show up at any moment. She had also made herself ready for a ghost, a shade she believed might just be her husband. She was certain the traveller she had seen in the orchard hidden behind Friar Rush's robes had been Teddy's ghost—if it was possible for a living man to leave behind spectral copies of himself. She thought if she could only get close to that evanescent creature, she might learn something. Something had happened to Teddy. Here. She was searching for something to take back with her that would make everything all right again with the real Teddy. But nothing in her wildest imaginings had prepared her for a talking hole. The experience left her quite undone.

It was still rainy the next morning but the air was soft, and the fog that muffled the hill was opalescent with trapped light—sunshine that promised to burn away the gloom by lunch time. The light, such as it was, strengthened her resolve. She could not leave now, abandon the search when it had really only just begun, sent packing by a trick of acoustics!

She spent much of the morning walking around the base of the keep, staring up at the little window sixty feet above her, listening. How it loomed—like movie music.

She explored the cellar for some kind of secret entrance to a secret stairway to a secret dungeon. She found nothing. By noon she had convinced herself that Mechelney had triggered the incident in the little room, but not electronically. Yelling at her had opened up a wound, another parcel of pain inside her, the contents of which she had not sorted through. There was nothing left but to confront the hole.

She made herself a good lunch and ate it in the growing warmth. Then, with a flashlight and a penknife concealed under her blouse, she re-entered the keep. Reaching the room at the top of the stairs, she walked bravely up to my mouth and shone her light down into me.

"Who are you?" she demanded.

"I am an oubliette," I answered obediently. "I am a secret pit, the only access to which is the hole at your feet."

Her eyes peered down into me, trying to make something out of the darkness her flashlight could not penetrate. "There is someone down there," she insisted.

"There is no one. Nothing," I replied tolerantly.

"I could get help," she said. "I could get you out." She heard her voice swallowed whole by the oubliette. She backed off.

I suspected she was trying to make sense of a talking hole. "Do not waste your time contemplating the mechanics of it," I said. (It had very little to do with her training, the cadavers she had mutilated in school. What did I exhibit of articulate musculature, clever flaps of flesh?) "Suffice it to say," I said, "that in my intimate association with man, some of him has rubbed off on my rough sides."

This prompted a response—laughter, or something like it. A wheeze, a chortled snort, and then a great wave of hysteria. I couldn't help chuckling myself but as I did so, her own laughter died in her throat.

"Don't you see," I shouted to her as she backed away. "I am laughing *with* you."

She did not return that day. She was up a great deal of the night, wasting her candles, writing feverishly in her journal. I sang to her in her snug room in the servants' alley. I called her name. "Alexis, come and talk to me. I'm so lonely." It was I who had been talking to her all along, she realized. All the voices at night she had thought were memories—all me. She had been tricked. She wrote with anger until her fingers were numb. "There is much I can tell you," I shouted.

Despite her lucubrations, she was in fine fettle when she barged in on me the next morning. She gave me quite a piece of her mind.

"Tell me about Teddy," she demanded.

"Teddy?" I asked.

She wandered around the room punching her hand into her palm. The urgency in her voice was punctuated by these little smacks of bone into flesh. "He was here," she said.

"Teddy," I murmured again, letting the breeze distribute little morsels of the name around the chamber.

"He used to hike," she prompted. "He was a speleologist, a spelunker. He had come to Somerset caving."

"Ah," I said. "I'm afraid you have the wrong end of the shire. Up Cheddar way...."

"He was here!" she reiterated, her fist smacking her palm sharply. "I've sensed him. I've even caught a glimpse of him." She was furious. I was enjoying myself. I enjoy getting a piece of someone's mind.

"Teddy...Edward, Theobald, Thaddeus...."

"Theodore," she interrupted. "Theodore Forgeben."

"A boy...."

68

"It was before I knew him," she said breathlessly, hopefully. "He would have been in his early twenties."

"Hmmm," I muttered in a perfect rendition of the deepest cogitation. The little chamber positively rang with pondering. "I seem to recall a spotty-necked character...."

"Adolescent acne scars," she said, hardly believing her ears. "But how could you have known what he looked like?"

"Oh, supplicants always find a way to describe their physical features to me, especially scars. It means so much to humans, doesn't it? Tell me what you look like, my dear."

"I am not a supplicant," she said coldly.

"Aren't you now? People who come to me usually have something pressing on their minds. Why, I could have sworn you were asking after one Theodore Forgeben."

"He was here, wasn't he?" she said.

"He was here," I allowed. "As you surmised."

She whimpered a victorious little whimper. She cried a little and laughed, congratulating herself and her instincts on her victory over the tyranny of common sense. She was quite pathetic. "Go on," she said at last.

But I would not go on. Not in the state she was in. To receive the full benefit of my attention the mind must be in a supple state. Alexis' mind was wound up like a spring. I decided to do a little unwinding.

"He was here," I said. "But alas, he died."

This snapped her out of her complacency. "That's not true," she said.

"Awfully gruesome business," I continued, while she tried to organize her thoughts.

"That's ridiculous," she cried, but there was room for doubt in her assertion and I hurried to fill it.

"Are you questioning my memory?" I crackled. "He got fouled up in his blasted ropes while attempting to explore my inner workings. He'd never explored a man-made hole before. Hanged himself. Kaput. End of story."

"That isn't true!" she roared.

"There you go again," I said. "If you know so much, why are you here and what is it you expect of me?"

"He didn't die here," she said. "He's still alive."

"Now, now." I spoke soothingly. "Denial won't fix it."

"I married him!" she shouted. Her strident appeal filled the room, bouncing off the walls and broken ceiling. She must have heard the phrase a thousand times over before the clamour died down. "I married him...I married him...I married him...."

"Ah," I said. "And then what happened?"

She realized immediately that I had been playing with her. She reined in her emotions and her voice went steely with control.

"Why do you want to know?" she said.

"I may be empty," I responded, "but I am filled with insatiable curiosity. I can't help wondering, for instance, why you are here right now pleading with me to fill you in."

"I am not pleading," she shouted, which set the room off again.

"We needn't fight," I said, when it was quiet again. "Let's make an exchange, shall we? You tell me what happened between you and Teddy, and I'll tell you what happened between Teddy and me."

I don't think she liked the sound of my offer. I heard her suck in her breath as if to argue. Then she paused, reconsidered, and began, tentatively, like a chess player not prepared to take her fingers off a pawn, to tell me a story.

"Teddy was under a lot of mental stress," she said.

"And?"

"He couldn't see it...."

"But you could," I advanced.

"I became frightened of him," she stuttered.

"So, wisely, you left him," I suggested.

"No," she said. "He left me!"

"But you are here," I pointed out.

"He was crazy!" she shouted. "Something happened to him, but he wouldn't own up to it. He was living with that something inside him and it frightened me. It wasn't his fault but it scared me stiff."

I said nothing. I had her knight *en prise*.

"I don't care if you believe me," she shouted. "You're nothing but a hole." She was, by now, greatly agitated. I was silent while she swallowed her heart. Such a big heart. Such a small throat.

"So," I offered, "it was not you he left but his senses. Is that it? And when you talk of him leaving you, you suggest that the leaving started a long time ago, before you had even met him. Would that be an accurate summation of our conversation so far?"

"It happened here," she said. Her breathing was ragged. She gasped for air. She could hear birds and water dripping and the wind. Ordinary sounds which calmed her. Then the wind picked up.

"The implication is that I was the one who drove him crazy," I said. "Is that what you think?"

She stuttered "yes", and went silent. Obviously the interview had taken a turn she had not expected. "Oh please," she said, "tell me what happened." Her voice was soft as rain. "If I knew what happened—what's happening—I'm sure I could help him."

She seemed docile enough but I waited a moment longer. I am a connoisseur of all that is poignant. "Perhaps if we stuck to our deal: *you* tell *me* what happened first," I asked.

"It's hard to say," she countered.

"Give it a try," I replied. "All I know so far is that he married you and then he went crazy."

She groaned. "Teddy was under a lot of mental stress," she began, but I was not about to listen to that medley again.

"You're stalling," I interrupted. "We were going to share secrets, remember? If you want to know mine, tell me yours."

"I don't remember," she said.

"What don't you remember?" I demanded.

"What happened," she replied.

"What happened when?" I pressed.

"What happened the night it happened," she said, weakly now. The chess game was in disarray; her pieces lay fallen all around her. Her queen was exposed to my attack.

"Tell me, then, what you know of that night," I asked.

"I'll tell you what I know," she said. "I can't remember much. I've been told other things that were supposed to have happened, but it's as if it happened to someone else. Not me."

"I know that feeling well enough," I said. "Nothing ever happens to me."

This seemed almost to amuse her. She was getting used to me. I liked that.

She tried to find the right place to start. "It had gotten to the point where, although I loved Teddy, I found the thought of making love to him unbearable. He frightened me. We fought and that frightened me more. Then, one night when the argument had turned bitter, as it inevitably did, he told me he wanted me to see a doctor. Me. He had already contacted someone. Suddenly it was all my fault. I was the one who was frigid. He would come along with me, he said, as if it wasn't his problem at all. I was furious. I went all to pieces. I lost my mind—I attacked him. Somehow...somehow I stabbed him. There was this wound under his heart. I screamed.

"I don't know what happened next. All I remember clearly is the feeling of waking up and finding him gone. I didn't blame him. I felt sick with the horror of it. I knew I had to find out what it was that haunted him. I had to make it up to him, you see. Do you see?"

"I don't see," I said, very gently. "But I hear everything."

"It started here," she said. "I'm sure of it."

"Sit down," I said, taming my voice to a benevolent purr. I waited while she dragged her heels to the little table. "I didn't lie to you earlier when I told you he died here," I said. I could hear her about to remonstrate and I cut her off. "*Part of him* died here," I said. She could not argue with this, for she had seen something of his ghost.

"I've come so far," she said. "I must know everything."

"Well, why didn't you say so?" I replied. "Everything is by far my favourite topic of conversation. I suppose it comes from being nothing, oneself."

I waited but could not get a rise out of her. Instead she started rocking on her chair. Back and forth, back and forth.

"It's really not much of a story," I began. "He wasn't here long enough for us to get to know each other as well as I would have liked. He came to climb. He climbed down into me, into my very pit, and there amidst the bones and mud and stones he found something quite extraordinary. He found a baby."

"A what?" Alexis asked, though I had enunciated the word most clearly.

"A baby," I repeated, giving each syllable its due weight.

"A skeleton," she said.

"No," I answered. "Newly dead. It had only recently been committed to my safe-keeping."

"Stop it!" she shouted. "How can you talk like that?"

"A girl from along the dyke," I said, ignoring her plea. "She had conceived it on the hill in the back of some pipe-fitter's car and brought the results up here to dispose of."

"That's horrible," Alexis moaned.

"But nothing new, I'm afraid. After all, I am a forgettery. This kind of thing is my *raison d'être*."

"Yes," she said, her voice tight. "Yes," she said again, louder and more painfully, as the picture in her mind expanded to take in the scene in the pit: Teddy in his web of ropes with the tiny corpse. For some moments the room was filled with low belly-aching and the clicking of the chair rocking. Then the noise subsided as the nurse in her repressed the image of an ossuary in the bowels of the earth and conjured up instead the sterile scene of an operating room; an abortion reflected in shining aluminum and staunched by bleached white hospital linen. In this way she absorbed the shock of the dead baby.

"And then what?" she asked, her voice blank, neutralized.

"He panicked, of course. Screamed his fool head off. He would have happily screamed the castle down around his ears to obliterate that thing at his feet. But nothing of the sort happened. After a while, he found the strength to pull himself out of me. He didn't hang around."

"No," she muttered.

She was breathing heavily, as if she had just climbed with him foot by gruelling foot: hands, rope-burned; legs, scraped and raw; eyes craving for light, even the dull light of my little cell.

"There," I said. "Is that what you wanted to hear?"

"Hardly," she said.

"But it is something of an explanation, isn't it?" I asked. "I mean, he hasn't gone caving since, I'll wager?" There was no answer, but then, sometimes silence is most telling.

I could feel her leaving me before I actually heard her. She left in pieces, her mind first, followed in a desultory fashion by the rest of her. "There's more," I called after her. "You haven't heard the half of it yet."

A few moments later she was outside in the courtyard. She was still there at twilight. By then the birds were screaming in the trees, having no memory of the previous night and fearing the worst. Alexis wrapped her arms around herself against the chill and watched the clouds gather, pink and purple, in the west. She craned her neck up to where the little bull's-eye window peeked from behind fall-dead ivy. Her eyes travelled down the steep side of the keep to where a baby lay forgotten by all but herself— forgotten even by Teddy because he could not live with such a memory. She envisioned his grim descent and grimmer return. He's still climbing, she thought. And could she live with the baby in the oubliette? She turned to the west, to her home. "Why didn't you tell me?" she shouted. But Teddy couldn't hear her. It was too late, already the middle of the night back home.

9

She might have left then, her quest complete. She had found a truth, as awful as anything she could have dreamed. Leaving crossed her mind and got lost in the traffic there; her mind, in this particular twilight, was a very busy intersection. In the end she stayed. She was exhausted and cold and insatiably hungry.

She ate like a fiend. Nothing could fill her. She ate all of a canned corned beef and most of a canned plum pudding. She ate all the eggs she had hard-boiled the day before and then, piling up the straw around her to keep warm, until she was half buried, she sat in a corner munching on soda crackers. She imagined flying to her sick husband's side. "I have found it," she would tell him. "I have found the talking hole. I know about the baby. It'll be all right." She tried to imagine the look on his face and was rewarded by a fleeting glimpse of her last night with Teddy. A glimpse of panic—a jagged shard of glass—a fragment—for her conscious mind would not let her see the whole pane. She tried to imagine telling Teddy's psychiatrist. The counsellor he had arranged for her to see. She imagined composing herself to appear sane. "You see, there is this castle. And in the keep is the entrance to an oubliette which can talk, which remembers everything. And at the bottom of the oubliette, in the dungeon, Teddy found a dead baby. Of course,

he can't remember because the memory is in the oubliette...."
The psychiatrist's office evaporated from her mind's eye. The idea
withered. "They will lock me away," she muttered. She recalled
telling her mother she was going to England to find herself a
consolation prize. Consolation. She wanted to laugh out loud at
the irony of it but she couldn't, for her tongue and throat were
coated with a thick and salty paste.

In the dark she made her way to the well where she drank
deeply but could not seem to drink enough. She up-ended the
bucket of freezing water into her mouth and felt her brain shrink
under the deluge. She imagined it shrivelling to the size of a
goat's cheese and rattling around in her skull. She put on all
her sweaters but still shook through and through. She cursed the
night that kept her there. Then it occurred to her to build a fire.
She had not done that yet. She had been careful to use her little
Coleman stove, lest Mechelney have her locked up for burning
his precious gold mine. Now she considered razing the place to
spite him. And to spite me, I dare say. She was greatly distressed
by me.

In the barn she found a pile of old wood that was dry. She
made a pyre in the alley large enough to burn a saint. The wood
burned splendidly. When the fire was high, she could see that
her logs had once been the kneeling pieces of pews.

Warm at last, she put on a pot of passion-flower tea to boil. She
drank it, leaning against the alley wall. She slumbered by the fire.
She awoke to the sound of someone approaching. Looking up,
she saw a woman through the flames. The woman was smiling
at the fire as though it brought back pleasant memories. She only
glanced at Alexis but accepted her presence as if she had known
she was there all along. She had long, thick, grey hair, tangled
with bits of root and leaf in such a way as to look decorative rather
than dishevelled—a tired Botticellian grace. Her hair framed a
lovely, oval, middle-aged face, with a pointed chin and set with
clear grey eyes. She wore a painter's smock. She warmed her

hands over the flames and rubbed her belly to transfer some of the heat there.

Alexis felt the need to explain the fire. "I was frigid," she said.

The woman's eyes engaged Alexis. "Any luck?" she asked. Her voice crackled pleasantly like the fire.

Alexis was not sure what to say. "I've talked to the oubliette," she said.

"Oh, that old trickster," said the woman. "No, I meant any luck with *him*."

Alexis sat up but held back her excitement. She took a nearby twig and poked at the fire until the twig was consumed. "Who are you?" she asked.

"I'm the one who should be asking questions," said the woman, but there was no malice in her voice. "It is my house," she said. "Or at least, I was the last official tenant."

"You are Elspeth Husted," said Alexis.

The woman nodded. "And you, young lady, are looking for someone, are you not? Have you found him?"

"Not since I came to stay here," Alexis answered. "Do you know him?"

The woman smiled. "Only to see him," she said. "There isn't much of him, is there?"

Alexis remembered her own fleeting glimpse of Teddy—the wraith behind the holy man's back. "No," she said. And then she recalled something I had told her. "Only a part of him died here," she said, echoing my words. The woman seemed to accept this explanation of Teddy's deficiency. Alexis added, "Also, he's very shy."

The woman smiled knowingly, as if shy men were a curse and a blessing. "I've caught sight of him from the ramparts," she said. "I don't go out much, though some of the others do."

"I saw him first in the orchard," said Alexis, wondering who the others might be but for the moment intent upon finding out what she might of Teddy. "He rapped on my door the other night."

The woman cast her a dubious look. "Oh, I doubt he did that," she said. "No men are allowed in here, dear. You're quite safe."

Alexis thought better of arguing. She had assumed it was Teddy and now there was more than enough reason to question her assumptions about this phenomenal place. For one thing, Elspeth Husted, according to Troubridge's information, should be a woman in her nineties. This was not a woman in her nineties, but somehow Alexis doubted she was an impostor. At Fastyngange, it seemed, time was not the same as at other places.

Elspeth did not seem entirely content standing there. Alexis was afraid she would leave and she was bursting for company, even if only the company of a ghost. "The oubliette told me what happened to him," she said.

Surprisingly, Elspeth threw back her head and whooped with laughter. "Did he now? How very co-operative of him."

Beyond Elspeth, Alexis heard a rattling and sloshing at the well and, peering into the darkness, she saw another woman who seemed to have been filling buckets but now turned towards the fire.

"He's a bloody liar!" shouted the water-carrier, rising under the yoke across her sturdy, rounded shoulders. She was dressed in an old woollen shift. Her hair was long enough to plait but not so long as to require attention. She approached them under the weight of her buckets, swaying and splashing with her gait. Her hips were slim, boyish.

"He lied to me at first," said Alexis, uncertainly. "He was just ragging me." The water-carrier came into the fire's shimmer, snuffled like a pig, and spit into the flames. Her shift was drenched, revealing a stomach still young and firm and breasts not yet declined by ripeness and gravity.

" 'e says anyfing 'e bloody pleases," she said. She lowered her yoke until the buckets, sloshing, stood on the ground. She looked up fleetingly at Alexis and then stared at the fire as if at fine clothing in the window of an extravagant shop. Her face was grimy and smeared with sweat. Despite the youthfulness of her figure her face appeared older than its years. Her eyebrows were thick and unplucked and there was a pale moustache over her full lips. But her eyes, Alexis couldn't help noticing, were as soft as the colour of new moss, flecked with gold. The pupils were dilated—but that hardly seemed the word—engorged—with longing. The water-carrier looked for a moment at the older woman's hands caressing her belly.

"Ooo, 'e'd talk the Blessed Virgin out of her frock, 'e would," said the water girl.

"Told me he was the keeper of the Grail," said Elspeth, smiling ruefully. "A veritable mystagogue. He was going to prepare me for it, he was. Told me ever so convincingly a story of the Glastonbury abbots bringing it up here from Chalice Hill to hide it from the treachery of robbers and tourists. There were tourists even back then, though they called themselves pilgrims. St. Joseph's Holy Crater right under my nose—can you imagine? He said it was our little secret."

The water girl squatted on her heels, scowled and spit again into the flames. The sputum foamed and hissed and vanished.

"Tell her about you and the captain, Sal," said the woman in the painting smock.

Alexis stared at the younger woman who she now knew must be Sally Bert. She had guessed as much. Sally, like a cautious animal, narrowed her eyes under the gaze. She looked back towards the kitchen as if expecting to be called, flinching as if expecting to be caned. There was no one there. No sound. "What 'ave you 'urd?" she said, turning back to Alexis.

"A sad love story," said Alexis, guessing now what had been the plight of the mysteriously vanished lovers.

"Tell her, Sal," said the painter. "She's almost like one of us." Sally grinned, which made Alexis' blood run cold.

I am *not* one of them, she told herself. They are ghosts. They had obviously been foolish, bewitched. She would not let a talking hole beguile her. She returned Sally's attention evenly. "I'd like to know what really happened," said Alexis. Sally's strong arms coiled around her knees.

" 'e'd tell you it was a romance," said Sally, jerking her head back to indicate the keep and its hollow keeper.

"The tower was boarded up in them days. I used to sneak up, to think, like, by meeself. I didn't know about the 'ole—'e was covered up. It was the captain 'oo discovered our empty friend. They 'it it off right from the start, I reckon, not that 'e ever told me about it till 'twas the end, like. The two of 'em 'atched up a scheme to drive me mad."

"But the love story," Alexis interrupted.

"Ooo, there was enuf of that in the beginning," said Sally. "I'll never forget one afternoon we were at it up there with 'im whacking away at me like a roofer at 'is tacks, when King James' men let fire on the 'all. Boom, boom, boom. There we were, me wif me pinny up over me 'ead and straw from top to toe, and the bleedin' keep tumbling down about our ears. Ooo, did I laugh— well, I'll tell you, it was all I'd expected—fireworks, like. I was in love wif 'im but not 'e wif me, as I soon found out. That's the day I decided to tell 'im about missing me monthly visitor."

Already Sally's story had taken a turn the legend had not. "He wasn't pleased," said Alexis.

"Pah! Not likely," said Sally. " 'e must 'ave stayed behind when I went back to the kitchen. Maybe it was then 'e discovered the 'ole."

Sally's forehead knotted in concentration. For several hundred years, thought Alexis, Sally has been trying to sort out what happened, how and why, and still it is a mystery to her.

It soon became apparent that it was only in the legend that the captain who had loved the serving girl was noble. When next she and her rebel lover met he talked of an escape plan, but it was only to build up her hopes in order to dash them again. He filled her mind with horrors: what the soldiers would do to her when they took the castle; what else they would do to her if they found she was carrying the child of a rebel. His stratagem, conceived with my morbid sense of purpose, was to instruct his naive mistress in death as he had instructed her in love. Day by day he set about fanning the flames of Sally's growing despondency, to the point that she would jump at the chance of dying with him. Literally. The idea was brutally simple. When the castle acquiesced and the keep was plundered, King James' soldiers would find the signs of Sally and the captain's love nest: her shawl, his sash, and the suicide pact bearing Sally's "x" under the captain's illegible scrawl. There was rumour enough in the castle to substantiate the evidence of their affair. Meanwhile, under the guise of making peace with God, the captain had been spending his days feathering a hidey-hole in the organ loft of the chapel. Secretly he stored food and supplies there against the day of his "disappearance".

"We met on the chosen night at the chosen time," said Sally, "and 'e brandished 'is sword at the same moment I brandished me stout rope. Ooo, what a quarrel we 'ad. Can you imagine? 'e fancied 'is neck too much to think of 'anging 'imself and I couldn't for the life of me see 'ow both of us could die on the end of one sword."

"How sick," said Alexis, fidgeting by now.

"Cried me eyes out," said Sally. "The bastard."

Alexis' temper rose. "Why didn't he thrust his sword into your heart and have done with?" She was appalled at the story, wanting it only to be over.

" 'e wasn't man enuf," said Sally, giggling. "In the end 'e 'ad to leave it up to 'is secret partner. There I was, cowering, not knowing what was to 'appen next, 'e was in such a rage. Then all of a sudden like, 'e kicks away the straw covering the plug 'ole and kicks the lid clear off its 'inges. ' 'ello,' says the 'ole, and, 'If you put your arms 'round each other and squeeze tight there should be just enuf room for the two of you.' Of course, it didn't faze the cap'n but I was pipped on the post, as you might say. The 'ole did the rest."

It wasn't difficult for Alexis to imagine my effect on Sally's modest intelligence. She could see her, trance-like, giving herself freely to the oblivion of that dark passage, while the captain looked on with relief, free at last of the burden of his debauchery and provided with a realistic enough escape.

"It's so sordid," said Alexis.

Sally only stared into the flames. Alexis tipped another kneeling piece into the fire. "Men," said Elspeth, and her eyes registered resignation rather than passion.

"So nasty," said Alexis, seeming to cast around for what it was that most infuriated her about the tale. "There is not a single redeeming feature to it," she said at last.

"The hole knows nothing about redemption," said Elspeth. "Bafflement and brutality. Nothing more."

The new log caught flame and crackled in the darkness between the women: Alexis, alive on one side; the ghosts on the other; and beyond them, at the end of the alley, black against the autumn night, tricked out in moonlight, the keep. Again Alexis' eye travelled up to where the windowed room was. Again her eyes travelled down the steep stone side, but this time following Sally's fall. She looked quizzically at Sally. Images of traffic accident victims in emergency rooms crowded her mind. How strange, she thought, that this ghostly woman shows no sign of her fall. But then, ghosts are counterfeits of the living, she reasoned, not of the dead. The answer did not entirely satisfy her.

Then from somewhere far off there came the sound of a baby crying. Startled, Alexis sat bolt upright, her eyes searching the castle, her ears peeled trying to pinpoint the source of the distress. But it echoed off the walls and battlements so that it seemed to come from everywhere. Sally sighed and stiffly clambered to her feet. She bent under the yoke and lifted the buckets of water she had collected at the well. "I'd best get back to me work," she said.

The distressed baby seemed to bother her no more than a clock striking the hour. Without so much as a glance in Alexis' direction she turned again towards the kitchen quarters and a moment later vanished into that dark doorway.

"I'd best see to the infant," said the painter.

"Is it yours?" asked Alexis, relieved that she would not have to hunt through the castle herself, for by now the cry had escalated into a wail.

The painter chuckled. "My goodness no, dear child. What would Mr. Husted say about that?"

"Is it Sally's?" asked Alexis, wondering with mingled curiosity and horror whether ghosts carried their babies to term.

Elspeth shook her head. "We're not sure who it belongs to," she said. "All we know is the baby is one of our kind—a survivor. The mother, it seems, was not. Until the time we are set free from waiting, we must care for her."

"When will that be?" asked Alexis.

Elspeth looked up at the dark keep and then back at Alexis. The fire had burnt low again and Elspeth's eyes were lost in shadows while her cheeks seemed to burn in the glow of the light at her feet.

"When we may once again enter the tower," she said. "For now the way to the oubliette is barred to us survivors."

"But why?"

Elspeth laughed. "Ask the hole. It's his doing." And then, before Alexis could pursue her line of questioning, Elspeth turned away. "Coming, little one," she said with a sigh.

The baby's howling cut through Alexis' senses like a buzz-saw but she could not let Elspeth go. "What do you mean 'survivor'?" she called to her, hopefully.

Elspeth glanced back. "Oh, we're special, dear," she said. "We survived the fall." She said more but Alexis did not catch it for the sound of the baby drowned her out. She closed her eyes and drew her blankets up around her head to make a cave. Desperately though she tried she could not quite help herself from thinking of the child as Teddy's baby. It was unfair of her, she knew; after all, he had only found it—if the hole's word was to be trusted.

Some moments later the crying stopped. Alexis lowered the covering from her ears and breathed a deep sigh of relief. She heard a sad and lilting lullaby: "Lullay my liking, my own dear darling," sang a tremulous voice from a nursery Alexis had not yet found despite her explorations. She settled back against the wall, wrapping her blankets around her, up to her chin, cold all over despite the fire. She felt utterly desolate.

"*We're special. We survived the fall*." The idea was monstrous. Lying broken and hopeless at the bottom of the oubliette—what kind of survival was that? And what had Elspeth meant about entering the tower again? Was survival a kind of failure? Must they jump a second time? Then it occurred to her that Teddy was a survivor by the same token, if only vicariously, for he too had stood at the bottom of the hole. He had escaped and yet part of him had not. Must he too enter the tower again? The idea struck her as the spark of a plan before she recoiled from it as horrible. The thought made her ache for him as she hadn't done in months. And she ached for herself, for she had stumbled, vulnerable, into this ghostly way-station in the middle of nowhere and it was night time and Teddy was in another country. It was too much. She was enfeebled—unengined.

The lullaby ended. Something like peace descended over Fastyngange. In the pocket of her sweater she found a small gritty tin of aspirins. She took two of them. They dissolved on her tongue as she tried to work up the spit to swallow. The bitter taste was reassuringly familiar. She settled down into her blankets. She watched the fire, pretending the sparks were stars. She made a wish.

From somewhere a long way off she heard an owl, though in her weary, beaten state it sounded more like many owls. Sleep overtook her; she imagined a pack of owls hunting together, swooping down in formation to carry her off.

Others came to her fire that night, others more timid than Elspeth or Sally. Alexis did not see them. She sank deeper and deeper, slow-falling into dreams she thought were her own but were mine. For, with the wind at my service, I spoke to her in her sleep. I filled her up with nothing until there was nothing on her mind.

In my dream, we were close. She moved into my chamber. She brought her little Snow White broom and swept away the cobwebs and dust of the ages. The loose masonry littering the floor from the keep's upper stage she pushed down the stairway, never thinking that she might block her one means of exit from the tower—her one *safe* exit. She brought up buckets full of water and swabbed the stone floor and then sprinkled it with wild flowers and fresh straw. In my dream she made a manger and moved in.

I cured her of her sojourns in the nearby towns. Wherever she shopped in my dream she ran into the Dickeys, who railed at her and chased her, trying to run her over in their rented car. Leaving Fastyngange became too horrifying a prospect to consider. Instead, she took to making midnight raids on the towns along the dyke. She became a scavenger, living on garbage, wild onions, and windfalls. She became drunk on juniper berries left fermenting on bushes. Like a hunted thing, she learned to fear and distrust mankind. "You are safe with me," I told her. "I can neither attack nor leave you. I am the essence of detachment." Less and less did she leave the tower. Closer and closer she moved to my side. She hung on my every word and if the wind stalled, leaving me speechless, she would blow across my lip so that I might finish what I had to say. Weeks passed in my dream while I regaled her with my violent past, my history written in blood, until she became inured to it. In my dream, nothing bothered her. She became devoted to me, sleeping, curled at my side, half of a parentheses to my full stop. She put aside her cause and lived in effect. In my dream she lived only to magnify my existence.

Like an intravenous poison I kept topping her up.

And then rain interrupted my alieniloquy.

The rain poured down in sheets unruffled by the smallest of breezes. In this way I was held at bay and Alexis managed, without ever quite waking, to drag herself from the dying fire into the buttery to her pile of straw. There she lay next to her empty food cans and cracker boxes and slept dreaming her own dreams for whatever comfort they might give.

10

She wasted no time, upon waking, preparing to leave. She fancied herself hitching a ride to Glastonbury, though she felt rested and frantic enough to walk the whole way. She imagined herself arriving, foot-weary, at the Marriotts' at tea-time, bathing in a hot, deep bath, and sleeping in the room over the kitchen. She fancied visiting Dr. Troubridge at Chewton Cottage and drinking strong coffee—how she longed for coffee now—while she told him her adventure. She longed to tell Troubridge about me. In the dull light she neatly folded her dirty clothing into her backpack, fighting off the urge to stay, ascribing it to an enchantment of this abandoned and wholly dangerous place. She concentrated her attention on a plan: she would bring Teddy back to Fastyngange, with medical help, of course, to confront the source of his trauma. She thought it was a good plan. She thought it was her own.

She had hung aside a going-to-town skirt, blouse, and sweater, just as she had done on her summer holidays at the cottage. Now as she turned to the door of the buttery to embark, dressed in these last clean clothes, her heart sank. For the shadows outside her door had re-arranged themselves and the twilight she had mistaken for dawn was in truth dusk. She had slept the day away.

The knowledge numbed her for a moment, but the falling dark soon mobilized her again. She marched from her bivouac and down the alley to the yard, her eyes straight ahead. She picked up a sturdy stick, wet with dew, in the alley—a walking stick, she told herself, though she took a mean swing at the heads of the tall grass as she walked through the yard. She was ready for anything.

And anything was ready for Alexis. He stood, in the bulky form of Friar Rush, directly in her path just outside the front gateway. She did not stop immediately, but walked resolutely towards him until she drew within a few paces of the castle entrance. From there she could see that the friar did not have his shy traveller in tow. But she could also tell that he was not alone. She slowed her pace. Rush, his fat fingers laced in prayer, bowed low. She heard his rosary beads clicking. From somewhere off to his left out of Alexis' vision a voice sniggered, and down the hill below the fat figure the bushes parted to reveal an urchin child in rags crouching in the grass, gaping up at Alexis framed in the gateway.

"What, leaving so soon?" asked the monk. "Did you get what you came for?" It was not so much a question as a remark calculated to amuse his comrades. The gaping mouth of the guttersnipe in the bushes twisted into an idiot grin and a sound like an ass braying issued from his tongueless head. Alexis could see a heavy cross dangling from a string around his neck. The sniggerer roared with laughter. Wielding her stick like a club, Alexis ventured nearer to the threshold of the gateway. Peering along the battlement she saw him, not ten feet away: a man in an executioner's black hood leaning against the outer wall. He was not tall but his naked arms were strong and folded across his leather jerkin self-consciously, to make the biceps stand out. On his ring finger he wore a gaudy chunk of jewellery. It caught her eye.

"It's a scarab, i'n't," he said. He fingered the ring near-sightedly, holding it up close to the eye slits in his hood. "A swap," he said. "For a merciful quick dispatchment." He sidled a little closer. "You see, I can break the ver'ibrae, which is right fast, or I can thro'tle 'em, which 'urts worse 'n anyfing."

Alexis did not intend to speak until she could do so without her voice trembling and giving her away. "You are ghosts," she told them, fingering her makeshift club.

The hangman looked her up and down. "I'm not one to turn down a wretch what needs a favour," he said, his hand stroking his crotch. It was Friar Rush's turn to chortle now.

Alexis remembered a sailor she had nursed, who, in his infirmity and impotence, had taken to sexually taunting her in just such a manner. It gave her a shot of confidence. "I'm not afraid of you," she said to the hangman.

"Good on you," said Rush. He held out his hand towards her, his fingers shaking. "And since this master of Scrag'em Fair does not put you off, come. I shall take you to your inamorato." The urchin scampered up the hill on all fours, to stand near the friar.

"I wouldn't if I were you," said a voice behind Alexis. She swung around, wielding her walking stick like a truncheon. "Fugh, watch that!" said the woman, arching her back as the end of the stick whistled past her face. "It's them what deserves a good spanking!" said the stranger, pointing out to the trio beyond the gateway. The woman's ample frame was dressed in nothing but petticoat and corset, from the top of which heaved breasts the colour of porridge. She was flabby-armed and gooseberry-eyed. Her copper-coloured hair hung in great tousled bunches around a pug-like face, heavily powdered and rouged. Despite her repugnant appearance, she was not intimidating, and Alexis turned her armed attention quickly back to the men outside the gate. They had moved, each a step or two nearer, but stood perfectly still now, like children at a game. "Not that that lot of lewdsters'd dare cum in 'ere," the woman said. The men laughed heartily at this.

"Lewdsters indeed," said the holy man.

"Listen who's calling the kettle black," said the hangman. "Maeve, the slutch—one of Blagdon's whores."

"A piece of chattel that somehow never made it on to the miller's inventories," piped in Friar Rush.

Maeve smiled. " 'e's the randiest of 'em all," she said, leaning her hand on Alexis' shoulder and pointing at the friar. " 'is marriage to our lady church is an open marriage, if you catch my meaning."

Rush chuckled. "Are you to take the word of a trollop over that of a holy man?"

Maeve squeezed Alexis' shoulder and whispered loud enough for all to hear, "I've been a trollop over that 'oly man often enough to know what 'e's like."

The men laughed uproariously, the urchin soundlessly, slapping his sides while his great cross bounced on his narrow chest. Alexis considered charging them, screaming a war-cry, her stick swinging, but as her eyes gazed out at the growing dark she sensed there were more of them. She sensed something else as well, something she did not understand but at which Elspeth and now Maeve had hinted: *though there were no gates to stop them the men could not enter the grounds of Fastyngange*. She hoped it was true.

"Come," said Rush, waving his arm at the women in the gateway. "You both shall watch."

"We'll watch, I'll wager," cried Maeve. "Watch our step!"

"Uu oond," said the urchin, his mouth puckering like a howling wolf. "Uu ooond!" He pointed towards the beech grove across the meadow.

"He tries to say *'the Wound'*," said Friar Rush, patting the boy on his head. The urchin flinched and darted out of arm's reach. Rush edged nearer to the women but Alexis could tell by his tentativeness and the way he gazed up at the teeth of the portcullis, fixed—corroded into place—above the opening, that he was uncomfortable so close to the gateway.

"Your lover will no doubt be there, Alexis," he said, hiding his trepidation. "He is drawn to the Wound's festivities. I've seen him. It might prove most educational to you in your quest. Hmm? It might be your one chance to get near him."

Suddenly Alexis heard a low chanting from the beech woods. Like owls. At the same time she felt Maeve's grasp tighten on her shoulder. "We can watch from the safety of the ramparts," said the woman. Feeling Alexis' indecision, Maeve looked menacingly at the trio of men. "Those nasties all get a bit squirish when the Wound's about. It wouldn't do to find yourself out among the likes of them."

By now the last bit of sun clung to the horizon, leaving behind it a sky battered and bruised from the ordeal of day. Alexis felt her courage draining from her. She allowed Maeve to draw her back into the castle grounds, to a steep staircase set in the curtain wall that led up to the rampart connecting the gate tower to the keep. Elspeth and Sally were already there, leaning out over the indented parapet. There was some wind, enough to sweep Elspeth's grey hair across her face and make Sally clutch at her shawl. There was another woman as well, removed from them, farther down the wall, whom Maeve identified in a whisper as the lady from Bath. The lady, tall and elegant in her carriage dress, turned her head slightly at their arrival on the battlement. Her face was hidden behind a veil.

"She let 'er chauffeur drive 'er up 'ere," whispered Maeve, with obvious relish. "Then when 'e'd 'elped 'imself to 'er ladyship's favours, 'e 'ied off back to Bath, an' she, either because she couldn't face 'er lord's disfavour or because she couldn't face 'er lord's feeble efforts in the sack, stayed on 'ere."

Alexis stared at the noblewoman. In the last of the daylight she could see that the white foulard of her skirts was faintly splattered with dried mud. Alexis looked back into the courtyard and imagined a lady there, standing back as her car—Edwardian and grand, blue with gold appointments—pulled away through the gate, through a puddle long since dried up, leaving Fastyngange and the lady, bespotted, never to return. The image faded as the chanting in the woods picked up, claiming her attention. "This must be so heavy for you," said Elspeth, slipping Alexis' backpack from her shoulders.

She saw a clearing among the naked beech trees, a circle of men gathering, sitting knee to knee around a bonfire which had not been there when she last looked. The men were as naked as the trees, their heads shaven, their bodies emaciated. There did not seem to be a leader, nor did they need one. They knew all the changes in their chant and ceremony. She counted forty men, singing in one voice. There was very little to their worship: an incessant drone, the odd gesture.

Down below her, Alexis' gaze wandered to the hangman, the urchin, and the monk observing the goings-on of the shavelings, whispering to each other now and then, looking up at her on the wall, sniggering behind their hands like boys in the back of a classroom. From her vantage point she saw other men: a soldier, half-dressed in armour, leaning against a boulder and sewing a leather thong; a fussy, scholarly-looking old man in tweeds, with a neat goatee and wire-rim glasses, his journal in his hand while he scribbled notes or sketched. There were more men in the underbrush or crouching in the meadow, like bushes in the twilight. At one point in their chanting the shavelings turned their heads, all of one accord, towards Fastyngange, and the men below the battlements turned with them, looking up at the women on the wall.

"See how they long to get in," hissed Sally.

"Professeur Flavigny, who is too old," said Elspeth, pointing at the scholar. "And that beggar child, who is too young." The tongueless boy grasped the weighty cross around his neck and hunched his shoulders as though he would hide from the women's eyes behind the rood. "None of them — no man of any age — can come into Fastyngange," said Elspeth. "It is ours."

Down in the woods the shavelings turned again to the fire, then each turned to his right and leaning forwards, seemed to kiss the upper arm of his neighbour. The kiss lingered. Some of the naked heads swooned and something like ecstasy seeped into their monotone hymn.

"Are they all survivors?" Alexis asked.

Elspeth shook her head. "Not them," she said. "You are not looking closely enough." Alexis strained her eyes and this time noticed that the men were insubstantial. She could see the flames of the fire clear through them. "Like your young friend, they all lost something of themselves here. More than he did, I'm afraid."

"The part of 'em what finks," said Sally. And Maeve made crazy circles around her ear with a fat finger.

"You see," said Elspeth, "there are shades of shades."

"Who are they?" asked Alexis, looking out towards the woods.

"Them's Woundlings," said Maeve. "It's a religious sect, if you please. They always appear right about now."

"It being All Hallowed E'en," explained Sally.

"The arse-end of Easter," said Maeve and rattled with laughter. One porridgy breast jiggled free of her bodice.

"They worship the wound suffered by Jesus during the crucifixion," said Elspeth.

And before Alexis could stop herself, she asked, "Which one?" The women stared at her as if her question had been disrespectful, saucy. The question shocked Alexis herself. It had seemed so important.

"The one caused by the spear in his side," said Elspeth.

" 'ere!" said Maeve, jabbing Alexis cruelly under the heart.

Alexis stepped back, her ribs smarting. "I'm a nurse," she said, as if to explain away her strange question as a nurse's desire for anatomical accuracy. Meanwhile, Maeve laughed at her and Alexis was forced to consider the physical strength of these survivors. And their unpredictability.

"They make much of entering the wound, walking through the wound into the body of Christ, there to take root in his fertile flesh," said Elspeth, frowning at Alexis, like a schoolmarm. If she had seen Maeve's wicked knock she clearly felt Alexis had deserved it.

They are turning on me for no reason, thought Alexis. But then it occurred to her, being alive—being alive on Hallowe'en— might well be reason enough. She had not realized the fall had advanced so far. She moved away from them a few paces down the wall, nursing her sore side. When she looked up again at the service in the woods, she saw a shadow moving among the trees.

"There! What'd I tell you," hissed Friar Rush, from directly below her. She glanced down at his bald pate. "Your *enfant sauvage*." Again Rush waved his arm at her, beckoning. "Come on. We'll catch him, shall we?"

But Alexis paid no heed to the monk. Her eyes clung to the spectre prowling closer to the periphery of the Woundlings' circle.

"Like little germs, they are," said Elspeth. "On a spear's-edge ride to eternity."

"Sordid affair," said Professeur Flavigny, "but not without a certain metaphorical intensity of vision, *n'est-ce pas?*" He had joined Friar Rush by the wall but addressed himself to Alexis. Distracted by him only for an instant, she looked up again to see Teddy stepping still closer to the Wound. Oh how she longed to get closer to him. The professor carried on in a voice as dry as dust. "How strange to worship Christ's wound, one thinks, and yet it was all that was left once the Roman Church had divided up the relics: the saints' tears, the nail, what have you." He suppressed a laugh behind his sketch pad at his blasphemy.

What did Teddy want with this strange cult, thought Alexis. For as she watched, he broke from the cover of the bushes and wandered, as though mesmerized, up to the very ring of the circle.

"They won't notice him," said Elspeth. She had left her spot to come to Alexis' side. "If you were as close as he is, you would see that their eyes are rolled back, the aperture of sight safely tucked away to avoid any confusion of focus. It was in that manner, blissfully blind, that they first found their way to the keep. They were alive then; they could come and go as they pleased. That is, until they found your friend the hole."

"The hole is not my friend!" said Alexis, turning to the woman, shocked at the cruelty in her voice.

Elspeth pulled wind-blown strands of hair from her face and stared at Alexis as though she were a long way off. "The hole became their Church."

"There isn't any room left in Jerusalem," said Flavigny tittering. The men had all been listening to the argument. They had gathered below—the soldier and others she could not make out in the shadows cast by the rampart wall. "To them, the oubliette was Christ's wound carved in stone," said the professor. "Those who leapt thought of themselves as human spears."

"The wound incarnate," said Elspeth.

"The wound that talks!" hissed Sally.

Alexis tried to block them out. Had Teddy fallen in with them, she wondered, watching him slowly circling the stoned, head-swaying shavelings. Had the hole lied to her? The night before the women had told her that the hole lied. Perhaps the awful truth was a different awful truth. Did it matter? Her mind was racing. Somehow it seemed to matter! Perhaps there never had been a baby in the dungeon. Maeve's rough hand on her arm yanked her back to the moment. Sally had grabbed her firmly by the other wrist. The women had closed in on her. "No fire between us now," whispered Sally.

Alexis glanced over the parapet and saw the men gathered below, like hungry dogs, waiting for table scraps. Even the lady from Bath had ventured a step in her direction. "Look at them now," she said. The voice coming from behind the veil startled Alexis, for it was like an unoiled hinge. She pointed and all eyes followed to see the Woundlings each bent over the arm of his neighbour again. "When they kiss in that manner," croaked the rusty hinge, "they actually draw blood through the skin."

"It's a kind of communion," said Friar Rush.

Suddenly Maeve was leaning over Alexis' arm—lips, teeth, pressed against her skin. She grabbed Maeve's hair and flung her head back. How heavy her head seemed. How powerfully the coiled muscles of her neck resisted. Yet they are ghosts, Alexis told herself, turning from them. She looked for Teddy, who stood in the open now, his pale ghost as naked as the Woundlings....

"You must speak to the hole for us!" insisted the lady from Bath.

"Plead for us!" demanded Elspeth. Alexis refused to listen to them. She closed her eyes. She focused on Teddy.

"We'd do it for ourselves, of course," said Professeur Flavigny, his voice whining.

"But we can't—none of us—get to it!" said the hangman through gritted teeth.

"In killing us," said Friar Rush, "he created us."

"We'd be nuffin wivout 'im," said Maeve, laughing harshly.

But Alexis wasn't thinking of the hole. If only I could talk to Teddy, she thought, blocking them out, the women pressed against her, pushing her against the rough parapet, leaning into her as though they might tip her over and tumble her into the men's hands and gaping mouths fifteen feet below. If only I could reach him, thought Alexis. And then suddenly she realized she could.

"Teddy!" she called. And Teddy jumped to hear her. It was as if the fire had leapt out and scorched him. His eyes searched the woods.

"Teddy!" Alexis shouted and this time it came out like a hysterical scream. The chanting stopped. The Woundlings, dazed and confused, looked around, some pointing towards the castle wall while others pointed at the intruder in their midst.

"I'm sorry about the wound!" cried Alexis. And with her fist she pounded the spot under her heart where Maeve had hit her.

Then several things happened all at once.

The baby in the castle screamed. Teddy dove into the underbrush, shavelings screeching in pursuit. And Alexis flung back the women crushing around her and rushed for the stairs leading from the rampart. The ghosts chased her; the men trapped outside the wall hollered for her capture. She ran to the only place she had been told no one could follow her. She ran to me. My ghosts made sure of that.

11

It was dark in my chamber, even darker down the spiral staircase where Alexis waited, stranded half-way between the viragos at the bottom and the hole at the top. From what she could gather, she was safe where she was, although, she had to admit to herself, she was hardly anywhere at all.

As far as she could tell, there were ranked orders of ghosts. There were lowly emanations like Teddy who had hardly died at all. Then there were the Woundlings, whose appearance was scarcely more substantial than that of Teddy's apparition. Each had plunged to his death in an ecstatic fulfilment of the cult's religion. They had not survived the fall. They were lesser ghosts than the so-called "survivors". The survivors were full-bodied, Alexis thought, and though she shivered violently, fell to laughing hysterically at the idea of a full-bodied ghost. Shades of shades. They were only more fully realized and protected. A better sort of ectoplasm, I could have told her, had she asked. But at that moment she would have none of me.

The survivors were at the top of the heap. They had died a lingering death in the oubliette, filling me with their cries and prayers. I had come to know them. They had died slowly in me and their beings passed into my own being, such as it is—this Alexis could almost grasp. It made a kind of sense.

It was not sense but urgent need which convinced her she was safe where she was at least for the time being. No ghost, not even my chosen ones—the survivors—could enter the keep—not a second time. The keep, after all, was reserved for the living, a last refuge for the besieged. A sanctuary, if a lonely one. I was there waiting in my small room under the window at the service of those who could not face the ghosts outside and had lost the will to continue living in a state of siege. Meanwhile below, the women survivors called the castle grounds their haunt and the men survivors lived on the castle's perimeter—my arrangement. For, as with the angels in heaven, Fastyngange in all its decrepitude was not without propriety. So Alexis was momentarily safe, though it could not have been a pleasant thought for her. "We've got your rucksack," Elspeth called up to her. "You must be so cold." Such a thoughtful chatelaine.

After a while the women ceased their caterwauling at Alexis to come down, though she could distinctly hear their shuffling steps in the whispering gallery below. Waiting. She prayed that their strength came from the night time and that she would live to see the day when she could quit the castle once and for ever. I called softly to her. "I can explain everything," I said.

Curiosity finally brought her to my room, though she would not venture past the last step. After the absolute darkness of the stairwell, the room must have seemed almost cozy—moonlit and with its little table and chair....

"Ah, Alexis," I greeted her warmly, I think. "Time for another session?"

"Who is the baby?" she asked, when she had breath for it.

"Didn't I tell you last night?" I replied.

I could hear her teeth chattering. I suggested that were she to take a seat at the table across the room she would be out of the draft. Hesitantly, edging along the wall, she did so. She did not trust me, but sitting at the table must have given her courage and she began to talk. She spoke as though she were interviewing an applicant for a distasteful job.

"Was he a part of the Wound?"

"Who?" I asked.

"Teddy," she replied—weary, her voice frayed.

"I thought perhaps you meant the baby," I said.

"How could a baby be connected with a religious cult?" she snapped.

I could think of ways—black, traditional ways—but she was not about to listen.

"You said only last night the baby was some girl's from along the dyke. Conceived in the back of a pipe-fitter's car, you said." She hurled this at me. "Well?"

"Well, what?" I asked. "I'm finding this a bit confusing...."

"Were you lying?" she demanded.

"Ah," I said. "Now we're getting somewhere." This seemed to throw her offence into disarray.

"What's that supposed to mean?" she said, more timidly now, her vexation having spent itself in her accusal.

"I would have thought it meant everything to you," I said, quite reasonably. "After all, if I am lying then—"

"No, stop," she said. "I can't keep this up any longer. Not now." Poor tormented thing.

I obeyed her wish and stopped, but not for long. "You could always check," I said. "On the baby, I mean."

For another moment the room fell quiet as she considered my offer.

"Where?" she asked.

"In the oubliette," I whispered. "The baby is still there. And once there, all your questions would be answered."

A cackle arose from the gallery below. The survivors had been eavesdropping and found my menacing solicitude unbearably funny. The effect of the interruption was to release Alexis yet again from my thrall. I was not particularly disturbed; it was plain that her mind was far from focused.

"They're very solid," she said, "for ghosts."

"To you," I answered. "Some would hardly notice them at all."

"Is it me?" she asked. "Or is it Fastyngange?"

"Something of both," I said. "There are all manner of ghosts, Alexis. As many ghosts as there are levels of hell to occupy. There are zombies of demon strength and shades evanescent as dusk. There are flibbertigibbets who flicker across the mirror when you are combing your hair, and succubae as heavy as gravestones who straddle a man's loins while he tries to sleep. The world of ghosts is not so uniform as the world of humans. A single human may be responsible for hurling many projections into the ether. He need not even be dead, as you have come to discover of Teddy."

Again a fight broke out below us in the gallery.

"What do they want with me?" Alexis demanded.

"The question might well be turned around," I replied.

"I want nothing from them," she said.

"But you must," I quickly pointed out. "Or they would not have made themselves visible to you. They would rather be left alone in their misery, unless they sense another soul as miserable as themselves looking for company."

"Is that what Fastyngange is?" she asked glumly.

"You all share something in common," I said. "Aren't you the least bit curious what that is?"

"We were all unlucky in love," she answered in a lacklustre voice.

"And don't you want to hear the stories of how they came to me?" I pressed on.

"No," she said, "I don't. But you're dying to tell me. You can think of nothing better to do than to gloat over your gruesome victories."

"I cannot *do* anything," I said. "I am nothing."

She went silent again, but in the silence the night and the cold closed in on her. She sang to herself, under her breath, to take her mind off her discomfort. She explored the room, as much to keep warm as anything else. How careful she was—filled to the brim with care. But the room offered no distraction, save one. With some trepidation, she raised her voice again.

"Is this where Mrs. Husted came to paint?" she asked.

"Only to draw," I answered. "It was too dark for her to mix her paints up here, and she demanded brilliance for her painting. She was always on the lookout for new angles from which to see the world. The limited panorama available from the *oeil-de-boeuf* seemed to entrance her. It made a perfect frame. A circle, you see."

"Yes," said Alexis. "I recognized the viewpoint from a work I saw of hers. But how could she have sketched at the window with you there?"

"She lugged two hefty planks up the staircase and laid them across my mouth," I replied.

"Then how did you get to her?" Alexis demanded. The choice of wording was shrewd.

"There was a crack," I answered. "I only need a crack."

"And, carelessly, she said something one day...," said Alexis. There was vehemence in her voice but also fatalism.

"People will talk," I said. "If they kept their loneliness to themselves, I would have nothing to say. I would be perpetually in the dark. But I can hear the most insubstantial of utterances. The minutest grunt, the feeblest sigh—each is as clear to me as a shout. A sigh is the crown of a larger unhappiness. Forceps are seldom required to draw out the whole squirming business." The significance of the image was not lost on Alexis. She did not speak for several moments, her mind occupied with that other baby whose effect on her husband had been so devastating, or so she believed. Certainly it had been on her.

"And you told her you were the guardian of the Holy Grail," she said, shaking the infant corpse from her vision.

"Poor Elspeth," I said. "She was alone much of the time. It was she who came up with the idea of the Grail. I merely—shamelessly, you will say—led her on. Her mind, that tireless fantasy, had manufactured a purpose for my existence. Something to justify her squalid obsession."

"But why?" Alexis demanded.

"Mr. Husted spent all of his time in Bristol," I replied. "Their honeymoon had been one of much cry and little wool."

"And what does that mean?" she said.

"It means their honeymoon was not unlike your own—"

"My honeymoon was fabulous!" Alexis interrupted. "What happened later.... What we.... I'm not going to stay here and be abused!"

I heard her chair squeak on the floor as she stood to leave. Then there came echoing up the stairs a guttural howl of laughter from Maeve followed by an invitation to Alexis which was not at all nice. Quietly, Alexis resumed her seat. "I don't have to put up with this," she said. "If I have brought these ghosts on myself I can make them go away."

"Perhaps," I murmured. "But for tonight, at least, you're safer here."

"Am I?" she said. Then her own mind, every bit as excitable as Elspeth's, conjured up a monster. She saw a hideous amalgam of the lives I had assimilated down through the ages rise from my gullet to devour her. She let it. She let it crash down the flimsy barricade of the table which separated us and swallow her whole. She pictured it again and again, scarcely breathing. I waited. Unmoving.

"Call them off," she said. "They're your ghosts. I have no control over them. Just as I have no control over you."

"Let me tell you something, Alexis," I said. "Not everyone can hear me. I only speak to those who come in search of something."

"And then you lull them to death," she said. She was not like the others, she told herself over and over. She was too sensible to be taken in.

"Sally Bert came up here alone with her thoughts," she went on.

"And found herself alone with mine," I added hastily. "But, as you may recall from her own touching account of the story, I didn't bother her at first. It was only later, when she had defiled her little funk-hole by sharing it with a lover—it was only then that I proved meddlesome."

"You despise love, don't you?" said Alexis.

"I know very little about it," I said. "Only the suffering of its conclusion. I wouldn't have learned much about love from Sally and her rebel, I can assure you. The two of them spoke in indecipherable bursts: huff and puff and huff. Not much company. Boring. Maybe that's why I came up with the notion of a suicide pact."

"Murder pact," said Alexis.

"Suicide," I countered. "You see, Sally only assumes her lover got away with his ruse, but my plan was even craftier than the captain dreamed. His own part of the bargain was only postponed."

"Do you mean he tripped or something?" said Alexis. There was new enthusiasm in her voice, as if the accidental death of the once noble captain would now come as an unexpected happy turn.

"More poetic than a mere accident," I proclaimed. "You see, the captain had held off the suicide game until the last moment. He knew the castle was about to fall—which it did soon after he had ensconced himself in the organ loft. The pact was found and it was generally assumed he was dead. His plan would have worked to a T if it hadn't been for the rats. Fastyngange was crawling with vermin in those days, but seldom did they find a store of food in such a delightfully safe location as the loft

105

of an organ. Not only had they eaten a goodly portion of the captain's stores, but they were reluctant to let him share, let alone stop, their unexpected feast. The captain, as you will have figured out, was a most cowardly sort. Within forty-eight hours he went berserk. Bitten all over, glassy-eyed and foaming at the mouth, he ran screaming from his hideout, through the church, across the yard, through the hall, and straight to me, the one friend he could turn to in his desperation.

"There were those who swore they had seen a rampaging ghost but I can attest to his substantiality."

Alexis was very quiet. For her the story was not yet over. Sally, after all, had been one of those who had survived the fall. In Alexis' all too vivid imagination she pictured Sally in the hole and the captain plummeting down on top of her. She felt the impact of his great boots on her own skull and her own slim shoulders. She felt herself caving in. The oubliette was filling up with carcases. Teddy would never get out—the part of him that was still trapped.

She sobbed for some time. "There, there." I murmured an avuncular blessing. "It is good to have a ready ear into which I may pour those stories which haunt me," I confessed, when her crying jag had run its course.

"How awful it must be to be haunted," she admitted, but I don't think she was really thinking about me.

The room became very still. A fight broke out in the whistling gallery and died down. The baby awoke and went back to sleep. Slowly, slowly, the night plodded on and there was not yet the slightest sign of light. She checked. She stood on the narrow rim of my lip as Elspeth had done so many years before and poked her head out of the window. No light.

She took to pacing. "Sit down," I said.

But she would not. She paced and sniffed. Finally, in desperation she spoke: "For God's sake, say something!" she demanded. She would listen to any voice at all in that darkness rather than listen to the thoughts running around in her head. So I told her the story of each of my survivors. There were twelve in all.

There was a Welsh stonemason who finished me off and whom I finished off. Drunk he was and the mortar not yet dry, when to amuse his co-workers he decided to inaugurate my completion. He pulled down his britches and piddled. He slipped on a puddle of his own making and followed his piss into his grave. Then there was Judge Jeffrey's cockney hangman whom Alexis had seen for herself. He let one of Sally's kitchenmates lead him by the cock up to the room in the keep. And the urchin who stole a cross from the abbot's newly furbished church and, having been given the cross, was committed by the holy fathers to the oubliette to think about his sins.

"Professeur Flavigny thought I was an oracle," I told her. "He spent days explaining the current art scene with the hope that I might predict the next trend and make him famous. The soldier, on the other hand, only thought I was an escape route." On and on I spoke. The bodies piled up.

"Go on," said Alexis, when it seemed I might stop. Perhaps she hoped to become inured to shock, the better to help her beloved, and apparently dangerous, Teddy. In any case, that one night we spent together at Fastyngange she proved herself a devil for punishment. When words failed me she talked about herself. And then in the early hours, despite her best efforts, sleep overcame her. She curled up as far from me as she could remove herself. "Go on," she said, yawning. So I did, until I had recounted all the survivors' stories. She dozed. It was a bedtime story. I was her Scheherazade, but in this inverted Scheherazade it was the listener not the storyteller who must eventually perish. That was my plan.

"Let me tell you about Friar Rush," I said, having reached the end of my list of infamy. She made no objection. I began.

"It was in the closing years of the Glastonbury Retreat, towards the middle of the last century. Rush heard me whistling a hymn one day. He could not know that I had listened to him muttering to himself as he ambled about in the gardens below. He was a man with a sharp ear and a sharper than average intellect, with too big a gut and too many questions. They were not questions he brought up in the refectory. They were questions he only referred to obliquely sometimes in confession. He was not a simple friar.

"The day he made my acquaintance I was whistling "Rock of Ages". It had been recently penned in the nearby Quantock Hills. All the monks were whistling it. It was a devout appeal chosen to pique the curiosity of a holy brother. When I first addressed him he denounced me immediately as the devil.

" 'But I am nothing,' I told him. 'Nothing but a hole.'

"Rush modified his charge. I was a conduit to hell—the devil's mouthpiece. I parried. 'But if I am the route to hell why is it that so many innocents have found their way into my keeping? Men whose only offence was to disagree with the lord of this place or the tenor of the times.? And not men only, but children.' I recounted the story of Sally Bert. Rush listened in silence.

" 'The girl was guilty of the sin of pride,' he blurted out when my account was complete. He was a little too quick in his denouncement. I sensed that sin was never far from Rush's thinking, as well might be expected in a holy man.

" 'Then plug me up at once,' said I. 'Gag the devil. Have me so filled with cement that the weight will crush the fallen angel's head once and for all.' I was most eloquent. 'But ask yourself these questions before you do,' I added. 'Why has no one else closed me up? Why am I still unfettered when a century of holy men have come to this place to pray and meditate? Are you the first to find me here? Why has no one reported me to the abbots?'

"Rush was silent. He knew the answers, or guessed at them, and he knew that he was as good as damned for knowing the answers. He kneeled for a long time staring up at the little hole of the *oeil-de-boeuf* window. If I was a conduit to hell then that tiny window clogged with ivy must certainly be a conduit to heaven.

There was the palest glimmer of a sunset in the window but there was no voice. Rush prayed ferociously. Had God whispered the slightest word to him he would have known his course, known his duty. 'Now, oh now,' he pleaded. 'If You are ever to talk to me, God, make it now.'

"Of course he received no guidance. I did not disturb his thoughts at this crucial moment. I couldn't. The wind had died completely. The room, I think, had never been so still. Had the poor brother not been so close to committing his own sin of pride he might have realized that God was speaking to him through the intensity of His silence. God was allowing the holy man the chance to hear his Saviour's voice in all the testaments he had committed to memory. But my voice was still fresh, still clamouring in his ear, and God's subtle strategy could not drown me out. 'Oh Lord. Why hast Thou forsaken me?' he thought, and was answered with silence. The moment of salvation passed and when I had breath enough to speak, I risked saying, 'God moves in mysterious ways His wonders to conceal.'

"Rush said nothing, nor did he leave. His vows were shattered in his failure to do so, or so he thought. He didn't leave because he tacitly agreed with me. Besides, he was already formulating the first question he would ask, his first wish. It crowded his better judgement and the learning of the years of his novitiate.

" 'Go on,' I said, recognizing all too well the signs.

" 'Tell me about *hell* ,' he ventured.

"And so I did—what I knew. What I had heard or could invent. Since he was so determined that I issued from that place, it was no use explaining to him that I knew nothing but what I'd learned from his fellow man. I made hell sound as he expected, with a few surprises so as not to disappoint him. He did not go to Vespers that night. He did not go to Prime. He listened to me throughout the night. By Matins it was too late. In his guilty mind the banishment was now complete. He had not simply bitten the apple, he had consumed it, core and all. The seeds of it were already buried in the lining of his stomach. Soon his new wisdom would take root in him. He could imagine the trunk of it already in his throat, swelling there, gagging him. All his training led him to believe that in communing with the devil his own destruction was complete. When his curiosity was sated and he was overcome with tiredness there remained only the final act of making himself one with his nemesis. He did not jump. On his knees he said a humble, contrite little prayer and then just tipped over the edge. I was not aware of his spirit funnelling up through me back to heaven.

"Alexis?" I said. Her breathing was soft and regular. She had taken so long to unwind. "It is time to give up this futile quest," I continued in a voice she had not yet heard, a voice modelled exactly on her own at its most gentle and persuasive modulation. "It is time to leave the Teddy of this world behind, to forget him. That is what the oubliette is for, Alexis. That is why you have come here. You knew it all along. Get up, Alexis. You are tired, you are mad. And the part of him you long for is waiting below. You are not comfortable on that cold floor."

She stirred.

"I have a bed waiting for you," I continued. "Softer than the bed at the Marriotts', far more giving than your marriage bed."

She moaned, slowly clambering to her hands and knees.

"That's it, dear," I coaxed, like a nurse with a tired old patient. "A bed. The softest bed of all. Softer even than the womb. And so close, Alexis. You can see it from here. You will be there before you know it. The truth will no longer matter."

She climbed to her feet and stood there swaying. "Doctor?" she said. "Dr. Troubridge?"

"I will lead you to him," I whispered. "Come."

She took a step. Then another. And then two more until she was standing next to me.

"One more step," I whispered. But she did not move. "He is near," I said. Then I heard the sound of her hand on her cheek. Once, twice. Again.

It was the sun.

A small burning mote of it like a freshly minted coin had fallen on her cheek and she was trying to brush it away.

"One step and the irritation will go away," I said, unable to keep my own irritation from my voice.

Perhaps my imitation of her voice slipped. "Who are you?" she murmured.

Then I heard it and sensed that she too heard it.

"No, don't wake up," I said, loudly. "You are so sleepy. So tired...."

But I could not drown it out. It came closer and closer shattering the peace of the castle, and snatching Alexis from my grasp. For it snapped her out of her sleep-walking. For one insane moment I even thought the noise might accomplish what my cozening could not, for she teetered on the very edge of me. Then she reclaimed her balance and her eyes opened in amazement to the light and her ears unscrambled the sound outside. There was what I would have called a lorry (and she a truck) on the hill.

12

"I have been trying to wake you," I said, in my own voice again. She was on the ledge, hanging from the sill, peering through the dried tangle of brown ivy down at the courtyard where the lorry had come to rest.

"It's Mechelney," she said. But even as she spoke I heard in succession the opening and slamming of two car doors.

"This can only mean trouble," I said.

"What do you mean?" she asked, for she had thought I meant trouble for her. I did not attempt to enlighten her for I was straining to hear what Mechelney and his accomplice were up to. The wind was high and snatched their talk away but what I heard was enough to disturb me more than I had ever been disturbed in my long life.

"Big trouble," I said.

"Mechelney is pointing things out to him," said Alexis, watching them from the window. "The other is writing things on a clipboard. He's wearing a hardhat."

At one point she slid away from the window. "He is looking this way," she explained. Under the circumstances, I couldn't help finding this amusing.

She had been away from civilization for some time now and had not liked or trusted Mechelney to begin with. She had made a bonfire of his stockpile of kneeling pieces. More important, she had made Fastyngange her home and saw these intruders as a violation. I supposed it was that which made her temporarily forget the ordeal of the previous night and kept her from calling out to them. Still, I was somewhat surprised that she did not immediately see them as rescuers. She was, after all, desperately in need of rescue. By the time the idea of being rescued occurred to her I had had plenty of time to think.

"Where are you going?" I asked, as she darted towards the stairs.

"Away from here," she said triumphantly.

"Without so much as a goodbye?"

"I owe you nothing," she said. She was already around the first turn of the staircase when my riposte caught her up short.

"And you owe Teddy nothing!" I shouted. She was still under my spell. I reeled her back to me.

"The stranger is a demolition expert," I said softly. "A wrecker."

She did not speak. I wondered if she heard me at all. "Alexis," I said in a sterner voice, "I need you. And you need me if you hope to rescue Teddy from his insanity."

Her silence was infuriating. I am patience personified, but then seldom is my very existence threatened.

"If I am destroyed," I said, "I will cave in on that part of Teddy which is still in the dungeon, transfixed. I am his only hope of recovery. Leave me now and you can kiss Teddy goodbye."

This time her silence was poignant.

"What am I supposed to do?" she asked. "Stop them? I only have a pocket-knife." Her voice was small like a child's but infused with a child's conviction. Despite my precarious position, I was moved to gentle, fatherly laughter.

"It should not come to that," I said.

"You have a plan?" she asked.

113

In truth I did not. But I had spent hundreds of years contemplating destruction; it seemed entirely likely I could escape my own.

"Yes," I said, "I believe I do."

Fastyngange was to be demolished the day after the following day, I had heard the men say. There was time. The idea came to me in stages. But first I had to convince her to stay. It was not easy. Whatever reservations she had had about making her presence known to Mechelney passed when the men drove off. I was passionate. "You have come so far," I told her. "You have done what a doctor could never have done. You have entered Teddy's reluctant madness and found the scent. You have followed his footsteps back to the scene of the trauma. You cannot turn back now!"

"You will help," she made me promise.

"I am your servant," I told her.

"It's the ghosts," she said.

"Two more nights," I pleaded. "I have complete power over them, as you guessed. I will not let them harass you. You are too important to all of us."

She went to the rampart to find her backpack. It was where she had left it. She went to the buttery and gathered some food she had planned to leave behind. She saw no ghosts—I made certain of that—though she felt them watching her. She came back to the room and made herself as comfortable as she could. There was no Snow White sweep-up, there wasn't time.

She began work right away and indeed her penknife was part of her arsenal. It was my intention that she should pry loose the stones that make up my miraculous mouth. It was just the beginning, of course. She worked late, without the benefit of more than her knife, a hinge, and a broken piece of iron rod she had found in the stable. She was up early the following morning, hard at work again. Mechelney arrived early too, alone.

She glared down at him from the little window. It soon became apparent that he was only there now to make one last raid. And what a rampage it was. I had never known him to work with such rapacious diligence. He picked and chipped at Fastyngange while Alexis picked and chipped far less effectively at me. She swore between her teeth each time Mechelney's pick came down. When the noise below let up, she looked out again with the hope that he was leaving, but he was only stopping for a sandwich. Then suddenly Alexis let out a little stifled yelp of excitement, and dashed from the room.

It seems Mechelney had wandered down the bailey to eat in the sun. Stealthily, Alexis made her way to his most recent scene of carnage, where she found the tools of his destruction. She would have liked to take the pickaxe, but thought better of it and took up only his crowbar. As she turned to go, she was startled by the appearance in her path of Elspeth. Her arms were crossed on her chest. But it was her eyes which commanded Alexis' attention and pity, for they were filled with fear. The brawler on the wall was once again the disenchanted and hapless wife.

"So this is what his meddling has come to," she said. Alexis did not stop to comment, afraid he might catch her there. She raced into the hall. The other ghostly women were at the windows watching Mechelney. They turned to Alexis.

"Stop 'im," pleaded Sally.

"Bash 'is bloody head in wif 'is filfy tool," growled Maeve.

The lady from Bath said nothing, merely adjusting her veil to conceal more properly all but the shape of her face. She moved, gold glittered on the tulle veil, and Alexis caught a glimpse of eyes brimming with alarm. Grasping her crowbar she raced up to the keep. The termagants were on her side, for the time being.

I bid her hide the crowbar, though I congratulated her quick-wittedness in seizing such an invaluable aid. I had advanced my plans in her absence, and had more pressing work for her. Time was now a more redoubtable adversary than old man Mechelney.

She must make herself presentable and set off for Glastonbury at once. She must get there during business hours, which necessitated hitch-hiking. She had several errands to accomplish, not the least of which was returning to Fastyngange in time to finish the removal of my mouth before the following day.

She slipped out just in time. Moments later, Mechelney, looking for his crowbar and suspecting treachery, journeyed up to the keep. He called up the stairs as he had done the time before, but this time he climbed the spiral stairs warily, stopping every few steps. Listening. How long had it been since he was last here?— not long enough by his way of thinking. I could hear the terror in his voice. He had been hardly more than a boy when he had come up here to find Elspeth Husted where no one else could find her, and the fire that had consumed the Mary Chapel still had been flickering in her vacant eyes. He had no idea what he might find this time. What he did find, I think, came as a relief. Alexis' soiled work clothes in a heap on the floor. The floor wet around the bucket of water she had used to wash herself before leaving. The bucket she had cut free from his well. He didn't find his crowbar. That much she had hidden.

The wind, playful and exuberant as a dog all day, turned into a wild thing with nightfall. It was almost eight when Alexis returned. She had accomplished her banking and rented a car as I had suggested. Taking her cue from Mechelney she drove up the hill and parked at the gate. She had to fight the wind to get out of her car, and once she had done so it flung the door shut impatiently. She set off in a run across the bailey, the courtyard, the anteroom to the hall. It was strange to hear the clatter of her shoes when I had become accustomed to the barely perceptible patter of her unshod feet. It was stranger still to come to grips with the notion that those fleet footsteps were among the last I would hear at Fastyngange. She ran across the great hall where I had, in time, heard the triple metre of the galliard and

116

the arhythmic clomp of uninvited troops. Alexis was still running, down the steps from the bridge into the whistling gallery, when she screamed. Then her scream was muffled by flesh and I was left to imagine for the time being what was going on below.

The man pinned her to his chest with a wiry arm, until her initial struggle weakened. Then he turned her roughly to face him.

"Ye turned out to be a bigger fool than I ever dreamed," he said. " 'ave ye any idea what ye've got yerzelf into?" Mechelney shook her and she folded like a rag doll. She was in shock. She had been returned forcefully to the world of men.

"Up there Mizzy," he snapped, pointing towards the keep. Mechelney squeezed her arms still more firmly. "Ye'r getting out of 'ere, right thiz minute. Out of 'iz way."

Alexis seemed to give up. She bowed her head and her muscles slackened. She became limp in his grip. He relaxed his hold on her. Then, as he turned towards the bridge, she tore herself free of him.

"Come back!" he shouted after her. From his pocket he produced a flashlight which followed her down the gallery. "Come back," Mechelney called again, and there was a note of desperation in his voice. "Ye need 'elp!" he yelled. At first he made no attempt to follow, so that she was well on her way up the stairs when he came in pursuit. She arrived breathless in the chamber and her first instinct was to grab up the little chair.

"Come here," I hissed at her. "*Put me between yourself and him!*" I whispered. She understood. Kicking off her shoes, she stepped gingerly onto the narrow ledge between the hole and the wall. A flashlight beam preceded Mechelney up the curve of the stairs. He stopped before he reached the landing. For a moment there was no sound but heavy breathing in the room, and outside, the wind's muffled howl.

"For God's zake, Mizzy," Mechelney said when he at last pinpointed her with his light. "Thiz 'az got to stop!"

"Leave me alone," she called back.

Mechelney advanced a step closer but still would not cross the threshold into the room. "You heard the lady," I rumbled.

"I'll not lizzen to the likes of you," Mechelney said, his voice quivering but resolute. "Whatever ye think of me, mizzy, ye muzn't lizzen to 'im." Mechelney cast the flashlight beam into Alexis' eyes. She turned away grasping the wall behind her. The light dazzled her.

"Tom Mechelney," I said. "You old rapist. Leave her to me."

"Ye bloody devil," Tom shouted. "I'll not leave 'er 'ere for ye to 'ave yer way with!" And with that he stomped into the room right up to my very lip. And that is when I shrieked, the most hideous, unearthly shriek imaginable. Alexis' legs went weak. She lost her grip on the wall and found herself falling—and then, for the second time, in the strong grip of Mechelney, who dragged her from her ledge, from my mouth, out into the room. Again she pulled herself away, but this time Mechelney made no attempt to stop her.

"Leave 'im to me!" he shouted over the noise of my howling. To his shock, Alexis made no attempt to escape but started hitting him with her fists. She screamed as she battered at him.

"Stop!" he cried. "Ye've got it all wrong, mizzy!" But there was no convincing Alexis. He pushed her off but she raged at him, ramming him against the wall and forcing the flashlight from his grasp. It clattered to the floor where it rolled in circles, spinning the room around in Alexis' eyes. Then suddenly a shadow came at her out of the wheeling light and something hard smashed into the side of her head. She found herself falling against the wall, the floor. "I'm sorry, mizzy," she heard Mechelney's voice from farther and farther away. "Ye can't be allowed to go on like this," his voice implored and the sound followed her down and echoed all around her. "I can't allow 'im to do this to ye," he said and she wanted to ask why he kept talking about "him" when it was

118

only a hole and the hole was no sex at all. From very far away she heard them arguing.

"Oh, Teddy, what have I done?" she moaned.

It seemed to her that she fell for a long, long time. No oubliette could be so deep, she thought and was encouraged. She was floating, she decided. And then it occurred to her, with a shock, that perhaps she had died in falling and was already a ghost. If it was true, then she should be thankful for being saved the bone-crushing blow of landing. The floating sensation passed and in its place she became aware of an enormous weight pressing on her, threatening to squash her. She pushed at it with all her might, but could do nothing to move it. She must, she told herself, and she heaved against it again, her head threatening to burst with the exertion. Then slowly she came to consciousness. She fought that, remembering what a painful place consciousness was. She lost the battle. She came to and found herself lying on her sleeping bag, pushing down desperately on the stone floor.

It was still dark. The wind had died down. The room was quiet. Her temple was bleeding. Mechelney's flashlight lay on the floor, weakly shining into her eyes. Mechelney was not there. She moved and groaned.

"I was wondering how long you'd be," I said.

"Where is—"

"Don't worry about him," I hastened to say. "He will not bother you again."

Alexis got to her knees, her feet. She found the bucket and tipped a mouthful of water into her lips. She was shaking all over and it was not from the cold. She sat heavily against the wall. "What happened?" she asked.

"It's all right," I said quietly, respecting her physical weakness. "You didn't kill him. They'll never blame you."

A thousand questions swirled around in her aching head.

"Pull yourself together," I said firmly. "There is much work to be done."

13

Alexis was ready when the demolition crew arrived in the morning. She had not slept but was as alert as a soldier waiting in the woods for the enemy tanks. Against such odds there was no hope of saving Fastyngange; I had accepted that all along. But there was a chance of saving me. To that end she had laboured until the wee hours. It had been the longest night of her life. Her faith in me was extraordinary but it had been gained at the expense of her natural hardiness. I still counted on her stamina to make my escape: in fact, the worst was yet to come.

I had guessed that my mouth was the only materiality I was dependent upon. True, the well of my being gives depth to my character, but that miraculous mouth stretched over any pitcher would still be able to talk—to be. This I had surmised. Alexis had to pry the stones free.

How feverishly she worked. If she had questioned the task presented to her, she did not question it again in carrying it out. I was a patient on the operating table. She was not able to — did not know how to — give up. The occasional moan escaped my dismembered lips. It startled her the first time. As if, indeed, a heavily anaesthetized patient had spoken. It did not sound like me, but only hideous and guttural like an uncovered sewer. Disenchanting. Still she persevered.

It took until the early hours of the morning to pry loose the twelve stones that form my magic circle. She hauled these off in several trips to her car. Then she drove the car back down the earthwork out of the way.

She saw no ghosts as she passed through the hall. There was no hangman at the gate, no shaveling in the beech wood. If there was, they hid from her. Perhaps they realized the end was nigh, she told herself. But their absence preyed on her just as their presence had done at first. She had become used to living with this egregious company.

It was dawn before she climbed back up to the castle. At the peak the shadow of Fastyngange rushed to meet her as it had done before. She did not re-enter the keep. She waited in the underbrush. Curling up in the dead leaves she drifted off to sleep. The drone of heavy wrecking equipment snapped her back to life.

The bellowing of the machinery as it climbed the hill seemed apocalyptic enough in this quiet place. Like a primitive, Alexis watched the demolition juggernaut roll by her hiding place. They wasted no time. Bulldozers crashed through walls King James' ballistics had only been able to dent. With winches the hall was collapsed in on itself, neatly, without drama. It was only a matter of hours before the crew was ready to tackle the keep. And it too offered little resistance. Explosives were placed strategically. A horn sounded the alert. The blast was detonated. The keep puckered—this was how she described it later—like a face holding back vomit. Then it caved in ignominiously, leaving a tower of dust in its place. My home for nearly a millennium crumbled in a matter of moments.

Alexis' heart sank. She was certain that my plan had miscarried and that all her work had been in vain. She trained her eyes on the cloud of dust and, as it settled, she saw it—she saw me. The workers didn't notice—how could they? They had neither the expectation nor the imagination nor the need. For one astounding moment I was suspended there in the clear sky. A hole. All my emptiness exposed, a long shaft of fetid air, full of forgotten screams and horror; a shuddering column on the top of that ancient hill, invisible to all but one. I stood there above the rubble of the castle, free, for one glorious moment. It could not last. I could feel myself sinking. She could *see* I was about to sink. My edges were being blown away. If I'd had a voice then I would have cried out: "*Alexis, now!*" But she knew without prompting. She stood up, with her back against a tree for support. She clenched her fists. She closed her eyes. She opened her mouth wide. She opened her body to me. By an immense act of will she opened up her heart to me. Me. Even as I was caving in I felt that attraction whisk me towards the beech wood. I rushed across the clearing like a small tornado, a purposeful gale. I rushed into her, the full length of me. All that I am of time waiting, ploughed into her enormous heart. Even though I had been preparing her for me all along, she grunted and collapsed with the impact. She tumbled over backwards in shock as I entered her mouth and ears and pores—all of her, a great sweep of cold nothingness. She lay amidst the roots of the tree, rolling and retching and holding her sides to keep from exploding. She writhed under the weight of me, wanting to scream yet clamping her mouth shut. And even with the pain there was already a taste in her mouth of what it was going to be like to be full at last. Teddy's name came up again and again. She was delirious. Perhaps my own ecstasy was mingling with hers. I was struck first by the warmth of this new home. All that streaming blood. I had never known until that moment of immersion in Alexis that in my entire life I had never been warm. Not for one second. The delirium passed, leaving her moaning in pain. Some of that moaning was my own. I was mortal, at last. The last thing she remembered was propping herself up on her elbows and seeing the workers stop for tea.

14

Alexis heard voices. But there was nothing new in that. She had been hearing voices for years and never so many as at Fastyngange. It was not enough to bring her around. The first sound she attended to was the chinking of masonry against masonry. It sounded a long way off, in Fastyngange, in the north-west corner of Somerset.... She was dizzy. She forced open her eyes and in her dizziness she mistook the shadowy shapes around her for shadows. The voices stopped. It was early evening. The birds were going mad again anticipating the night—though it was no worse for them than any other. Alexis blinked away sleep and tried to make the shadowy figures vanish or at least stand still. They would not. As consciousness seeped into her senses she recalled the workers. Workers, she gathered, a motley handful. Five of them. But why did they stand there? Couldn't they see she needed help? She hitched herself up on her elbows. She opened her eyes wide.

They didn't look like workers. They looked like soldiers after a battle they had lost. Or one of them did. He stepped back, turning away from her gaze. He looked down on himself sorrowfully. His torso was encased in a shell of battered armour, the rest of him was in tattered strips of clothing, bandages streaked with grime and caked with blood. Beside him stood a boy. His hair was matted with cobwebs, thick with masonry dust. Finally Alexis noticed his one arm, withered to the bone, and slung in a cast. His back was bent with the weight of a cross he wore on a string around his neck. Alexis had seen the cross before; she couldn't quite remember where. Not on this boy, she thought, and yet....

Her limbs buzzed with pins and needles. She straightened her back against the beech tree. One of the five, a woman, cried out with fear and edged away, back towards Fastyngange. *Fastyngange*. It was a ruin, a heap of rubble. Adjusting her eyes to the twilight, Alexis scanned the wreckage. There was no sign of a demolition crew. She stared at the castle, reconstructing it in her mind. I was captivated. *It was the first time I had seen my ancestral home*.

Alexis' eyes returned from the moonscape of dead rock and fell on the figure who had cried out in fear. She cringed under Alexis' gaze. She pulled a decrepit shawl around her bony shoulders. The deep curve of her bosom seemed preposterous on her skeletal frame. Then Alexis noticed the swollen belly under the girl's shift. Though she moved and apparently carried life in her, her belly looked more like a cancer on a sapling, a gall. The girl whined and flicked her hand at Alexis.

"Stop staring at her," one of the others whispered.

Alexis' eyes picked out the speaker. He raised a hand in front of his eyes as if expecting a blow. He wore fingerless string gloves streaked with gore. His face was covered in sores and remnants of a clotted beard. He wore a filthy tweed suit jacket and a pair of breeches. His stockings trailed behind him in a long thread. Stuffed in his pocket were a pair of spectacles like Professeur Flavigny's, Alexis recalled. This hideous broken creature must have stolen them, she thought.

Alexis pressed her back against the tree and edged herself up painfully, slowly, with the patience of a cicada. They watched her as if they were watching a magic plant spring up from the ground; a clinging, climbing thing; a parasite. At full height she was taller than any of them. They shrank from her.

"What do you want?" she asked.

"*Alors*! She's got it," cried the one in string gloves indignantly. "She's got it somewhere and she's going to tease us!"

Then from behind the man with the string gloves another of them pushed forward, near her. There was no mistaking him. It was the hangman, but transformed. Wasted almost beyond recognition. His sack with its rough holes for the eyes and mouth was rotting. Spikes of black hair shot through tears in the weave of the sacking.

"We wan' it *back*!" he said. His voice stung like the grating of a broken loudspeaker.

"I haven't anything of yours," said Alexis. Her scrawny inquisitor flinched when she spoke.

" 'ive it 'ack!" said the boy with the cross. He spat at her feet and scampered out of range. Then there was a shout from the ruin. All eyes turned to that quarter. Alexis saw nothing. But the little brutes around her started to murmur excitedly.

"Over 'ere!" yelled the hangman.

From behind a jagged pile of rubble a figure arose, silhouetted against the dull sky. The failing light revealed him, dressed in a robe. He was larger than the others and rose like a dark planet from the broken mountain of stone. He looked down across the meadow towards them. He turned and shouted, in a voice like a foghorn, "They've found something." Then he beckoned unseen bodies with an arm that rose from his robes, an arm that was only bone.

Others quickly found the planet and began to tramp with him towards Alexis. As they walked they searched the rubble at their feet, stooping now and then to turn over a stone or a broken length of timber. One of them wore a full-length dress and picked her way through the rubble with the help of a skeletal parasol. One of them carried a baby.

125

Alexis whimpered as the terrible company moved closer.

Now and then their spindly shanks gave way under them and they tumbled over. All but the planet. As he drew nearer, the five around Alexis grew bolder. The tongueless boy edged close to her, tittering madly, and jabbed her in the side, though he screamed in pain when he touched her and pulled his hand away as if scalded. Whimpering, he tucked it back into its sling of cloth.

"Tell us what you done wiv it!" demanded the hangman. He threatened her. The huge scarab in its gold nest glinted on his misshapen fist.

"We know what you are," keened another, in a voice so shrill it made Alexis wince. This started them howling and cackling, which in turn promoted the rest of the tribe to howl and cackle. Alexis clapped her hands over her ears, so intense was the wailing as the two parties congregated. There were a dozen of them in all, and the planet pushed his way through them until he stood face to face with Alexis. He called for quiet and got it, but it was an electric silence, crackling and ready to explode.

"It's 'er!" the hangman squealed triumphantly.

The scabrous head of the planet rose from the cowls of his robe, which Alexis could now see was a monk's sackcloth habit. He composed his face. He smiled, but there was too much tooth and gum showing for the smile to be truly considered benign. One of his eyes was dead.

"Perhaps you can help us," he said. His good eye travelled over Alexis' body seemingly independent of the planet's control. She remembered the day in the orchard when he had propositioned her in the name of a shy tourist, the night at the castle gate.

"Remember me?" asked Friar Rush, leaning towards her. Alexis pulled away from the stench of him. "Not quite what you expected," he said, winking impudently.

"Not quite as she imagined, you mean," croaked Maeve, elbowing her way to the front. Through the tears in her petticoat Alexis glimpsed withered, leathery dugs hanging on a washboard chest. Maeve arched her shoulders and piled her ragged copper-coloured mane up into a grotesque bouffant. "What, not as luvly as me wraith?" she simpered. "Never thought I'd live to see the bleeding day!"

The others roared and screamed with laughter, a sound that made Alexis' teeth water.

Her eyes returned to Rush, pleading for an explanation. "What you saw of us before tonight was only apparitions," he said. "Something the hole conjured up for your amusement."

"As we were, like," said Maeve, tilting her chin defiantly. "When we was bee-you-ti-fool!"

"An enchantment," said a shaking voice from the ranks. Alexis' eye picked out the remains of Elspeth in her painting smock, her hair grown thick down to the middle of her back, the colour of unpolished silver. Her face, alone among the ghoulish lot, seemed almost human. But then, thought Alexis, she has been dead a lot less time than the rest. It was she who carried the baby. It lay still against her shoulder, tiny and swaddled in a blanket. It did not move.

Don't wake up, Alexis pleaded silently with the sleeping infant.

"He's good at enchantments," said Elspeth dolefully.

"And lies!" screamed Maeve, which started them all complaining at once. "Bleeding 'ole!"

"Quiet!" shouted Rush.

When they had obeyed him, he spoke again. "What have you done with it?" he demanded in a sharp whisper.

"She's hidden it!" someone yelled.

"Hold your tongue!" bellowed the planet, and this made them scream with laughter again. Maeve fell on her knees in front of Alexis and waggled her tongue at her until the planet cuffed her to one side. She still laughed uproariously, rolling on the ground; laughed until she cried. Her eyes bled viscous tears like egg white down her scabby cheeks.

127

"Insolence!" cried Rush, and, lashing out with his hand, cuffed Maeve again. This time she moved out of the planet's range to the fringe of the group. Alexis watched her nervously slink away into the shadows.

Friar Rush turned his unnerving one-eyed gaze back on Alexis. He pressed his nose up to her own and she flattened herself against the tree. "Have over with it," he rumbled.

"I don't know what you want," said Alexis. But she did have an inkling and Rush must have seen it in her eyes.

"The hole," he hissed.

"*Our* 'ole," said the hangman, prodding her with his foot. It might have been a straw, though the hangman had seemed to kick her with some vehemence. I could waste the lot, she thought, and it gave her a sense of hope. And then, out of the corner of her eye, Alexis saw Maeve move suddenly, flinging something her way. A stone flew invisibly out of the night, grazing Alexis' cheek and clattering against the tree trunk. She screamed. Then there was a silence like death as the blood trickled down her cheek and collected in a warm pool at the corner of her lip. The blood frightened and then seemed to excite them. The urchin growled loud in his throat like a cur. And then the baby leaning on Elspeth's shoulder moved. It turned its wobbly head and glared with unfocused eyes at Alexis. Its face was as sharp as a bird's. Its mouth opened like the voracious beak of a wingless nestling. Then it screamed. A blood-curdling scream that cleaved Alexis' senses like a scalpel blade. Heaving herself forward with all her might, Alexis shoved the planet back into the crowd pressing around him. He toppled like a dessicated roll of paper, like an enormous wasps' nest. She might have put her hands clear through him. Others fell like dominoes. Ignited, Alexis turned and ran.

A piercing ululation followed her down the hill. Missiles, bits of the demolished castle, ricocheted off trees as she crashed through the dry leaves of the wood. She heard them crashing after her, but the sound was lost in the pounding of her heart and the thumping of her feet on the grassy slope of the earthwork. She felt it again, the urgent tug of gravity pulling her away from the insanity above. And I, *I* was in rapture! The exhilaration of moving through space! Then suddenly we were flying, but only for a moment. The ground came up to meet Alexis with a force that knocked the wind out of her. She had stepped in a rabbit hole and fallen flat on her face. She rolled over quickly and Sally was there, over her, the ratty tail of her shawl bumping against Alexis' face. Then Elspeth, with her wailing bundle, was standing over her as well.

"Where shall we stay?" she asked. "We must have a home for the baby!" Her lips were hideously chapped, mouldering away.

"I can't help you," Alexis cried, and squirmed out from under them. Elspeth made to hand her the bird-like baby, but she rolled away.

"We need you," they cried, and the sky around Alexis' ears seemed to crack and fall in sharp splinters, so dreadful was their wailing.

She ran.

At last she reached the rutted path which had once served as the driveway to Fastyngange. In another moment she raced between the twin oaks that formed the threshold of the property. She turned out onto the country road. Fastyngange Hill lay between her and the moon now. There was little light, only the palest of reflections on the far shore of the Parrett, which lay along her course. The river was swollen with fall rains and lapped against the shore. She heard that and nothing more—not a bird or animal.

Then, from the side of the road, there was a crashing in the bushes just ahead, and another of the survivors, the soldier, broke through the gorse, dragging great trailing lengths of it caught in his hair and embroidering his limbs. The tangle had brought him to his knees; Alexis flew past him while he was trying to pull himself free of the knotted vegetation.

"It's not you we want!" he called after her, his voice heavy with grief.

Not me, thought Alexis, but what is in me.

Others appeared like a wall ahead, armed with sticks, but in front of them, walking towards her, was Elspeth, weaponless except for her foster child. Alexis did not stop.

She charged through the blockade, scattering them like bowling pins. They moaned and bellowed like sick cows as she pulled away from them.

Finally she saw the silhouette of her car. It was parked on the verge by the river where she had left it on that fine September day a million years ago. She piled in. In a moment the car screamed up onto the road, spitting mud clots left and right and spraying the windshield with a fine brown speckle. Fear clamped her foot to the floor. She remembered some time later to flick on her lights. As she did the tangled figure of the undead soldier in the gorse turned towards the glare, imploring with his hands. The bandages around his face had caught in the briars. They were like the ragged wings of a bird in a fisherman's net. He floundered and flopped helplessly in her vision for a startling moment and then he was left behind.

The car swerved violently—Alexis was shaking so—but bit by bit she regained control. By the time she reached the turn onto the Burrow Bridge her breathing had returned to normal. She slowed the car to a stop and, resting her head on the steering wheel, she closed her eyes for a moment.

She wiped the scratches on her face and arms with the tail of her torn blouse. In the corner of her eye she caught a movement in her rearview mirror. She swung violently around and stared down into the back seat. It was empty.

She pulled herself together and drove to Glastonbury. Once there she drove straight to the Marriotts' bed and breakfast where she had reclaimed her room the day before—as I had instructed her to do. She warded off the old couple's kind solicitations and went straight to bed. Her old room above the kitchen unchanged; the bed turned down, the heater requiring only small change to warm her. How very pleasant it seemed, though she hardly noticed. How very pink. Alexis fell out of her clothes and fell, exhausted, into the bed. We were very tired.

15

Alexis slept. She awoke to the sound of hammering. From her window she could see Mr. Marriott in his workshop at the bottom of the garden. The sun was lost to view; she had no idea what time of day it was or, for that matter, which day. She bathed, and marvelled at how skinny she was and at the scratches on her weathered fingers. She made herself respectable and went downstairs.

She stood in the front window of the sitting room, looking out at Jerusalem Street. The season was long over. Glastonbury had been returned to the natives, who had packed away their neat little garden patches and flower-filled window boxes until the next tourist season. The sky was overcast. Alexis heard a hand-bell and watched a knife sharpener push his portable grindstone up the road. Seeing Alexis in the window, he stopped and started pumping his treadle, hopefully. She had no knives to sharpen. She felt a guilt out of proportion to the situation, as if she did have a knife and was hiding it from this poor man out of meanness. She stepped back out of the window into the shadows of the room until she heard the mournful bell clanging again and finally fading into the ordinary sounds of an ordinary day. Alexis remembered her pocket-knife too late, but it was chipped beyond repair.

Isabelle, having heard the bathwater running, had set another place at the kitchen table. There were only the Swedes with them now, but they wouldn't be back until late in the evening. It was five o'clock, tea time. The kettle was whistling when Alexis entered the dining room.

"Duncan," she heard Mrs. Marriott calling through the back door. "Well," she said, seeing Alexis peeking almost fearfully around the door. "Welcome back dear. Sleep well?" Alexis said she had; she hadn't, though, and Mrs. Marriott knew it. She had spent several anxious moments at Alexis' door the past night. It was like having Jill at home again, she had told Duncan, upon returning to bed. It reminded Duncan more of when Isabelle's mother was still alive. Especially the moaning.

"Good to see you back among the living," Mr. Marriott said brightly. He washed his hands at the kitchen sink and sat down to tea, chattering away despite furtive glances from Isabelle. "Here, I've saved you a cutting from the local paper," he said, leaving the table with his meal half done. By a smile that was equal parts anguish and sympathy, Isabelle was able to convey to Alexis her despair with Duncan's meddling.

"See," said Duncan, propping a newsprint clipping against the saltshaker in front of Alexis. He resumed his seat but sat with his cutlery poised, waiting for Alexis to respond.

It was a picture of a castle in a ruined heap.

"Is that the property you took a fancy to?" Duncan asked. Alexis nodded, though it was hard to recognize it as Fastyngange. The brief article outlined the politics that had led to the demolition of the castle: a blot on the landscape; potentially unsafe; a possible site for a park....

"Pity," said Isabelle.

"Must have just about broken your 'estate agent's' crotchety old heart," said Duncan, laughing, recalling a happier time.

Alexis looked down at her plate. Very slowly it was all coming back. Not Mechelney's heart, she thought, but Troubridge's, for sure. How she longed to see him now, but how terribly disappointed he would be with her. To have let this happen. Looking up again she was favoured with a glance from Isabelle that was meant to be taken as "I understand." Duncan was hacking away at his chops.

"I have a pal in customs," he said. "With guests staying here from all over, there are always queries about this or that. I don't think we'll have any problem with your stones."

"He's made them a lovely packing crate," said Isabelle.

"Lord, but they're heavy," said Duncan between mouthfuls.

Alexis couldn't eat. She had thought she was ravenous, but something stirred in her, making further ingestion a risky proposition. She suppressed a moment of panic. "Thank you," she said, being careful to take them both in with her glance. "You've been so kind."

Duncan shook his head and averted his eyes. Alexis had turned quite pale. "All part of the extended warranty," he said, a little too heartily. "Tomorrow, if you like, I'll take the whole shebang down to the shipping office."

"We sent most of your baggage and parcels on ahead to Southampton," chirped Isabelle. "Like you suggested."

"The S.S. *Northern Lights*," Alexis remembered just in time.

"Of course the ship doesn't leave for another week," said Duncan, "but it's best to be early in these things."

"Yes, of course," said Alexis. "What would I do without you?"

"Time to get yourself all rested up and ship-shape," said Duncan, laughing mildly at his own joke.

"How lovely to be crossing on a steamer," said Isabelle. She was thinking of the healthy sea air. "So few young people travel that way any more."

She began to clear the dinner plates. Dessert was already out. It had been out when Alexis sat down, as was the Marriotts' custom. Custard adorned by two soggy ladyfingers, sticking up as if a chocolate lady were going down for the second time beneath the yellow waves.

"If you'll excuse me," said Alexis, getting up awkwardly from the table.

"Of course, dear," Isabelle said quickly, before Duncan could remonstrate. She helped Alexis up.

"The missus and me would be...we were thinking we might drive you down," said Duncan, half out of his chair.

"If there isn't someone...if you haven't other plans," added Isabelle.

Alexis embraced Isabelle awkwardly, for her hands were full of dirty plates.

"You are both very sweet," she said, and turned to the hall, the stairs, and her room.

Alone again, Duncan and Isabelle exchanged glances but said nothing until their custard was finished.

"I think you may be right," said Duncan, wiping his chin with his napkin. "Man trouble."

Isabelle held her teacup thoughtfully between her fingers. "It's more than that," she said. Duncan gazed at her questioningly. "And she on the rebound and all," said Isabelle. "Poor dear."

PART 2

WINTER CROSSING

16

The old drunk had been scratching at a scab on the back of his hand. This absent-minded occupation had opened an old wound. He sucked it. The blood was salt, not like at church where the blood was sweet. Unfortunately at church there was never enough. No matter how clean he scrubbed himself to please the priest, no matter how beatifically he arranged the expression on his face to prepare for the miracle of transubstantiation, the cup passed by in a glimmer of silver and was gone.

A streetcar rolled by on Queen Street, one long and cluttered alley below where the old drunk sat. The clatter aroused him from his train of thought. The night was wearing away with still no sign of light. Maybe this would be the morning the sun did not rise. The thought sat in his mind like some heavy packing crate that would take too much energy to move. He longed for the hole to speak again. It had remained silent now for some moments. The drunk missed the voice. It was not a comforting voice — certainly it had nothing comforting to say. But it was something. Remembering how in the hole's story Alexis Forgeben had blown across the stone when the wind died, the old drunk crouched with his chin to the ground, intent upon priming the pump in the same way. He blew. The hole coughed and wheezed.

"Your breath is like death warmed over," said the hole. The old drunk scuttled back a foot or two to safety. He clapped his hands. Again he remembered camping—how you moved close to a dying fire only to find the embers hotter than the flames.

"Your story—" he said.

"What about my story?" interrupted the hole, querulously. "You find it hard to believe? You think I'm making it up as I go along? Am I just a little too omnipresent for your liking, perhaps?"

"Hell no," said the drunk. "I was just going to say, it's pretty miserable." The old drunk sniffed and pulled his knees up to his chest, smarting a little from the hole's attack.

"Where was I?" grumbled the hole.

"You were coming to Canada in a packing crate," replied the old drunk.

"Wrong!" boomed the hole. His voice sounded like a bell ringing the half-hour. "I was coming to Canada in a young woman."

"Oh yeah, that," said the old drunk. "But I can't get over the idea of you in a packing crate."

The hole made a snorting sound. "You have probably spent some time in packing crates yourself."

The old drunk could not tell a lie. He nodded sadly.

"It was a mortification," said the hole.

"You didn't like being in the girl?" replied the drunk, incredulously.

"I suppose you would find it desirable," said the hole, "but it was hell to me. Or at least, it grew to be. It was all right at first. What is it they say about the cardio-vascular system? End to end a woman's veins and arteries would form a line with which you could rope the moon? Well, as extended as Alexis may have been inside, she was not big enough for me. I grew homesick. I can assure you that these stones, my other nature, spent as little time crated up as possible."

140

The old drunk was startled. "You mean something happened on the ship?" he asked.

"Oh yes," said the hole. "And there's time enough to tell it if you'll stop this wrangling."

"I'm stopped," said the drunk.

"Indeed," said the hole.

17

The gangway pierced the biscuit-coloured shell of the S.S. *Northern Lights* amidship and half-way up its steep side. She was not a sleek vessel, not under the November skies that hung like damp, smudged sackcloth over Southampton. In Alexis' travel brochure the *Northern Lights* never docked but sailed, unfettered, a jewel in a Caribbean setting, floating on a sea like molten gold. Alexis found the real ship almost comfortingly prosaic in this North Atlantic harbour. Never more so than when she stepped from the gangway into the entrance lobby. The scene was like nothing so much as a school the first day of term. There was something about the shrillness of the passengers collected in gaggles, giggling or laughing out loud too heartily. There was something of student-like bluster and self-conscious vigilance. Was this the Baltic or the North Sea deck? Was one's room fore or aft, and was it called a room? The purser stood on guard outside his office with his hands easy behind his back and a carefully tailored expression on his face: I am here to serve, the face seemed to say, but it was vouchsafed in the weary manner of a principal before the first assembly.

The Marriotts had accompanied Alexis to Southampton. Now they shepherded her through the bustle of the lobby, suffering vicariously all of her trepidations and an envy which was entirely their own. Duncan found the lifts. He had served in the navy during the war, he explained, pressing the "down" button, the "close" button. Isabelle nodded to Alexis, verifying her husband's claim. "I travelled on the *Anconia* to visit my sister in Montreal," she added. "It was posh in its way but nothing like this." She gestured at a scallop-shaped light fixture.

Alexis' was an inner cabin on the White Sea deck, the least expensive accommodation available. Korrie had offered to kick in the extra for an outside stateroom above board. Her mother, despite her wealth, was not overly indulgent by nature. Her generosity, Alexis had learned, was prompted more by the horrifying prospect of her daughter closeted away like a novice in a cell. Alexis had resisted the offer. The return voyage by ocean liner had seemed an extravagance that was at once romantic and somehow pathetic. She had justified the expense only so far. She could afford to pamper herself but she couldn't bear the embarrassment of her pampering being subsidized. It became too much like treatment then, which in turn made the sorrow and anger of what had happened too much like a disease. She had assured her mother she would not closet herself away, but her candour had only helped to substitute one uncomfortable vision for another in Korrie's eyes; her cabin merely a place to nap between liaisons, a cubicle in which to change from bathing suit to party dress. But there wasn't to be any swimming and there wasn't to be much in the way of partying either. It was a winter crossing, not a regular excursion.

The liner had been in dry dock at Kristiansand, Norway, most of the summer and fall. Ultimately it was bound for Miami and the Caribbean. But Alexis would have long since disembarked in Halifax when the *Northern Lights* resumed its cruise trade. She had deluded herself, constructing a voyage out of travel-brochure fantasy. The voyage had seemed so far away when she had booked it, the size or shape or prospect of her cabin mattered very little.

The White Sea deck. Duncan led them down a passageway which jogged twice inwards towards the foremost reaches of the ship: cabin 201.

"Isn't it lovely," said Isabelle, before the door was fully open. No worse than a condensed, windowless motel room, Alexis thought to herself. The walls were coffee-cream coloured. A double bed with a bright red coverlet filled the forward end.

Duncan crawled across the bed and rapped on the forward wall. "This here's the collision bulkhead," he announced. "Nothing up ahead but bow and anchor."

Isabelle frowned at him, then, turning, smiled expectantly: Alexis had discovered the flowers. Mums in a little plastic galleon with a card from "Is and Uncle Duncle". She hugged them both.

The flowers sat on a dresser to the right of the hatchway. A mirror rose to the low ceiling, reflecting the already faded yellow of the mums, a white phone, and an ice-bucket in the ship's blue and gold colours. An air duct crossed the ceiling above Alexis' bed. The room was sweltering. Alexis looked, without success, for something to adjust. To the left of the hatchway was a desk upon which sat a television set. Beside the desk was a door to a cramped bathroom with a shower. "The head," Duncan announced, beaming mischievously, a sailor again. He danced a hornpipe and ducked inside, locking the door behind him.

Isabelle distractedly plucked the dead petals from the flowers. "We supposed it might need a little brightening up," she said.

Alexis turned on the television. There was only one station. It provided a colourful view from a porthole of a south sea atoll, complete with anchored yacht and blowing palms. Under this pleasant vision ship news rolled by. Alexis read the announcement of the captain's cocktail party which would commence at 1700 hours. Ruefully, she recalled her vision of what the crossing was to have been like. She sank back onto the bed, her eyes glued to the imaginary porthole, while Isabelle pushed the suitcases about and took stock of the cabin's limited storage facilities.

The toilet flushing interrupted the calypso Muzak drifting from the TV. Duncan emerged from the head looking pleased with himself. Fighting his way past Isabelle, he perched on the bed to watch the television.

"Very comfy," he said encouragingly.

Isabelle hoisted him by the arm and guided him towards the door. "You go make yourself comfy elsewhere," she said. "Alexis and I have got work to do." Duncan resisted his expulsion good-naturedly. Isabelle closed the door behind him and hefted the biggest suitcase two-fistedly onto the bed beside Alexis. Alexis, sulky as a spoilt child, merely moved her leg to accommodate it, but made no move to help. Isabelle did not seem to expect her to. She took a loosely wrapped tissue package from the suitcase.

"Where shall I put your smalls?" she mused. It was not really a question, evidently, for she chose a drawer beside the bed.

"Smalls, tops and bottoms," said Isabelle indicating which drawer held what. "Shoes?" she said to herself, before picking a spot under the desk. "And your frocks," she said, her voice strained as she climbed to her feet. She hung them on wall hooks at the foot of the bed. Then she plunked herself down beside Alexis and took her hand. "Cheer up, luv," she said. "You're not the first woman it's happened to."

Alexis looked at her cheerlessly. She patted her stomach, the resting place of the baby she had told Isabelle she was carrying. It was not difficult for her to act newly pregnant. I often positioned myself just so in her abdomen, without mass but with great weight.

"When you get back, there'll be time enough to make up your mind," said Isabelle. It was the same thing she had said when Alexis had let her gently pry the story out the first time. It was as Isabelle had suspected. She had not been shocked. "I'm not as old-fashioned as that," she had said. She had also promised not to tell Duncan. As far as Alexis could tell she had kept her word. Towards the end of the stay Isabelle had felt bound to say she hoped Alexis would keep the child—Teddy or no Teddy. Alexis had assured her that while she felt every woman ought to have the right of choice in such matters, for her abortion was out of the question. Isabelle had been pleased, as Alexis had anticipated she would be.

They watched the TV in silence. Alexis laughed at something on the screen. Isabelle got up to store the suitcases. Alexis stopped laughing. Calypso Muzak reclaimed the room.

Alexis turned off the television and found her way to the head. Isabelle listened to Alexis' dry heaves and when she re-entered the room, she folded her in her arms. How dry her hair had become, thought Isabelle. "Everything's ship-shape," she said. "A cup of tea is in order."

They found Duncan on a bench between the elevators, smoking his pipe. There was still time before departure for a drink, he informed them, and led the way up to the Valhalla Lounge in the after end of the Boat deck. It was domed in glass but the lights were on, attempting to dispel the gloom of winter twilight. There were trees in bright Mexican ceramic pots.

The lounge was crowded and noisy. They found a table up against the back end, looking out over the North Sea deck and the swimming pool. It was empty. A young red-haired woman in a rose-coloured cardigan sat on the edge of the deep end, her arms crossed against the cold. Beyond the railing the Channel was dappled green and grey like camouflage, prepared for war. Duncan and Isabelle didn't seem to notice. They ordered long colourful drinks with umbrellas. Alexis ordered tea. Isabelle nodded her agreement. Best for the baby that she not imbibe.

Isabelle seemed intent on brightness and chattered away aimlessly, her eyes never resting a moment as they roved the room. Alexis could imagine the old couple on tour in whites and floral shirts. Better they than she, she thought. It was not just the trip that bothered her. It was what must happen at home.

146

"Nice to see a chaplain on board," said Isabelle. Alexis followed her gaze towards the bar. A tall, well-fed, silver-coiffed gentleman in his fifties was making the rounds. He might have been a tour director, so smoothly did he manoeuvre his portly frame from party to party, his tanned hand floating up into the air in lazy gesticulation, landing lightly on a shoulder, leaning against a chair back. "Seems a clubbable sort," said Duncan. "For a Holy Joe." Alexis could not hear the chaplin through the excited chatter in the room, but she could imagine his voice, as sweetly flowing as the lines of his honey-coloured Bond Street suit. He wore dark glasses. The face under the silver hair was as round as the moon. Alexis turned her attention to the emptiness of the pool deck. The redhead was gone. Alexis gazed at the Channel.

"Welcome aboard."

The chaplain was shaking Isabelle's hand, clasping it in both of his while she explained that really only Alexis was to be a "parishioner" on the *Northern Lights*.

The man wore a warm false smile. "Larry," he insisted. "You must call me Larry. Well, Mrs. Forgeben. It seems I am to keep an eye on you." He shook her hand; his was powdery soft.

Alexis nodded hello, but her gaze fell short of Larry's eyes. She saw only his immaculately starched collar, his silver hair curling against his lapel.

"I shall look forward to talking with you," she said, glancing quickly at where his eyes must be, behind the dark glasses. This accommodating friendliness was intended as a parting gift to Duncan and Isabelle. They seemed pleased.

A bell clanged noisily.

"Battle stations," said Larry, chuckling. All around them drinks were hoisted in final toasts and drained hurriedly. It was time for visitors to disembark.

18

Alexis stood on the gangway for some time, watching the Marriotts fade out of her sight and her existence. Larry had made quite an impression on the old couple. Isabelle talked of him as an old trustworthy friend. Her obvious relief that he would be there to watch out for Alexis helped to uncomplicate the goodbyes. They were warm and relatively tearless, mercifully free of the weight of intimacy which had bound the two women over the last week.

Alexis felt exhilarated at seeing them go — exhilarated and guilty. The easy enjoyment that had characterized her stay with them before Fastyngange had been impossible to duplicate. In desperation she had dreamed up the pregnancy. The charmer at the hostel, the trip to Cornwall, the romantic thatched cottage by the sea, the argument, the leaving—it had all seemed plausible enough. A lot more plausible than the truth. Now she dared, for the first time since her dark conception, to consider the future freely. Three days and four nights, the crossing would take. Getting me to Teddy, the mountain to Mohammed. It was the thought of bringing home a cure, however demonic, that had convinced her to take me in.

The air was chilly but Alexis was reluctant to enter the ship. Nor could she leave it. Were she to disembark now, she would do so without the stones that formed my mouth. She could not do that. She watched the longshoremen load the ship. A port cargo was open near the stern. A derrick on the dock lifted flats of stores and baggage to the opening in the ship's side. Alexis strained her eyes to see a wooden crate unlike any other among the bins and boxes and colourful trunks. Gulls wheeled around the hoisting cables, squawking excitedly. Others sat in ruffle-feathered ranks on a nearby gantry crane. From time to time one or another turned its disinterested gaze on the lone figure leaning against the gangway railing. She was unaware of their surveillance.

The port cargo closed. The cranes swung away.

"Ma'am...ma'am?"

He had spoken several times. She stared at him, wondering why she should know him. But he was only a steward bidding her follow him back into the lobby. He left her with a quick bow and hurried off.

The lobby was quite empty now. School was in session. An attendant sat at a computer terminal behind the glass window of the excursion office. In the bookstore an old man perused paperbacks at the mystery shelf. At the end of the lobby in the clothing boutique a fat, worried-looking woman tried on something chic and shapeless in pink. Alexis wanted to be alone. It came over her in a wave. She longed for my little shadowy round chamber in the keep. Small and damp and comforting. She could not imagine returning to her cabin. She felt quite sick.

A map was mounted on the wall by the purser's door. She went off in search of the infirmary. It was one deck up. She stood outside the pebble-glass door with her fist poised to knock. She heard no sound from within. No shadows crossed the glass. No one passed her in the corridor. The ship seemed deserted. She entertained the notion of a kindly doctor: Oskar Werner in *Ship of Fools*; someone to replace Dr. Troubridge, lost to her for ever now. She would never see Chewton Cottage again; it already seemed like a dream. But if not Troubridge, then someone.

Someone to give her something for her affliction—drugs or sympathy. A purge.

The idea had not occurred to her until that moment. I spoke to her along her skin, moving like a wind-snake over a frozen pond. She withdrew her hand from the door. I could not speak to her directly any more, but I could warn her. She hurried off.

A spiral staircase led to the Sunburst Dining Room. She continued on her slow turn of the ship. Her spirits revived somewhat when she stepped out onto the promenade. Southampton was slipping away.

The promenade was wide and partially enclosed. The deck was marked with lanes for joggers. Teddy had jogged. She had joined him at it for a while, but running never delivered her the high it did him. He kept her at it—it would come, he promised. She quit anyway. She knew it bothered him that she stayed slim and healthy without apparent effort. Towards the end he ran more and more and greater distances, until he was never in bed when she awoke or when she returned home from working the night shift.

Until that last night. I could feel the turbulence of its memory in her. I could sense a truth she had not divulged to me at Fastyngange. It took all her effort to keep it from me. It was locked deeply away from my covert probing. But I worried away at the lock to the door of that room. I am a jealous hole. I live on secrets. Thrive on secrets.

Alexis turned from the sight of the island pulling away from her. She climbed a companionway to the uppermost deck. The Sun deck. It was empty. There was a miniature golf course, a little green island of artificial turf badly worn, torn in places. Beyond it there was a door to a solarium. The door was locked. A sign indicated the hours at which men and women respectively might work on overall tans. Alexis read the sign through the cloud of her own breath; another rude joke. Her teeth were chattering but she was loath to return indoors. Already the harbour smells of

150

pitch and rubber and dust were fading. She could smell the sea, the greenness of it—the smell of the growth beneath the surface flow. It disturbed her. She could see cars moving silently along a shoreline road. But all she could hear were ship's engines and the occasional squawk from the gulls that drifted in the air above the ship's wake. They did not flap their wings; they were like streamers. Alexis walked closer to the ship's starboard rail. By the lifeboats she was able to squeeze past the railing. She checked to make sure no one was watching. The deck was empty. Past the railing she leaned against the boat chock that cradled the lifeboats. Her heart was pounding. Grasping the cold steel of the davit crane, used to lift the lifeboats out to sea, she was able to lean out over the water. For one dizzy moment she hung there with the shell of the ship curving away to the roll of Channel water ploughed from the ship's path. Then she pulled herself back to safety, gasping for breath and chilled to the bone at the force of the impulse that had made her do such a thing. Her breathing restored, she stayed a moment longer, leaning against the boat chock. Her eyes surveyed the lifeboat machinery. Everything had been painted over a hundred times. Every gear and pulley seemed fixed solid by generations of disuse. Tiredly she slithered from the platform back onto the deck. A man in a long tweed coat stood with his back to her, reading the sign by the solarium. His hair was tousled, blown about by the wind. As she watched, strands of it blew away across the deck. The man did not seem to notice. Alexis found her way quickly back to the body of the ship.

She headed down to the White Sea deck. As she stepped from the lift, her eyes were dazzled by the lights from the beauty salon. She stopped for a moment. The lift doors shut behind her. The salon had been dark earlier but now it was brilliantly lit, as if Caribbean midday sun had somehow sliced through three floors of steel to cheer on those about to be shorn and made beautiful. There were no customers in the glass booth, only a hairdresser sweeping in a desultory manner. On a hook by the door, Alexis recognized the rose-coloured sweater of the girl she had seen sitting by the empty pool. The girl looked up suddenly, sensing Alexis' presence. Her hair had appeared chestnut in the open air, but in the garish reflected lights of the salon it seemed neon red. It was tied in a complicated braid which had come undone. The girl pushed a strand away from her face. Her eyes were hooded, weary but expectant. Her lips were like a piece of fluff from the sweater, pale and chewed ragged. She could not have been more than twenty. The girl glanced past Alexis. Her gaze faltered, then her eyes filled with alarm. All at once the lift chimed and its doors opened behind Alexis, startling her. Before she could move, a body crashed into her. She stumbled forwards, felt herself falling headlong. Hands grabbed her firmly by the waist, stopping the fall, holding her up. She flinched and the hands relaxed their grip. She turned to see the face of a young man.

"I'm sorry," he said. "I wasn't looking." He began to smile. Alexis mumbled an apology, not waiting to see how the smile ended. As she turned into her corridor, she glanced furtively towards the girl in the glass booth, in time to catch a spasm of anger cross her face. At whom the anger was directed, Alexis could only guess. She locked herself in her cabin.

She lay naked, spread-eagled on the bed. The cabin seemed even hotter than before, and in the heat she could smell its last tenant. She could smell the cigarettes he had smoked. She knew it was a man. She had called the purser upon returning to the room. Something was to be done about the heat later. For the time being, lying perfectly still seemed the only solution.

Something also had to be done about the captain's cocktail party. It was half over. Two frocks hung at the end of the bed, awaiting Alexis' choice. She had not worn a dress since some time in August. She knew either of them would look equally ridiculous on her, hang from her as shapelessly as they did from their hangers. She stared down the length of her body. But for her extremities, she looked as white as a grub. Her breasts were like bleached calfskin purses. Her sternum, ribs, hips, and knees seemed alive under the lifeless integument of her skin. She recalled tales of prisoners in the Orient tied down over bamboo groves. It is said you can hear bamboo grow. She wondered if her bones, like shoots of bamboo, might grow through her—slow arrows. If Teddy could see her now, she thought, a pile of living bones. Suddenly she curled into a tight ball, her knees up hard against her chest. She could feel me probing upwards, shoving her organs aside, climbing up to the air. I was suffocating inside her. That was why I punched at her so. The room was stifling. She clambered from her bed, catching at her breath. She would have to go to the party. It was no use attempting to be alone. She was the last person on earth she wanted to be left alone with.

She took the nearest frock and climbed into it. She brushed her hair, though it had lost any semblance of shape or curl. She was ready, she supposed. Then she sat on the bed, unable to move.

She turned on the television, expecting a south sea atoll. Instead she got a party. The camera scanned an enormous, sparsely filled room, lighting momentarily on a grinning face or a couple dancing to the dance-band music coming from the stage. A few children in party dress played tag among their elders. Alexis recognized the craggy face of the captain in his dress uniform, chatting amiably with passengers. The party, Alexis realized, was in progress. She plumped up her pillows and sat back to watch. There were really very few people. The ship held six hundred, but there couldn't have been more than a hundred in the lounge. Alexis imagined others, like herself, in their cabins glued to their TV sets. Already waiters were cleaning away glasses and preparing the room for dinner.

The camera turned its attention to the stage. There was a four-piece band in white tuxedoes with blue and gold trim. The camera settled on the saxophonist as he glissandoed into a solo. Alexis turned up the volume. It was the young man from the lift, the one who had stopped her fall. The camera closed in on his gaunt face. His hair was yellower than she remembered. But he had been wearing a hat, a beret, she recalled. Or maybe it was yellow in the dazzle reflected off his sax. In any case, she now saw that his hair was long, tied back in a ponytail. His eyes were tightly shut behind glasses with clear plastic rims. Under the golden arch of the saxophone, Alexis could see the whisper of a yellow beard on his narrow chin. He raised the instrument and held one last, long blast of a note which hung like a bold flag over the band's accompaniment. His face was red and strained. He held the single, achingly rich note through a long diminuendo while the bass player sitting next to him took over the solo. No one clapped. Perhaps no one had noticed the soloist but Alexis. The screen filled with the bald black dome of the bassist hunched over his instrument. Alexis watched only the sax player in the corner of the screen. He had stopped playing. She watched him open his eyes and look around as if awaking from a dream. Something awakened in Alexis too.

19

Alexis arrived in the dining room for the tail end of the party, in time to grab a martini from a passing tray. She was disappointed; the sax player was nowhere to be seen, the drink nowhere near as refreshing as it appeared. She drank enough of it to sink her teeth into the olive, which she nibbled to the pit. She was still carrying the pit when she sat at her table. She planned to deposit it in the ashtray as soon as the boy across from her stopped glaring. She put his rudeness down to overly vigorous pubescence.

He introduced himself as Sven Nordquist. He was the son of a shipping company executive, on his way to visit his mother in New York. "I will practise my American on you," he said. Having implicitly justified the act as an educational experience, he then proceeded to talk a blue streak.

The woman to Alexis' right leaned over and whispered in her ear, "He seems to have learned English from American sitcoms." The woman's perfume surprised Alexis. It was like a dry, warm summer's day in the meadow overlooking the lake. She remembered the last time she had sat up there watching Teddy waterski behind her father's big inboard.

Sven's attention was first drawn to Alexis' dreamy smile and then to the whisperer with the buttery blonde curls. When she shared her trivial confidence, her breast had pressed against

Alexis' arm; when she withdrew, she had unwittingly trapped the young Norwegian in her ample cleavage. She adjusted her shoulder straps but could not shake him off. She didn't really seem to mind. Gloria, as she introduced herself, didn't seem to mind much of anything. She accepted Sven's attention and Alexis' inattention equally. When conversation resumed, Alexis leaned over and whispered in Gloria's ear, "He must have learned that slack jaw from the sitcoms as well."

Gloria was in real estate in Vancouver. The trip was a prize for having finally got her company gold card.

"Gold card?" asked Sven.

"For selling a million dollars' worth of property," said Gloria. "I'll show it to you later," she added, winking at the boy mischievously.

"I won a prize too," said the man to Gloria's right. He seemed utterly disconsolate. He was a stocky little man with a barrel-chest. His jacket did not fit him or else he was unaccustomed to it, but either way, he wriggled awkwardly as though it were a hair suit. His name was Morgan. He was a barkeep from Bangor, Wales, he said. The mere mention of the Maid and Crow brought a tear to his eye. Gloria prodded him to talk about it, and soon Morgan was animated enough. Sven recovered sufficiently from the enchantment of Gloria's bosom to resent the attention she paid the Welshman. The studied flat, nasal tone of the boy cut into Morgan's sing-song chatter as he tried to regain the real estate agent's attention.

"I didn't see you at the captain's do," said the woman to Sven's right. She was the same woman Alexis had seen in the boutique. She had bought the pink dress but did not seem happy with her purchase. Alexis wondered if her husband disapproved of it. The couple, she sensed, had argued recently.

"I had a toothache," said Alexis.

"Ah," said the pink woman's husband. It turned out he was a dentist from Des Moines.

"I don't have my kit with me," he told her, "but I'd be pleased to poke around."

"A shame to suffer," said the wife. The dentist sat on Alexis' left. By the way he edged his chair towards her she was afraid he might just begin a probe at the table.

"It's nothing," she said. To give her prognosis force she announced herself to be a nurse. "It's nothing," she repeated, "that a martini won't cure." The others at the table thought this entertaining—all except for the dentist's wife who was arguing in a whiny voice with a waiter. It seemed she was on a salt-free diet and the kitchen had not been informed. The table fell silent, which only embarrassed the dentist's wife more. So Gloria asked Alexis what she had been up to in England. "Castle hopping," Alexis replied, to which Gloria admitted to having been "millionaire hopping".

Sven, who had been gulping down glasses of wine, became even more garrulous as the dinner wore on. He began to talk of his parents' squalid divorce. He refused to have the floor usurped from him. The others turned to their meals or leaned back in their chairs the better to hear brighter chat at nearby tables.

Only the forward end of the dining room was occupied. Alexis counted: eighteen tables accommodating six passengers, twelve tables for four. At the captain's table she saw Larry, dressed in black now and holding court by the looks of it. She caught Morgan staring at her.

"What castles were you hopping?" he asked. A drop of wine sat on his thin lip like a bead of blood. Alexis rhymed off several popular tourist attractions. She did not mention Fastyngange.

"Do you know of Tatws Rhost?" he asked. It was a castle in Anglesey near his pub, he claimed. Alexis had not heard of it. The dentist from Des Moines felt sure he had. Morgan smiled to himself.

"Far too many castles in England," mumbled the dentist's wife. Then the dentist claimed Alexis' attention. He smiled in a practised way to reveal a glint of gold. Sven picked up where he had left off with his mother's drug problem. The dentist's wife stared intently at her ice cream as if to will its calorific content away. Her unhappiness was infectious; Alexis began to feel it. She had drunk the martini—that might be it. It was hard to say. Her sense of well-being was a precarious candle of a thing whose light was eclipsed with ease by the slightest darkness in her own disposition or in those around her.

"She's living with a tennis player now," said Sven enthusiastically.

"How tedious for her," said Gloria, leaning forwards to allow the boy a better look down her dress, hoping it might gag him again.

Sven gulped down what he saw. Morgan hooted. "That shut him up, it did."

"There's a movie on the Bridge deck," Sven mumbled, glowering at his beefy neighbour.

"We should all go," said the dentist, turning to Alexis. He had made several such communal suggestions to the group, always addressing his importunate overtures her way. "That is, if your sensitive condition will allow it."

Alexis thought that she didn't think it would. The others were already getting up to leave. She had eaten very little of her meal. She suddenly was afraid of these innocuous people, of what might happen were she to lower her guard. *Afraid I might speak to them.* She broke out in a cold sweat. Gloria looked concerned. "I'll be all right," Alexis said, and left the room hurriedly. She didn't wait for the lift but took the spiral staircase down to the Baltic and then the stair-tower down to the White Sea deck. Opening the hatchway, she found the dentist stepping from the lift, wringing his hands in an energetic display of concern.

"I believe they have some facilities in the infirmary. I could give you a thorough going over," he rattled. He was very much out of breath.

"The toothache was a sham," she told him as they reached her cabin door. Looking at him she could almost see his heart beating against his ribcage. "I've lost someone," she said. She didn't want to take out her key in his presence, and so they stood in the cul-de-sac in deafening silence. The dentist patted her hand. She felt me growing inside her at his touch and it frightened her.

"We all need one another," the dentist said, his tongue clicking miserably. He squeezed her arm while she tried not to flinch. "I believe in the communal organism," he stated firmly. He made it sound like something with a lot of legs. "Caring is a responsibility," he said. He laughed self-consciously. "But you know that, being a nurse and all."

She recalled a shy pathologist who had spoken of nurses with just the same hopeful inflection in his voice. The dentist was rubbing her arm without daring to look at her. She said nothing, not wanting him to mistake speech for dialogue. She would simply have to wait him out. Meanwhile the pressure inside her mounted. Suddenly down the hall a vision in pink appeared. The woman stopped twenty feet away, her hands folded in front of her. Alexis saw in her face a look of trepidation or what was little more than dread deferred, mingled with profound humiliation. What hideous, loathsome creatures men are, thought Alexis, as she watched the dentist deftly fish his wedding band from his jacket pocket and slip it back on his scrawny finger. Alexis had not noticed it at dinner, if indeed he had worn it. Now the sight of it astonished her, for it was not simply a gold band.

"Hold the Aspirin against the cavity," he said in a clinical voice. "In that way you'll get the greater benefit of its analgesic power. Well, goodnight, Mrs. Forgeben," he said, patting her arm again, this time in a brotherly fashion. He left. Alexis heard him use the same cheery tone on his wife. He called her Rosemarie. She heard his tone alter as the couple jogged out of her view. She leaned against her doorjamb, reeling. The ring had been a scarab. The scarab of the hangman.

159

20

Alexis did not wake in time for breakfast. She had stayed up late writing in her journal. When she woke up her journal was open in her lap and the TV showed people gambling in a floating casino. They weren't people on Alexis' ship.

A steward in the main lobby suggested the Horizon Café for a snack. She saw the other steward, the one who had surprised her on the gangplank at sailing time. She kept out of his sight. She recognized him now as the knife-sharpener on Jerusalem Street. There were gypsies around Glastonbury, Duncan had warned her, and she had thought the knife-sharpener one because of his dark-haired hands and dark skin. How imploringly he had gazed at her on the gangplank. He was one of them, one of the ghosts; or, more properly, one of my ghosts occupied his body. Which one, she did not know. Staring at every face she passed, she found herself reliving the mad race from Fastyngange and wondering which innocent-looking passenger—the man in the Disney World T-shirt, the woman reading Tolstoy—might suddenly pin her against the wall and demand the hole from her.

With this thought uppermost in her mind, she was alarmed to hear the report of guns as she stepped out of the lift onto the topmost deck. Several men were skeet-shooting off the bow. She recognized Morgan's back immediately; she didn't notice the dentist until she had drawn quite near. It was his turn to shoot. He was quite a shot. One, two, three clay pigeons burst over the green sea. His wife was sitting nearby in a deck chair, knitting something for an infant. She was wearing a blouse printed with pussy cats. Shirt-sleeves. And for the first time Alexis realized the air was balmy. The sun was high. The sky was blue.

"A warm current, miss," said a steward as he helped her open a deck chair. "It won't last," he added, depositing a blanket at the foot of the chair. "But might as well enjoy it while we can." He frowned at the wild look she gave him.

Alexis ordered coffee and muffins. She leaned back in her chair clutching her cardigan around her, for she was not entirely in the lee of the wind. She dozed for some time, almost peacefully, letting the ocean air work its healing magic on her ragged nerves.

A squeaky wheel disturbed her rest. The noise stopped quite near to where she was lying. She opened her eyes to see a woman opening a portable lap easel and a folding stool near the railing. A pram was parked beside her. Alexis sat up, her eyes not leaving the carriage. If there was a baby in it, it did not stir. The fear that had clutched her heart at the sight of the pram eased up. Her eyes wandered to the painter at work, to the sun on the bright blobs of colour the woman squeezed onto her palette — cerulean blue, peacock green, viridian, and ultramarine — sea colours. The baby stirred and Alexis found herself grasping the arms of her chair. But the woman rocked the pram, her eyes never leaving the water or her watery impression of it, and the baby slept on.

It is just a baby, Alexis told herself. And though nothing had been "just" anything for some months now, it was difficult to work up a flap over such an innocent scene. She drifted off again and opened her eyes only when she heard the pram squeaking again, glad, despite herself, that it was leaving. But it wasn't. And the baby was sitting up staring at her, sexless in its white bonnet. Not a muscle in its small round face twitched. She fully expected it to scream, to open its beak like the thing at Fastyngange, and to

161

break her heart with its howling. She sat perfectly still. The painter painted. The baby stared. The sun shone and the ship rolled. It was finally the fixedness of these things which alarmed Alexis into action. She gathered herself together and flung herself from her chair. She didn't look back to see if the child's eyes followed her retreat. Nothing, she thought — nothing human — could remain expressionless for so long.

She wandered aimlessly and found herself in the Valhalla Lounge, now empty. She passed through it to the steps that led down to the swimming pool where she had seen the hairdresser sitting. The deck seemed empty, as she had hoped it might be. But when she reached it she found a massage parlour, and by the open door sat a large, squarish woman with straw-coloured braids, wearing a starched white uniform. She cupped an aluminum reflector under her fat chins; her cheeks were the shape and colour of boiled beets.

"You look all done in," she called pleasantly to Alexis. She introduced herself as Linn, the masseuse. Linn's buttons looked as if they might burst at any moment from the pressure placed on them by her robust figure. She was in good humour, joking about the weather, the empty pool, the half-empty ship. "No appointment necessary," she said, pointing to her sign, and then she shepherded Alexis into her parlour. Handing her several fluffy towels she showed Alexis the changing room, showers, and sauna.

The sauna was stinging hot. Alexis could hardly breathe. She was going to leave when Linn peeked through the door, grinned, and splashed a ladleful of water on the stones. A wave of steam obliterated Alexis' view of Linn's retreat. She closed her eyes and hung her head. She leaned heavily forwards on her knees. She heard whispering. She opened her eyes and looked around the clouded room. It was empty. The heat made her groggy. She leaned her head against the hot cedar wall. The whispering continued, voices escaping from the heated stones of the furnace.

She gave up all hope of making it go away. It rolled over her: the heat, the anonymous voices. She felt certain she would faint. Then a draft of cool air heralded the return of Linn, who gathered Alexis' loosened limbs together in a heap and half-carried her out to the massage table.

"We reshuffle the deck," said Linn, as she vigorously rubbed Alexis' body with strongly scented oil. "See what kind of hand we come up with, yah?" Soon her meaty fingers were hard at work, remoulding what flesh Alexis still had on her slim frame.

Linn asked Alexis about herself, where her cabin was, how she was enjoying herself. Then she squeezed the answers out of her like toothpaste: nur-urse, Ca-na-da, White Sea, lone-ly.

"There really is a White Sea," said Linn. But all Alexis could think of were the aches that Linn was digging up — aches that were months old and as stone-weary as Fastyngange. "It opens into the Arctic Ocean," said Linn. "Out of the top of Lapland. Such an empty place."

To Alexis' astonishment, pain was seeping out of her pores under Linn's ministrations. Any moment, she thought, any moment she will reach it. And suddenly, her heart froze. Linn must be one of them. "Stop," she moaned. But Linn only chuckled. With her strong fingers she was attempting to break clear through Alexis' tired flesh to let me seep out. "No," Alexis cried, unable to move, part of her longing to be released of the awful thing.

"Deeper," said Linn.

Alexis squirmed but she was too drowsy to escape. She moaned. How could a spirit be so strong, she wondered, but then reminded herself that it was the spirit's host who was massaging her, kneading her, while the ghost of a survivor moved the sausage fingers. And all the time Alexis wrestled with these thoughts, Linn pressed and poked and talked about Iceland, which she said was her home. "Tonight," she said, "sometime about midnight, we will pass under Iceland." With a great effort Alexis rolled herself off the massage table away from Linn's

163

groping hands. On legs of rubber, she stumbled to the change room. "We haven't finished with you," said Linn.

Inside the change room, Alexis grabbed up a chair, preparing for attack. But Linn did not come after her. She changed quickly. Stepping out into the massage room, she looked around but did not see the masseuse anywhere. She heard the sound of muffled laughing. She threw open the sauna door and the laughing retreated behind a translucent wall of steam. Alexis ran from the parlour out onto the deck, where she stood in the cooler air breathing deeply, deeply. She mustn't let them take her over like that. They need me, she told herself.

On her way from the massage parlour, Alexis passed a man on the stairs. He was wearing a tweed coat and smoking a crooked pipe. His chin jutted out like a shovel. He smiled at her. She recognized him and glared back. On the way to Southampton, just outside of Dinton where they had stopped for lunch, Duncan had passed a car stalled on the motorway. The driver had looked up at them from under the arch of the car's hood. She remembered the crooked pipe, the smile on the shovel face.

Returning to her cabin, she found a man there. He stood on her bed with a section of ductwork in his hands. His face was filthy with dust and sweat. The room was as hot as before. The name on the worker's uniform read "Alfred".

"The problem appears to be local," he said, grinning behind a cigarette. He hurriedly put it out, begging her forgiveness. He offered to leave.

"Might as well get on with it," she said between clenched teeth, wondering if she was to have a moment's peace.

She made her way back to the topmost deck. The skeet shooting was over. The painter and her child were gone. She lay back on her chair, feeling exhausted, and looked out to sea. She tried not to think of ghosts. Of anything.

There were five rails before her, like a musical stave. The waves rose and fell in the cadence of the rolling ship. Alexis tried to hum the melody of the waves against the stave until the pastime became monotonous. The song never seemed to change.

Her eyes drifted to the stern. The ship had lost its train of gulls. She could imagine the last of them turning back at Land's End, when the ship passed that promontory early the previous evening. She strained her eyes to see the country she had left behind. She saw nothing. There was a night between them. There were two more nights at sea ahead. Two more nights with them, and then what?

She had not slept well and, hoping to take a siesta, she wriggled down into her chair, but a patch of white paint a foot long on the railing caught her eye.

"It's called a holiday," said a voice nearby. The Reverend Larry was sitting in the deck chair to her left, tipping a waiter who had brought him a drink. He had not been there a moment earlier. He was in a blue silk shirt and a pale blue cravat. The rims of his dark glasses were cobalt-coloured. "That strip of white showing through the paint," he said. "It's called a holiday, meaning the sailor who was painting the railing took a holiday instead of painting it."

She stared at the priest. His cheeks were powdered. His entire cheery face seemed composed, from his capped teeth to his silver peruke. "So it seems I'm not to be left alone," she said tartly, turning her attention back to the sea.

"There was a time when this ship was bright white from stem to stern," said Larry, ignoring her and gesturing as he might have done from a pulpit.

Alexis did not look his way. "I asked in the purser's office," she said brusquely. "There is no chaplain on this crossing."

"Ah, that's right," he said. "And not an entire crew either, for that matter. This is no ordinary voyage."

Alexis chose not to respond. The priest took her silence to be an invitation to go on. "There are few ocean liners still left on the

Atlantic ferry," he said. "But how they capture the imagination: inspiring ladies, leviathans, express greyhounds...."

"And what is the *Northern Lights*?" Alexis asked.

Larry smiled indulgently and whispered behind his hand. "An old tub," he said. "In dry dock, in Kristiansand, they found out just how old." There was an intention in the statement which caused Alexis to glance his way. "The deep cut of anaerobic corrosion in her hull," he continued, his eyebrows raised behind the rims of his glasses. "Too deep and too widespread to consider another overhaul."

He paused and put his fingertips together in a parody of prayer. "Anaerobic corrosion is a fascinating phenomenon," he said. "It is brought about by sulphate-reducing bacteria that thrive in most harbours of the world. If a ship could only stay at sea, she might last for ever."

Alexis found his fey voice and the anticipation intolerable. "The ship is doomed? Is that what you are trying to say?"

"It will not see the Caribbean again," said Larry.

"I gathered," said Alexis. "Will it see Halifax? Or are we to perish on the high seas? What's the plan?"

"We will all perish sooner or later," said Larry. "Dying comes naturally to us—"

"Oh, cut the crap!" Alexis shouted. A passenger going by hurried on his way. "I know who you are," she whispered. "Your charade doesn't fool me."

Larry chuckled lightly. "Do you indeed?" He sat up, yawned, and stretched his coiled hands in front of him. "This is a tired old ship," he said. "After Halifax it will be sailed to the New Jersey ship-breaker who has purchased it for scrap metal. I learned that, in confidence, from the captain."

Alexis snorted. "I could have predicted it," she said. "Your voice is remarkably like the hole's voice, or maybe the hole's voice is a lot like yours. Same delivery. You've given yourself away."

Larry chuckled again. He was sitting on the side of his chair now, and he leaned towards Alexis. He took off his glasses. "Look, here," he said. His face was carefully, discreetly made up. His eyes were cyanine-blue, flecked with green. One of them blinked. The other sat perfectly still—a well-constructed blind jewel. "Let us not beat around the bush any longer," he said.

"What do you intend to do?" she asked.

"What do *you* intend to do?" he replied.

"Nothing," she said. "I have nothing for you."

He smiled. "A clever bit of double-talk," he said. "Worthy of the master. Tell me, what is it like to have so much of 'nothing' inside?"

"You'll never find out," she said, staring at him until, with a smirk, he replaced his dark glasses and climbed to his feet.

"We will have to talk about this later," he said. "But right now I have an appointment to keep. There is an excellent masseuse on board. Did you know? Ah! I see by your expression you do know. Under her capable hands I recall what it was like to feel myself. Good day."

With a contemptuous bow he walked away. Alexis wondered why he had not pressed her, but she was captive, after all. Escape from the *Northern Lights* was even more impossible than escape from Fastyngange.

21

They are all here, she thought, but she must have said something else because the bartender refilled her glass.

The fine weather had persisted through the day. Picture clouds hung over the glass dome of the Valhalla Lounge like freshly washed laundry on invisible lines.

In her journal, Alexis made a list: the Reverend Larry, the dentist from Des Moines, the gypsy steward, the shovelfaced man, the painter, the baby, Linn the masseuse; seven—which left five survivors unaccounted for. She looked around the busy room. No one looked her way. The late afternoon crowd chatted gaily. Alexis should not have sat at the bar. There was a mirror in which she saw herself whenever she looked up, and each time she suffered the same painful shock. By the third drink she could give form to her predicament. I am dragging around an entourage of ghosts, she thought, and I look dreadful.

She tugged at a strand of hair in the fringe that hung like a limp curtain across her eyebrows. "Snip, snip." The voice reached her before the face that suddenly swam into focus in the mirror. Gloria was leaning over her shoulder making scissor cuts with her fingers. "This needs some TLC," she said, grabbing Alexis by the scruff of her neck. It might have been rude—it was certainly surprising—but Gloria's candid smile made it seem like nothing more than the simple truth. Alexis closed her journal. She made a face at the faces in the mirror, Gloria's up next to her own like a portrait. Beauty and the Beast, thought Alexis, grimacing.

"I didn't see you come in," Alexis said, as she moved her purse from the stool next to hers.

"That's because I was already here," said Gloria. She was dressed in red and yellow—flamboyant and desirable. Her makeup, to be charitable, could have been described as unre-strained. She wore too much liner, too much paint, and looked fabulous, thought Alexis, unable to resist grinning at her new ac-quaintance. Gloria held up a half-empty glass of something as red as the polka dots on her wide-collared blouse, and indicated a table occupied by several men. One of them was the bass player from the band; another, the drummer, Alexis seemed to recall. The sax player was not there, and, curiously, the reminder of his absence hit her the way seeing him again might have done.

"They play in the Midnight Sun Bar," said Gloria. "You should see them."

Alexis grimaced again. "I live to party," she said gloomily.

Gloria's response was instantaneous. She downed her drink, stood up, and took Alexis firmly by the arm. "Come on," she said. Alexis' resistance was more vehement than she intended, causing Gloria to unhand her. They apologized simultaneously.

"It's the gold-card school of getting things done," said Gloria. "I thought an appointment with the hairdresser might cheer you up." There was not a shred of resentment in her voice at being snubbed, and Alexis apologized again.

"I'm on edge," she said, and hated it for an equivocation.

Gloria sat down again and looked closely into her eyes. "You're frightened, aren't you honey?" she said, so that only Alexis could hear. Alexis nodded her head.

"Of me?" Gloria asked. Alexis looked at her closely. If a ghost had taken over this exuberant soul, then it must have been a powerful spirit, she thought.

169

"No," she said, and was pleased to hear the ring of conviction in her voice. She downed her own drink and, smiling, took Gloria's arm.

"Actually, this is a trap," said Gloria, as they passed through the doors from the lounge. She looked stunned as Alexis pulled away from her. "What did I say?" she asked, with such earnestness Alexis could only take her arm again.

"Don't talk to me of traps," said Alexis.

"All I meant was that while you sit there getting coiffed, I can natter away to you," Gloria explained as they entered the lift. "I like a captive audience." Alexis pushed the button for the White Sea deck and sighed.

"Be nice to talk to someone real," she said.

Gloria laughed. "Oh, I'm real, all right," she said, giving Alexis' arm a squeeze. Alexis dared to believe it was true.

"Are you open?"

The hairdresser looked up at the face in her mirror, startled. She put down her comb as though she had been stealing it from her mistress's boudoir.

"Take a seat," she said in nasal Liverpudlian. Gloria guided Alexis to the seat and parked herself in a chair by the window looking out on the lobby. She picked up *The Tatler* and began a running commentary on the faces there present and the money, or lack of it, behind those faces. She seemed tremendously knowledgeable about money and people's worth.

Alexis was turned around in the reclining chair. The hairdresser's name was Sandra. It was stitched in gold above her bosom. Sandra lowered the chair, tilting it back until Alexis' head fit snugly in the sculpted sink. Sandra's eyes were dull with boredom. Baleful. Alexis tried to smile; drink made her sleepy. Sandra turned her attention to the stream of water from the tap, adjusting it to the right temperature. Again Alexis gave herself up to the luxury of physical attention, this time with a bodyguard on hand.

Her bodyguard chattered away, while Sandra's scrawny fingers worked up a sweet-smelling lather in Alexis' limp hair. The fluorescent lights buzzed, Alexis' stomach rumbled. There was no other sound but Gloria and the rush of water in the sink. She made herself stay awake long enough to tell Sandra what she wanted done. "Yes miss," said Sandra with each direction, each change of mind. Finally she began. Sleepiness now overcame Alexis. Her head drooped, the scissors snipped. Sandra's crepe-soled shoes squeaked. Gloria's voice soothed, soothed. Alexis began to fall. Off the ship. Down the oubliette. She had leaned out too far, she could not keep her balance. She flung herself backwards in the chair. The scissor blade creased her scalp. She screamed.

"Oh Lord!" screeched Sandra. Alexis pressed her hand to her head against the blinding pain. The temporalis muscle, the zig-zag suture linking the occipital bone to the rest of the skull—she could see them, text-book graphic, in her mind's eye.

"She lurched!" cried Sandra. "Honest. I couldn't help it!" Gloria had grabbed the scissors from the girl and, at the same time, collected a towel which she pressed against Alexis' wound. The blood came fast, but that was only normal in the head. What a fool she was, thought Alexis. When would it sink in? She could trust no one on this trip. No one!

Sandra was whimpering. "Really, miss, I didn't mean to— "

"Like hell," Alexis interrupted. The girl crumpled in the corner chair, sobbing. Alexis no longer knew what to think.

"Now, now," said Gloria. She took control. She got Sandra looking for a first-aid box, which she found in a cupboard and opened at Gloria's command. Alexis looked at Sandra in the mirror. Without knowing why, she found herself despising the snivelling wretch. The accident was her own fault, she supposed, but the girl's fecklessness elicited nothing of sympathy in Alexis. The thought made her stronger.

"Here, I'm the nurse," she said, taking over the first-aid kit. Meanwhile Gloria took the scissors and snipped away at the hair matted with blood around the wound.

"I can't let you go out like that," Sandra whined, looking at Alexis' hair.

"Why in heaven's name not?" said Gloria, her own equanimity fully recovered. "We'll peroxide the short side—"

"We *are* peroxiding the short side," interrupted Alexis, pouring more of the bubbling liquid from a brown bottle onto a fresh towel.

"There, *voilà*," said Gloria, taking Alexis by the shoulders and making her confront her image in the glass. Carefully she put down the makeshift dressing. Alexis had to laugh, despite herself, at the lopsided effect of Gloria's shearing. Sandra had stylishly trimmed one wing; Gloria had clipped the other. "This kind of thing is all the rage in Vancouver," she said. Sandra had quit sobbing and was sulking in the corner.

Alexis climbed out of her chair, anxious now to leave the scene of the attack, no matter how comical Gloria made it seem. As they left Gloria returned to Sandra and patted her on the shoulder. "Oh, buck up," she said in a cheery voice. "No harm done. Is there, Lexy?" Alexis looked at the girl, who returned her gaze with trepidation.

"Tell your friends," said Alexis as evenly as she could, "I will not be intimidated." The girl looked with panic at her and then at Gloria. Gloria looked at Alexis quizzically. Alexis didn't try to explain but turned and left.

Alfred had gone. The air conditioning had apparently been fixed, for the room was frigid. Alexis crawled under her bedclothes fully dressed and curled up like a cat in the enormous purring hull of the ship. Her teeth chattered. Her head throbbed.

Later at dinner, the dentist's wife was shocked when Alexis explained about her hair. She had been for an appointment only an hour before the accident. Gingerly she touched each fluffy bubble on her own head, imagining the fate she felt she had so nearly missed.

Sven was dressed in a black turtleneck, trying to look as mature as possible. "You look like Hypnos, the Greek goddess of sleep," he said, proud of the stir his analogy produced. "She had only one wing. I've been reading a lot on ancient gods and goddesses lately."

He spoke to Gloria, but she was too under the weather to play goddess or coy mistress. After leaving Alexis she had drunk the afternoon away. Morgan, bartender that he was, seemed to find her condition amusing. He chattered on about this and that, oblivious of the pained expression on his neighbour's face. He talked about the fine weather. "Oh, that's it," said Gloria. "It's the sun. Where he comes from, it doesn't shine."

The dentist was quick to smooth over the off-colour remark with a suggestion of games they might play that evening. Alexis noticed that the scarab ring was turned inwards, showing only a gold band.

Again she declined to join the others, but stayed behind, glad to be alone with Gloria again.

"I owe you an explanation," she said.

Gloria shook her head and winced with the effort. "You don't owe me anything," she said. "You're paranoid; it's rather outré in this decade, but I recall the signs with some affection from my youth."

Alexis sighed. "I suppose I am crazy," she said.

"Hey," said Gloria, "as some sixties savant said: 'Just because you're paranoid, doesn't mean someone isn't following you.'"

Alexis wanted to go on, but Gloria's face was grey with discomfort. She has her own problems, thought Alexis, and decided not to burden this kind woman with her own. "My husband used to talk about the crazy sixties," she said.

"Ah, your husband. Now tell me about the break-up," said Gloria, smiling expansively through the pain of her headache.

Alexis looked perplexed. "You've told me about everything in your life but why you're not living it at the moment," said Gloria. She collared a waiter and ordered a Scotch. "For the Aspirins," she explained, holding up two tablets for Alexis' inspection.

"I don't remember it very distinctly," said Alexis, and Gloria winked.

"Keep it up," she said. "Forgetting is much overlooked as a remedy. Better still, lie!"

Alexis laughed. She jiggled and this jiggling was a new sensation for me—not entirely pleasurable.

"I'm serious," said Gloria. "Test out different lies the way you would a pair of shoes. Settle on the most comfortable and don't worry about the expense. You're the one who has to wear them, so get the most for your money. Hell, I've got a closet full of them."

The waiter returned with the Scotch. Gloria swallowed her pills and downed the drink. "Did he leave you?" she asked.

Alexis grinned. "Do you want the truth?" she asked.

Gloria returned the grin.

"Yes," said Alexis. "That's what I'm telling myself for the time being. You guessed?"

Gloria shrugged. "I'm good at my job," she said. "My married clients come back when they each want something smaller."

Alexis didn't want to think about living accommodations. Gloria patted her wrist. "You know what I tell my clients? Don't move into something too small."

"I have this hole in me," said Alexis, staring at Gloria, daring her to be one of the survivors. Gloria stirred the dregs of her Scotch with her finger. She smiled distantly.

"Don't underestimate a hole," she said. "It means there's somewhere left to fill up." She laughed lightly. "Wouldn't our horny young Sven love to hear this," she said. Then she got up to leave. She took Alexis' head in her hands and kissed her on the forehead. "Take it easy, Hypnos," she said and left the room

174

wobbling on her spike heels. Alexis watched her depart. She
would have to be careful. They would not all try an open attack
like Linn or Sandra. They would try to frighten her like Larry, try
to corner her like the dentist, or try to melt her like Gloria, if
Gloria....

Feeling somewhat more in control, Alexis wandered about
the ship, looking for crowds and avoiding long corridors. Good
babies would be sleeping by now, she told herself. She feared
the baby most of all.

She did not return to her cabin until ten. There she showered
and dressed. Of her two frocks, one was chic—she had worn that
to dinner the first night—and the other was flirtatious—fuchsia
silk jacquard, boldly printed in orange floral splashes and emerald
tracery. She had liked it in the store, but looking in the mirror at
it on, she saw only her washboard chest. She lost her nerve and
then recovered it—dug a fine black shawl from her drawer and
pinned it at the shoulder. She wore one of a pair of earrings Teddy
had given her—a dangly gold loop with a small loop inside. She
wore it on the wounded side of her head. An attempt at balance,
if not symmetry.

She heard the band while she was still in the lift. The saxophone player was wailing high in his register. The bass sounded
like the slightly crazy heartbeat of a fetal child, dangerously
fast, thumping and pumping to keep something both fragile and
volatile alive. The sound grew louder as the lift rose, thrillingly
loud as the doors opened on the Boat deck. God, how she had
missed live jazz! She had forgotten. She entered the Midnight Sun
Bar. There was scarcely a soul there. A stage for the band, turned
in on themselves, oblivious of their tiny audience; a handful of pa-
trons here and there, oblivious of the band. A Sikh and a Chinese
girl dancing alone on a postage-stamp dance floor.

Alexis found a table by a starboard window near the stage.
The saxophone player turned to the room. He was playing a
soprano. He was dressed in a dark green shirt and a thin yellow

175

tie, and wore his beret. The five musicians had put aside their formal work clothes and apparently their formal repertoire: the pianist played huge dissonant chords; the drummer's hands flew over his kit like a cock-fight; the bass player was like a squirrel defending his territory, thin fingers racing up and down the fret board. Then the straight, gold wand of the sax player cocked up; once, twice, and all together the musicians came tumbling down their separate scales into the coda, the end.

Alexis clapped loudly. The only one in the place. The band applauded her. The sax player smiled—a huge, warm, rubbery smile—and counted in a Latin number.

Alexis was pleased with herself. She ordered a ridiculous drink that was more like a fruit salad. There was a little blue light at Alexis' table. The whole room was blue with the blueness scattered around by a mirror ball. Outside the black sea met the black sky almost seamlessly. She tried to stare through the blackness, looking for Iceland. The Latin number ended. The Sikh stood like a soldier; his dance partner stared at the floor hoping the next tune would come quickly. A group had gathered at the bar. The sax player announced a break. He had an accent, Alexis noticed—northern European. He came towards her table and she clapped again, pulled out a chair.

"My falling lady," he said, taking the chair. He took off his beret and combed his hair with long, pale fingers. His hair really was yellow, she noticed. Strong as mustard. He had abandoned the black ribbon which had kept his hair tidy in a ponytail. It was shoulder length, ragged.

She had recognized the first piece she'd heard: "Cecil Taylor?" she asked. He seemed pleased, astonished. He called out to the others sitting at a table littered with beers.

"A fan," he said, pointing at her. They raised their drinks to her.

"A man I used to know liked Taylor," she said, blushing. "My name's Alexis Forgeben."

176

"Andrzej Howlonia," he said. "But you must call me Howl. That is what my friends call me. Because when I am cooking they say I sound like a timber wolf."

She could see something of a timber wolf in the cut of his jaw. But his eyes were soft, the colour of a northern forest.

"You weren't cooking at the captain's cocktail party," she said.

He frowned. "But you weren't there!" he said. "I looked everywhere for you."

The blush spread like waves from a stone, spilling over Alexis' face and down her neck.

"On the television," she said. "In my cabin."

His frown softened to mocking reproach. "For the captain we play 'Hello Dolly'. But up here we play for us. And now for you."

He got up and headed towards the stage. For a moment she thought he was going to play a solo just for her, but he was only recovering a Heineken he had left on the piano.

"What were you doing in England?" he asked. She thought for a moment, uncertain of what to tell him.

"Looking for someone," she said.

"Romance?"

"Someone who went missing," she said. "A tourist. It's too complicated."

"Are you a detective?" he asked.

She laughed. "*You're* the one with all the questions," she said.

So they talked about music. How easily it came back to her. Then, all too soon, the bass player, Benny, came to their table and dragged Howl away. Midway through the first number the Chinese girl left the Sikh on the dance floor looking at his watch, while she got her purse from the table. She passed Alexis and their eyes met. Alexis recognized the expression: the tranquilized patient on the way to surgery and not quite under yet. Dating on the high seas—not quite like the brochures! Alexis began to feel sad. It happened far too easily, and against all her wishes: a melancholy I could manipulate far more readily in my new locale.

She shifted her chair so that she was sitting in the shadows. She leaned her head against the cool window. The cut on her head was throbbing; the cool helped.

The set wore on. A few more people arrived in the bar, but no one, apparently, to listen to music. Howl announced the Zoot Sims version of "Somerset". He looked her way, but despite the title of the song she assumed he was addressing her only in recognition of the fact that she was the band's sole audience.

When Howl introduced the next number, he looked her way again, but this time there was no mistaking his intention. "This is a Richard Rodgers tune I picked for an angel I had the good fortune to rescue the other day. It's in F minor, close enough to G to be home for the sax. Beautiful and as the man says *doloroso*. It is called: 'You Have Cast Your Shadow on the Sea'."

He played tenor. The opening was lush, opulent harmonically. There was no fanfare, but Howl played with a kind of contained fervour. He seemed to taste each note; he wasn't blowing notes but sucking them into himself from the glistening rim of the instrument's golden bowl. He was sucking in the blue-turning darkness. Sometimes he bent low to dig up a rich vein of sound, a buried bone he would worry like a dog, flinging it about in the air. His face would distort: puffing up like a courting frog one minute, cadaverous the next.

The song seemed to focus Alexis' sadness. She had been sure she wanted this man but now she was not certain. She feared it was I who yearned for him. She wanted to leave, but waited out the song. When it was over and Howl, spent, had mumbled good night to the empty room, she waited still.

The band started to pack up. Howl downed his beer in one large gulp and rejoined Alexis. He put on a smile.

"That was beautiful," said Alexis. "Thank you."

"It wasn't beautiful," he said. His voice sounded edgy. He was frustrated, Alexis could tell, but not with her. "It was just jazz," he said, grinning maniacally. "My father didn't want me to play it. He said it was the devil's handiwork. Maybe he was right."

"It's never quite good enough?"

"Something like that," he said. "Your friend tell you that?"

She nodded.

His fingers drummed nervously on the table's edge. His toe was tapping.

"I've seen this before," she said. "The body keeps playing when the gig is up."

Howl laughed. He took this to mean in her musician friend; she meant in the operating room.

"I wish I was big!" he said suddenly.

"A star?"

"Hell, no," he said, astonished by her misinterpretation. He puffed out his cheeks and held out his arms to embrace a whale. "Big!" he said. "Then I could really blow a tune, blow out the rafters. Blow my brains out."

"It's hard to come down, isn't it?" said Alexis.

He nodded, not looking at her. Sniffing. Looking around impatiently before glancing her way again. "Are you doing anything?" he asked.

She thought of all the appropriate answers, rejected them, shook her head. "I don't sleep very well, anyway," she said.

He smiled. "Me neither. So let's not sleep together, how about that?" His mouth was too big for his face, comic in motion, sensual in repose. "You have to see my flags!" he said, touching her cheek. He didn't wait for a response but went to the stage to pick up his instruments.

She watched him gather up the worn cases that contained his three horns. He had a comb in the back pocket of his jeans. She could count the teeth on it. He handed her the case with the baritone saxophone in it. A tear had been covered with electric tape. Well travelled.

They set off. She had pencilled Gloria's name onto the list in her journal, lightly, so that she could rub it out without a trace to remind her of her lack of faith. She wondered if in the morning she would be pencilling Howl's name there too. Her ghosts had so many methods of getting to her but so far Howl's was the only one that was irresistible.

22

They passed the lifts—decisions about where to get off would have to be made too quickly. Under a white light in the companionway Howl examined Alexis' cut. She felt his finger gently follow the line of the gash. He looked pained when she explained the incident. Then his exploring fingers started the loops of her earring spinning in opposite directions.

"Your friend?" he asked.

"For Mother's Day," she said, but made a wry expression. It was a joke. She told him about Teddy—what she wanted him to know. They had been married less than a year and were now separated. He was crazy and played keyboards.

"Ah, that explains it," said Howl. "The melody gets lost so easy with all those notes. You need a man with a horn." He was so comfortable with his arrogance, Alexis noticed.

They stepped out onto the deck. The night was overcast, moonless, starless. The bartender was leaning against the rails, smoking, sucking in the quiet.

They walked to the end of the deck and looked down over the stern: Bridge, Boat, and North Sea decks, stepped like an empty Babylonian garden. They put down the instruments. Howl wrapped his arm around Alexis, against the cold. She told him about "singing the waves" from her deck chair that morning. From where she stood she could see the spot on the pavilion where she had sat then, where Larry had sat. There were no chairs there now.

They walked along the port side of the ship. Howl pointed over the railing. "Look at this," he said, and Alexis peered into the dark expecting to see the face of a man overboard in the black waves below—such was the cast of her mind. But Howl had meant to draw her attention to something much closer at hand. He pointed to the planking on the floor beneath their feet. "That last seam," he said, "between the planks and the gutter; you know what they call that?" She didn't. "That seam is called the devil," he said. Alexis stared at the place he indicated. The ship's period of roll leaned them out now so that the black waters loomed into their down-turned vision. The ocean, she noted, was growing choppy. There was only the thickness of the ship's shell between the devil and the sea.

"What does he look like?" Howl asked.

She looked at him and he held his face as still as a mirror. "Like you," she said, "but older." Her fingers pushed away the hair from his neck, held it away from his face. The resemblance was uncanny.

"But he plays keyboards," Howl said pointedly.

"He played his way across the ocean on a ship like this," she said. "It was his first gig. Before I knew him."

A door slammed shut. The bartender had gone. Alexis and Howl recovered the horns and sauntered back inside.

They walked slowly, tier by tier, down through the ship. They heard laughter in a stateroom. A steward passed them with the remnants of a late supper on a tray: a champagne bottle, two glasses, gritty bits of caviar, and cracker crumbs. Alexis looked down as the steward passed and saw his face distorted amid the clutter on the silver tray. Mentally, she added him to her list.

At the stairs on the White Sea deck, Howl kissed her. There was no embrace—their hands were full of saxophones—but his lips seemed to pull her towards him. He was playing her, she thought. In F minor.

"I have an outer room," he murmured between kisses.

"And I *have* to see your flags," she anticipated him. She followed him to another set of stairs she had not seen before, which led down deeper into the ship. She had thought all along that her own cabin was on the deepest floor.

"I am in a licensed officer's quarters," he said. "The crew are lower still." She had not dreamed the ship could be so deep.

His cabin was in the extreme forward reaches, almost directly under hers, as near as she could tell. She tapped on the forward wall. "Collision bulkhead," she said, mimicking Duncan Marriott's authoritative voice.

"And ahead of that?" he asked. She shrugged her shoulders. He put his saxophones away. "It is the place where the anchor cable is secured in its locker," he said, opening a porthole. "It's called the bitter end." She looked at him to see if this was meant to elicit some response. Apparently it was not. Just nautical information—like the devil.

He bent down and drew a large black portfolio out from under the bed. She sat dutifully on the scratchy, khaki, sailor-issue blanket. "Look at this," he said. He held up a two-foot-square sheet of paper for inspection. A red diamond sat on a white background. The colour appeared to be heavily encrusted wax crayon. She could smell it—like childhood—in the room.

"Ship's flags are wonderful," he said. "This is F—Foxtrot. Flown by itself it means 'I am disabled, communicate with me.'"

He carefully returned Foxtrot to its tissue paper envelope and pulled out another—horizontal stripes: orange, blue, green. The wax was in relief, since it had been applied so thickly.

"What is that one?" she asked.

"D—for Delta," he answered. "'Keep clear of me, I am manoeuvring with difficulty.'"

"I'm getting the message," she said.

183

He knocked on his locker: slap, knock, knock. "I am manoeuvring with difficulty."

On the side of the bed she made the same signal. He put down the picture and joined her. He buried his head in her shoulder. He kissed her. His hand stole under her shawl, into her dress, to her breast. She held his head tightly in her hands, arching towards him, fitting him as if they had worn each other like this for years. His leg wound around her leg until his knee rested high up against her thigh. Her mouth opened, his tongue entered her, probing. She felt an urgent wave begin to mount in her, to roll through her being. She thought it was desire —it was *like* desire—but suddenly, with horror, she realized it was something else! I was rising through her, in full flood, and she knew why: to escape! She clamped her teeth shut at the last possible second. He jumped back. She looked at his startled face. There was blood on his lip. Her eyes filled with tears. With her hands she brought his head back down to her shoulder. She held him there tightly while she sobbed.

"Don't do that again," she said. "You have no idea what could happen to you."

She cradled him, rocked him, felt her tears gather in hot pools between their cheeks. Slowly his breathing became regular, the respiration of sleep. She moved slightly under his weight, moulded herself to his contours. She curved herself into Howl's lean body. In his sleep his fingers tapped her lightly, opening valves in her skin—still playing. She relaxed and settled into the deeper resonance of this nameless deck below her own. She wanted another blanket. There was one at the end of the bed, but she couldn't reach it with this man on her. Nor the light switch. How had she let this happen?

She dreamed herself back on the Boat deck where the lifeboats waited, painted into their holds. In her dream the ship was white again, the *City of Sandakan*. Alexis was alone. The ship was listing badly. She could hardly keep her balance but she stepped around the protective railing and walked up to the edge, her bare feet up against the devil. She could see where the ship curved in to the keel—the tumble-home. Then when she was at her greatest pitch, Alexis leaned out over the edge of the ship, casting a huge shadow before her onto the grey waves. She fell. But even as she hit the freezing surface of the water the shipboard alarm went up. Three long blasts, over and over. "Man overboard," someone shouted.

The simple code was fragmented as wave after wave rolled over her. Under the waves she heard only the ship's turbines thundering. At first she did not struggle. The impact of the fall and the intense cold numbed her. Then she heard a splash nearby and coming up she saw Howl, his yellow head bobbing in the water. Then he was gone, or she was, lost in the trough of a wave. He called to her. He caught sight of her again and swam up the steep side of a wave. Coldly, she watched him thrashing at the water. Why does he fight it, she thought, and allowed herself to sink again out of his sight. It was not peaceful, not yet, but at least it was dark. Then all of a sudden he was over her, dragging her back up to the air. She screamed and spluttered and fought him off. Suddenly the air was criss-crossed with spotlights. Life preservers descended like a flock of clumsy birds, landing noisily in a ring around her. She heard a lifeboat being lowered from its crib. Ladders appeared on the ship's side, so many of them the ship looked like the walls of a beleaguered castle. So much effort, she thought, for one small life.

"Leave me alone!" she screamed at her rescuers. Howl paid no attention. He grabbed her single wing of hair and began to drag her towards the ship. She struggled out of his grip, dragging him under. He fought his way free and swam to the surface, gasping for air. He wrapped his arm around her neck and held her in against him so tightly she choked. She weakened. She could not stop him. And in her submission to this man instead of to the sea, *my* voice inside her was at last able to well up, forcing aside her own small voice.

"Help me!" I cried. "Save *me*! Get me out of her!"

Alexis' throat almost cracked with the outburst. Revived, she struggled again. Clamping her mouth shut defiantly, she threw off Howl's hammer-lock and propelled herself back down into the darkness. She would fill her hole with water; I would never speak again. She would drown me. But Howl had her again and this time he pulled her up over the gunwale of a lifeboat. Then before she could fight him off he was over her, his mouth on hers, pumping air into her stinging lungs.

"Help me," my voice groaned from its own darkness in her belly. "Help me...."

The voice woke her. She found herself staring into the startled eyes of Howl, hovering over her. He was on top of her. He was inside her. But even as she stared wild-eyed into his face, she felt him grow limp and small until he fell from her like a slug from a wet stone.

He drew away from her.

"I was asleep," he said. "I didn't know what I was doing."

She tried to calm him, to tell him it was all right. That she had wanted it—him—still wanted him. But all that came out was a dry rasping sound. "It was a dream," she told him. He was at the foot of the bed, his back against the wall. She reached out to him but he flinched. She retreated to the head of the bed.

"I'm sorry," he said, when she was as far away from him as she could get.

"It wasn't me," she said. Then she began to cry again. She wept and wept. He came to her and it was his turn to take her head in his arms and cradle her. She could feel his trembling through her own. She wanted to tell him something—anything—but the tears would not stop. She had swallowed an ocean in her dream and now must cry it out of her system. She felt his tumescence, sticky wet against her thigh. Her hand went to him but he resisted

186

her attempt at stimulating him as futile. And when it sunk in she howled at what had happened and what had not. "It wasn't me," she said.

23

Tap, tap, tap. Tap, tap, tap. Someone was rapping on the cabin door. Where can I hide, was Alexis' first conscious thought to find its way out of the confusion of sleep. Under the bed, replied her unconscious mind, with the flags.

Tap, tap, tap.

She forced her eyes open. She was alone. She was in her own cabin. "Room service," a voice called. She recognized it.

"Coming," she said. She struggled out of the tangle of bed-clothes. The room was swaying. She found her dressing gown, but fell back on her bed. She could hear china chinking together outside the door. She had not ordered room service.

Finding her footing again, she made her way to the door. When she unlocked it, it fell open to reveal Larry holding a tray covered with linen. He bowed stiffly, a distorted smile playing around the corners of his mouth. He was without his dark glasses.

"There are various forms of stewardship," he said, as he steered his way past her. The floor tilted starboard and they both lunged forward towards the chest of drawers. Alexis picked up the Marriotts' vase of flowers and pushed aside the ice bucket, making room for Larry to deposit the tray. She searched for a spot to put the vase until she realized that the flowers were dead. She threw them, plastic galleon vase and all, into the pail.

"You won't want to go up there," said Larry, rolling his one good eye upwards. "We're into a head sea. The effect of the turbulence is magnified at each stage of the way up." Larry dragged a chair out from the desk and parked himself squarely in it. "I ate my breakfast early, as is my wont, in the café, and was flung about like a watchman in a crow's nest."

Alexis found her watch by the bed. It was afternoon. There was barely a full day left before they docked. "Are we still on course?" she asked.

Larry smiled at the plangent note in her voice. The smile did not last long. She turned her attention to the tray. Removing the warm linen cloth she found a basket of croissants, little pots of fruit preserve, shavings of sweet butter, and an enormous carafe of coffee.

"Wonderful," she said. "Thank you." She turned to Larry but the expression on his face was stern. She helped herself to a bun, slathering it with butter and preserve, while Larry poured them each a coffee. She tried to eat but her mouth was like chalk. She accepted a cup of coffee but her hand was shaking so badly she had to put it down on the dressing table. The steam clouded the mirror.

"We need to talk," said Larry, sipping his own brew, seemingly unaffected by the rolling ship or the serious nature of his visit.

"Yes," agreed Alexis without looking up. She dared to glance at the priest again, and gasped. He was dangling an earring in his free hand. Loops within loops. Instinctively she reached for it. He snatched it away. His manicured fingernails glistened as he made the piece of jewellery bob up and down before at last relinquishing it to her grasp.

"Where did you find it?" she asked.

"Presumably in the same place you lost it," he replied. She made a series of connections in her head which must have played in rapid succession across her face, for Larry said, "You needn't think that musician is one of us." There seemed to be genuine distaste in Larry's voice.

"How do I know?" Alexis demanded woefully.

"Why do you think I am here?" said Larry. He took a napkin and dabbed at his lips like a woman setting her lipstick.

"I am not sure," said Alexis.

"Well I'll tell you then, shall I? I am here precisely because this Howl fellow is *not* one of us. He is an unknown commodity. You are, to be frank, enough of a problem without an ally."

"Thanks," said Alexis.

Larry seemed not to hear. His lips made a moue of displeasure. "We heard something quite disturbing last night, Alexis. There was a spy at your lover's door, you understand. The spy heard the voice of a very familiar and very *weak* friend. 'Help me, help me!' the voice cried. Put a fright into him, I can assure you, poor creature.

"Some of us," Larry went on, "are not as well endowed mentally as others—if you get my meaning. We all heard the hole give you its last instructions before Fastyngange was destroyed, but not all of us fully comprehended what then followed." Larry made it perfectly clear he was not among those who had been deluded. "The impression among the ranks was that you were under the hole's guidance in some mysterious way; that you were harbouring it. Until last night, that is. Now the very dimmest of us is aware that you are carrying the hole inside you."

The priest inspected her now as had done Friar Rush on the hill on All Hallows' E'en.

She tried to see the rotting death's head behind his well-kept skin. He was wearing cologne. She tried to detect the scent the cologne was meant to hide.

"Obviously," he continued, "one would not expect the hole's voice to amount to much carried in such a thin-walled, if charming, vessel."

Alexis imagined the priest himself at Howl's door, on his knees at the keyhole. "It wants out," she said.

"That is only too heart-breakingly clear," said the priest. "It is afraid of you. Afraid of what you might do. And—speaking for the group—that frightens us too."

Alexis steadied herself to respond. "You won't dare kill me," she said.

"No?"

"You can't," she said. "You don't know what will happen to the hole if I perish."

The priest smiled, recognizing the challenge, and even welcoming it. He chuckled. "You figured that out early," he said. "It was, if I'm not mistaken, one of the first entries in the journal of your trip. The pipe fitter, Alfred, read it there."

Alexis felt foolish at still being surprised. "You would kill me, wouldn't you? You'd like to."

Larry laid his hand on his breast and nodded his head sadly. "Of course we would, dear," he said. "We do not like being stranded. None of us likes this masquerading about. We are stowaways. Not just on this ship but out here in the real world. Borrowing the bodies of stewards and dentists, of Sikhs and balmy Welsh bartenders. No, I suppose you have only guessed the most obvious charades. We are never entirely sure we might not be found out. We want our home back. Is it so much to ask?"

"And that is why you are here now?"

"It would be a particularly generous gesture on your part," said Larry. The irony in his voice, the matching rows of neat little teeth in his smiling mouth, both frightened Alexis and gave her courage. I am alive, she told herself. I am stronger than they are.

"You will have to wait," she said. Her eyes gave away her rekindled determination. The priest changed tack.

"There are those among us who are very bitter; who see you as a most insidious interloper.

"I have attempted, as the group's spiritual leader, to make it clear that a rash move could leave us eternally stranded in this purgatory. On the other hand, a rash move from you, a suicidal leap, would leave us equally at sea—if you'll allow me a joke at such a moment." His smile was perfunctory. "I cannot be everywhere at once. And I cannot be responsible for one of my fellow survivors letting fear or frustration cloud his or her better judgement. It would be to your advantage to move with great caution from now on. We do not intend to lose you at any cost."

Alexis ate the remainder of her croissant and washed it down with lukewarm coffee. "You have been very patient with me," she said.

"We know all about patience," Larry replied unctuously. "But surely you do not intend to carry the hole with you to the grave?

"Imagine it," he continued, enjoying the vision he had conjured up. "Laid out in your best clothes and lowered into the ground. The faces of us ghosts looking down on you, transfixed with loathing and terror. I at your head saying the burial service, flinging dirt down into your eyes." Alexis blinked and Larry's vision came to her. She tried to find her parents or Teddy among the mourners, but if they were there at all they were crowded out by the gang she had dragged with her from Fastyngange.

"Alexis?" said the priest. He raised his voice: "Alexis!" She imagined it to be part of the funeral rite—a call to the deceased, one last-ditch attempt to raise her up. Then the priest was not saying anything from any prayer book, but railing at her instead, and she found herself not in a grave but in a tiny, windowless cabin in a ship making a winter crossing. Larry was shaking her.

She pulled herself free of his grasp. "I am not carrying the hole for me," she said. "I am carrying it for someone else. It is not mine to give away," she added defiantly.

"Neither is it yours to take!" Larry snarled. "Give it up now. Think! You will be free of us. Once in the oubliette we will be gone and done with. Forgotten." Larry's good eye suddenly brightened. "You could suck it back up again once we had used it."

"And then release you all over again when I get home? No thank you."

"Either way," said Larry, "we survivors will not let you out of our sight until we are reunited with our proper darkness. We will dog your steps, plague you. We will be your unholy disciples."

The thought was not a comforting one, but stubbornly Alexis held her ground. "I will give it up when I am good and ready," she said. "I will carry it to term."

Larry flung his napkin on the silver tray and rose to leave. He glared at her, then strode across the cabin to the hatchway. He turned her way while his hand recovered his dark glasses from an inner pocket. "I have warned you," he said. Just as he put on his glasses she saw an expression pass over his face she had not expected to see. It was neither rage nor keen disappointment. It was panic. He slammed the door shut behind him. His panic chilled Alexis to the bone.

24

There were hand-written warnings up by the lifts, the entrance to the dining room, and anywhere else they might catch the public eye. The last-night bash had been cancelled due to the storm.

The rough sea had calmed somewhat by nine when Alexis made her way up to the lounge deck, but there were few passengers about. She overheard a rumour that damages in the kitchen were responsible for the party's cancellation. She was disappointed. A party might almost have been safe. She could have sat near the band, spent the wee hours with Howl. She no longer wanted to spend much time in her cabin—not alone, at least. She had stayed there for some time after Larry had left, but the rumbling white noise of the ship proved to be composed of a thousand disquieting sounds refracted to her attention through the prism of her door. Her hearing, she had noticed lately, was acute. It was my hearing, in fact.

She made her way to the secluded lounge where she had attempted the previous day to write in her journal. She stood at the windows overlooking the forward weather deck. It was a desolate sight, awash with spume, glazed with ice. The rain on the sea had stopped. It moved like something swollen. The clouds hung in tatters, bruised purple.

If I were to give it up now, she thought, it would all be over. The suicidal dream of the night before had come back to her when she was alone again. She had resisted my dark cozenage, though she had found something like solace in my eternal morbidity. Death, she recalled me saying, was not my *preoccupation* but my *sole* occupation. She had resisted the urge to complete my longing while I was outside her. Now, after only a week with me inside, she had become infected with a death-wish that was not her own. How long she could stop the infection spreading from her dream-consciousness to her waking consciousness, she couldn't be sure. And now, she was threatened from the outside as well. Larry had threatened her.

A hand touched her arm.

In a single wild motion she swung around, grabbing the wrist of her assailant and flinging it away, while her freed arm lashed out where it might be expected to make contact with his eyes. Instead it was frozen in mid-flight by a sturdy grasp. Howl stood, his head out of reach of her swing, his eyes as watchful as a cat's. A crazy cat, she understood in that instant, but a beautiful one. His grip on her wrist was like steel. She dropped her head and turned away to the window. She leaned her forehead against the glass and got her breath back.

"What is it?" he asked. Again he touched her; tentatively his hand slid around her waist. She pressed his palm against her stomach. She could feel the sinewy muscle in his hand, the bones of him. He was real; she had to believe that.

"It's too complicated," she said.

"Does it have anything to do with the girl following you?" he asked.

Alexis turned to him, then looked past him through the empty lounge.

"She's gone now," he said.

"Who?"

"The hairdresser."

Alexis took Howl's hand tightly in her own. He began to talk almost desperately. "I caught her out in the passageway peering in. She ran off before I could speak to her. She was following you, wasn't she?"

Alexis nodded her head.

"That cut on your head...." Alexis peered up to Howl's eyes; she nodded again. "Christ, I've been such an idiot!" he said. Alexis looked at him quizzically. "I think I have something to do with this, though God knows I wouldn't have believed she'd go so far."

Alexis was about to stop him and try to explain, but she could see him settling his face for a confession.

"I made friends with her when she came on board," he said. "It was a few days before sailing. She was new, seemed lonely."

Alexis could not keep her skepticism from showing.

"Friends," he reiterated. He held her chin so that she could not avoid his eyes. His lips twisted into a self-abasing grin. Then his eyes travelled to the scar under her scalp, and the grin faded. He looked guilty. "We had lunch a couple of times. I showed her around. Honest, that was it."

"Did you show her your flags?" Alexis asked.

Howl didn't smile. "She wouldn't have understood," he said.

"She'd have understood your cabin," said Alexis.

"She is not well," he said.

"I'm not well," said Alexis. "That didn't stop you."

It was meant as a joke, but Howl looked clear through the mischievous grin on her face. "You are..." he searched for a word "...possessed?"

Alexis smirked. "Sleep with a girl and suddenly you're all cheek."

"But is it true?" he asked, unperturbed, his voice calm. He might have been commenting on a headache. She looked at him closely. He was not frightened, but intrigued.

"Something like that," she replied. She wanted to tell him more. He seemed to know that.

"I thought about it all night," he said. "Then when I saw Sandra just now, I wondered if there was some kind of connection. If maybe she was possessed in the same way but doesn't understand it or has just gone right out of her mind. Because she is crazy—not like you—really mad. She thinks she's pregnant—"

"Stop!" Alexis' hand covered Howl's mouth. Pregnant? Her head was spinning. She needed to think. "Pregnant?" she asked.

"That's what she says," said Howl. He had slowed down. "She claims it's my baby, but that's ridiculous. We've only known each other a week."

"Sometimes women know these things," said Alexis.

"But we never slept together," said Howl.

Alexis tried to picture Sandra, but could only see the pregnant hag at Fastyngange. Her mind reeled back still further to Sally Bert. In her mind's eye their faces became one. Newly pregnant when she jumped to her death, surviving the fall—how long? Long enough to be crushed under the weight of her rat-bitten captain? Then two hundred years of waiting, for it suddenly seemed perfectly clear that no child could be born into purgatory. And now, out again in the real world. What, in the name of all creation, might be born after so long a gestation?

"Tell me what is going on?" Howl asked.

She looked blankly into his face. Then slowly she wound her arms around his neck. She bent his head down to her lips. She tucked strands of yellow hair behind his ear and began to tell it to him, in a whisper. It began with Teddy, so she started there. She told him what she thought was everything, though it was really only as much as she could tell. She leaned against his lean body and he held her around the waist like a fine, long instrument. She could not see his eyes glistening with excitement as she described the hole entering her and how it was to be disgorged.

"You have been very brave," he said, when she was finished.

"Or damn stupid," she replied.

"You must love this keyboard man a lot." There was something distinctly off-putting about his enthusiasm, Alexis thought. But then it might have been worse. He might have raced off to get help. Surely there was somewhere secure on board for the safekeeping of lunatics. Looking into Howl's eyes, Alexis wondered if it was her lunacy she saw there—transferred in the telling of her outrageous story—or his own. He took her hands in his and held her eyes with his own.

"You must spit it out," he said.

"I won't," she said. "Teddy's life might depend on it."

"*Your* life depends on your spitting it out, now, as soon as possible," he countered. "You can always take it back in."

Alexis went weak at the thought of it. She remembered the sheer brute force of the black whirlwind. "I was unconscious most of a day," she said. "There isn't time. No, it's impossible."

He took her in his arms. "Listen to me," he said. She shook her head but he shook her harder. "Listen!" His eyes grew hard but softened immediately. "When I surprised Sandra in the hall, she had scissors with her. She had them clutched like this—" he said, rolling his strong hand into a fist. "They don't care. Whoever that poor girl was, she is this Sally Bert monster now and *she* hates you."

Alexis tried to imagine the pain of being stabbed. She had dressed stab wounds at St. Michael's. It was a downtown hospital; there were street fights and muggings. She remembered the face of a rubby who had died in her arms.

Howl clicked his fingers three times as if counting in a song. "The painter woman at the castle; she said they would only be survivors until they were able to jump again."

He looked into her eyes to see if she understood. She did, but after a moment she shook her head. "But how?" she asked. "I need the stones."

Howl jumped to his feet. "Leave that to me," he said. "I have friends on this ship from the bridge to the hold." Then he sat beside her again, scarcely able to conceal his excitement. "I have a feeling it will not be as bad as you think."

Alexis was puzzled by him. Suspicious. This could all be an elaborate plot. Howl read her indecision. He stroked her hair.

"I believe your story," he said. "Isn't that enough for you?"

She shook her head. "It only means you're as deluded as me," she replied.

He laughed. "This thing—this hole—it has captured my imagination. I tasted it—remember—on your lips, in your mouth. I sense what it wants." This admission did not encourage Alexis. Howl stammered impatiently. "You dreamt of the sea," he pressed. "The hole tasted something in your dream, something powerful and vast. Something it longed for. The sea."

Alexis nodded slowly, sensing that he was on to something, but too tired to know what. "The hole's yearning is only theirs," he said slowly, as if working out a precarious equation. "For hundreds of years these 'survivors' have waited at the bottom of the hole on the hill. But in the sea," he said, "in the sea they would be free."

"What is in this for you?" she asked.

"Teddy may not want you back," he said, shrugging his shoulders. "Despite all your help, he may decide it is safer to stay crazy. Then maybe you will think of me?"

How am I supposed to think, she almost said. For he had turned his eyes on her and what little bit of reason she might still boast turned to liquid under his gaze. She wanted him desperately then—would have had him right there—her buttocks on the railing, her back up against the cold spume-covered glass. I won't bite this time, she tried to tell him with her eyes. No alien voices—promise! But don't ask me to think, she begged him. He embraced her but gently, like a fragile thing, when what she wanted was excavation! He brought her down gently.

They sat for an hour while Howl hatched his plan and Alexis collected herself. Then he left and she wandered off like a heat-seeking missile looking for other flesh-and-blood passengers. She knew most of the hunters now: Larry, the dentist, Linn, Shovelface, the knife-sharpener steward, the painter, the baby, Morgan, Alfred, the Sikh, Sandra—eleven. There were twelve. Who was the twelfth? The other steward she had seen carrying the late-night snack? She had thought him a possibility, but she had suspected half the people on the ship. One hunter unaccounted for. She found herself regarding the passengers. Everyone looked drained after the storm. They were all too self-absorbed to return her gaze.

She eventually found herself in the Horizon Café drinking Scotch with her back to the wall like Jesse James. The café began to sway. The ship entered another storm.

Though the rocking made her sick, she did not dare go to her cabin. At six-thirty she fought her way down to dinner, for a change of scenery. She did not imagine she would be able to eat. She wondered if Larry would have told Morgan and the dentist of their meeting. Would it change their attitude towards her, to know she knew? The dining hall was even emptier than usual. The captain was not at the head table; an emissary from the bridge apologized for his absence. There was no danger, he assured those hearty enough to make the journey up from their cabins.

Before the officer could sit down, a man spoke from the floor. "Why is the ship rocking like a rocking horse?" he asked.

The officer grinned reassuringly. "That is under control," he said. "You should notice a difference shortly."

There was an audible murmur of dissatisfaction with this response. The officer was forced to take his feet again as the hostility of the small crowd grew.

"It has to do with weight distribution in the holds," he said patiently. "There must have been a general shift of the cargo

200

towards the stern during the earlier storm. We are trimming the cargo and fuel at this very moment."

This seemed to satisfy the rabble, who settled down to talking among themselves.

"Actually we're hogging," said Gloria. "And from what I hear, it's damn unusual for such a light run."

"Why are you whispering?" demanded Rosemarie. There were only the three women at their table, but Rosemarie had chosen to sit at her own place across from the others.

"I was just saying I'm going to sleep in the cinema on the Bridge deck," said Gloria. "With my fur coat and my galoshes."

Rosemarie looked confused and put-upon.

"The lifeboats are nice and handy on the Bridge deck," said Gloria, blithely unperturbed. "It's my instinct for real estate. I'm not sure if women and children first still counts for anything these days," she added.

At that moment a waiter brought them each a sandwich wrapped in Saran wrap. The kitchens were indeed not working to full capacity. But, he added quickly, the captain had opened the bar. Rosemarie ordered a gin and tonic and bid the waiter remove the sandwich plate. She looked gloomily at the other two women.

"My husband isn't feeling well," she said, though neither of them had asked. "He isn't himself lately," she added apologetically.

Alexis picked at her meal. She was uneasy. About the night ahead. About Gloria. About not trusting Gloria. "What is hogging?" she asked.

"The opposite of sagging," said Gloria, cocking an eye. "Actually, this ship is known to hog in a head wind but not as much as this."

"It's the shifting of the cargo," said Rosemarie, taking a swallow of her gin as though it were medicine. "You heard the officer."

"Maybe," said Gloria.

"I figure the captain knows what is going on better than a—a real estate agent," said Rosemarie. Gloria shrugged. "Well, it stands to reason," Rosemarie continued, desperate now for assurance. Gloria put down her sandwich and, rounding the table, she wrapped her arms around the dentist's wife. She hugged her and petted her broad back. The woman whimpered, downed her drink, and left. Alexis listened to the swishing of her legs as she waddled away.

"You shouldn't have teased her," said Alexis, when Gloria resumed her seat. The two women ate in silence.

Finally, Benny, the bass player, signalled her from the hall that it was time. Gloria looked devilish. "My, my," she said. "Just like a horn-player to send the rhythm section out on a roundup." Alexis blushed, as she excused herself.

She and Benny strolled down to Howl's cabin. She wondered what Howl had told him, why he had not come himself. Benny leaned against the wall outside Howl's cabin as Alexis tapped out their signal. Slap, knock, knock.

Howl was in a merry mood, a boy-scout mood. He had uniforms for them: baggy grey denim overalls, boots, and, for Alexis, a cap to hide her hair. Her name tag read "Jerry". She wondered if Jerry worked with Arthur.

"If anyone asks," said Howl, "you're in reefer maintenance." She memorized this strange occupation without asking more. The less there was to know, the better. Meanwhile Howl prepared a further surprise: makeup. She was to enter the nether regions of the ship in blackface.

"Gimme five, bro'," snapped Benny, tickled by her getup. Then he looked her over more critically. "The nose notwithstanding, you make a passing good spook," he declaimed. The bass player was to follow Howl and Alexis at a discreet distance, to make certain they were not followed. After they left the stair tower, she never saw him again.

Alexis had been dubious about the costumery: both their need for it and its effectiveness. They had to pass through the ship, after all, and in her three days on board she had only once seen a maintenance man in the passenger section, and that had been in her room (and he had not really been a maintenance man at all). To her surprise, as they made their way to the dining room, they more than once met workers passing this way and that through the deserted corridors, carrying tool boxes and lengths of wire, taking readings off instrument panels, and talking over walkie-talkies to some central command. The storm and the ship's unusual action had resulted in its being taken from the passengers' control by the crew. There wasn't room for appearances in a crisis. The passengers were now no more than cargo.

Looking as if they were going somewhere on some important task, Alexis and Howl crossed the empty dining room and passed through the swinging doors to the galley. The thick carpeting gave way to linoleum the colour of dried turd; incandescent lights in scalloped glass and chandeliers gave way to banks of fluorescent tubes in fixtures swinging from the low ceilings. Immediately Alexis' attention was drawn to four men in yellow slickers, wearing oxygen masks, and fighting a blaze in one of the stoves. The scene was like something from Hieronymus Bosch. The white foam from the fire extinguishers oozed down walls and counters to the floor where it floated on several inches of water that other workers were trying to mop up. The floor was awash with garbage and escaped vegetables; a cabbage rolled towards Alexis like a bowling ball and thwacked into the wall.

Howl took her hand and led her through the flotsam and fumes. It would have seemed strange to see two workers holding hands, had anyone paid them the slightest attention.

Through a second set of doors they entered the messhall. There was nothing of panic here, only shouts of annoyance directed at the swinging, flickering lights from employees trying to read poker hands while preventing the kitty from sliding off the table. The only smoke in the air was cigarette smoke. Through a long cafeteria-style hatchway the conflagration in the galley could be seen by anyone, but the off-duty staff cast their eyes on their books and their games and their beers. In an alcove several sailors cheered and jeered as one of their mates shot down marauding space aliens on a video screen. They spoke Norwegian. Through a third set of doors, Alexis and Howl passed into a corridor painted two shades of brown—like a school, complete with locker-lined walls. A man stood stripped to his underwear at a locker alive with pink pin-ups. At his feet in a puddle lay a pile of soaking work clothes. An old man grinned at Alexis from the doorway of a laundry room, showing off teeth that were no longer there. Just beyond the laundry room, Howl turned down a short corridor leading inboard to the centre of the ship. He pushed through a door with a prominent sign restricting admission to a very limited category of people.

25

Alexis found herself on a steel-grated stage built around a metal casing the size of a smokestack. A stairway wound down around the casing. She heard the thrumming of turbine engines underneath her. The grating buzzed in resonance. They began their descent.

Work boots clanged on the stairs below. Alexis shoved her hands in her pockets. Her black face moist with sweat, she looked down at her boots. Two men passed them on the stairs, their faces about as black from grime as Alexis'.

"*Hvordan har De det?*" said Howl, in a friendly way.

"*Ut slitt*," said one.

"*Sulten*," said the other. They laughed.

Alexis and Howl continued down the service trunk without meeting another soul. Alexis concentrated on counting the stages of their descent. She counted seven. Then they were at the end and Howl opened a gas-tight door that closed behind them with a sucking sound, like a large rubber kiss. They found themselves on the narrow landing of a steep fire escape that led down to the very floor of the ship. The noise was terrific, for they were in the engine chamber. Eight turbines versus the Atlantic. They hurried towards the stern, then through another gas-tight door in a bulkhead which mercifully closed the noise of the engines off behind them. They found themselves in a long corridor. Steel stanchions rose to the left and right, supporting lofts loaded with cargo. There were ladders at regular intervals. Naked lights illuminated their path but very little else. There was a large black tunnel to their right running down the ship's centre from the engine room. Its roof slanted down to less than shoulder height at the further bulkhead. There was a low door set in the curved side of the tunnel.

"What is it?" she whispered in his ear.

"The shaft alley," said Howl. "Where the drive shaft leads down from the engines to the screws." His face relaxed into a nervous smile at the look of horror on her face. He took her hand. Alexis stared up into the open hull, the massive steel ribcage rising from the keel to engulf her. Huge cant beams extended out radially from transom beams to the outer edge of the first full deck, three loft stages above. It was like the dome of a grotesque cathedral. Everything was coated with green fireproofing. It hung like dirty stalactites from the shadowy ceiling. The smell was sharp in her nose.

"Come on," said Howl. His grip on her hand tightened. They passed through another bulkhead into the aftmost section of the ship. The shaft alley slanted lower and lower towards the floor and the propellers fighting the sea. This last section was quieter than the two previous ones. Alexis could hear the sloshing of bilge water. The floor area was divided up into "offices" of cargo by shifting boards made of wood. It was like a maze, an extended stable without horses, in the belly of the ship.

"It's over this way," said Howl, impatiently tugging on her hand. She resisted him. "What's the matter?" he asked. Her eyes searched his. His gaze flickered away.

"Come and see," he said, taking her hand in both of his and pulling her on like a stubborn donkey. She wanted to go back but something drew her towards his destination, something other than Howl. She let him lead her through the maze of loose luggage to a far corner.

It was darker here. Howl took a flashlight from his worksuit. In the dimly lit corner Alexis could see what looked like straw; it was like the manger in a Christmas pageant. She took the flashlight from him. She saw that the straw was actually excelsior. Duncan's crate had been opened. She advanced into the makeshift room and saw what had been hidden from her view and what she now knew had drawn her against her will: the stones from Fastyngange laid out in their magic circle, the size of a manhole. She immediately felt the overwhelming desire to retch, and turned away from the stones. Howl, guarding the exit from the room, stared at her wide-eyed.

She glanced at him without daring to open her mouth. She could feel the nausea rising in her. She dropped the flashlight on the floor.

"It's for your own good," he cried. "It's just for now, until we land. I knew as soon as you told me about it that this was the only reasonable thing to do."

But she shook her head violently, fighting convulsion. There was nothing reasonable about it. She couldn't go through with it, she thought, knowing full well she could not avoid it. In the light from the floor—for neither of them had recovered her flashlight—she saw on Howl's face a look of almost idiotic joy. She wanted to call him a bastard and a fool for his plan, but if she opened her mouth now it would be I who spoke and she had no idea what I might say. She only knew I was rising in her. She felt herself trapped inside the cave of her own body as the black tide rose higher and higher. And still Howl was yammering.

"They will come," he said. "They will know it is here. Then when they have jumped and are part of the sea, you can recover the hole. It will work," he said. "And if you are too weak...." He paused. "If you are too weak then I will carry it for you."

For one startled instant Alexis' nausea ceased. She went cold all over. She stared unbelievingly at Howl. He looked frightened.

"I'm stronger, don't you see? The hole recognized that when it called out to me in your dream. 'Get me out of her,' it said."

Alexis stared at him. His face was filled with desire. He was crazy. He had been all along, perhaps that was what had drawn them together.

"The hole sensed me," he said, "through you."

Then Alexis fell to her knees under a shocking wave of contractions. It was all she could do to crawl to the circle of stones. She did not move so much by her own volition as by the attraction of the mouth waiting across the floor. She lurched forwards the last yard or so, until her mouth hung over the cold, sharp lip.

I rose through her like a black wind. She felt as if her face were peeling away from her skull to make her mouth larger and larger. Any moment, she thought dizzily, the twenty-two bones of my skull will crack open and explode. I was drilling up through her like a tornado. The brightly coloured excelsior began to whirl in the air around her. Duncan's crate began to slide away across the floor until it smacked up against the aftmost bulkhead. Other things began to move. Piles of luggage swayed and toppled, smashing to the ground. Howl backed up against the wall of the ship. He watched the top of a crate burst from its wrapping, releasing a swirling flock of white linen into the air. Soon all the air in the hold was dancing with clothing in a multi-coloured whirlwind above the circle of stones. Then the sound of the wind was overcome by a grinding hiss worse by far than the propeller shaft. Howl covered his ears. The ringing grew so piercing he had to fall to the floor and curl into a tight ball. He found himself screaming to try to equalize the pressure in his head. Looking towards the still prostrate Alexis, he saw the floor between the stones growing white hot. The tornado of clothing was a three-storey column rising above the circle—a column that seemed to

208

be drilling a hole in the ship. As Howl watched, the column sank from his view. The noise seemed to follow it through the newly drilled hole, leaving only a choir of echoes coming from the rows upon rows of intercostal stages in the huge open section of the ship. Then the ringing died. A box toppled somewhere far off. Glass was heard to smash in another section of the ship. Howl's flashlight, which had been rolling in circles on the floor, came to a stop aimed at Alexis. She rolled away from the stones and lay exhausted on her back. Her eyes felt glued shut. Her teeth felt as if they might fall out. Howl moved towards her cautiously until he was standing over her. She sensed him there but could not respond. He hardly noticed her. His eyes were fixed on the hole in the thick crust of the ship. He could see the ocean; it splashed up into the hole, sizzling on the hot sides of the shaft. Somewhere a bilge pump kicked into action.

It was not the same to lose the hole as it was to take it in. Alexis found herself recovering more quickly than she expected. She lay very still. She kept her eyes shut, letting the numbing pain in her skull disperse.

"I had to see it," she heard Howl say. Then another sound caught her attention. It was the distant kiss of a gas-tight door. Howl knelt beside her. "Shhh," he said.

Alexis gathered herself together and, with his help, climbed to a crouching position. His appeal for silence had been unnecessary. There was not a sound in her capable of escaping into the air.

Alexis had crept away from Howl and wedged herself into a spot between two tall crates from where she could see the entranceway and the hole. Just in time. They came through the hatch into the last section of the ship. She recognized all but one until that one was within a few feet of her, and then she saw it was the captain of the *Northern Lights* himself. The twelfth ghost. Who, she wondered, was piloting them in the storm? They had come directly from their beds and baths—some in pajamas, some naked—drawn home. Drawn to me, escaped into the world again.

I took the liberty of being the first to speak. "Where am I?" I demanded groggily.

Sandra screamed. "It's 'ere! It's 'ere!" Whoever Sandra was, it was Sally Bert ascendant in her now.

They moved with one accord towards the sound. Howl backed up until he could back up no farther. He moved across the hold in the opposite direction from Alexis' hiding place.

Sandra burst ahead of the others. "Our luvly 'ole," she said. "Our luvly 'ome." She didn't seem to notice Howl at all. Larry glanced at him as the others filled the area between the shifting boards. They made straight for me and crowded around, like spectators at a cock fight, shoving, vying for position.

"Give me room!" I said. "You're stifling me!"

Sandra fought her way out of the crowd and looked around, up into the lofts, into the corners. "Where's Miss Fancy Arse?" she screamed. Alexis edged silently out of view towards the end of her hiding place, nearer the corridor.

"Where is she?" said Sandra, finally acknowledging Howl's presence.

"She was frightened," said Howl. "She jumped."

Sandra looked confused and then disappointed. "She what?"

"Don't wail," said Larry. "It's what she's wanted all along." Several of them cackled at this.

"She'll like being dead," said the dentist.

"*If* she jumped," said Larry. Then they all began to argue among themselves, while Alexis slipped out of her hiding place and gained the cover of another crate five yards closer to the hatchway through the bulkhead.

"Did she jump?" asked Larry, but he did not direct his question to Howl. The others stopped talking and listened for my response.

"There was so much excitement," I said. "I'm new at this transplant business. She may well have done."

"Don't play games with us!" shouted one of them.

"Liar," called another.

Others joined in, berating me while one or two of them pulled away from the group and began to search the hold.

The dentist started back up the corridor. He had a score to settle; dying could wait a little longer after having waited so long already. From where she hid Alexis could see the dentist coming towards her. Though he seemed not to see her, he held his head up, sniffing the air like a hound. He had in another incarnation been a hangman, she recalled, and though he had scarcely had to hunt for his prey then, it was possible, faced with fear on a regular basis, that he had developed a keen sense of smell for it. Closer he drew, drawn by killer instinct, until he stood not four feet from Alexis. She was weighing the possibility of making her break for freedom when suddenly there was a clatter and a splash and a deep-throated yell. Morgan had jumped. Others now battled for the chance to follow. The dentist turned and watched the skirmish around the hole with delight. He even clapped his hands. He seemed to have forgotten completely his vendetta and, as one after the other of his ghostly companions delivered themselves of this stormy world, he could resist no longer.

Between splashes I spoke. "Come my poor wayfaring children," or some such bilge. It was hardly necessary; they needed no further inducement. Soon, to Alexis' amazement, they were almost all gone, all but the painter and the baby. The painter stood naked, with the naked child staring down the hole. The hold grew strangely quiet. Go, thought Alexis. Go! For she had been watching the baby ever since the dentist's attention had been diverted from her. She pleaded silently that they would jump and when they did not her patience failed her. Without thinking she stepped from her hiding place.

"Please," she said. "Go away."

Howl, who had drawn near the painter and the child, turned towards her, as did the ghost. The painter smiled and held out the baby for Alexis. "There you are," she said to Alexis. And Alexis slowly advanced towards them. The baby's feet kicked and his tiny fists punched the air excitedly. It was a he, she could have noticed now that he was dandled before her, but as she drew near her eyes were not on his genitalia or on his young-ancient toothless face but on something else: a mark under his heart. A wound.

"Don't listen, Alexis," said Howl, rushing towards her. "The baby is dead, Alexis. Years ago." He stepped into her path. "Let it go." She fought him aside; her eyes never leaving the scar. The baby gurgled. The painter laughed.

I, for my part—not wanting to be left out—called to her: "Alexis, this is your chance."

But Howl kept her from me. "It is not your responsibility!" he said. "It is not your baby." With uncanny strength she pushed Howl out of her way. He grabbed her arm and she dragged him with her until she was an arm's length from the child.

"Touch it," said the painter. "It no longer hurts him."

And Alexis tried to touch the wound under the heart, but her fingers fell short. Howl wrestled her back.

"This is all so painful," I said. "Come, Alexis. Surely you have had enough. In me you can be with the child for ever. Think of that."

By now the baby was struggling in the woman's arms, wanting to be free. Alexis watched its tiny face grow redder and redder and knew what must necessarily follow. She struggled to free her hands from Howl's grasp but he held her tightly, having no idea that all she wanted to do now was cover her ears. And then it was too late. The baby screamed and the scream was like a siren.

Howl, caught off guard by the astounding shriek, lost his footing and Alexis pulled herself away. For a moment she stood transfixed by the cry. She stumbled backwards and then, picking herself up, she ran. Covering her ears she ran for the corridor that led from the hold. I called after her. The painter called after her.

Howl called after her. But all she heard was the baby. Whatever had possessed her to want the child vanished. She raced for the engine room, for the noise that might block out that scream of immortal innocence.

She raced clear past the fire escape which had led her to the hold. She crossed the engine room on a catwalk. She flew through the hatchway of a second bulkhead and then a third. The scream echoed after her. She climbed a ladder to a loft. If only I can keep moving, she thought. To get away, farther and farther from it. She climbed three storeys, slipped on the top rung, and dangled for a moment in the darkness. If she fell, the sound would die, she reasoned, but could not be sure. With a last burst of energy she clambered to safety. She was dizzy but ran on along the narrow steel walkway, running on the adrenalin rush of her near fall.

It was some time before she realized that she had left the screaming behind her. She distrusted her own ears. It was still there, like the stars in the daylight. She slowed down anyway, almost ready to drop. Finally she pulled open a hatchway and found herself on a floor that was not grating, though not one she had ever seen before. She leaned against the door for a moment, gasping for breath. She listened but could not distinguish the sounds of the ship from the sounds in her head; in her head the baby was still after her.

She pulled open another door and found herself in a vertical service trunk, much smaller than the one by which she and Howl had entered the hold. She began to climb. She thought of Howl and her legs went weak. But there was nothing she could do for him.

It was really just a spiral staircase leading up to somewhere well forward in the ship. She had lost all track of distance in her escape. The service trunk had no other entrances. The walls close around her were lined with great multi-coloured bundles of electrical wires. She assumed it was to service these that the trunk existed at all. In the warm darkness she imagined herself climbing up through the spinal cord with its network of nerves delivering sensation to the body. If I climb high enough, she thought, I will reach the brain. Her weariness was making her faint. Her legs were giving way beneath her. She was hallucinating. Perhaps there is no end, she thought. Perhaps the mad little undead dentist had throttled her and, being too busy to notice, she had kept on running. At least I am heading heavenwards, she thought, but it would be hell to be trapped on a stairwell whichever direction it headed.

Then at last the stairs ended at a little platform. There was no doorway. But in the low ceiling, under which she could not stand at her full height, there was a manhole-sized hatch. She decided to lie down on the little platform and rest. The platform was plenty large enough to curl up on.

She was much higher in the ship now, and as soon as she lay down she found herself being flung from side to side. She didn't mind. It was no worse than going to bed horribly drunk.

The hole. She had let Howl talk it out of her and she had lost it. "I'm sorry Teddy," she mumbled, drunkenly. She heard a door open at the bottom of the stairs. She pictured Howl standing there looking up. She imagined him climbing, climbing, and as he climbed in her tortured mind his features aged and his skin ruptured until it was Teddy coming home late from the club and she, drunk in bed, waited for him, frightened to death. No. She shook the vision from her mind and it was Mechelney on the stairs, Mechelney's voice calling up to her. "Ye can't keep this up, mizzy," he shouted. And then it was Dr. Troubridge coming to her. "You will be careful, won't you? There have been incidents...."

It was all coming unravelled. "It's what I have to believe for now," she mumbled, but "now" was running out. There wasn't much left of it. She would soon be home. Inexorably "now" was being brought home to her, or her to it.

"The hole," she murmured, feeling sick from being tossed around. Dr. Troubridge will want to hear about the hole, she thought, and against the rocking of the ship and the crazy spinning of her head, she climbed dizzily to her feet. The hole was back, behind her, but she was too confused now to have any idea where she was or where she was going. As hunchbacked as Quasimodo she heaved with her shoulder on the exit above her, but without moving the heavy cover. Then her fingers scrambled with the metal dogs which battened the manhole cover in place. The hatch cover seemed to fly away into the freezing night. Alexis shinnied up and out and found herself on the weather deck. The storm was raging. The wind cut through her like a thousand blades. The deck and all the deck machinery were coated in ice. She lost her footing and slid first this way and then that. She gave up holding on. The ship would shake her off, just as she had shaken off the ghosts of Fastyngange. Why fight it? She found her feet one last time and through the freezing rain she waved up at the bank of lights that was the bridge. Then once again her feet were swept from under her. Her head hit the deck and she remembered nothing else.

A call went down from the bridge. Someone had left the top off the booby-hatch.

26

Alexis woke in the infirmary. She didn't need to see to know: the tight fit of the sheets, the unforgiving pillow, the sharp tang of smells, the unforgiving light. Through blurry eyes she recognized the pebble glass of the door on the other side of which she had stood the day of sailing and had hoped for a kind doctor.

Without moving a muscle larger than those controlling her eyes, she tried to assess the damage. She ached all over; that was the good news. She could not feel the cold weight of a cast on any limb. There did not appear to be tubes transfusing liquids into her blood. She allowed herself to fidget minutely, waiting for the stab of pain indicating a rupture of some kind. Nothing.

Her fidgeting must have been more noticeable than she intended it to be. A cupboard door closed and a face swam into focus over her. The face was framed by a nurse's cap. "Welcome back," said the face. The accent was Canadian.

Alexis grunted. Her lips were salty. Her mouth and throat were numb. The nurse brought her a glass of water. Alexis sat up and drank a thimbleful. Over the nurse's shoulder, across the cabin, a porthole let in a stream of sunlight.

"May I get up?" she asked in a gravelly voice.

The porthole framed low hills, pines weighed down with glistening snow, trees bare but shining with a coating of ice, like nets of light. The sky was blue.

"Home," she said.

The nurse smiled. "We'll be docking in less than an hour. You don't look too wobbly. How are you feeling?"

Alexis thought for a moment. "Famished," she said.

"I'll see what I can do," said the nurse, and headed for the door. Then she turned. "A table-mate was by this morning to see you. Gloria?"

"Yes?"

"You were friends with the saxophone player...."

There was no alarm but no expectation in Alexis' voice when she replied, "How is he?"

"I'm afraid he's dead," said the nurse. "I'm sorry."

"How?" asked Alexis dispassionately.

"He was found in his room. It looks like it might have been a massive heart attack. No visible wounds. There will have to be an autopsy in Halifax."

They will find nothing, Alexis thought. "May I see him?"

The nurse, true to her training, saw nothing unusual in her patient's request. "Are you sure you're up to it?"

"I am a nurse," said Alexis. The other woman nodded that she understood this fact. "He saved my life," she added.

The nurse looked at her patient standing by the porthole in her shapeless green hospital shift. "You'll need to wear something warm," she said. She went to the closet and took out Alexis' own dressing gown and slippers. Then she pointed to a door at the other end of the room. "I'll be back in a few minutes," she said.

The room off the infirmary was cool, a tiny windowless morgue with a single gurney. Howl's face looked as if he were blowing a very high, slightly sour note on the saxophone, pushing hard to make it tuneful. She had seen other corpses with such a look of agony, as if they were still waiting for something to happen.

217

Alexis listened to the outer office. The nurse had gone. Hesitantly, she placed her thumb on Howl's chin. She pushed it down slowly.

"I was wondering how long it would take you," said the mouth without moving. It was remarkable to Alexis how very little Howl's accent influenced my voice. "Congratulations," I said.

"Was that meant to be cruel?" she demanded.

"Cruel?"

"I didn't mean to kill him," she said.

"Nor did you. He killed himself," I said. "No, no. My congratulations were sincere. You have rid yourself—and me, I might add—of that plague of ghosts."

"Have I?" Alexis asked.

"All gone," I said exuberantly.

"Why should I believe you?" she asked. "You lied to me. You probably lied to Howl. You lied to all of those hideous creatures. What makes you think I will ever trust you again?"

She pressed Howl's mouth shut, closing me off from her behind the wall of his teeth. She sobbed deeply. She was talking to a dead man and for some unearthly reason found this more poignant than talking to a mere ghost. She controlled herself. There wasn't much time left.

"He killed himself for you," she said. She took some morbid delight in holding the corpse's mouth closed so that I could not answer. But there was too much she needed to know for the game to go on long.

"How do I know the ghosts are gone?" she demanded, opening Howl's mouth.

"Look for yourself," I said. "Ask your friend Gloria who showed in the dining room for breakfast and how changed they seemed, as if they had just woken up from a bad dream: the captain weary after a stormy night in an old tub; Morgan, a rather cheery soul, after all. And the dentist—well, a dentist—a bore but not a lecherous bore."

"And the baby?" said Alexis, making herself ask.

"Still there," I replied promptly. "The changeling only a bad dream; all the hosts a little disoriented but otherwise themselves.

"Howl was right," I continued. "It's something to do with the sea. Heaven knows how long they might have waited in Fastyngange to be released. They guessed that, you know. That's why they got so edgy. They didn't like this trip. You should have let them have their way from the start. It would have saved a lot of trouble."

"The baby was wounded," she said. "Who could do a thing like that?"

She was not addressing me. She was miles away and drifting, and my life depended on her. "As for Howl," I said drawing her back to the face before her, hoping there was enough residue of life in it to bring her back, "he was bound and determined to get to know me. Had he, in his day, wandered up to Fastyngange, I would have had him in no time. But you have changed all that. Now that I'm portable, so to speak, people like Howl feel they have a choice to possess rather than be possessed. A dangerous alternative. You'll have to be careful."

"Why did he do it?" she asked, the wounded baby forgotten for the moment.

"He said with me inside him he'd blow the stops right out of his horn. Aptly put, I'd say."

"Why does it have to be so violent?" said Alexis, after a moment.

"All these quests are," I said. "Single-mindedness of purpose leaves behind it a path of casualties."

"*But I didn't kill him!*" she pleaded, squeezing her eyes shut.

"Of course not," I consoled her. Letting my voice drop, I allowed the conformation of Howl's vocal cavities to affect my utterance. Some bit of him clung to those three words, for when she addressed me again it was with something akin to tenderness.

"I can't take much more of this," she said. "I seem to be running all the time."

"It will not be so hard from now on," I said, borrowing Howl's sweet voice to lend my promise veracity. "With the ghosts gone I will not be so difficult to bear."

"But you are dangerous," she whispered.

"And you are so close!" I hissed back at her. "You are home, Alexis. On your own turf."

"Shhh!" she whispered, clamping Howl's mouth shut. The nurse had returned to the outer office. She was talking; there was someone with her. There was no more time. Alexis had to make the decision for herself. She did. But how is it to be done, she wondered. Then she remembered kissing Howl, and me rising in her to meet him. The thought of consummating that embrace now made her feel ill. She looked down into Howl's anguished face. It was Howl she would be kissing, she told herself. One last kiss. Shaking, she bent forwards and kissed his cool lips.

I travelled into her, not like a thunderous thing but like a slick-skinned, slightly electric eel. It was done in a moment. She did not feel faint. I had been right about that. She looked at Howl's face one last time before turning from the gurney. His face was sweet with repose. She began to cry softly to herself. Now I would always taste to her of Howl.

27

It was Gloria's idea to take a room in a hotel. She convinced Alexis to come with her. The nurse had brought her back to the infirmary and she had stayed with Alexis, helping her pack and disembark. The captain had shaken hands at the gangplank, looking peaked, glad to be docked. They saw the dentist and his wife leaving the boat, arm in arm; the dentist looking, as the hole had predicted, like a man freshly woken from a dreadful dream. Rosemarie, looking tearfully content to have him back, waved happily at her two tablemates: "Thank you, girls," she called through the crowd on the gangplank.

Alexis searched the crowd for the baby; Gloria in tow did not know what to make of her friend's excessive concern. Then when the child was located at last (in the arms of a grandparent) Alexis would not go near it, could not bring herself to so much as say goodbye.

Gloria changed her flight to Vancouver. Alexis had been planning to take the train home — one last romantic gesture — but she had not bought a ticket. Too weary to resist Gloria's kindness, she accepted the overnight accommodation arrangement, though there was a brusqueness to the woman's generosity which disturbed her. She realized on shore what she had not realized on shipboard—that if Gloria was not a ghost she was, at least, a stranger to her—beautiful and kind, but an unknown commodity. There had been too many strangers. Alexis was tired of strangers.

The room overlooked the harbour. A storm settled in; the water took on the same dull lustre as the battleships at the naval base. The sky was black with snow. Gloria opened the bar in her room and mixed them drinks. She ordered supper from room service and when it arrived and they were comfortably seated by the window eating, she said, "Now I think you really do owe me an explanation."

Alexis had suspected her friend's benevolence had a price. But she was reluctant to speak because of what had happened to Howl. It was what had happened to Howl that had pricked Gloria's interest. So Alexis told her story in an abbreviated version.

Gloria did not respond as Howl had done. She sat very quietly, her hands folded in her lap. There was no mad twinkle in her eye. She had left her meal half eaten. "I think we should phone Teddy," she said. "Tell him the good news." Alexis didn't think that was possible. "Then don't you think we should phone Teddy's doctor?" Gloria asked. With a growing sense of panic, Alexis suggested it could wait. But Gloria persisted. "I can help," she said. "What is his name?"

Alexis would not look at her. She looked out at the leaden sky. She shook her head. Gloria took Alexis' chin in her hand firmly. "Your nurse said you kept going on about a Dr. Troubridge. Asking for him. Have you a phone book?" she asked.

"Why?" Alexis asked.

Gloria leaned on the arms of Alexis' chair. With her eyes no less than her body she held Alexis captive. "You're home now, honey. I think it's time to call the doctor," she said. "I'll do it if you like."

Alexis sagged in her chair. Gloria found her purse and pulled out a small black book with worn edges and loose pages. Alexis grabbed it from her. She clutched it to her breast, resisting Gloria's gentle appeals.

"It's all going to come apart now," said Alexis.

Finally she gave in. Gloria opened the phone book to "T". She phoned a number in Toronto. "Dr. Troubridge, please," she said.

Alexis looked out at the ferry scuttling across the bleak water from Bedford. Gloria's conversation faded into the background until it became one with the hum of the heating. At long last it ended and Gloria was kneeling in front of her looking at her, with an expression of curiosity and consternation. It was an expression Alexis had got quite used to before leaving. "This must have been one helluva ordeal for you," she said. "They've been worried."

Alexis nodded. "What else did they say?" she asked. "Did they warn you I was dangerous?"

Gloria's face belied any fear on her part. "Are you?"

Alexis shrugged her shoulders. "Not to you," she replied.

"And what about yourself?" Gloria asked.

Alexis frowned. "I'm not suicidal, whatever he thinks."

Gloria patted her hand and sat back in her own chair. "What are we going to do with you?" she asked.

"Did he say anything about Teddy?" said Alexis.

Gloria nodded but said nothing.

"What?" Alexis demanded, sitting upright in her chair. "Is he all right?"

Gloria nodded again. She sighed. "The doctor says he's gone to England."

Alexis' face clouded and then, unexpectedly, brightened. Teddy was better and there was still time. It wouldn't all have to happen at once. Unexpectedly she laughed. "He won't find it there now," she said, and for an instant she beamed radiantly. "I've brought it home, haven't I!"

Gloria patted her hand and said, "The doctor is looking forward to hearing from you."

PART 3

THE ROOM AT REST-HARROW

28

The old drunk was getting hungry. Listening to the hole talk made him think of the hole growing in his own belly. He had had a good feed the night before, mid-booze-up. He had left the guys at the tavern and stumbled over to Mary Magdalene's near the mission for the Women's Guild Pancake Tuesday. The head of the Women's Guild was a personal friend. She'd always give him a coffee for free after Sunday mass when the churchgoers crowded down into the church basement to let off steam. The old drunk stayed well out of everyone's way, in a corner where his attire and smell weren't likely to offend the regulars, and Father Mowbry always came over and gave him a hearty handshake and sometimes slipped him a dollar or two. He made about as much coming to church as a choir boy. But he had surprised the head of the Women's Guild and Father Mowbry the previous evening by paying for his own supper.

Times were difficult at old Mary Mags. Everyone had to do his part. There had been a fire. Some of the roof had caved in. There was smoke and water damage. Father Mowbry had been particularly eloquent in his sermons lately, as if the fire had been some kind of message from above.

"How much longer have I got?"

The old drunk, dragged from his reverie, looked down at the hole at his feet and then up at the sky. He had taken the opportunity during one of the hole's infrequent breaks in its story to make himself more comfortable. He had piled up discarded pelts against a packing case. Now he swivelled in this throne to face the east. But he could not see dawn from where he sat. For that matter, he couldn't remember ever having seen dawn in the city—not until it was fully broken.

"Old man?"

"I'd say about an hour," said the drunk, guessing.

"Just enough time," muttered the hole. Then it added, with an oily and completely feigned humility, "That is, if it is your wish for me to go on?"

The old drunk pondered this question though he was sober enough by now to recognize the wheedling tone as anything but flattery.

"That depends," he said.

"On..." the hole invited, provocatively.

The old drunk growled. "Whether the girl gets out of this alive," he said, and was rewarded by a shiver of something like power if he could but have recognized it as such.

"Didn't I tell you it was a romance?" said the hole.

The old drunk chuckled at the indignation in the hole's voice. "It ain't like any romance I ever heard," he said.

"But the night is not over," replied the hole, hastily. "And it will be over before I can finish if we go on like this. Don't you see, I *must* finish. You are my sole jury," the hole added, and in a tone of abject toadiness, it continued: "My very existence, as humble as it has become, depends on your grace, my man."

The drunk reclined on his throne savouring the hole's plea. It had been a long time since anyone had depended on him for anything. "I've always wondered what jury duty would be like," he said. "A pal of mine once made a killing on a murder trial—sat there for three months raking in the dough."

"Yes, yes," said the hole.

"Okay," said the drunk, sensing the hole's impatience and not certain any more if he could risk annoying it. "But your story had better end on an upnote or this jury'll bring in a charge of mischief in the first degree."

"Oh, we can't have that," said the hole and began to speak again, hurriedly now.

29

From the window Alexis could see two loonies in the park, playing tennis without a net. The men were inadequately dressed against the cold, one in an old sweatsuit with torn sleeves and the other in a stained raincoat. One wore his hair long, kept out of his eyes with a headband. Both their weatherbeaten faces sported crusty old beards. One was barehanded, the other wore woollen gloves out of which raw red fingers poked to grasp his battered catgut racket. One of them wore sneakers, the other plain black loafers which he continually lost chasing dribblers. There were plenty of dribblers. The ball had little life left in it; the men, not much life to lend it. The November wind kept grabbing the dirty orange ball from them and flinging it around the chain-link compound. Alexis could hear them shout to each other from time to time above the dull roar of traffic on Queen Street: "Love fifteen," or "Game point." The game moved along briskly without a net to worry about.

"Mrs. Forgeben?"

Alexis turned from the window. The receptionist stood beside the door to the office's inner sanctum.

"Dr. Troubridge will see you now."

Alexis hesitated. She had already seen him once since her return. Very little had happened. They had only felt each other out that day. It would not be the same this time—she felt sure of that. He would be probing today. Still, she thought, there is Fastyngange to entertain him with. She found herself remembering the morning she had stood in the vestibule at the Marriotts', hoping Isabelle would catch her before she could steal away to Fastyngange. She would not escape this time. She felt a moment of panic replaced almost immediately by a strange elation. She clutched her purse and walked resolutely into the doctor's office, even managing a tight smile at his receptionist as she concentrated on not wobbling on her high heels. It had been a very long time since she had worn heels and she had lost her mastery of them.

Straight-backed she lowered herself into the faded brown leather seat beside Troubridge's desk and, folding one leg carefully over the other, she arranged the pleats in her dress. He did not notice. He was writing something in a folder, though he had looked up and smiled at her as she entered, in a way that was as neutral as his grey suit and his brown wood desk and the room that had once been a ward. She was sure it had been a ward; she could smell the disinfectant behind the diplomas and the framed Klee prints.

She had forgotten how much like a lawyer he looked, with the controlled grey at the temples, the sharply cut lapel. He mumbled an apology as he dotted the "i"s of a report. Then he closed the file and placed it in a black briefcase open on the floor beside him. He clicked shut the gold clasps and gave each combination lock a tumble before turning his full and—so his expression would have her understand—undivided attention to his patient.

"Alexis," he said, leaning back in his chair, his hands clasped behind his head, "you look rested already. Things must be good at home?" His grey eyes twinkled. He was looking forward to the session with her, she thought.

"Things are fine," she said.

"Good, good," he said hurriedly. Itching to get at her, she thought. She was not displeased. In fact she found his attention gratifying. "Ready to begin?" He did not take her approval for granted but waited for a nod before turning on his tape recorder.

"Where were we?" she asked.

He seemed to like her choice of the first person plural and adopted it readily. "*We* were sitting in front of a fire at Chewton Cottage," he said, grinning slightly.

"It doesn't surprise me," she said, "that you find the doctor the most interesting part of my story so far." She had adopted a mildly disgruntled tone of voice which Troubridge took in good humour.

"We're a vain lot," he said, smiling.

"You find my other Dr. Troubridge amusing?" she said.

"Yes, I do," he answered frankly. "So do you, I think. He is a charming fellow, after all. An excellent cook, a good listener, a devoted gardener. Roses. A rose-covered cottage. Lovely."

"But you don't believe it really exists," she said. "Or Fastyngange either, I suppose. I have made them up."

The doctor leaned forwards, his hands clasped together on his desk. She noticed his manicured nails. "At this moment, what I believe isn't really important," he said. "But real or not, this other doctor is a very fine specimen of humanity."

"You make him sound like something in a petri dish," she said.

The doctor, however, was not inclined to keep up the banter. "Psychoanalysis itself is a fabrication," he said, "and a highly useful one."

"So that's what you think of *my* Dr. Troubridge. He is a useful fabrication," she continued lightly.

Troubridge weighed his response. "I believe he is a fine specimen of a man," he reiterated. "An advanced manifestation of what we call in my business transference. Patients sometimes think they are falling in love with their analysts. Far from being an impediment to the process of healing, it is often a positive sign. We tend to see transference as an indication that the patient is serious, is ready to enter into a meaningful phase in her relationship with her therapist."

"I don't love you," said Alexis bluntly. "I don't even like you."

"No," said the doctor, unable, she noticed, to resist a professional smirk at the gibe. "But you loved this other Troubridge who lived in a peaceful, storybook cottage, who shared your obsession for an alarming and secret castle, and who, being retired, had all the time in the world for you and only you."

"Loved?" Alexis asked. "Have I fallen out of love with him, or do you mean he no longer exists?"

Troubridge shrugged. "That's up to you. But whether he exists or not and whether Fastyngange exists or not, I want to hear all about them."

"You needn't drool," said Alexis, grinning ruefully. "You look like you're gloating. Am I to become a paper in a journal? Will you become famous now, doctor, with a neurotic behaviour named after you?" She found herself thinking of her own dear Dr. Troubridge with his little bound journal on Fastyngange, the cover the same grey as his eyes.

This Troubridge would not be ruffled. "If I turn you into a paper I shall be sure to entitle it 'The Fastyngange Syndrome', if you like."

"The Fastyngange Syndrome sounds fine," said Alexis firmly, as if they had reached a deal. "I should be credited as a research assistant. I'm the one who did all the leg work."

Troubridge agreed but added, "You *and* this other Dr. Troubridge—let's not forget him—who wouldn't pry but wanted so much to help you."

"And who didn't feel the need to subject me to a battery of psychopharmacological experiments," said Alexis, needling, her voice on edge. "And when that failed, shock therapy."

"So you do remember something of what happened before you left," said Troubridge, his eyes locking hers.

"The room brings it back," she replied.

"Good," he said. "It didn't last week."

"Being *dragged* from the room," Alexis added, her voice cracking. It was coming back to her even as she spoke: the wild tantrums, but most of all the silence. For an uncomfortable moment she was afraid the silence would return and claim her again.

"Let us go back to Fastyngange," said the doctor, seeing the anguish in her eyes.

Relief surged through her. She could talk about Fastyngange. She launched in with a sense of urgency that propelled her story further and further from the dreaded silence. She had the story down pat. She recalled every detail. She had practised on Howl and then Gloria. Now it all seemed as if that had been in preparation for Dr. Troubridge. Her body jerked violently: once, twice.

"Are you all right?" the doctor asked.

She must talk, she told herself. Having nothing to say had turned into hysteria and hysteria into incarceration and incarceration into withdrawal and withdrawal into regression and regression into a kind of pathetic, borrowed sanity and sanity into release into her mother's—not her husband's—care and release into escape from it all to England and that—well, that was what she was here to talk about. She was back and the nothingness in her had gained form in her time away. Nothingness had gained a voice.

She had hated this Troubridge but she returned to him readily enough, albeit trembling, glorying in having something to tell him. It had not gone well the week before and she had left the session feeling cheated. She had watched Troubridge's face keenly when she started telling him of her odyssey, her quest. She had looked for signs of curiosity, horror, enlightenment, compassion. She had seemed to see nothing. He had stared at his desk most of the session as if reading a score he had composed, mildly titillated at subtleties in her performance, mildly annoyed at hesitant passages. In the outer office that day, the receptionist had been printing out some interminable paper. The word processor had chattered away, back and forth, boustrophedon—like oxen plowing a field. Troubridge might as easily have been listening to it as to her for all the astonishment that registered on his face. Perhaps, Alexis had thought, he has a place where he keeps astonishment—beside his second pair of contacts in the washroom vanity.

She had wanted to break through his smugness. She now saw that he was with her, the score abandoned, and it occurred to her that perhaps, in his professional, glossy way, he had been as frightened of their confrontation the previous week as she had been. Now she would captivate him, she thought, for she had reached the point in her story where she finally entered the keep and confronted the oubliette. The talking hole. He interrupted her, as she fully expected he might, but she was surprised at what feature of her story had claimed his attention.

"Mechelney again," he said. "He keeps cropping up. It was Mechelney who called to you in the keep?" She nodded, eyeing him suspiciously. "Did he come up?" he asked.

She shook her head. "I'll get to that in a minute if you'll let me continue," she said.

"Yes," said Troubridge. "Of course."

She continued, remembering every word I had spoken to her on that first encounter. "If you think you have nothing to learn from a hole," she recited, "then I suggest that you have not examined your life closely enough." She looked at the doctor then, almost triumphantly. See what I have brought you, she was thinking. Well, just wait until I reveal what else this hole had to say. But to her surprise Troubridge's mind was not on the hole.

"Did Mechelney *ever* come up to the keep?" he asked.

She did not try to hide her annoyance. "In the end," she said, "which I will never reach if you keep interrupting."

"Tell me about the end," he insisted, leaning forwards, elbows on his knees. "Make a leap."

"The story isn't about Mechelney." She cut him off petulantly. "Isn't the story good enough?"

"It's remarkable," he said. "I trust the story. There's a maxim—have you heard it?—'Always trust the tale, not the teller.' "

"Thanks for your vote of confidence," Alexis replied tartly.

"I don't trust your interpretation of what is and what isn't important about your incredible story, Alexis. Interpretation is my job, isn't it? Isn't that why you are here?"

She did not favour him with an answer. The doctor was intrigued, but his line of questions unaccountably alarmed her. "You're missing the point," she said, shaking her head.

"Please," he said, his voice imploring and at the same time comforting, "tell me what happened when Mechelney came up to the room in the keep, and I promise we'll get back to the oubliette later. You've got to admit a talking hole is going to take a bit of time to get used to. Tell me about this estate agent fellow. Him, I can deal with. Indulge me."

His hands were holding hers. She hadn't noticed until then. Noticing now, she wondered if anything else had happened without her knowing. Had he called the orderlies? Was he holding her still until they arrived? But his hands didn't feel like that; they were cool, relaxed. She could slip her fingers out of his grasp easily. She looked at his face. She wondered if there had been some kind of scuffle or encounter between them, for his hair was tousled and for a moment he was the kind gardener of Chewton Cottage. She could have told *him* anything he wanted to hear. The pent-up resistance streamed down her arms into her hands and into the doctor's cool fingers. She let go.

She recalled the night Mechelney had trapped her in the whispering gallery and then followed her up to the keep. She remembered the fight, and falling, and waking up to find him gone. She remembered what I had told her then: "Don't worry

236

about him. He'll not bother you again." She had concluded the worst.

All the time she spoke she stared at her hands held in the doctor's, hypnotized by them, quietened. Her hands were still rough next to his, but they were healing. The nights of digging up my circle of stones had damaged them irreparably, she had thought. But now, not three weeks later, the chipped and torn fingernails were pink and glowing, and the bruised and chafed skin was recovering.

"I didn't kill him," she said calmly.

"No," said the doctor solemnly. "You didn't."

"The hole did," she said, glad to have the doctor concur with her, but equally concerned that the blame should fall where it belonged. She was disappointed when the doctor seemed uninterested in her accusation. He paused and tensed. Though it did not show in his face, she could feel him readying for combat. She slipped her hands out of his and he gave them up carefully, like fine stemware.

"Do you recall ever having met Mechelney before the afternoon you discovered Fastyngange?" he asked.

"He's not important," Alexis replied calmly but firmly, refuting the challenge in his voice. "It's the hole that is important. It's the hole that told me what happened to Teddy. That's what this is all about! Or don't you want to hear?"

"I think you know I do," he said, but his tone was perfunctory, as if what he thought didn't really matter. She glared at him and under her gaze he smoothed his ruffled hair back into place. The kind Dr. Troubridge faded away in the gesture and she suffered the sinking feeling she would not ever be able to recover him. The strangely mingled panic and elation that had struck in the outer office returned. "Do you remember Mechelney?" he persisted. "*Try to remember, Alexis.*"

She didn't want to remember—not when it was put to her like that. She wanted to tell him a story. She could remember her story in the most painstaking detail. Why wouldn't he shut up and listen to her story?

"Your landlord," he prompted. "Do you remember him?"

"No," she said. "You've got it wrong. He was the estate agent, or that's what he called himself. Fastyngange wasn't really his—"

"You were fighting with Teddy," Troubridge said, his voice tolerant but unyielding. "You started to scream and your landlord came up to see what was the matter. Mr. Mechelney."

"He had no right!" Alexis said, angry at this imposture. "He was a meddling old bastard. He acted as though he owned the place."

"He did own the place," countered the doctor. "Your flat on Queen Street. He was afraid for you."

"He had no right to interfere," she said, shaking violently now. "That's why the hole got him," she cried. "If he hadn't come up into the keep he'd still be alive. The hole was only trying to protect me." She broke then, and began to cry.

In her mind's eye she saw the keep crumbling again. Troubridge got her a drink of water, tap water, and while she drank it she longed for the bracing coldness of the well water at Fastyngange. But the well was gone now, as was the castle, and suddenly she was sobbing softly at the thought of all that cool, clear water clogged with debris.

"It was destroyed, you know," she said. "Fastyngange. Demolished. He won't ever find it."

"Teddy?"

She nodded, frowning through her tears. Who else might she have meant? Why else had he gone to England? If only the doctor would let her explain what happened.

Troubridge wheeled his chair directly in front of her. She sniffed, and took a Kleenex from her purse. "I wonder," he said when she had composed herself again, "I wonder if you are well enough now—for I think you are brave enough—to try something with me, Alexis. I wonder if we can begin to wedge into your story another story."

"Your interpretation?" Alexis asked, suddenly tired.

The doctor shook his head, but he smiled conspiratorially. "Not my interpretation but Mechelney's. And Teddy's for that matter, though he was reluctant to give it."

"Teddy wasn't there," she said, but her heart wasn't up to quarrelling.

"Perhaps not at Fastyngange," said the doctor, "but at the flat, the night of your breakdown. You've heard this account before, but let me refresh your memory. May I?"

She cast him a sullen look. "I suppose this is going to be the truth," she grumbled, investing the word "truth" with all the disdain she could muster—which wasn't much. She was tired of chasing it around in circles. She wanted the game to speed up.

The doctor said, "Around here the truth is just another way of looking at what happened."

She shrugged her shoulders. "My doctor used to say that," she said. He laughed at the ridicule in her voice as if they were sharing a huge joke. He resumed his position behind the desk, though some of the authority that place had commanded seemed to have been displaced in rolling his chair over to comfort her. Alexis did not feel quite so distanced from him any longer. She sat up straight again. She even managed to smile. "Okay," she said, "wedge," liking the feel of the word in her mouth—firm yet soft-edged, snugly fitting.

"I'll tell you what I know and you stop me any time you want. All right?"

"All right," she said, leaning her head back on the chair.

"You and Teddy lived in a flat above a store on Queen Street," Troubridge began. "A taxidermist's shop, owned and operated by one Arthur Mechelney, who was your landlord. He liked you two a lot, helped you renovate the top floor. He still does like you, I dare say. He is not dead."

Troubridge waited for her to remonstrate. Her gaze shifted from the ceiling to her lap, glancing his way for only a fraction of a second, only long enough to search his eyes for disapprobation. She found none.

"Well?" she said, her voice resentful but under control.

"Mechelney knew you were having troubles," Troubridge continued. "He had heard you arguing. He had even heard you scream from time to time. He didn't really want to interfere but he became so worried that he collared you on the stairs one evening to talk to you about it. He hadn't meant to, but he caught you by surprise and you lashed out at him. You argued. He said some things in anger. He was on his way up to your place to apologize later that night when he heard you and Teddy fighting. In renovating the flat, there had been a lot of insulation put in to keep the sounds of the city out and the sounds of Teddy's band rehearsals in. He suddenly realized that what he heard from time to time was only the tip of the iceberg. Listening to you outside your door he became frightened—so frightened that he broke in. That's when you attacked him, or so he says."

Again the doctor paused, allowing her a chance to modify the story. She looked steadily at him. She was not on trial, she reminded herself. She said nothing.

"In the struggle," the doctor continued, "Mechelney, in self-defence he claims, threw you against a wall and you were knocked unconscious. When you woke up in hospital you were sure you had killed him."

"Who?"

"Mechelney."

"And Teddy?"

"You refused to see him," said Troubridge. "You were afraid of him; said that he had it in for you because you had wounded him. Teddy claimed to have no idea what you were talking about. You started screaming about a wound. 'Get him to show you his wound,' you shouted at your attendants. The wound you had ostensibly inflicted on him in your fight became a predominant motif of your disturbance."

"And had I wounded him?" Alexis asked.

"Not that we know of," said Troubridge.

"Did you look?" she demanded.

"Not personally. But he was examined at the hospital, when you were admitted. There were no signs of violence," the doctor explained. "Later you confessed to one of your nurses that Teddy had 'hang-ups', though you wouldn't go into details. The arguments had been about sex."

"I know that!" she snorted. "We couldn't make it. Why do you think I traipsed half-way around the world to find this place, Fastyngange? That's where it started, you know. That's where Teddy's problem began. I tracked it down."

"Do you want to tell me about it?" Troubridge asked.

The question was posed so delicately her suspicions were immediately aroused. "You were giving me *your* version of the story," she snapped.

"Not mine," he corrected. "Mechelney's and your husband's."

"And what's Teddy's version of our 'problem'?" she demanded defiantly.

"Should it be different from your own?" Troubridge replied evenly, refusing to tip his hand.

"Just tell me!" Alexis shouted, and wished immediately that she had not. She sank in her chair, her head in her hand. She sipped some water from her glass and tried to rein in her breathing. She didn't look at Troubridge until she had more or less regained self-control.

"Would you like to stop now?" he asked. She shook her head. He did not seem convinced about going on and she wanted him to, despite everything. There was, she was beginning to see, a kind of logic to the contradictory stories.

"I tell you what," she said, looking at her watch and managing a weak smile, tinged with desperation. "There's still time enough for me to tell you what the hole said about Teddy, and for you to tell me his version. What do you say, doc?"

241

"Why the hurry, all of a sudden?" he asked, but she didn't stop to answer.

She told him what I had told her. How I had teased her cruelly before relenting and telling her of Teddy's descent into the oubliette. Then she told Troubridge about him finding the dead baby there. "There was a baby among the survivors," she said. "And a baby on shipboard. This baby is important," she said. "It explains everything," she added. "You see? It *was* all Teddy's problem but now that you know the cause of it, surely you can do something. We could come to you together. Wouldn't that be good?"

The doctor was stroking his chin. He too gazed at his watch, calculating. He looked at Alexis and made a decision.

"I'll tell you this now to think about," he said. "You've come a long way but there is still a long way to go. Do you agree?"

She nodded her head obediently. The doctor cleared his throat.

"Your husband came to me several weeks before the night of your breakdown," said Troubridge. "He made the same offer you just did. He wanted to arrange for the two of you to come in together for sexual counselling. At the time he claimed you were frigid."

"That's ridiculous," said Alexis. "And you believed him?"

"I hadn't even met you," said the doctor.

"I mean later," said Alexis, leaning forwards, her fists on the edge of the doctor's desk. "After my accident—the fight."

"I still could reach no conclusion," Troubridge went on. "But, seeing the state you were in, I convinced Teddy you should be committed for observation here at the Institute. Your stay here was marked by anaesthesia and convulsions. You were cataleptic. I could get nothing out of you. Nothing but silence interrupted by screaming fits. Until last week I had not heard you utter more than a few words at any one time. Until today I have never heard you acknowledge there was any problem at all. Teddy did warn me that you had become quite morbidly obsessed about your sexual inadequacy—"

"But it was *his* problem!" Alexis interrupted vehemently.

"Alexis," the doctor replied soothingly, "I am not here to sit in judgement. Sexual dysfunction is inevitably a complex matter. It may very well have started out as Teddy's problem, but you must admit, it has become your problem now."

She was not so incensed that she couldn't recognize a masterful piece of understatement. "If it was purely his problem," the doctor continued, "then yours is a case of the most extraordinary empathy."

She could tell by the cadence of his voice that the session was nearing an end. She wouldn't get the whole story out today; she'd have to carry it around for another week, probably more. Maybe for ever.

"Are you still with me Alexis?" he asked.

She did not speak for a moment. She was watching as a door opened in her mind's eye.

"I can remember the flat," she said meekly. "I remember exactly what it looks like. It's just that I don't remember what happened happening there. Does that make any sense?"

"Yes!" he said, more ardently than she had ever heard him speak. "That is why it is important that you remember what happened at Fastyngange," he said. "Fastyngange *is* what happened! Do you understand?"

"Fastyngange is what happened," said Alexis.

"I promise next time I won't interrupt you." She pressed an imaginary stop button on the edge of the desk just as the doctor pushed the real one on the tape recorder. He smiled at her.

"In the meantime," he said, "I want you to try to hold on to what I have just told you. I don't ask you to believe it, only to keep it in mind. And I, for my part, will bend my mind to an adulterine—is that the term your other Troubridge used?—castle called Fastyngange and the talking oubliette in the keep."

He sighed, exhausted. Then he stood up. Alexis followed suit, not as tall as when she had come in. He guided her towards the door. "You said the castle had been demolished?"

"Yes," she replied.

"Sounds promising," he said. But he stopped her half-way to the door and examined her face. "Do you want me to get you a room in the hospital?" he asked.

"I came here voluntarily," she said defensively.

He assured her, "I only meant it as an option—no drugs, no shock."

She shook her head. "That won't be necessary," she said, careful to make her voice sound convincing.

He looked relieved as he opened the door to the outer office. "I'm sure you are better off with your mom than here," he said reassuringly. "Mrs. Harptree...." The doctor handed Alexis over to his receptionist who did not notice Alexis blush at the mention of her name. "Ms. Forgeben will be back in three days?" he said, turning to Alexis for confirmation. Not a week. There must be something in that.

A date was entered in the book while Alexis waited with becoming docility. Then she was led to the door and let out into the hall. She stood for a moment in the hallway. Dazed. What the doctor had told her sat like a massive weight in her mind—something too big to disregard and difficult to know where to store. It was not news. She had heard it before but it had happened to someone else, surely—not her, not like that. Perhaps she felt me creeping through her towards that weight of fact, circling it like a dog, sniffing it, trying to figure out what to make of it. Somewhere in the Institute a scuffle broke out between a patient and her attendants, and Alexis hurriedly made her way from the outpatients' wing into the chill of the late afternoon.

It was already growing dark but the tennis players were still at their futile game. "Hey!" One of them beckoned to her, his fingers clinging to the chain link of the fenced court. He seemed to want her to join them. Any number could play their game, it seemed. She shook her head. She held her collar tightly closed at her neck and with her head bowed against the wind headed out to the street where she had parked Korrie's car.

It had been quite a session. But a couple of things bothered her as she pulled the car into the rush-hour traffic. She wondered if she should have corrected the doctor's impression that she was staying with her mother. And she wondered whether she should have made it clear that although Fastyngange had been demolished the oubliette at its heart lived on.

30

The train trip from Halifax to Toronto a week earlier had been like a descent into an abandoned mine. The morning sun, bright on the St. Lawrence, had turned the copper roofs of Quebec City to fire. By Montreal a red dusk had settled on the Laurentians; by Toronto the darkness was comprehensive. There had been no snow in the city but the air was heavy with warning: bitter, damp, and polluted.

Her cabby had been talkative. She had tried to put him off by telling him she had just returned from a quest. As it turned out, he had been on a quest of his own. "If you don't mind," he had said, "I'll share the experience with you." The cabby's quest had taken him to Schenectady on a bus, where he had learned that doctoring was just a phase of his ego journey. So he had quit med school and moved to an ashram in Buffalo where he had fried his brains. He was only driving a cab for now, he had said. He sang in a gay men's choir, he had told her, having first checked in his rearview mirror to make certain she was harmless.

It had been Friday. The cab had crawled along Front Street behind a herd of limousines backed up outside the O'Keefe and St. Lawrence centres. Alexis had listened to the cabby's ego journey all the way across Front Street past the culture jam and the specialty shops—this one selling door knobs, that one selling lamps—until they had at last turned down into the Don Valley heading north on the Bayview Extension. The darkness and perhaps her complete lack of response had finally shut the cabby up.

Now she turned onto the extension with the darkness closing in again.

The cars had been legion on the expressway across the river that night, heading south on that artery from the suburbs to engorge the heart of the city. Weekends. Alexis had remembered nights of jazz and breakfasts lasting long into the afternoon.

Alone heading north, the cab had sped past the lights of Cabbagetown twinkling in the trees above the ballpark, then under a silver subway train crossing the valley on the viaduct. A long, familiar turn had pressed Alexis into the corner of the seat as the cab had crept silently under the lights of Rosedale—fewer than the lights of anywhere else in the city and higher in the trees, closer to the stars—what stars there were. How few stars the city commanded, Alexis had thought. Not a holy place.

Again, she made the long slow turn under Rosedale, but this time without the centrifugal dislocation, for her hands were on the steering wheel.

"What did you find?" the cabby had asked, a little sadly. "On your quest."

"A hole," she had told him.

"Isn't it just like that," he had said.

They had climbed out of the valley's darkness and passed the pretty shops of Friday-night busy Bayview Village. There were already Christmas decorations everywhere. Stopped in traffic, Alexis had watched an author signing books in the Sleuth of Baker Street. She had wondered if she had read this man, for there had been a time when she had haunted the Sleuth. That night she had found herself yearning for a good mystery. Something light and with a neat solution.

Then the commercial district had dropped behind them and a series of hills had signalled the neighbourhood in which Alexis had grown up: great sprawling houses receding farther from the road as they grew in size, built low to advertise the expansiveness of the properties upon which they squatted. The cab had swung right off Bayview, right sharply again and again and once more, always right, right into the Graingers' driveway. Twin spotlights above the two-car garage met the taxi's headlights, illuminating the seamless, shiny blacktop of the drive. Hadley resealed it every summer, himself. He kept the outside of the house in apple-pie order.

Alexis had paid the cabby and had tipped him handsomely. He had given her a poster advertising a Christmas concert the choir was giving. She had promised, most unconvincingly, to try to come. He had recognized her insincerity and given her a sour look. "Merry Christmas," he had said. Then, as he had driven off into the weekend, she had wished she could go with him, for he was as harmless as she was. It might have been fun. She had only been home an hour and already she felt left behind.

Her parents' home: biscuit-coloured brick with white shutters and Hadley's immaculately landscaped shrubbery—like a wreath, Korrie liked to say, around the house.

Alexis pulled into a doughnut place. She needed to stall her return. How could she have thought the house would be empty?

She had noticed there was another light on in the kitchen while she was searching for her old set of keys. She had assumed they were on a timer, like the spotlights. Her parents were in Florida at their winter home. She had prepared herself for the drill she must follow upon opening the door. The alarm switch was inside the vestibule closet in the upper right-hand corner. There was a thirty-second delay. She had unlocked the door, flung open the closet, pried up the metal cover of the alarm, and tripped the switch. Then she had listened to the quiet for a full minute—the buzzing quiet of a house that was so electronically equipped it was almost a machine. The ordeal of getting in had exhausted her. Wearily she had carried in her bags, kicking the front door closed.

But even before she had turned on the hall lights she had known there was someone in the kitchen. There had been no sound, no shadow, just a presence not wanting to be found out. Under the hall mirror stood a semi-circular table with a chair to either side. Flung across one of the chairs had been a fur coat. Then stockinged footsteps could be heard crossing the linoleum. A woman had appeared at the doorway and stood there staring out at Alexis, a rolling pin in her hand. She was a slight thing, wearing a neat burgundy-coloured suit and a blouse tied in a floppy bow under her wrinkled chin. She wore fat pearl earrings. Over the suit she wore one of Korrie's aprons. Her hair was pumpkin orange and sat on her head like a shiny helmet, not a strand out of place. For as long as Alexis could remember, this woman's hair had always looked like this. The fear on the woman's face had melted and she had laid her hand heavily on her heart. "*Oy vey*, Alexis," the woman had said, laughing to let off pressure.

"Mrs. Fleischman?"

Alexis had found she was quite giddy and had to sit down on the chair by the mirror.

"A fright I must have given you," Mrs. Fleischman had said, chuckling. "Let me get you a glass of water." She disappeared into the kitchen.

Alexis had closed her eyes. When would it stop? She had come home for a spell of total quiet, a retreat — even if it was a buzzing, suburban kind of retreat — and already she had been scared out of her wits.

The doughnut place was crowded. Alexis ordered a ridiculous pastry and a large coffee and retreated to her mother's car. It was an almost spitefully adolescent act — a deliberate after-school ruining of her appetite. Mrs. Fleischman would not be amused.

"I'll take your bags," Mrs. Fleischman had said, returning to Alexis in the hall with a tall glass of water. And Alexis had not been able to stop the woman from grabbing up her overnight case. "The pink room in the front, right?" The woman had confided this last piece of information with an indulgent smile, as if to say, "We all had pink rooms when we were girls."

Alexis had leaned her head back. The faded wallpaper of the hall was comforting. She had known it all her life. The pattern was raised but the flocking was worn in places. Korrie was as meticulous about the inside of the house as Hadley was about the exterior, but somehow she avoided redecorating the hall year after year. These faded palms were a sacred grove in which the diminished household gods resided. But it had seemed to Alexis that night that the grove had been violated.

From where she sat on that first night back, Alexis had been able to see her graduation photograph in its gold frame sitting on the table beside the couch in the living room. She hadn't needed to see it closely to recognize the plump cheeks and waved hair. But she couldn't really recognize the person at all. She was a ghost of her former self.

Again Mrs. Fleischman had returned, fanning herself from the exertion. "I'm fine now," Alexis had said, claiming the other suitcase. Mrs. Fleischman had seemed relieved.

"Mrs. Fleischman—"

"Please, dear, call me Belle."

"Belle—"

But Belle had interrupted her. "You're probably wondering what I'm doing here, right? Well, I dropped by to look after your mother's plants—so beautiful, she keeps them."

"But doesn't Theresa do them?" Alexis had asked.

"Oh, Theresa comes in now and then to dust and such, but the plants, *bubeleh*—the plants need a friend around. You know what I mean?" Suddenly Belle had looked grief-stricken. "Feh!" she cried. "Listen to me. You come home to your mother's house from a long trip and here I am yak, yak, yakking. I'll fix you something," she had said, heading into the kitchen. Before Alexis could speak, Belle had called back to her. "It's no trouble, dear. No trouble. Go wash up. It'll just take a minute."

Alexis had washed up in the cramped bathroom off her childhood bedroom. When she had returned, the table in the kitchen nook had been set for one and Belle was taking a filet mignon from the broiler. There were canned mushrooms and peas, and a tall glass of orange juice. Belle had sat across from her, beaming, while a frozen apple pie defrosting in the microwave.

"It's what your mom would have wanted," she said. "Now eat."

Despite the entirely unexpected reception, the food had tasted better than Alexis could remember food ever tasting. She had thanked Belle, who was pleased. In this familiar, if sterile, kitchen, with the Wallaces' lights across the backyard and the Mandels' poodles barking to be let in, Alexis had let the strangeness melt away. She had spent far more time in Belle's kitchen. Elizabeth, Belle's daughter, had been Alexis' best friend through grade school. While Korrie's kitchen was a machine, a model of efficiency, Belle's kitchen had always seemed a wonder to Alexis, cluttered and bright and redolent of baking and soup.

Belle had laughed. "That kitchen," she said. Then she had recalled the girls making a cake and how they fought with Elizabeth's older brother Steven and mercilessly baited little Simon—Simon who was at UBC now, studying architecture. "All the birds flown," said Belle, with the long face she had been working on as long as Alexis could remember. It was an expression derived from years of "Girls, girls—leave those shoes on the porch!" and "Go catch fairies in the ravine but don't let them loose in my kitchen!" The ravine, reached through a hole in the hedge of Elizabeth's garden, had been the path to school, a place of twig huts and confessions in the long grass. A place of necking with Darryl Somebody, taking turns.

Belle had tactfully asked about Teddy. "Your mother told me there were problems," said Belle. That was all Korrie would have told her, for it was all she told herself—problems, like cockroaches, or a difficulty with the plumbing. Nothing about hospitals, nothing about hysteria.

"Best to forget," Belle had said, making Alexis a second cup of instant decaf from the boiling-water tap Korrie had had installed. Convenience. But how very hard to forget, Alexis had argued. "And don't I know?" cried Belle, raising her hands over her head. "Leo leaving me with three children, for that blonde you-know-what in Denver! I know all about forgetting," she had claimed. And then, out loud to Alexis, she had remembered and remembered.

Alexis' mind had wandered. It had been a frosty, clear night. Mr. Wallace had come out into his yard and, standing under a floodlight mounted on a post, had watered the rink he made each year for the boys. Surely the boys were grown up by now, she had thought, but then she remembered how Mr. Wallace watered his garden all summer, always late at night. Watering rinks and gardens was a harmless enough obsession.

Then Belle and Alexis had taken apple pie and coffee into the living room. The walls there were coral, the lush pile carpet, sand. Belle had sat on the long sofa under Korrie's seascape. Korrie had got it for a song at an auction. She had felt it to be a bargain since there was at least fifty pounds of oil paint in just the waves, let alone the lowering sky. Belle's orange head bobbing before the murky grey-blue water had looked like a rubber life-raft on the sea.

Alexis had sat in Hadley's La-Z-Boy by the bookshelf which contained thick Book-of-the-Month Club novels. Hadley never chose them; they just arrived and he read them. No fuss.

The two women had fallen into a companionable silence. The room was comfortingly prosaic. Most everything was of good quality but little taste; the decorations of an unschooled eye with money's access to value. Swinging around in her leather chair, Alexis had made herself at home again, a girl again—around and around. She had reviewed Korrie's beloved collection of china figurines that cluttered the valance over the entrance to the hall. How Alexis had longed for the statuettes as a child, when she was not allowed to play with them. How she had come to despise them as an adult: their rosebud lips and insipid smiling eyes. Her glance lit on one of a little tow-haired boy in lederhosen with a rope coiled over his shoulder and a mountain climber's pick in his hand. Teddy had given that one to Korrie. Teddy, the spelunker. Alexis had thought it deceitful, for he hated the statuettes as much as she did. Korrie had loved it. Everyone loved Teddy.

Belle had left about ten. They had made plans to have coffee together another day and Belle had asked, if it wasn't too much trouble, if she might continue to do the plants. "I know you," she had said at the door, grinning. "You have a black thumb." And Alexis had been forced to acknowledge the fact. It was always a little frightening what the mothers of old friends remembered. She had watched Belle in her high heels and fur coat pick her way carefully through the icy patches on the driveway and head down the street to her own empty house, two blocks away on the edge of the ravine.

Alexis had drawn a bath. Korrie had had a special deep bathtub built for relief from her arthritis. Alexis found a mystery on the counter in the big bathroom. A Michael Innes. One of Belle's, she had concluded, for she remembered swapping mysteries with her while Elizabeth ranted about "literature". Alexis read it in the bath; how comforting it had been—the plot hardly mattering, for there were lots of teas and Palladian vistas and witty dialogue.

The following day, inspired by the novel, Alexis had walked down to the village, to the Sleuth, and bought an armful of detective stories, including something new by Parker for Belle, who, she remembered, liked her shamuses hard-boiled. She had stopped at Wright's Feed and Seed to arrange for firewood to be delivered. She had bought cognac at the liquor store. She had picked up some things at her mother's greengrocer, and everywhere she had been recognized and welcomed home. She had returned to the house and read away the day while a beef stew from Korrie's infinitely deep deepfreeze thawed for dinner. She had written a letter to her mother at the kitchen table to say she was home. She had always done her homework at this table. She had felt herself regressing. She had slipped comfortably into an uncomplicated past. Then, when it could no longer be put off, she had phoned the Forgebens. It had only reminded her that she was not at her own home at all.

Frau Forgeben could not have been happier to talk to her and called her husband to the phone. It had dawned on Alexis that they thought she was still in England—"Such a good connection, yah?"—and they were so glad to hear from her and pass on Teddy's itinerary. He was to be in London for a recording session, then Bradford for a jazz festival, and Edinburgh and home in two weeks, in lots of time for Christmas. He had tried to reach her, Frau Forgeben had told Alexis. How pleased he would be when she showed up out of the blue! Alexis had not bothered to disenchant her mother-in-law with the truth. It was easier to be so far away. Christmas? Of course she would come, she had told them, remembering the previous Christmas with affection. All the family from Kitchener and Papa played polkas on his clarinet with Teddy's accompaniment. Papa recalled it for her. Teddy had joked: "For a plumber, Papa, you make a pretty good clarinetist." Papa, undaunted, had gone off to the closet and brought out a battered and dusty old saxophone which he had played until the whole family hooted at him to stop.

"Remember zhat?" Papa had said on the extension.

"Now I do," Alexis had told him.

Christmas. Mama Forgeben making Black Forest cakes and Papa with his stubby pipe-fitter's hands being "Opa" to the three grandchildren. Only Teddy of the three boys had yet to produce,

254

a fact which got Alexis the odd poke in the ribs. How could she forget that? "How could I miss Christmas with you?" she had told Frau Forgeben, who seemed to have put completely out of her mind the six months of separation she and Teddy had gone through, let alone the circumstances which had led to their parting. A squabble, a row—that's how Frau Forgeben would think of it, Alexis had thought when she had hung up. Some squabble.

Off the phone she had thought of Teddy taking a very long side trip on his way to Bradford. She pictured him making a wrong turn, walking over the ruins of Fastyngange, and she had prayed that she had left nothing there to harm him. No pits concealed by broken stone. No ghosts. The Wound: were they still there? She prayed not.

Alexis finished her coffee but it did not wash away the queasiness brought on by the pastry. A great blob of it had stained her skirt; her face looked bilious in the rearview mirror. So much for teenage pranks. Angrily she turned on the ignition and squealed out of the doughnut shop parking lot.

The week had passed comfortably enough. The firewood had come and Belle had come and, with the exception of the appointment with Troubridge that Gloria had made for her while they were still in Halifax, it had been a time of peace and blessed quiet. I had lain low. Waiting.

Another week. And now a second session with Troubridge had come and gone with something curiously like a breakthrough, thought Alexis as she turned her mother's car off Bayview into the angular spiral that led to her natal home. She found herself thinking about Christmas at the Forgebens'—about eating too much hazelnut torte—and daring to think life could be so normal and boisterously happy again. Then she saw the new tire tracks in the light snow on the driveway. She parked and saw marks which were not footsteps, but drag-marks leading to the front door. She opened the door and felt me rise darkly in anticipation.

I rose up to her eyes to peek out through those portholes at the hallway strewn with excelsior. And in the centre of those paper entrails was the box Duncan Marriott had made for her out of the kindness of his heart.

31

Belle stood in the living room wringing her hands, looking both excited and apprehensive. She had laid the stones in their magic circle in the bay window and had moved potted plants into an ornamental arrangement around the perimeter. "I couldn't resist," said Belle, giggling. "Sort of a grotto, isn't it? I hope you're not angry," she said, meeting Alexis' eyes. Alexis' mouth was clamped shut. "It was strange; I don't know what came over me. I thought it was going to be furniture or something.... Is it?"

Alexis' eyes closed and she broke out in a sweat as she tried to hold me back. I pressed against her teeth. Her teeth hummed, and some of that humming slipped out.

"I can put it away again, dear, but it's so intriguing and the rocks so pretty. Oh, such a hoo-ha," she said plaintively, covering her mouth with her hands.

Then Alexis could hold me no longer. She crossed the room and, on her knees, delivered me back to my true nature. She hung her chin over the stones. The darkness swirled up out of her. Out of the corner of her eye she watched the hem of the drapes flutter. That was all. Her mouth was full of throbbing coldness for just a minute and then it passed. The circle of sand-coloured broadloom turned the colour of toast and Alexis' nose filled with the acrylic stench of its burning. A new blackness grew between the stones.

The smoke alarm went off and Belle cursed it mightily as she fanned the front door open and closed to quell the noise. The cold air gave me the opportunity I had longed for.

"Well, well, nice to speak to you again," I said. "How jolly nice of you to reunite me with my corporeal self. Crated up like some archaeological specimen in a museum basement, not deemed quite interesting enough for permanent display."

The smoke alarm stopped buzzing and the front door was closed, choking off my supply of moving air.

"Did you say something, dear?" said Belle, peering around the living room entranceway. Alexis shook her head. "I couldn't hear you above the racket," Belle apologized, still upset at her meddling and trying to make amends.

"It's nothing," said Alexis.

It was something quite horrendous, Alexis' expression informed Belle, but she was too upset at her meddling to know what to do. She got a broom and dustpan and cleaned up the hall while Alexis sat on the floor in dazed silence. Belle did not return and a few moments later Alexis heard the television in the den. *The Chains of Tomorrow*. She and Belle had watched the soap opera together the previous afternoon and Belle had told her it was the only one she kept track of. Alexis opened one of the side-lights of the bay window.

"How charitable," I said.

"You sound just like me," Alexis replied.

"What did you expect?" I said peevishly. "The ghosts you liberated out at sea took a great deal of me with them and in my long confinement I have replenished myself. It's really quite simple."

I continued to grumble in my new all-too-familiar voice. It reminded her of catching herself talking in her sleep; waking with a startled "What was that!" only to find it was her own voice that had wakened her.

I scolded her. "You have been denying my existence," I said, sounding like a schoolmistress. "You felt you could ignore me as long as I was just an indefinable singing in the blood, instead of something concrete. You felt you could assuage me somehow with cups of tea and cozy meals by the fire and books. But I am more than just an unquenchable yearning for mystery books, Alexis. Tsk, tsk."

At that moment the door to the den opened and Alexis, hurriedly closing the window, composed herself cross-legged by my silenced orifice. Belle entered the living room with her hands humbly clasped before her. "I am sorry, dear," she said. "It was just that the CN people said they had already given you two warnings to pick up your things. I was afraid they might auction them off or something. Are you very angry with me?"

"No," said Alexis, sighing. "No." She held up her hand and Mrs. Fleischman crossed the room to take it. Her hands were as dry as dust.

"And you so sick and all," said Belle.

"Pull up a chair," said Alexis. And when the woman was sitting expectantly, Alexis opened the window.

"This is becoming insufferable," I said.

Belle beamed. "The hole!" she said. "Where'd it come from?"

"A long way off," I answered.

"It talks," said Belle.

"Given half a chance," came my retort.

"How clever," said Belle, clapping her hands soundlessly. "You're no *kalike*, Alexis! Is it ventriloquism or what?" she asked.

"*It* is an oubliette," I interrupted. "Or what is left of one. I don't need Alexis in order to talk. I can be heard by anyone with a mind to listen."

Just then, Belle jumped from her chair with a little gasp. "The commercials are over," she said. "You must come and see,

Alexis." Belle, thinking Alexis revived, wanted nothing more than normality again. "Come," she said. "Terry's in such a jam!" And when Alexis declined, Belle scuttled back on her own to the safety of the den.

"I thought I could sort it out for myself—with the doctor's help," said Alexis.

"Ah, Dr. Troubridge," I said. "Is he making much progress?"

"Troubridge says it's me who has the problem, not Teddy. But that's not true, is it?"

"Take my advice," I said. "Forget for a little while longer. Push it back. It is not time yet. In the fullness of time, Alexis, it will be clear."

"I feel like I'm living in a dream," said Alexis.

"Or living out a dream," I said, "which may not seem much different but implies some kind of an end. But this is not the time for teleological niceties. You have been living by fiction and now it is catching up to you.

"You need me for a little longer. Bring me up to date. It is no use trying to sort through these modalities, willynilly. Let us explore the shallow waters, the recent past, the past you have kept from me for your own foolish reasons. Catch me up to date—meticulously, mind you—and I will make it good for you."

"Yes," said Alexis, chastised.

"Talk to me," I said. "Tell me everything since Fastyngange. *Remember*."

Alexis took a deep breath. She summoned up the spirit of Fastyngange—the quietest place she had ever known. The spirit whistled through her like a cleansing wind, emptying her. She began the winter crossing.

She reconstructed the S.S. *Northern Lights* rivet by rivet, and animated it with passengers and crew. I was acquainted with all the players; I had seen them through her eyes and heard their voices ringing in her ears. But her telling of the tale would keep her occupied at my service and give me the chance to recover and reflect. How I had missed the pleasure of quiet reflection living in her!

Alexis warmed to what had seemed a tedious task. She became lost in the tale. Or, to be more precise, she became lost to the present and found herself vividly in the past. Her parents' home and her housemate seemed to disappear. How easy it was to take her over.

Belle's soap opera ended and she left, quietly, after watching from the hall for some minutes. Whatever was going on in the living room, she did not want to disturb it. Alexis and I talked long into the night.

I was thirsty for detail and Alexis dragged it up by the bucketful. Then she would rest while I savoured the contents of the bucket, each drop, elixir. I gained strength from her disclosure. My voice darkened, though it never recovered the velvety baritone of my castle existence. There was too much of Alexis in me now.

And there was further reason for having her retell our adventure. There was no denying that multiple transplantations had weakened me. My prodigious recall of my own past was still intact, but I had trouble with short-term memory. Time and again Alexis was called upon to repeat some part of her story. This did not frustrate her nearly as much as it did me. Paradoxically, she found herself becalmed, reviewing the turbulent crossing. It was over, the ghosts vanquished. To relive it held no surprise. As long as she concentrated her attention on that episode, she could almost convince herself she was safe.

Apart from the annoyance of a faulty memory, I found the retelling of the adventure at sea a kind of sport. Often and accurately I predicted the outcome of some turn or crisis in the story. "I recognize that," I would say, for if I had forgotten a moment here and there I knew the story by feel. Alexis' narrative coincided with my emotional experience of the story under her skin. When an aspect of the tale did not feel right, did not exactly jibe with my inchoate sense of it, I would hound Alexis until she got events in the right order. She found this eerie, as if I were a child who could recall the womb, its prehistory. Yet it made sense, this inner dimension.

"Things do not happen *to* you," I said. "Things happen through you. The reverberations create a pattern in the senses, in the blood, that is no less real and a great deal more continuous than those units of time, those consciously distinguishable incidents, which make up a story."

And perhaps more trustworthy, thought Alexis. The mind can play tricks with a hand of consciously distinguishable cards. The blood never lies, she thought.

On went her story. She arrived home. She visited Troubridge. "So there are two of them," I said. "How confusing for you."

It was early in the morning. She had found the cognac and sat sipping it, wrapped in a blanket against the winter cold seeping through the window. She said nothing for a moment. She swirled her drink in her glass, her head tilted down towards the fragrant fumes. "Did you ever meet Troubridge?" she asked. "The Somerset one, I mean?"

"Ah, yes," I said. "We have more than a passing acquaintance."

"But if he knew about you," she said, "why didn't he warn me?"

"Perhaps," said I, "he felt you must find out for yourself."

"I could have died."

"But you didn't," I said perfunctorily. "Now remind me what else the doctor had to say...."

By three she had retold the entire story of my time in her. She was too tired to go on any longer. She wanted to close my window but I begged her not to. She relented, feeling guilty about ignoring me since her return. She made her way off to her pink bed, turning out lights as she went. I settled in to a spell of quiet, of reacquainting myself with myself. But in no time she was back. In the dark she crawled into the room, breathing heavily, and knelt by my side. Hiding behind the foolish jungle setting Belle had created for me, she peered out at the wintry night. There was someone at the foot of the driveway. I knew this. I had heard the someone arrive.

"It's Belle," whispered Alexis. "Standing in her fur coat with a kerchief on. She's in rollers. Staring at the house. It's you, isn't it? She wants you."

"That may well be," I said.

"But she is a friend of mine!" said Alexis, incensed and frightened. "Leave her alone!"

"She is old," I said. "She is alone."

Alexis did not speak for a moment. I could tell why. Through the moaning of the wind in the gutters and the brushing of the evergreen shrubbery against the glass, I could hear footsteps retreating.

"She's gone," said Alexis, sitting up with relief. But the relief was short-lived. "She'll be back," she said, more to herself than to me. She had seen the look on Belle's face. "What am I going to do? Why do I keep you? You're dangerous."

The answer was on my lips when she shut the window with a resounding bang.

"Can you hear me?" she said, although she knew I could not answer her. "I know what I have to do," she said. "I know where I can take you." I did not like the tone of her voice. She sounded, despite her tiredness, like someone who wanted to take things into her own hands.

32

Mechelney Taxidermy stood in a row of dilapidated shops just west of Queen Street's trendier shopping and club district. Alexis parked her mother's car, crossed the street, and peered in the shop window. There was a cruel-mouthed muskellunge mounted on the wall, an owl on a varnished branch, a ferret, a fox. There was even a brindle bulldog curled up beside a tatty lynx. The lynx snarled, the claws of its raised paw extended. The claws stuck out at all angles, greatly diminishing the ferocity of the stance. Beyond the display window stood a grizzly bear, semi-rampant, leaning against the wall for support. His snarl needed adjustments. Alexis was recalling the first time she had looked in this window when suddenly the bulldog uncurled and started to bark. He lunged at the glass, pawing to get out, to get at Alexis who stood petrified at the window. To the left of the shop was a peeling yellow door, hanging open on its hinges. Alexis went in and pulled the door shut behind her. She leaned against the wall of the entranceway trying to get her breath back and waiting for the dog to stop.

She was standing at the bottom of a narrow, steep stairwell that climbed two floors in a single interrupted flight. A light bulb swinging in a lazy circle on a long cord illuminated the landing at mid-flight. The door through which she had come allowed grey street light to penetrate to the level of the third step through a pebbleglass window that was cracked and taped. She stood on a warped linoleum floor in a puddle of muddy water. The floor was strewn with junk mail. The entranceway reeked of male cat.

Alexis climbed slowly to the landing, her hand scarcely touching the railing, her ears attentive to the squeaking stairs. The spiral stairs at Fastyngange never squeaked. She seemed to welcome each familiar sound. She wanted to name them: grumpy, wink, slouch, crack. She arrived at the first landing. There was one door—the door to Mechelney's apartment, though he spent most every day and most of each night in the shop below. His door was numbered 1. There were two doors at the top of the stairs: a blue one leading to a storage space, a red one to her and Teddy's flat. The number on her door was 2B. Mechelney was a Brit, and did not consider the street level a floor. "It's the flights what count," she remembered him saying. It was coming back to her.

She had not seen Mechelney in his shop and now she screwed up her courage to knock on his door. She didn't get the chance. A voice from above arrested her fist.

"Az I live and breathe!"

An old man stood framed in the red doorway at the top of the stairs. He leaned forward with one hand on the railing; he carried a toolbox in the other. He wore a white shirt and a dark tie. His pants hung loosely from suspenders. His nose was sharp like a raven's, his hair as black as a raven's.

The man started down the steps. He wore rubber boots—he always wore rubber boots—and they were wet. The stairs creaked dangerously under him, though Alexis doubted he weighed much more than she did. She remembered him now; the gruffness of his voice did not frighten her.

"You wouldn't happen to have a room?" she asked.

The man inspected her with his raven eyes: how much sawdust would it take to stuff her? Would he leave her mouth closed or open? The fingernails would need replacing—they were chewed to the quick. Alexis tried not to flinch under the scrutiny. Tried not to laugh. He looked up at the red door at the top of the stairs. He looked back at her as if estimating whether she would fit through that door or, for that matter, whether she could climb so high. He scratched his chin.

"Zo ye'r back," he said at last, his voice stern.

She could never have hugged Mechelney—he would not have stood for it—but she did reach out and squeeze his arm. She wasn't able to speak. He couldn't quite look at her, not straight in the eye. It was an uneasy reunion. He put down his toolbox on the landing. "I was jest fixzing the tap in the bathroom being az 'ow 'iz lordzjip asked me to git to it. Can't be wazting good 'ot water.

"Cum, I'll zjow ye if yer like," he said. And leaving his toolbox on the landing he slouched up the stairs again, Alexis following, trying not to cry with relief. She had been afraid of seeing her landlord again, afraid of what he would think of her. Afraid he would not let her into the building.

"Thiz 'ere I fixzed too," he said, clicking the bolt on a shiny new gold lock on the door to 2B. The door was punk—a good heave would open it—but the lock was impressive all the same. Alexis wondered if there was a new spare key and whether it was where they used to keep the old one, but she didn't have time to stop and check. Mechelney was off down the hall to the bathroom. She crossed the threshold of the apartment into a flood of memories no lock could have held back.

The corridor had not been renovated. It was dim and dirty and long, with three doors off it to the left. The flat stretched from the alley to Queen Street in the front. A tall window behind her led to the fire-escape overlooking the alley. She and Teddy had sat out there on hot nights, drinking beer in the dark. There was a back room which was hers for her books and her bits and pieces of antiques; Teddy had put a sign on the door: "The Shambles". Mechelney passed the door to the enormous

266

windowless bedroom with a skylight and a ladder up to the roof, where she and Teddy sunbathed nude, and then there was the bathroom, into which Mechelney now turned. A pair of Teddy's pyjamas hung over the shower rod. The room smelled of Teddy: his aftershave, his body. She found herself breathing him in deeply, not able to suck in enough of him but pleased to be reminded of him all the same. Mechelney turned the tap on the graceful, if cracked, old free-standing sink. On and off several times. The water gurgled and spluttered out, yellow with rust and then clear.

"I'm going to miss the drip," she said.

"Nay, lazz," he said laughing. He caught her eye in the mirror over the sink but turned to leave the room. He waited for her in the hall and closed the bathroom door after her, as though he were a landlord showing a prospective tenant a property. The gesture disturbed her.

"Will you have a coffee?" she asked, turning immediately into the enormous front room overlooking Queen Street, which served them as kitchen, living room, and studio.

"Nay, lazz," he said, and she could tell that there was something he wanted to say, to ask, and she was not sure she wanted to hear it, whatever it was. She was looking through a cupboard for the coffee when he cleared his throat.

"Mizz Alexziz, if yer don't mind. There'z thingz we should zay."

Things we should say, she thought. How eloquent. She stopped her frenzied search and, heaving a long and noisy sigh, turned to her landlord.

"I've kind of barged in, haven't I?" she said. "Didn't phone or anything."

"Doz 'e know ye'r 'ere?" asked Mechelney. "Thadz all I wan ta know."

She shook her head. "I missed him," she said. "I mean, I missed him leaving for England. That's where I was."

"Oh aye?" He seemed to brighten at this.

"In Somerset," she said.

"But thatz where I'm from," he said, and she nodded. "Oh aye," he said. "Therz bin Mechelneyz in Zomerzet zince the dawn of time, I don't doubt."

"Yes," she said. She wanted to add that she had met one, his double, but where would that get her? He had more to say, she could tell by the way he was looking at his boots. She spoke first.

"I wanted to phone, but I was afraid you might not talk to me, so I just came. I'm...not the same.... I'm..."

He waved away her weak attempt at an explanation. Then he looked her in the eye. "Who of uz iz still the zame az we were?" he asked.

There seemed nothing left to say and yet he still stood there. She was afraid he wanted her to defend her right to be in the apartment and she could not do that. It was her home—her real home—but it was his building and she had gone crazy there. Made life difficult for everyone. She was still crazy. She was between two worlds, equally real, and unable to leave the one behind to take up citizenship in the other again. Not yet. How could she tell him that? She was not the same. So much had happened. It was not over but, surely, Fastyngange had been the worst of it.

"I thought perhapz you'd bin in the 'ospital all thiz time," he admitted abashedly.

"Oh no," she said, and immediately wondered if that was quite the answer he had wanted to hear. "I...recovered some months ago. I was away...."

"So you zaid," he replied. He took a deep breath. "Well, I can't ztand around 'ere all the day," he said, rubbing his large strong hands down the front of his pants. He smiled without catching her eye and turned towards the hallway.

"Mr. Mechelney," she said, stopping him from leaving. He looked at her this time. "I owe you an apology."

"Oh dear, Mizz Alexziz—"

"No, I do," she interrupted. "It must have been horrible for you. You are probably still scared...." She couldn't continue in that line for she would have to admit that she was scared herself. Scared of what might happen, of what she might do. Scared of me and what *I* might do.

"Itz me who ought to be beggin' yer pardon," he said. "It waz an awful night, that; one I'll never ferget. But ztill and all, I had no right to use zuch violence; to be zuch an animal. I'm afraid it was yer accident—my pushin' ye like that—what made ye go, ye know...."

"I don't think so," she said. "There were other things."

"Yez, mizzy. I zuppose there waz." He recalled something of what he had heard at the door that last night and his face clouded. He didn't want to hear more.

She shook his hand firmly, steadily. Held it. "It won't happen again," she said. He looked at her as if he wanted to believe what she was saying. Then he left.

He sauntered down the hall only to return a moment later with a shiny new key. "Welcome back, then," he said. There was a sigh in his voice as if he already regretted his decision. He passed down the hallway and returned a third time. "I'm usually around if ye need me," he said.

"Oh, I don't do much hunting," said Alexis. They both laughed out loud at this old joke, and then Mechelney left for good. She was alone.

It hardly seemed as if Teddy could have been away two weeks. There was a coffee cup in the sink—a last mug before leaving for the plane? There were scribbled notes for a piece of music on the piano. She tried to read it, played a chord that was surely wrong. Gave up. There was a book open beside his chair: Bachelard's *The Poetics of Space*. It had been left open a hundred times before in just that same spot on the camel saddle. She picked it up. There were newly scribbled notes in the chapter called

"The Phenomenology of Roundness". She placed the book down where she had found it. She wondered if his new score was about roundness.

On the west wall there were two drawings. They were framed, part of a series: a red diamond on a white background, and horizontal stripes in orange, blue, and green. She had forgotten what they stood for now, but she recognized them. All these little parts of the story, all jumbled up inside her head, bits of glass in the bottom of a kaleidoscope. She tried to think of Howl now but she could only see Teddy. Howl, Mechelney, Troubridge; fading, fading....

At the window she picked dead leaves off a plant and looked out at the busy life on Queen Street. The light was tepid, distilled through the layers of winding-sheet in which winter would wrap the city for months to come. But if the sky was funereal the street was not. It seethed with salt-encrusted cars and leather-encrusted punks. Hawkers and rubbies and minor mafiosi rubbed shoulders with racks of dresses wheeled out into the cold for quick sale. Then she noticed that the plant she was pruning was dead, and with a laugh to herself she emptied it into the garbage can under the sink. A fresh garbage bag waited there.

Alexis strolled around the flat picking up this and remembering that. She turned on the radio to CBC Stereo but they kept interrupting the talk with music, so she turned to a news station but the news was repetitive. Nowhere near as entertaining as a talking hole, she told me later, when she installed me in a corner of the big front room. It was the radio which reminded her of me. She missed me.

It took her many trips back and forth to her mother's car before she had carried up the last stone. If anybody noticed her they said nothing. In this part of town people walked around with stranger bundles.

Quite out of breath she pieced together my magic circle. Then she closed her eyes and emptied me into my new home. There was no skull-splitting maelstrom. When I had left her she felt drained, but that seemed as much a product of the day's exciting events and the trips up and down the stairs as of my passing. Wearily she watched as the floor miraculously darkened between the stones. There was no sound, only the not unpleasant odour of burning wood. She dipped her hand down into the new darkness. She leaned out over the stones to look down. For a moment she almost imagined the hole might open out into the apartment below, allowing her to see into Arthur Mechelney's world. But of course the hole did not work that way, she told herself. It carried its own darkness about it.

I did not speak. The flat was well insulated, and she had taken that into account when choosing my site. Directly above the stones a broken window had been covered, long ago, with a campaign poster stuck with masking tape to the glass. Alexis lifted a corner of the cardboard. A draft swirled into the room.

"I do hope this is it," I managed to say, my voice not at all strong. "I do hope it has occurred to you that each time you suck me up and spit me out, a little of me is dispersed into the air."

She told me where we were. "This is it," she said.

But I was angry at being carted around. "You'll be the death of me," I said, yawning.

She laughed at this, a little too heartily for my liking. Then she told me about Mechelney, about the dog in the window who she thought had been Troubridge's dog. So much was still confused. "How awful," I said, "to be the pet dog of a taxidermist."

We talked. And as we talked it became painfully obvious who was the host and who was the hostage. I no longer had her where I wanted her, and I was weak from all the moves. We talked.

But gradually she grew sleepy. She drifted off and then woke herself. It was only three in the afternoon but already winter was squeezing the last light out of the day. Night was never far away in the city in the dead of winter. She curled up on a colourful rug beside me with a fat cushion under her head. She closed her eyes. She fell asleep. In her mind's eye she saw the animals in the shop window below. She saw herself reflected in the glass, saw the startled look on her reflected face when the dog barked at her and sent her scurrying deeper into the recesses of sleep. Narrowly she escaped the brindle bulldog and his yellow fangs. But deeper sleep took her backwards in time, deeper and deeper with the dog nipping at her heels. Down the hole to the inevitable oubliette at the bottom. The place of forgetting. She didn't dare go that far, and her conscious mind yanked her up again and again.

And while she slept fitfully I drilled my way down through the successive floors of Mechelney's dreary establishment and rooted myself in the earth. The earth was cluttered with the rotten footings of buildings that had once occupied the site, pipes gurgling with sewage and hissing with gas—hardly earth at all, but man's subterranean support system. It all made me sad. I prattled on in a foolish manner about my beloved Fastyngange, hoping to infect Alexis with my distemper. She slept on.

It was sometime in the middle of the night when she awoke. The breeze had dropped. My tirade had diminished to no more than the hissing of the steam in the radiator. Then she heard someone on the street below turning the knob on the taxidermy shop door. Silence. The knob on the appliance store, the Chinese grocery. The footsteps passed. It was not Teddy, not yet. She lay back down and heard the sound of jazz drifting through the window from one of the all-night clubs down the way. There was a sax—Howl howling, she thought. But when she listened more closely she realized it was a synthesizer. Such are the discrepancies of a mind casting about for bits of the true picture. The image of what happened. A mind drawing closer and closer to the place of impact.

She picked herself up, shivering from the cold. She scratched a porthole in the frost and looked out. The street always changed its makeup for the night, she recalled. First it was alive with

272

bumptious punkers and then, as the evening progressed into the wee hours, half dead with drunks and bag ladies rooting through the bins in the doorways and alleys. Alexis stared out of the darkness of her room into the semidarkness of the street. She remembered the crazy people. There was one across the way now: an old woman stalled in the doldrums, waiting for the wind to catch her shopping bags and push her on her way. There was a man leaning on a lamp post sorting through change that wouldn't buy a mickey from a cabbie's trunk. And in a shop door down the way, a lanky boy in a lumber-jacket with his tight jeans rolled up to reveal army boots. To Alexis he looked as if he was wondering whether it was late enough yet to go home. He was a skinhead and the sight of his baldness through the plume of his cigarette smoke startled her. He seemed agitated. One knee wouldn't stop shaking; his eyes scanned the street, back and forth as if he were watching a steady stream of cars go by, when in fact there was little traffic. She could not take her eyes off him. Then for one moment he seemed to look directly at her—though he could not see her in the darkened room, she prayed. Still his gaze rested on the place where her face showed through the porthole. Then suddenly behind the boy the door of the darkened shop opened, and a mate dressed identically came out carrying a bundle in both arms. Together they ran off down the street, turned at the first alley, and were gone. A robbery. The boy had been on guard, looking out for anything suspicious. That was all. That was why he had stared at her, she told herself. Probably saw the clear circle in the frost, not the face behind it. And yet.... Alexis tried to get her breath back. She had shaken the survivors but she was not at all sure now whether she had shaken the Wound.

33

"Did you ever have a baby?" Troubridge asked. He turned from the window where he had been pruning a prized bonsai tree he kept on the ledge. It helped him to concentrate, he had told her. Alexis, sitting on a couch nearby, watching him, shook her head. "Were you ever pregnant?" he asked. Again she shook her head. He turned to the bonsai and gently poked at a root with his sharp-nosed shears. The tree was over a hundred years old.

It was early afternoon and the sun reflected brightly off the new snow on the windowsill. She could not see the features of the doctor's face in the glare. The tiny tree set in its ornamental garden was a silhouette. "Not that I remember," she said, trying to laugh off the inanity of her obstinately blank memory. She had told him everything that had happened to her in Somerset and on the *Northern Lights*, and up to the time she had uncrated my stones at the flat on Queen Street. She recalled it all in vivid, lurid detail. But her life before Fastyngange she remembered only as it reoccurred to her.

"I have had access to your medical records," Troubridge said matter-of-factly. "But I wondered if perhaps you had miscarried at some time before seeing a doctor."

"The baby in the oubliette," she said.

He nodded, taking a small brass watering-can with a long snout and gingerly—stingily, she thought—watering his miniature garden. He wiped his hands clean and joined her. The tape recorder sat on the coffee table between them. "If you'll pardon a pun in bad taste," he said, "there would seem to be a baby at the bottom of this mystery. But whose?" he asked.

She shrugged her shoulders. She wished right then that she could claim the baby as her own—adopt it. It would be so convenient. But she had never conceived, she was sure of it. Her body had its own independent memories, free from the vagaries of her mind. From the look on his face, Troubridge did not think the baby was hers, either. He chewed his lip a moment. She sat quietly. She had told him everything she could.

"And this hole," he said. "Is it in you now?"

She shook her head. "No, it's at the flat." The doctor appeared to have asked only in order to confirm the facts. "But last time?" he said. "And the session before that?"

She nodded. "The stones hadn't arrived yet," she explained. Looking at his puzzled face, she realized how difficult it must be for him to grasp.

But a smile interrupted the look of consternation on his face. "Well, that explains your present attitude," he said. He meant her physical attitude. She was sitting Indian style, in her jeans, her shoes on the floor. She had taken seriously his request to make herself comfortable. She was comfortable for the moment.

"It's better when it's out," she said.

"But it would be best to be rid of it entirely," he concluded. "And that will happen when...."

"I'm not sure," she said.

"But you *hope* it will happen when you have forced Teddy to confront the oubliette."

She frowned. "I don't want to force him to do anything. It would be *best* for him, if he would," she huffed.

"You seem reluctant to let it go."

"I'm not sure how I do it," she said. "That's all."

"Ah hah," said Troubridge. "I can help you there." She seemed surprised. "The hole has already apprised you of the procedure," he said. "When you first set it up in the flat what did it say?— something like: 'Each time you move me, a little bit more of me disperses into the air.' Surely this voice is giving you the key to its own dissolution."

"But I can't keep moving," she said. "I'm home now. I want to stay home. And it isn't just a voice. There are rocks. Twelve of them."

"You can't just leave it somewhere, rocks and all?"

"Not yet," she said.

"But is your home big enough for you and Teddy and this hole?" Troubridge asked.

"I will only keep it until Teddy has seen it," she said, in a tone of voice that was meant to be uncompromising. She felt her mood shifting, sliding. A moment earlier, while he was tending his potted garden, she had felt completely at ease. "And why, exactly?" the doctor pressed. "What is the purpose of this confrontation?" The doctor had Jekyll-and-Hyded himself into a carping, poking lawyer again, and Alexis began to grow increasingly nervous. She unfolded her legs, sat up straight.

"I've told you—"

"Yes," said Troubridge. "You feel it's *his* problem to begin with. I'm entirely willing to believe there is some truth in this; I've told you that. This 'Wound' "—he intoned the word—"this Wound may well be the manifestation of some trauma in Teddy's life which you have picked up on and which has become, through transference, a trauma in your own life. A wound. A baby with a wound under its heart."

"I'm trying to think," she said.

"Something Teddy has put out of his mind. Something you want desperately to put out of your mind and cannot, so you have done what seems the next best thing. You have forgotten it. And now you are contemplating giving it back to Teddy. You intend to make it *his* trauma again. Make him relive the incident the hole speaks of which you are convinced is the source of his — and by transference your — unhappiness."

"No! It's not like that," said Alexis, rising to the attack. "I don't want him to suffer. I just know that baby must be confronted. Maybe it was his — did you check *his* medical records? No. Of course not."

"What might we have found there?"

"I don't know," Alexis answered truculently. "A scar, maybe. An old wound. Did you ever think of that? Maybe you'd have found a scar if you had bothered to check. Here," she said, poking herself in the ribs under her heart.

"Like the spear in Christ's side," said Troubridge softly. Arrestingly.

But Alexis would not be quelled, did not even seem to make the connection. "He can bloody well go and find this baby," she said. "After what I've been through, it's the least he can do. Whatever this baby is—whoever it is—this time he will know about it—he'll know what's down there. He'll be prepared. He can bring it up with him and it can be buried properly."

"But the baby on the ship, the 'survivor' baby," the doctor interjected soothingly. "Has it not been released into the sea like the others?"

Alexis cast him an annoyed glance. "Things are not the same in the oubliette," she said. "Maybe it's still down there. I don't know."

"And the other ghosts? Them too? Will Teddy have to confront them?"

Alexis looked away and tried to make sense of it. No. There would be nothing there. She felt sure of it. "No," she said. "But Teddy can't *pretend* there is nothing there. He has to go down and see for himself. If the baby is not there, well, that's the same thing, near enough."

277

"Is it?" Troubridge persisted. "A dead baby and a baby who isn't there—are these the same phenomena?"

Alexis glared at the doctor. "Are we just about finished?" she asked coldly. He smiled at her; a goddamned superior smile, she thought, which only infuriated her more. He turned off the tape.

"Yes. We are almost finished. For good."

Alexis was caught off guard. He had given her every right to get angry. It didn't mean he had to give up on her.

"It's not what you think," he said, standing, stretching.

"What isn't what I think?"

He sat, leaning towards her. "We—you and I—aren't going to get to the bottom of this. Not here in this room. The hole is back at your place. The answer is down there. I'm too old for such a trip. You are young and strong but lack experience. Teddy, on the other hand, was a caver. He's probably rusty, but he's in good shape. You are absolutely right. He must go into the hole and recover whatever it is that's down there."

Alexis stared at the psychiatrist, dumbfounded.

"What's the matter?" he said, picking up the tape recorder and heading towards his desk. "I'm agreeing with you."

"No you're not," she said. "You're making fun of me. Treating me like a headstrong child."

Troubridge shook his head. "No I'm not," he said. "I think you've got a point. You've done your part—the legwork, as you put it. If the man loves you—and I think he does—he'll have to rise to the challenge. It seems only fair."

"It *is* there," she said. "Come and see it."

The doctor shook his head.

Alexis was on her feet. "You're just going to send me off like that," she said. "Teddy comes home tomorrow. He'll be home tomorrow night! Shouldn't I have some downers or something, just in case? Besides, he'll be tired, suffering jet lag. I can't make him go down the hole in that state."

"Alexis, calm yourself." Troubridge rested his hand on her shoulder. She pulled away, sulking. "I assure you that I am not intending to be patronizing," he said. "I only said we won't find the answer here in this room. The answer is between those stones, down that hole you have suffered and borne back with you from Fastyngange. I sincerely believe that you can handle this yourself from here on, though I will be on stand-by if needed."

"Well, I wish I was as sure of myself as you seem to be!" she said, frightened now.

"You escaped Fastyngange with your life," said Troubridge, "and the castle was destroyed behind you. You lost your entourage of borrowed ghosts somewhere on the ocean. You met and loved, however ingloriously, this Howl man who reminded you so much of your husband, who was perhaps a simulacrum of your husband. He too perished. The *Northern Lights* was scrapped. These places and people have been useful to you and when their use ended, they have been left behind—which is as it should be. I am convinced the hole will go the same way. I'm not sure how, but I have faith in your resourcefulness."

"Simulacrum?" she murmured. On her lips it sounded like a drug.

"A deceptive substitute, a shadowy likeness."

Alexis thought of Howl. She could still feel him: she had seen the comb in his pants pocket; carried his saxophone; lain in bed with him, under him. She could remember the weight of him. The memory was not shadowy. He was more real to her than the girl in the gold frame by the couch in her mother's living room—the chubby-cheeked graduand, proudly clutching her R.N. certificate.

"The parts to the puzzle are all there," said Troubridge, intruding on her thoughts.

"Where?" she asked, and then coloured, for she had not been paying much attention to him and had thought, for a moment, that "there" was a real place.

He did not answer, but led her towards the door. They parted. Mrs. Harptree ushered her out the door as she had ushered her in. And that other Harptree, who headed the Historical Society in Somerset—the one who had put her onto the master historian of Fastyngange? How did it all go together when there were two pieces for each gap in the puzzle? As she stepped out into the winter, she thought of the stone circle in the corner of the living room and began to shiver. She had tried to tell him. He knew. Troubridge knew about the oubliette and had let her go.

She had taken her mother's car home one sunny day. She had had it washed and waxed. Her mother was fussy about such things. She had even paid the frozen wad of parking tickets that had accumulated under the wiper. When she left Troubridge's office she started for home, but she didn't go directly there. She walked all the way to Yonge Street, to St. Michael's Hospital, where she had worked until the night of her breakdown. Then she walked back, the darkness growing around her, the night not falling but moving in—into her lungs and her bones. She came, sometime well after supper, to The Crater, a jazz club where a sign on the window announced the Teddy Forgeben Trio, opening that weekend. "Back from a triumphant tour of Great Britain!" the sign claimed. She had to laugh at that. The door was open and the bartender, catching her eye, waved a glass he was cleaning at her. He nudged a guy at the bar—a musician friend. He waved, a champion's wave with his hands clamped together. Nobody seemed to know she had ever gone.

Finally, when her feet had become wet and then frozen, she made her way home. She met Mechelney locking the door to his shop. He wore a long coat and was carrying a battered old suitcase. He seemed disturbed.

"Claire iz zickly again," he said. Claire was his elderly sister who lived up in Sudbury. He would be away for the weekend.

The dog was with friends. He wished her luck. His eyes gave him away. He was flying the coop.

She watched him cross the street through the gusting snow and climb on a streetcar that rattled off towards the bus station. Then she opened the door to the stairs. A man was there. He was buttoning his coat up, a wretched old army coat with a fresh dark stain down the front. Steam rose from the floor. He grinned at her, toothlessly, and pointed up the stairs. "Youze live up top?" he asked. She pushed past him without answering, wrinkling her nose—not afraid of him but only wanting to get past his stench.

He called to her. "What's it like?" he asked. She stopped in her tracks and, turning, looked down at him. He was smiling up at her like a death's head, his eyes filled with a tender delirium.

34

In the week I spent in Alexis' flat, I came to loathe the city. I was distracted by the voices that bellowed, hawked, and squabbled on the street. I could hear everything, you see — each shuffling drunk, each sashaying hooker — nothing escaped my attention. It was a torment. Late-night streetcars terrified me. The mournful bell reminded me of the plague wagons, for the plague had not missed even so remote a place as Fastyngange. Alexis, on the other hand, felt at home in the clamour of the downtown. The rattling trolley shaking the building to its foundations was a sound that had worn a place inside her hearing, where it fit exactly. To me it was an infernal reminder of the juggernaut, the mighty wrecking machinery that had ripped my ancient home from me.

Back in her real home, the home she had made with Teddy, Alexis had become almost content. She left me from time to time to shop or see a movie, but despite her buoyant spirit, I sensed she was still in my thrall. But for Troubridge, she spoke to no one else. Her trips into the world since her return to the city were perturbations in an otherwise tight orbit. She was quite content. That is, until the night after her third and final bout with her analyst. She returned late; I had begun to worry, for normally she was anxious to get back and tell me all about her session. I heard the exchange with Mechelney on the street and I could tell that he would have been happier not to have run into her as he escaped for the weekend. He didn't want to be there for Teddy's return, I gathered. Alexis got the same impression. But there was something else bothering her landlord which she knew nothing about. Voices. He had been having the strangest dreams lately. Sometimes while he was at work—awake. Sister Claire's illness may well have been a fib. But he was getting away none the less.

I heard the encounter with the drunk on the stairs. That *was* interesting. He too had heard voices. Alexis had clattered up the stairs after the confrontation and slammed the rotten old door shut behind her. She was thankful for Mechelney's new lock. Shiny and gold, it almost looked invulnerable.

She made herself supper—made quite a clamour with pots and pans. She was upset, but she was not prepared to divulge her problem—not in so many words. I could guess. In less than twenty-four hours *he* would be walking in the front door. He would be surprised, perhaps shocked, perhaps even frightened, to find her here. And she, for her part, would be—well, would still be mad—her mysterious breakdown still an enigma. She was angry with Troubridge—irrationally angry, she admitted—because she had wanted to be "herself" again for Teddy's return. She managed to laugh at this when she told me. "It's not so much to ask," she said, slamming the cutlery drawer shut.

She related bits and pieces of her session with Troubridge to me but I could tell she was otherwise engaged. She paced around, pounding her knuckles into her palm. What memories that brought back. At midnight she made herself a cup of smoky Lapsang Soochong tea and stood at the window in the dark. She went all quiet. Very quiet.

"What is it?" I asked, though I could guess.

The robber boy with the shaven head was standing across the street, his eyes on her window. She waited, out of his sight, hoping for his partner-in-crime to appear and explain his presence there. But as the moments ticked away it became obvious to her that there was no burglary afoot. The boy was on his own this night. He made no move to cross the street, but neither did he leave his post. There were others: neighbourhood irregulars, crazies, whom she had passed often enough and distributed spare change to from time to time. She got the uncanny feeling they were standing sentinel, a grubby army laying siege. From directly below her window one of them, a harridan in a purple wig and wearing a green garbage bag over her winter clothes, called up to her. "What's she saying?" Alexis whispered.

I mimicked her sluggish nasal accent: "Whad's id like? Huh? Whad's id like?"

"That's Gladys!" interrupted the drunk. "Hell, I know Gladys."

"What a coincidence," said the hole.

"And the one who was pissing on her door, that sounds a lot like Wet Willy. He's always doing stuff like that."

"Curiouser and curiouser."

The drunk laughed self-consciously and peered around him in the dark. Any minute now the guys were gonna jump out— Surprise! He lowered his voice. "Are you trying to tell me they're part of some kind of conspiracy?"

"I'm telling you what Alexis saw," said the hole.

"That's crazy," said the drunk. "Gladys and Willy in some organization. Hey, Willy can't even organize when to relieve himself."

"Let's just call them volunteers," said the hole.

"Hah," said the drunk. "Gladys and Willy—part of something. That's a hoot."

"They're part of this story," said the hole, in a tone of voice which was intended to shut the drunk up.

"Come to think of it," said the drunk, "I haven't seen Gladys around lately."

The hole recommenced.

"I'm not moving," Alexis said. It was three in the morning by now.

"Of course not," I cooed. "They aren't like Belle Fleischman. They aren't loved ones to be protected from me. To hell with them."

"That isn't the point," she snapped. "This is my home. This is where I belong. I will not be driven away."

"And the street is their home," I countered. "They will not be driven away either."

"That's fine," she said. "They can have it. But I will not let them come up here. And I will not be intimidated."

"You are so thoughtful," I said. She swore at me then, said she'd had enough empty compliments and phoney encouragement from Troubridge that afternoon. "I mean thoughtful to me," I said. "Protecting me, like this." She lit into me then. Said all manner of vile and hurtful things. Said she should never have let me talk her into bringing me back. Said the idea of Teddy confronting me was sheer lunacy. She went on quite a roll and when it was done, she was exhausted and angry at herself, and subdued. I suggested a brandy.

"Where would you take me, if you had to go?" I asked, when I heard her pour herself a second snifterful. She said she didn't know of anywhere else. "There must be somewhere," I prodded, ever so delicately, not wanting her to go on another rampage. "There must be somewhere like Fastyngange," I said, and must have sounded quite feeble in my longing for it. She considered the question. She told me of a castle in Toronto, somewhere named Casa Loma, and, a little drunk by now, laughed at the idea of my going there. I soon saw why. It was a place reduced to the most wanton public traffic. A place for wedding receptions and visiting hordes of Girl Guides. No place for a hole like me.

"Somewhere far away," I said. "Deserted, preferably. Grand." She thought and thought, until I wondered if she had fallen asleep, but her hazy mind finally alighted. I was sure she would think of somewhere. There is a Fastyngange in everyone's life.

"Rest-Harrow," she said, her voice fairly quivering with excitement.

"Rest-Harrow," I reiterated. "It sounds wonderful."

"It was," she said. "Like Fastyngange was wonderful: tumbledown, irrelevant, an ancient trifle."

"You *must* take me there!" I said ardently. "It sounds perfect. Perfect."

"Rest-Harrow," she murmured, paying no attention to me. I heard the brandy bottle upended, emptied into her glass.

"It's strange you have not mentioned this place before," I said, my voice as excited as her own. "I demand to go there. Now. Alexis?"

But she did not budge. And so I asked if she might at least indulge me and take me there in spirit. She was happy to oblige. Filled with Dutch courage, she whisked me away.

Rest-Harrow was a country mansion near her parents' cottage on Lake Huron. She described it in loving detail: massive without grandeur, the façade prosaic despite the ornamental brickwork and stern despite an abundance of gables. The fenestration, she told me, was so ill-proportioned as to give the impression, even on the sunniest of days, that the house was sinking. Inside idiosyncrasy prevailed. Walls veered left and right with the logic of a carnival funhouse, and windows were scattered randomly as if they had lighted on the house of their own accord. Glass butterflies.

There was a vast and ramshackle octagonal barn surrounded by an ancient wreckage of farm equipment. There was a duck pond overgrown with cattails and encircled by hawthorns. But most prominent of all, towering above the house, there was a hill unrivalled in the surrounding countryside.

As a child, Alexis had christened it the Doctor's Head, an early example of her imaginative relationship with the landscape. She had called it that because a cowpath meandered up from the barn behind the house and forked just where the hill grew steepest. The resulting paths half girdled the lower slopes, the one fork leading to a southern pasture, the other ending in the woods at a rocky gash in the hillside. The gash, according to child Alexis, was the doctor's right ear. The cowpaths formed his stethoscope, as if the doctor were listening to the pulse of the inhabitants in the house below. Alexis, as a teenager, had mapped out the extent of this geomorphological oddity. There was a jutting chin thicketed with sumac, and a protuberance that might well suggest a vestigial nose, albeit broken. Brush grew thickly about the temples, and on the eastern slopes the woods gave the doctor a veritable mane of rich green hair. But it was the dome of the hill which lent the metaphor its greatest verisimilitude. No trees grew there and its conformation was that of a balding wise man. Through the sparse pale grass, as transparent as any skin, could be glimpsed a skull of granite.

Dwarfed and overshadowed by the giant head, Rest-Harrow sat, according to Alexis' childishly romantic cartography, directly on the doctor's heart.

Elizabeth Fleischman, staying at the cottage, had been the one who had found the way in. There was a storm shelter leading to a cellar under the kitchen, and, in an abandoned hand-operated tea elevator, a ladder of sorts—the exposed wooden framework of the shaft. Through it the girls found their way up into the kitchen with its rusting hulk of an Aga stove.

She and Elizabeth had made a play house out of Rest-Harrow, moving bits and pieces of furniture into the one room that best suited their needs: an oddly shaped parlour. There was a fireplace and a little ramshackle table and chair in this parlour and a broken-down pedal organ from which they could squeeze the odd grunt or groan, and sometimes even a wobbly, dissonant chord.

"Many years later, I took Teddy to Rest-Harrow," she said. They had made love there. After that, whenever they stayed with her parents, they found the time to get away to Rest-Harrow. Alexis never told Elizabeth. She felt, so she told me, as though she had defiled their play house by taking a lover there. But she did. Something about the smell of woodrot, I suppose, made the discomfort exhilarating. She remembered a storm. It had snuck up on them from the flanks, deflected by the Doctor's Head. How the house had creaked and shaken, she recalled. A Great Lakes squall and she and Teddy on the rug together expecting the whole place to cave in on them at any moment and not caring! "We were 'riding bareback'," she said, which, I learned, meant not using birth control. That, so it seemed, had been as much a part of the thrill as the storm.

She found another bottle. Opened it. Drank. She wandered around the room. She played a chord on the piano. "The wind was so strong the old organ began to moan," she said. Then she sat on the floor, her back up against the radiator.

"It was the last time we went there. We had been married, but not long." Her voice went all hollow. She admitted it had seemed strange to come back; vain, somehow, to try to recover the passion, the secret pleasure of the place, when it had been an illicit escape from board games with Hadley and Korrie.

"There was a muffled thump," she said. "Low. A sound under the noise of the storm."

Low as it might have been, this thump had interrupted their philandering. It had come from the fireplace. Naked, they had knelt on the hearth, side by side, to find a tiny bird, a nestling, which had fallen to its death down the chimney. Teddy had taken it up in his hands though she had not wanted him to, and he had teased her, she a nurse and all. Used to this kind of thing. She had touched it in the end. Its skinny naked body had been warm under her fingers. "It dampened our fervour," she said, with a laugh which died in her throat.

She didn't speak for some time after that. No doubt the talk of love-making had reminded her of the man who was to return in not so many hours.

"Will you ride bareback tonight?" I asked.

She didn't think this very funny. She suddenly began to shake with dread. "Jesus Christ!" she said. "Jesus Christ!" ·

She became enraged at me for making her think of Rest-Harrow. She had locked Rest-Harrow away in her mind. Then she ranted at me for keeping her up, when she had meant to be rested for Teddy's return. For the second time that night she took her anger out on me. Then, when she was reduced to a gasping wreck, she taped up the cardboard in the window, muzzling me.

She looked outside one last time, perhaps to shake her fist at the motley army of spectators in the pit, only to find them dispersing. They had hung around to listen to me, she realized. Not that they could really hear me from down on the street, but they could sense me speaking. I spoke to their loneliness and their alienation. Unwittingly she had helped to hold them there by giving me the wind to speak.

Alexis cried softly to herself to see them go. Turned away so easily, simply by closing a window. And when she was alone, really alone, in the bed under the skylight, she whimpered to herself, "What am I going to do?"

35

The day, I'm told, bloomed like a rose. A rose dipped in liquid nitrogen: perfectly frozen in colour and bloom but ready to explode into petal dust at the slightest touch. The weather man on the radio said a nor'wester was coming. Alexis listened to the radio the entire day as they updated the forecast. She seemed to forget all about me while the storm brewed.

When she woke up she had launched immediately into cleaning. She cleaned the flat methodically, from top to bottom, from stem to stern. Not a spider's web survived the sweep of her mop, nor a dust mote her cloth. When the flat was sparkling, she changed and went to Kensington Market. She came home with a thousand delicacies: fresh fish and coriander, wine and brandy to replace the previous evening's immoderation, and chocolates. Again she puttered, before making one final trip out into the gathering darkness and gusting winds. She came back with a pane of glass.

She set to work immediately, replacing the campaign poster over my breathing hole. She had to straddle me. It was inviting.

"Ah," I sighed, rejoicing in the cold draft of air that swirled into the flat. "That's more like it," I said.

"Enjoy it while you can," she muttered, chiselling away at the dried putty.

"You have quite an evening planned," I said, ignoring her attempt at a threat. "Will you wine and dine him first?" I asked, "and then spring me on him? Or will you get straight to the point?"

She huffed and puffed, scraping clear a place in the sash for the new glass. She ignored me. The wind was high—a storm wind.

"Have you been thinking of this Rest-Harrow place?" I asked.

"I have. It sounds just the place for me. Out of the way, I mean. Secluded. Peaceful. No thundering trolleycars."

"There isn't time," she grunted. And then, before I could persuade her to reconsider, she placed the glass in its frame, leaving only a trickle of air from around the edges of the pane. I was reduced to a whisper.

"It would be easier to leave," I hissed, like steam. "You could abandon me there, or stay, as you wished."

She started humming to block me out. She punched and pummelled the putty until it was warm, and then, inch by inch, she pressed it home, blocking out the buffeting wind and obliterating my proposition.

I fully expected to hear a bath being drawn when she left the room, but to my surprise her steps took her to the room at the end of the hall, the shambles. The window must have been open in that room, for a succulent ribbon of air reached me in my corner of the studio, and a ribbon is all I need. She rooted around in her study and there was much bumping and thumping, and then I heard something being dragged out into the hall and towards the front room. It was heavy, whatever it was. Breathing deeply, she pulled the weight towards me.

"What is it?" I asked. If I startled her, she was not so startled as to bother shutting off my source of air. I heard a heavy lid open, and the rattle of chains. "Alexis," I said in my best parlour voice, "you may well be displeased with me, but it is no use denying my existence."

"It's his spelunking gear," she said. I might have guessed. Shortly I would certainly have recognized the medley of sounds I had only heard once before in my life: the ropes, the pitons, the karabiners.

"How thoughtful," I said. "You are preparing everything for him in advance. It is just as well; he may be faint of heart."

She did not speak, not in words, though her breathing gave her away. Then I heard her placing new batteries in the helmet lamp and lashing the ropes to the radiator.

"So," I said.

"The more I've thought about it," she said, buckling herself into the leather belt and harness, "the less it seemed to be Teddy's problem."

"But it is some of him, down there. Surely he ought to be the one to recover it," I suggested. She didn't answer right away. It was as if she had not spoken to me at all. "Alexis," I said, a little shaken.

"I don't believe you," she said.

"You will soon find out that it is true," I replied.

"If you know what it is, tell me!" she said.

I could sense her reluctance to go and preyed on it. "He is the caver, Alexis. Let him do it for you. It's his problem, whatever Dr. Troubridge says."

"It *was* his problem," she said, tugging on her lifeline, once, twice. "It's my problem now, isn't it?"

"As you wish," I replied. "But you've left it rather to the last moment, haven't you?"

She did not comment further but went over the edge, gasping as though she were plunging into a pool of ice water.

The darkness gathered around her like wool, warm and suffocating, until she was fully dressed in it. She could see only what lay directly before her eyes, which was not wool-like at all; neither was it brick or stone, as she might have imagined, but the glimmering black surface of nothing. She touched it with her hand; it was as hard as glass.

I could not talk to her when she was in me any more than I could when I was in her, and it must have crossed her mind how ironic that was. How she must have missed me as she let out her line and lowered herself farther and farther into the abyss. Once the light of the room above had been left behind she lost all track of time. She might have been descending like that, length by gruelling length, for months or years for all she knew. It hardly mattered any more.

Finally her foot touched something jagged and the smooth darkness of nothing gave way to rock which scratched her arms. A comforting pain. She touched it and her finger was instantly black with soot. Then her feet—one, then the other—touched down, crunching softly onto a solid surface. She bent down and picked up a handful of coal. With difficulty she turned herself around and found there was a low entrance into a dim and shadowy chamber. Shadows meant light; she crouched down and entered it, standing up cautiously and turning to the source of the light that came from behind her. What a mind-numbing jolt she received when she saw the *oeil-de-boeuf* window of the keep at Fastyngange. Then a second and equally devastating shock-wave turned her bruised legs to jelly as she recognized the window for what it really was: Elspeth Husted's brilliant distemper miniature with its little light on above the mantel in Bob Troubridge's front room. She was back at Chewton Cottage.

The light on that porthole drained away, replaced by a larger light, and turning Alexis saw Bob Troubridge at the door, his finger on the light switch.

"Ah," he said. "Welcome back."

She stood there, her rope, like a slack umbilical cord, hanging from the fireplace opening, while the doctor, his fingers fumbling, removed the helmet from her head and patted the chair where she might sit. He took the other chair and immediately—rather nervously she thought—began to load his pipe, which he took from the pocket of his old gardening sweater.

"How is it possible?" she said.

Bob smiled, sucking the flame of his match into the bowl of his pipe until the tobacco glowed and his face reflected that glow. "This part of the world," he said, "is riddled with underground networks of caves and rivers and swallets too deep to make ready sense of. I tried to indicate as much in the introduction or, as you so rightly put it, the overture, to my little book. This is a place, Alexis, which quite confounds the mind."

Alexis stared around the little room lined with books in glass cupboards. So neat. So unlived in. She remembered the dining room—would the table still be set, the cozy fire there still burning? She found herself shivering. "Couldn't we go somewhere else?" she asked.

The wise old face looked pained behind an aromatic smoke-screen. "We could," he said. "But I'd rather you didn't."

"But it's cold," she said.

"This room was once my consulting room, before I retired," said Troubridge. He paused. "You and I had some pleasant moments together in the warmer reaches of the cottage, but I do not think we can return to that, do you?"

Alexis did not answer immediately. Then, without really wanting to, she shook her head. It was then that it occurred to her, exploded into her thoughts, and had she not been sitting the momentum of it would have sent her reeling. She found herself glancing back over her shoulder at the light in the doorway through which the doctor had entered the room, as if at any moment someone or something might enter and drag her away. Troubridge, watching her closely, waited for her to speak.

"Out there," she said feebly, gesturing towards the hall, "out there is Chewton Cottage, and Judge Jeffreys."

"Yes."

"And beyond...," she said, though this was the hard part.

"Go on," he said.

"Beyond that," she started again, "the Marriotts' on Jerusalem Street, and...and...."

"And Fastyngange," he said. "You are absolutely right. Out there is Mechelney, the estate agent, and beyond his Somerset, an ocean not unlike the Atlantic whereupon a liner named the *Northern Lights* might be seen to plough towards Canada. On that ship, Howl plays in the band. And beyond the ocean, on the other rim of the New World, Gloria sells real estate in Vancouver and waits to hear from you—"

At this point Alexis could not hold herself in. "No. Not Gloria. She was real."

The doctor raised an eyebrow, quizzically.

"She phoned the doctor for me—the other Troubridge."

Troubridge held her eyes in his gaze. "Perhaps," he suggested. "Perhaps she motivated the call. But it was you who called from Halifax, I think you will find. She is real, if you wish her to be. But only down here. You could call her, if you want to. There is a phone by the stairs. You could call the Marriotts and reserve Jill's room above the kitchen, if you like. They'd love to see you." There was a gravity in the doctor's voice which belied the kindness of his invitation.

"But if I do...," she said.

"Then you will have chosen to live in the past," he said. "That is what is at the bottom of the oubliette. A past that never was, but that was real enough that you could spend the rest of your life living it."

"A crazy woman," she said.

He nodded his head. "Absorption into madness," he said.

"And if I am to live in the real world...."

"Then," he said, "you will have to leave me and this world behind and climb back up the shaft which led you here in the first place."

Alexis sat, staring at her smudged black hands on her knees. Her eyes wandered to the fireplace. Where had she seen it before? She bent on her knees to the hearth. "This fireplace," she said.

"You recall it?" he asked, leaning forwards. She nodded, but that was not entirely true for she could not, in truth, *recollect* it, but only recognize it as something she should be able to remember. The doctor chuckled at the look of puzzlement on her face.

"Everything down here," he said, "has been borrowed— no, that does not put it forcefully enough—appropriated— commandeered—from the world you know. The world in which you grew up. Down here are all the little rooms where you have stored your life away behind you while you went on about the business of living it. Then, when it became too much to bear, you found yourself banished to this place where, to your confusion, nothing was in quite the same place you had left it. Who would have thought the past could have a life of its own. But then—this fireplace. *Think*, Alexis."

But she already was thinking. Her mind was racing, stimulated by *our* discussion of the previous evening. The discussion I had so brilliantly engineered, had she but known it. A secluded place, a Fastyngange from her own past, where I might find some solitude. Why, she thought, had she not recognized the fireplace before, when the doctor had shown her Elspeth's painting? Before she had ever suffered to meet me.

"Rest-Harrow," she said. "The parlour at Rest-Harrow."

"And what happened there?" asked the doctor. She told him, as she had told me, and as she did so she tried desperately to see how a dead nestling could have weighed so heavily on her mind, for surely that was the lesson of this hearth.

"It wasn't so very awful," she said.

"Not on its own," said the doctor. "But while you knelt there by the fireplace, Teddy and you, you were not looking at the bird, were you. You were looking where you always looked at him when he did not notice. When he was naked."

Her brow creased in consternation. "Tell me," she said. "There isn't time. He will be back any moment. Maybe he already is back. Tell me!"

Troubridge shook his head. "This is the past, Alexis. The answer is here, if you but grasp it."

She closed her eyes and cast her mind back. The two of them at the hearth, Teddy and she, and he picking up the dead bird in his cupped hands, his long-fingered hands, looking giant. But it wasn't his hands she saw. In her mind's eye, her gaze wandered. Surreptitiously, guiltily—for this was something unsanctioned even by the intimacy of their marriage—she gazed at his chest, at the wound under his heart. Her eyes always went there when he was naked. "The scar," she said. "I see the scar."

"What scar, Alexis?"

"Where he was attached to her," she said, squeezing her eyes shut, trying to hold the image of the wound. Three inches long.

"Attached to whom, Alexis?"

"To his sister," she said.

"More than twins," said the doctor. "Joined. But he had the health to survive the lesion of their separation."

Her vision of Teddy faded. And there was the baby. The baby he had abandoned when, screaming, he had climbed out of the oubliette. The part of him he had left behind and had learned to live without. But whom Alexis could only forget and therefore endure because it lived on as memory in her deepest self. This twin who might have been her own sister.

Then the doctor was behind her, his doctor's hands were on her shoulders, squeezing comfort back into her. Her head drooped under the doctor's healing hands. The other Troubridge could never have touched her like this.

"It should be easier now," he murmured. She drifted. At one point she half-opened her eyes expecting to be in the therapist's office in Toronto, but saw only his twin, the kind gardener of Chewton Cottage. She closed her eyes wearily. She still had such a long climb ahead of her. The thought made her weak. She sagged and the doctor, with an effort, helped her back into her chair. She stared at the fireplace but saw nothing now. Nothing.

36

She had no idea how long it was before she came to, came back from wherever it was she had travelled. To her shock she was still at Chewton Cottage. Troubridge was slouching comfortably over one arm of his chair, his pipe between his lips, puffing away thoughtfully. He smiled as she turned to him.

"Do you remember now?" he asked.

She did.

"Can you remember that last time in the room at Rest-Harrow? When was it?"

"June," she said.

"And your breakdown?"

"The following March."

"Nine months," he said. "A woman who has an abortion sometimes suffers around the time her child would have been born. You conceived on that last visit to Rest-Harrow, Alexis. In that little parlour with its rickety table and chair and broken pipe organ. You conceived of a baby who was not your own, a baby who was already long dead but who had left its mark on your husband."

"A baby who fell from the nest," she said.

"Yes," he replied.

"But I wouldn't let it die," she said.

"You protected that changeling with your life. It was growing inside you and lest he interfere with it, lest Teddy disturb it, you would not let him near you. The thought of him making love to you became disgusting."

"It would have been incest," said Alexis.

"But he died anyway," said Troubridge.

"She," Alexis corrected.

The doctor shook his head. "No, Alexis—he. Conjoined twins are always the same sex. They are monozygotic—formed from a single egg. You must have known that from your studies," he said. "It was never a sister you lost, but a brother, Alexis."

"A brother," she said.

"An identical twin to Teddy," the doctor added.

Very slowly Alexis nodded her head. "Why did I make it a girl?" she asked. The doctor had no answer for that mystery.

"I protected her from Teddy all those months. I wouldn't let him near me while I thought I was carrying his sister. And then when she died I thought I wanted to die with her. But it was a him."

"And when you got to Fastyngange you found you didn't really want to die after all," said Troubridge.

"I only wanted Teddy back," said Alexis.

"Fastyngange is a melancholy place," said the doctor. "The beginning of the end for some."

"But not me," she said. "I came back."

"And Teddy will be back," said the doctor, rising from his chair, "any minute now. You had better go to him. You are strong enough? Here then, let me help you untangle this rope. The climb won't be as difficult as you expect. This equipment is old but sound.

"All right then? A kiss. Goodbye."

"Goodbye."

It all happened far too quickly. She could not find words to say to him. She was overcome with urgency. All she could think

300

of was getting back to the flat to tell Teddy. She climbed like a demon, and as she climbed the events which had taken place in the doctor's front room, the oubliette—wherever it was—began to fade. As she climbed, hand over hand, she found herself thinking inconsequential thoughts: whether the wine should have been left by the window to keep cool but not cold; whether the salmon had been overcooked. She had not wanted to spoil its appearance by tasting it. But what if he had eaten on the plane or drunk the whole way back!

Before she knew it, when she arched her head back there was a sparkling dime of light above her in the darkness. Light that did not come from her helmet lamp. The dime grew until it was a plate and until finally she could see the edges of the stones themselves, the rim, and her free hand was reaching up to grab the lip and heave herself up into the living room. My lip sharp enough to cut, but she was protected by a caver's gloves.

"So," I said, my voice a little slurred, for she had displaced several of the stones in clambering out of me.

"So," she answered, out of breath. She was tearing off Teddy's climbing gear and flinging each article into the tin chest as she did so.

"So now what about this folly?" I asked. One of her oversized boots landed in the chest with a resonant thump.

"We'll have to talk about it later," she said. The second boot landed in its battered repository. "Right now, I'm busy," she said, and her voice was ripe with elation.

"Oh, of course," I said. "Now it's going to be all Teddy. Not a second thought for the hole, who made it all possible."

She seemed to find my ill humour comic, but not worthy of response. I started in again but by now she was dragging Teddy's chest across the floor at such a pace and with such a racket that my weak voice was lost to her. I was just about to summon up all my energies and scream when a clatter came which stopped us both in our tracks. The door at street level slammed shut. Then there were footsteps on the stairs—not one pair but many—and then, while this sound was still registering, the sound of someone pounding on the door, then the door splintering and crashing open against the wall. Boots approaching.

Alexis stood perfectly still, knowing the footsteps were not Teddy's and knowing there was nothing she could do about whoever it was because they were coming down the hall, several of them, many of them. When they arrived at last they found her sitting on the tin chest bolt upright, wondering how she could have regained her sanity and lost it again so fast.

But it was not shades or shavelings who finally appeared around the doorway. A scruffy head turned until its eyes located her, at which point a hand, ostensibly attached to the same body, shot out and tore off the head's snow-covered toque. Another head appeared, the harridan's, until, with much whispering among themselves, a dozen intruders had seeped into the room like sludge and gathered, dripping, around the table Alexis had set for two.

"Sorry 'bout the door," piped up the nearest, nervously pulling at the toque in his hands. But he did not look at Alexis. All of the ragged assembly's attention was fixed on the hole by the window.

"It was the storm," said another, and, looking out the window, Alexis saw a white wall of snow blurring the street lights and obliterating from view the far side of the street.

"We got cold," said the burglar boy. His skinhead glistened as though he wore a close helmet of ice.

Alexis recognized the tennis players first of all. Then she saw they were all street people, the crazies, who had been her constant companions since she had moved back into the studio.

"You aren't ghosts," she said.

"Hell no," said one of them. "Not yet." One or two of them chuckled uncertainly.

"Come in, come in," I said. The draft from the stairway had given me a new life. A murmur passed through the shabby crowd.

Wet Willy stepped forwards, his fly down, his fedora in his hand. "We sorta figured der was some'n like dat around here," he said, pointing towards the corner. Pointing at me.

"We hear sigs," said Gladys. "We hear real good," she added, tapping a cabbage ear. It was a cabbage ear that had been left out in too many frosts.

"We smelled it," said another, with a silver beard like God's and a face like a gnarled root. He tapped his nose.

"That's Saint Klaus!" cried the old drunk. "Is he in this too?"

"Everyone," said the hole expansively. "Everyone is a part of the story now."

Alexis approached them. "What do you want?" she asked. None of them seemed actually to have thought this out.

"They are volunteers," I suggested. "Don't send them off just yet. They have come for me."

One of the crazies clapped.

"What the fuck do we do with a talking hole?" grumbled another.

But the one called Saint Klaus made his way through the damp bodies towards the hole, munching on a celery heart he had picked up from the table, and peeked down into my warm darkness. "We'll take this off your hands, if you like," he said.

Alexis stared at the bearded old man.

"You see?" said I. "I told you they had come for me."

"What the fuck do we want with a hole?" said the same disgruntled voice that had complained earlier, but now with his mouth full of bread. Someone else poured a glass of Beaujolais.

"Oh, we'll take real good care of id," said Gladys, adenoidally, staring down into my depths.

"I can tell you stories," I murmured to her. "Romances. You like romances, don't you?"

"You mustn't listen to it!" said Alexis, stepping backwards towards me, as if to shield me from their eyes.

"You see how generous she is?" I said.

"It's just dat she feels such affection for youze," said one of them.

"It is not affection!" Alexis' retort silenced the noisy assembly. She turned on me. "You will trick them. You will suck them in. They are miserable enough without your interference."

"Now wait a second," said Wet Willy.

"Where does she get off?" someone mumbled.

"You were quite miserable when you first stumbled on me," I said, taking charge. "In fact, I would say you were suicidal, Alexis. Would you agree? While you were suicidal I urged you on. I urged you to forget, forget it all. But you fought back from the edge. You decided to *remember*. And then, with my enormous memory, I helped you again. I am without prejudice in these matters—life, death—it's all the same to me. It's the one who turns to me who must decide. I haven't from the start let you confuse me with justice or mercy. I am an oubliette. A conveniently large hole with an insatiable appetite. Make of me what you will. And let all who come across me in their travels do the same."

There was silence. Someone rubbed a stubbly chin. Someone munched on a carrot stick. Gladys had tears in her egg-white eyes.

"Id souds real good, eh?"

"Yeah," said Saint Klaus. "Miss," he said, his face twisting into a grin, "begging your pardon, but we don't need protection from something like this hole. Can't you see that?"

Alexis looked at his world-weary old face and realized that whether he needed it or not he had long since stopped listening to helpful advice.

304

"A little distraction would do us a whole world a good," continued the saint. The others agreed, noisily.

But Alexis wasn't yet convinced. She was recalling what had happened to Howl. She reminded me of Howl's heart attack in rather lurid fashion. One of the rubbies whistled. Another chuckled.

"I was much stronger then," I said. "Besides, Howl was selfish. There's no reason why these people here can't share the responsibility of carrying me away, since you seem to have had enough of me."

"Yes," she said. "I have had enough of you. Enough to last a lifetime."

"And you won't take me to this glorious house in the lee of the 'Doctor's Head'?" I asked. "This Rest-Harrow?"

"No," she said. "I will never take you in again."

"So how do we do it?" said one of them, impatiently.

Alexis supervised the operation. Those who could, carried the stones. Then, on their knees in a ring around me, as though I were a tiny drinking hole in the savannah, a number of them sucked me up. One of them felt dizzy and had to be supported. Another grinned foolishly as if drunk. The hole in the floor into which she had poured my darkness vanished, like ink sopped up by a sponge. Then, in a parade half giddy and half solemn, they filed out of the apartment. Standing shivering at the top of the stairs, she looked down on the snow drifting through the opening at the bottom.

"How can I thank you?" she asked her pathetic benefactors.

"How the fuck should we know?" said the angry one, but he was kicked in the leg.

"We need dis hole," said Gladys, "ta keep us company."

"That oughta be enough fer now," said Wet Willy.

"Be careful," warned Alexis.

The crazies promised they would, but mostly they laughed.

The rabble was almost at the bottom of the stairs when Teddy walked in off the street, his long hair windblown.

"Outa my way, scout," said the first of the street people, who hefted three of the heavy stones. Teddy, flattening himself against the wall, dragged his suitcases out of the man's path. He looked up the staircase and did a double-take to see Alexis there.

"What is going on?" he cried, his face a confusion of elation at seeing her and annoyance at the rumpled and threadbare parade.

Alexis laughed and there was nothing hysterical in it, which only made her laugh louder and more joyfully. It was like the laughter which had burst forth from her when, having glimpsed Fastyngange for the first time, she saw something more comic than grand, more like farce than mystery.

"What is all this?" Teddy asked, picking up on her laughter, letting it infect him and soothe his annoyance. He edged his way up to the first landing.

Saint Klaus was just passing him at that moment. "We're helping the missus out," he said. "She's paying us to move some garbage."

"But what—"

"Them's rocks," said Willy. "Nuthin' ta git yer pants in a knot over."

"Y'dink w're steal'n sump'n?" Gladys asked, sidling up to Teddy and pinning him against the railing.

Alexis looked on. She could never have engineered such a reception party, not one so perfectly grotesque and amusing. The residue of fear at his coming slipped away, dissipated. She skipped down the stairs to rescue him. "Welcome home, darling," she said, as she took the largest of his suitcases and toted it, two-fisted, up to the flat. "New lock," she said, pointing out Mechelney's handiwork, and this only brought on a fresh burst of laughter, for the lock was bolted firmly to a shattered piece of wood which hung away from the door at right angles. The last of the volunteers shook Teddy's hand, and handed him an empty wineglass and a crust of bread.

"Come," said Alexis from the top step, when the troops had finally passed out of the door and there were just the two of them, alone again. "Tell me about your trip," she asked.

"Tell me about yours," he said, dropping his other case and carefully wrapping his arms around her.

"Later," she said, closing the door after him and leading him by the hand to what was left of the supper she had laid out on their finest wedding-present linen. The volunteers had helped themselves, but there was enough left and there was more where that came from and they didn't feel much like eating in any case. It had been a long trip. It was enough to be home again.

"Now wait a sec," said the old drunk. "Hold on a mo'. How do you know what they ate or didn't eat? You were out on the street by then. Gone. Kaput."

"Ah, but I can imagine," said the hole. "Can't you imagine?"

The old drunk looked up at the window that opened on to the fire escape. It was dark. He supposed he could imagine what happened. But the story was still so incomplete. "It's Ash Wednesday," he said. "This all happened before Christmas. Whata you been up to the last few months?"

"Now *that*," said the hole, "*is* boring. Suffice it to say that through some miracle of coincidence your rummy friends deposited me here in one piece, so to speak, when they had had enough. A few of them are wandering around to this day with a little of me inside them. A little goes a long way.

"So here I am, where they found me, more or less, at the foot of Alexis' fire escape. She, I gather, is too busy these days for the likes of me."

The old drunk stretched hugely, yawning and wiping out the hole's reply.

"...my redemption," said the hole.

Light was seeping into the alley. Somewhere behind him, in a place the drunk had never been, on the city's eastern flank, dawn was creeping. "You can't redeem a hole," he said, but that set him on a completely different line of thought. "At least, I don't suppose you can," he said.

The hole sensed indecision, and behind it the more powerful fragrance of salvation. "You must save me," it cried. "The castle in town. There are so many mysteries still left unsolved. Admit it, you have a million questions you are dying to ask me. Put me to use. I will be your counsellor, your confidant, your confessor."

The old drunk snorted derisively. "But you're a liar," he said.

"A sin of the inveterate story-teller," said the hole, rapturously now, throwing everything into his suit for salvation. "The lies, don't you see, which lead to the sad, occasionally hideous, truth.

"But if you'd rather, I can just as easily lead you away from the sad truth. Distract you. Yes? I will tell you anything you wish to hear. I will be your protector—think of that! You have enemies, I assume...."

The tirade continued while the drunk painfully marshalled his thoughts. He was thinking of Mary Magdalene's. He'd ask God, or maybe just Father Mowbry, what to do. Then it hit him. The idea hit him square in the forehead like a brick, stunning him and then making him laugh out loud at the sheer unadulterated poetry of it.

"You think I am funny?" said the hole, pleading now. "Fine, I shall be your comic relief."

"No way," said the drunk, getting to his feet, chuckling still, tickled at his bright idea. "I got other plans for you," he said.

He looked down at the circle of stones. There was enough daylight now to see them clearly. How beautiful they were. Blue-grey HamHill stone, carved nearly a thousand years ago. He could see the sharp lip time had eroded, a circle within the circle.

"What are your plans?" asked the hole. "Rest-Harrow, perhaps? Or the Fastyngange in your own life. Somewhere where you were truly alone—"

"You'll see," said the old drunk, interrupting.

"Ah, but I cannot see," said the hole. "I can only help others to see. I am a telescope, bringing into focus things that are far away."

"More like a whaddayacallit," said the drunk, sauntering away. "A periscope."

"Don't leave," called the hole.

"I'll be back," said the drunk.

Epilogue

The forty days of Lent passed and then Christ got killed all over again and it was Holy Saturday. At Mary Magdalene's all was in darkness, to begin the ceremony of light. Behind the soft wall of darkness, a large congregation waited. The noise at the back of the church indicated the wait would not be long. The parishioners stirred.

The pascal candle was lit, the only light in the tall, cold building. It was held, its base in a water-filled basin—the ancient precarious equation of Easter. Fire and water. The procession began slowly towards the front of the church.

The old drunk sat at the back in the shadows near the font. As in the days of ancient Rome, Holy Saturday was *the* night for baptisms. In this case, only one, but the old drunk didn't want to miss a moment of it. He couldn't resist a proud sideways glance at the new font, for which he, the old drunk himself, had provided the rim of beautiful old blue HamHill stones. The basin, smooth and white, awaited the holy water which would anoint the head of the child. The old drunk chuckled. He didn't know the child but he knew the font. He wondered what the font was thinking about just then.

When the service ended, he walked down to Queen Street. There was a hint of spring in the air, a good, hard, smacking hint. He parked himself across from Mechelney's Taxidermy. The lights were on upstairs. Then, as luck would have it, Alexis came to the window to look out at the rain. If she noticed him, an old drunk, she didn't show any signs of concern. Then a man came up behind her, or so the drunk thought, for all he really saw was a shadow and her responding to the shadow, her head lolling back, eyes closed, withdrawing from the window, embracing the shadow, or so it seemed to the drunk. And that was that. A romance after all.